COLD MEDINA

COLD
MEDINA

GARY HARDWICK

A DUTTON BOOK

DUTTON

Published by the Penguin Group
Penguin Books USA Inc., 375 Hudson Street, New York, New York 10014, U.S.A.
Penguin Books Ltd, 27 Wrights Lane, London W8 5TZ, England
Penguin Books Australia Ltd, Ringwood, Victoria, Australia
Penguin Books Canada Ltd, 10 Alcorn Avenue, Toronto, Ontario, Canada M4V 3B2
Penguin Books (N.Z.) Ltd, 182–190 Wairau Road, Auckland 10, New Zealand

Penguin Books Ltd, Registered Offices:
Harmondsworth, Middlesex, England

First published by Dutton, an imprint of Dutton Signet,
a division of Penguin Books USA Inc.
Distributed in Canada by McClelland & Stewart Inc.

First Printing, February, 1996
1   3   5   7   9   10   8   6   4   2

REGISTERED TRADEMARK—MARCA REGISTRADA

Library of Congress Cataloging-in-Publication Data:
Cold Medina / Gary Hardwick
p. cm.
ISBN 0-525-93919-9
1. Afro-American police—Michigan—Detroit—Fiction. 2. Gangs—
Michigan—Detroit—Fiction.
3. Detroit (Mich.)—Fiction.
I. Title
PS3558.A62368C65 1996   95-32878
813'.54—dc20   CIP

Printed in the United States of America
Set in Transitional 551

Designed by Jesse Cohen

PUBLISHER'S NOTE

For Susan

Cities rob men of eyes and hands and feet,
Patching one hole of many incomplete.
                    —*James Russell Lowell*
                      "The Pioneer" (1847)

Human blood is heavy; the man who has shed
it cannot run away.
                            —*African proverb*

Prejudice is like a hair across your cheek . . .
you keep brushing at it because the feel of it is
irritating.
                            —*Marian Anderson*

PART I

CHOCOLATE CITY

Rollin' on the River

The island was packed.

A night breeze came from the west, carrying the scent of the river to the shore. The park pulsated with the energy of the crowd jammed inside it.

The crowd was young and mostly black, but white faces could be seen here and there, cruising the drive for action.

Music blared out of vehicles parked along a circular drive. Rap music. Thumping bass lines, funky rhythms, and throaty, angry vocals. The differing beats rose like thunder, a defiant imbalance of sounds.

The air smelled of the river, fast food, marijuana, and beer. Within the darkness, small pipes were lit, their flames flickering for an instant then disappearing like fireflies.

It was ten-thirty on Belle Isle Park in Detroit. Prime time. The long concrete drive called the Strip was filled with young folks hanging out, cruising, and getting high.

The police drove through occasionally, keeping an eye on events. They were booed, cursed, and generally disrespected in the process.

Beyond the party on the Strip, further into the park, a young black man sat on a picnic bench in an old gazebo, oblivious to the celebration half a mile away. A large flashlight sat next to him on the end of the table, its beacon cutting a passage of light. In the light, the man counted a huge wad of cash. It had been a good night.

He'd made the rounds in record time and he was pleased with his success. He was good, he thought, but you had to be good to run the action on the island. There was a police station on Belle Isle, and a dealer had to be smart to move the product and evade detection. The cops were big, mean bastards and you couldn't tell which ones were tight with the crew. And if you got caught by one who wasn't, he might not bother to arrest you. He might just take you somewhere and beat the shit out of you—or worse.

Times were good for Floyd Turner, called Big Money Grip on the street. He got the nickname because he always packed a large wad of cash. He was the best roller in his crew of dealers.

His crew didn't really have a name, but they were unofficially called the Union. They ran most of the drugs in the city. The lesser crews and independent rollers stayed out of their way and took the leftovers.

Grip didn't take no shit and minded his own business. That's how you survived. The crews had their own code of honor and he never violated it. Most of the rollers were fools, he thought. Just punks with a little money waiting to get shot by a cop, another roller, or some bitch they couldn't handle.

He had ten young rollers working the island. They ranged in ages from twelve to twenty-one. They were smart and ambitious. Some he even called friends, but he never liked anyone to be around when he counted the take. He always counted his money first, then checked on the others. This way, only he would know exactly how much he had, and if he was in need of cash, he would skim a little off the top and no one would know.

Tonight business was good. The black folk were buying in volume. The white suburban boys and their pale girlfriends who cruised the island were shelling out the cash, too. The white kids usually just came to buy, then headed back to suburbia with its green lawns, and station wagons.

Many of the white kids were what they called wiggers, or white niggers. They adopted the cultural trappings of inner city blacks, the clothes, the music, and hair styles. They rejected their parents' middle-class values and sought the edginess of being black.

The wiggers loved to come to the city on their little adventures. They could buy the stuff out where they lived, but that was boring. Better to come to the city, where the animals live. Grip didn't mind, though. They paid in cash.

He finished counting his take and stuffed it into a large leather pouch. The Belle Isle crowd was really putting the shit away tonight, he thought.

Grip sold crack which was called base, rock, juice, or the ever-popular shit. He also dealt a little weed called indo, chronic, or just plain smoke. The names were always changing in drug culture. Currently, he was a roller, because a drug dealer was said to be rolling out the product, or rolling in the money. Dealers were called slangers, ballers out west, or clockers on the East Coast. As the culture embraced different themes and icons, everything changed. Except the job. The occupation of dealing drugs could never change.

It was ten forty-five. Grip decided to wait an hour before going back out. Then he would go for the big time score—midnight. There was something about the witching hour that made people crazy for getting high.

Grip was too smart for the pitfalls of drug dealing. He had ten years in the game and counting. He didn't even break the time the cops busted him. They beat him silly, then stole all his money and drugs. He was praised by his peers for his strength and honor. He knew then that he'd move up eventually to manager. That's the way it was in the drug business. You roll the product, don't talk to cops, and you get rewarded. At the ripe old age of twenty-three, Big Money Grip was looking for a promotion.

Something moved. The sound was sharp, cutting through the silence. Grip sprang to attention. He searched the area, hand on the gun in his waistband. He couldn't tell exactly where the sound had come from and the noise from the Strip was too distant to be heard.

Grip took out his gun. He stepped from the concrete gazebo to the grass. The earth felt good under his new basketball shoes. He followed the flashlight beam, walking toward his truck.

Maybe it was just an animal, he thought. But he didn't like taking chances. Nobody knew where he was, not even his own rollers. The light cut through the darkness, but revealed nothing.

"If somebody out there, you don't wanna be fuckin' with me!" Grip yelled. He flicked the flashlight back and forth around the truck. "I'll bust a cap in yo' ass, as sure as I'm standin' here!"

Silence. Grip took another step. You had to intimidate when you were in danger. That was one of the first things he'd learned in the business. He moved slowly, his muscles tense. He brought the light to the side of his truck. Its cherry red body gleamed.

He wasn't afraid to shoot whoever it was. He'd killed before. Grip guessed that if someone was out there, it couldn't be a cop. They never came this far into the picnic area at this time of night. They knew all the sales took place on the drives. It might be one of those undercover bastards, but they wouldn't be out this far either. No, it wasn't the Hook, as the police were sometimes called. They wouldn't play games like this.

Grip traced his steps back to the gazebo. It was probably somebody's mutt-ass dog or a raccoon, he reasoned. He sat and stretched his arms upward, yawning. He was beginning to feel a little tired. He didn't sleep much. Rollers never did. Selling drugs was a twenty-four-hour-a-day job.

Grip placed the gun on the table with the leather pouch of money. He had a lot of time before he had to get back out there. Grip took out his pipe and pulled his private stash from his hip pocket. The small white rocks briefly caught the beam of the flashlight in their plastic container as he placed them next to the crack pipe. He picked out a nice fat one.

Grip did not see the man crouched beyond the gazebo on the far side of the wooden picnic tables. Hidden behind a series of large steel trash cans, he was only a few feet away.

The crouching man was dressed in black and knelt as if praying. Silent and motionless, he could have been a large rock or a mound of dirt. His pulse was slow and steady, his breathing thin, noiseless. He'd been following the drug dealer all night, watching him sell death along the Strip.

As Floyd Turner dropped a rock of crack into his glass pipe, he heard a rumble at the end of the table and saw the shadowy figure spring to its full height, winding upwards, like a thick, black spider.

Grip stood and reached for the gun. He had to take his eyes from the shadow to locate the weapon, and in that instant, the man was upon him, springing across the tabletop in a fluid motion. Grip was knocked to the ground.

Grip saw a reddish flash as the force of a blow hit him squarely in the face. Strong hands grabbed his throat and pulled him up to his feet. Grip's body stiffened at the hot pain of a knee in his groin. The wind flew from his body and he fell back on the ground in a sorry lump, holding his balls.

The killer stood above Grip breathing hard, heart pumping. The killer removed a large knife from his clothing and stepped closer to the man on the ground. Grip sensed him coming and tried to roll away. The killer kicked him hard in the ribs. Grip grunted loudly and rolled over, grabbing his side.

The knife struck. Grip howled in pain, trying desperately to crawl away. But the killer followed. With a quick jab, the knife was in Grip's face. Grip tried to cover with his hands, but the killer's strokes were too quick, darting between Grip's bloody fingers. Grip rolled over, hiding his face.

The killer pulled back, then braced his foot in the small of Grip's back and plunged the knife deep into the dying man. Grip's mouth opened in a wide, soundless scream, straining the skin at the corners.

The killer watched a moment, then removed the knife. He braced himself over Grip then struck with the blade again and again.

Finally, the killer paused, breathing heavily. He brushed sweat from his forehead.

"Dirty hands," the killer whispered, then cut Grip's throat.

The killer watched the life flow from the trash beneath him. A breeze flared up and the killer briefly smelled the scent of the river.

He jerked himself back into the moment, removed another tool from his jacket and knelt by Grip's corpse.

He finished his work and walked off into the night.

2

Wake Up Call

He is in a large room, a pen of some type. His limbs are heavy. He struggles and hears chains clanking together. It's a sick, filthy sound. His vision is obscured by a dirty, tattered cloth wrapped around his face, but he can see shadows moving in the room and insects scurrying on the edges of the fabric.

Suddenly, he's aware that the pen is filled with bodies—writhing, dark figures moaning and calling out in pain and despair. He moves his head, struggling to loosen the cloth. It recedes a little—and then he is rushed by a flood of smells: urine, sweat, excrement—blood. With his toes he feels the thick wetness of the dirt floor and creatures, rats maybe, running over it.

He can see an opening in the room. It is a door, and a dim, gray light comes through. Each time it opens, tall figures come through, grab a dark body from the floor, and take it out. The victims scream an ungodly sound each time.

Beyond the opening, he hears the shouts of a crowd, but their words are muffled. Again and again the tall men come and remove bodies, each time coming closer to him.

He tries to wake himself. He knows it's only a dream. He tries to shake his own consciousness to force the dream to break. He searches for memories of reality, proof of his other existence. But he can remember nothing of his life. And no power he can muster will break the fabric of reality. He has always been here. It is real. He is here, in chains, lying in his own feces. He begins to cry, and struggles while the chains sing their awful song.

The door opens again. They have come for him this time. He watches the tall figures come through the doorway. He cannot see their faces, but knows they are smiling, laughing at him. He is struck again by the smell of the place. Something gnaws into his leg, the pain is sharp and hot.

He screams, a last desperate attempt to escape, and something crawls into his mouth. He chokes on it. He spits it out and faintly tastes its coarse flavor.

When he recovers, the men are upon him. They grab him and lift. The chains sing again. Something falls from his leg and he hears it plop onto the ground.

The men drag him toward the door and the dim light in the doorway is frightening, pulsing with life. Voices yell on the other side of the door, shouting numbers.

"Five hundred!"

"Six hundred!"

He knows where he is and despairs. At the edge of the hideous door, he hears someone whisper to him, but he is not sure if it is one of the captors. The voice is cruel, and familiar.

"End of the line, nigger."

He is pushed into the light. . . .

Tony Hill sprang up in bed, his mouth open in a soundless yell. His heart raced and he was wet with sweating. He checked the room as he always did after the nightmare, looking for specters.

He was home in bed, his wife Nikki sleeping next to him and his son, Moe, wedged between them like an intruder. The sight of his family drew him slowly into reality and calmed his heart.

He had never been a slave and yet the nightmare seemed real, as if from some past life. Bondage, vermin, chains, the clarity of the moment was frightening. And strangely, it was the light in the doorway, with its awful, glowing hatred, that was the most hideous sight.

Tony had tried desperately to stop having The Dream, as he called it, but it kept coming back, breaking free of each mental barrier he created, like a freight train hitting a picket fence.

The phone rang. Tony caught it in mid-ring, trying not to wake his family. He was surprised at how quickly he had grabbed the receiver.

He scanned the room again and caught the clock radio. The red numbers glowed 4:10 A.M.

"Hello? . . . Yeah, this is Inspector Hill," he said.

The voice on the other end was not familiar, but it possessed a timbre of dread and urgency that he had heard a thousand times. And before the words were out, he knew someone had been murdered.

The flashing lights of the police cruisers danced on dark trees as Tony pulled his car into the area on Belle Isle where Floyd Turner's body had been found.

Tony got out of his car, and for a moment he felt he was walking through ripples of time as the grim faces of uniformed officers and coroner's aides blended into a hundred memories of a hundred crimes past.

Tony had been notified that there had been a death and the police were in a stand-off with the probable killer. He walked up to the scene and a tall black man broke off from a group of officers and intercepted him.

"You in charge here, brother?" asked the tall man.

Tony smiled a little at the sight of his partner. Jim was a black lieutenant assigned as an assistant to Tony. They were supposed to function independently, but their friendship had melded the relationship into the traditional partnership. Cops couldn't break old habits.

"What we got here, man?" Tony asked. He walked with Jim toward the line of police cars forming a barricade. Tony took out his Beretta 92FS. There was no immediate danger, but it was another old habit.

"We got a stiff and the perp," said Jim. "Two officers got here while he was robbing the corpse. He pulled out a gun and the uniforms backed off. The perp got caught before he could get back to his car. He's hiding behind that row of metal garbage cans."

"Any shots fired?" Tony asked.

"Nope. He's saving 'em I guess."

"How long he been holed up?"

"Uniforms got here about two hours ago." Jim said.

"Hostages?" Tony asked.

"No, it's just him back there."

"Any use talking to him, you think?"

"You know these young boys nowadays ain't got no heart," Jim said. "We'll have to go hard on his ass."

"But if he didn't fire on the uniforms, maybe he didn't kill the guy there."

"Look, this is drug related," Jim said. "And I bet this guy has been through the system before. He's got nothing to lose."

"You a mind reader now, Jim?"

"What the fuck is that supposed to mean?"

"It means, we can't suppose any of that. If he killed the man, why was he still here? He could have popped him and took off. . . ."

The other officers watched their argument without concern. Partners going at it was normal. They kept their eyes on the perp and waited for Tony and Jim to complete the cycle.

". . . I say we try to take him," Jim said. "We surround him, move in slowly, and if he fires, so be it."

"You ready to take that bullet?"

"You know it."

Tony looked at Jim. He was ready, crazy bastard. And he was probably right. The rollers of today were often ready to die or kill at any moment. They didn't give a shit because they knew death was in the contract when they signed up. An aggressive posture was called for.

"Let me talk with him first," Tony said. "No reason to have a dead witness unless we absolutely have to."

"He's a perp, not a witness," said Jim.

Tony didn't answer. He grabbed a bullhorn.

"This is Inspector Hill, Detroit Police. We already have you for killing your boy there."

"I ain't killed nobody!" the perp yelled from behind the cans.

"Then throw out your weapon and come out."

"How I know you won't shoot me anyway."

"You don't. But we damn sure will if you don't bring your ass out."

"I . . . I got me some demands."

"That's a dead body out there." Tony said. "There's no way we're letting you walk."

The perp was silent.

"We could wait him out," Tony said to Jim.

"Sure," said Jim. "He'll pass out from hunger in three or four days."

"We can't sit here all night screwing around with this guy," Tony said. "And if I call in SWAT, there won't be enough left of him to put in a baggie."

"OK, then let me go for him and you lay back," Jim said.

"Thanks, but I have another way," Tony said. "Tell the uniforms to move laterally but to stay out of the line of fire."

"What good will that do?"

"It'll give this guy the feeling that we're moving in."

Jim pulled a uniform aside and gave him the order.

Tony put his Beretta away and lifted the bullhorn. "OK, we're tired of this shit! You got a minute, just sixty seconds to come out."

"This is bullshit," Jim said. "He won't fall for it."

"He's scared. He'll go for it. Besides, he's not worth getting a cop shot, even if it's you." Into the bullhorn, Tony said, "We're coming to get you. If you shoot, my men will kill you. So, you can deal with me or the men with the guns. OK, people move in!"

Jim signaled the uniforms. They moved in circles around the perp, but did not come any closer.

"Forty-five seconds!" Tony said into the bullhorn. "Throw out your weapon."

The garbage cans hiding the perp knocked against each other. The uniforms stopped, then continued to circle.

"Hey! Back the fuck off!" the perp yelled.

"Too late," said Tony. "Thirty seconds!"

"What are you some kinda fuckin' nut, I gotta gun!"

"We have them too. They use hollow points. Pretty messy. Fifteen!"

Tony and Jim stepped out from behind the cars.

"Ten, nine, eight. . . ."

"OK, OK," said the perp. He stood up with the gun dangling on the index finger of his right hand.

Tony and Jim drew their weapons. The perp was right in front of them, about twenty yards away. They moved in, keeping a bead on the man.

"Hold fire!" Tony shouted. To the perp he said, "Drop the weapon, now!"

"I didn't kill him," the perp said.

"Drop the fucking gun!" Jim said.

"I just got here and . . . there he was—"

Tony signaled Jim to stop, then he walked on. "Put the gun down, son," Tony said in a softer voice. "It's over. Just drop the weapon." Tony lowered his gun. To Jim he said, "You got him?"

"I got him," Jim said, keeping his gun on the perp.

Tony walked closer. He kept his eye on the perp, knowing Jim was watching the gun in the perp's hand.

Tony got to the man and slowly removed the gun from his finger. Two uniforms rushed out and grabbed the perp and quickly hand-cuffed him. The coroner's aide and his crew hurried to the corpse.

"You're the luckiest bastard on two feet, you know that?" Jim said.

"God looks out for babies and fools," Tony said.

"Goddamned inspector walking out without a gun. What's this department coming to?" Jim said.

The two uniforms brought the perp to Tony and Jim.

He was a thin, black kid about seventeen. "I didn't do nothin'," he said. "He was like that when I got here. I swear."

"He been Mirandized?" asked Tony.

"Yes sir," said a uniform.

"Who are you?" Tony asked the perp.

"Alonzo . . . Fields," said the kid. His voice was shaking, desperate.

"What happened here?" Tony asked. He knew that anything Alonzo told him would be thrown out by a judge even though the kid had been given his rights.

"Like I said, when I got here, he was dead. So, I was just gonna lift some jewelry off him, you know."

"See anybody?" asked Jim.

"Naw, but there had to be somebody 'cause I swear on my mama, I didn't to it." Alonzo was near tears now.

Tony could see now that he was not a killer. He'd seen enough hard cases over the years and this wasn't one of them.

"Who is he?" asked Tony.

"Shit, you don't know that truck? He's The Grip. Big Money Grip."

Tony knew the name. One of Detroit's finest dealers. "You one of his men? You in the Union?"

"No, I'm just hangin' out, you know. I ain't with them. Besides, everybody knows there ain't no Union."

"Right," Tony said. "These officers are going to ask you some more questions." He walked away.

"I didn't do it. You believe me don't you?" said Alonzo. "I was just gonna take his watch, you know."

"With a gun? Yeah, we know," said Jim. "Take his ass in."

"But, what about my car, I left it—"

"That's the least of your worries," said Tony.

The uniforms carted Alonzo off as Dr. Ralph Neward, the assistant medical examiner, walked toward Tony and Jim. Neward was a smallish man with thick, black hair.

Tony and Jim watched Neward approach as they had so many times before. But this time, he looked different. His chubby face was red and his eyes contorted into circles of dread.

"Inspector Hill," Neward said. "I think you should see this."

Tony, Jim, and Neward walked over to the body. The corpse was on its stomach, spread-eagled and it was a mess. The dead man had been ripped to pieces. Skin hung in flaps, bone could be seen in places, and blood was everywhere, dried and brownish.

"What is it?" Tony asked.

"It's his hands, sir," Neward said.

"What about them?" Tony asked.

"They're gone. He doesn't have any."

Tony and Jim both knelt closer to the corpse. It was still dark and there was so much blood that it was difficult to see anything. When they were upon the body, they saw that the hands of the dead man had been cut off, severed at the wrists.

Tony stood. "Jesus," he said.

"Why do I get the feeling this is going to be a lousy day?" said Jim.

"The forensic techs will need to do a lot of work here," said Tony. "Don't move the body until they're done."

"Yes sir," said Neward.

"Tell your boss, Dr. Roberts, we'll be calling on him bright and early," said Tony.

The forensic technicians began their delicate task of searching for evidence. Tony and Jim watched with grim faces.

On the horizon, the first rays of morning glowed yellow and orange. Tony turned his face toward the light and quietly cursed.

3

1300

The First Precinct police station at 1300 Beaubien had seen better days. It was old and overdue for refurbishing. Its brick surface wore the dirt and soot of many years. Police cars surrounded it on all four sides, as if protecting it.

On the fifth floor of the building that everyone in Detroit called Thirteen Hundred, Police Inspector Tony Hill was drinking his fifth cup of coffee. He'd been in his office since capturing Alonzo Fields and securing the crime scene on Belle Isle.

Tony was the leader of the Special Crimes Unit, an elite group of detectives drawn from the citywide force. They handled all the nastiest cases in the city: mass murder, drug gangs, serial rapists, child molestation, and any other crap that flowed down the pike. The officers affectionately called the SCU the Sewer, because that's where all the shit landed.

The last two leaders of the SCU had gone on to better things. One was now on the City Council, the other in the state House of Representatives. Tony had no such aspirations, but it was nice to know that he could.

Only heading the mayor's personal police force, the SS, was more prestigious than the SCU. But then again, he thought, you had to be borderline crazy to be one of those SS guys and he wanted no part of it. A veteran cop named Walter Nicks was the current leader of the SS and he had one foot on psychosis and the other on a rusty nail.

It was only seven o'clock and the day was already sliding downhill.

Tony's wife, Nikki, had gotten onto his ass about sneaking out in the middle of the night again and someone had ripped the city's number one street dealer to shreds.

Detroit didn't have gangs like other cities, wearing colors and spray painting tags. Motown's gangs were smart, young businessmen, overachievers, who banded together for a specific purpose.

The Union was the result of that mentality. A collection of three big drug crews under a truce dating back to the late eighties. The Union split the city into sections and stayed out of each other's way. This made the drug trade more profitable and less dangerous. They were smart, efficient, and ruthless. Finally, black people had come together, but unfortunately it was as a pack of criminals.

Tony was already thinking that Floyd Turner's death might be a hit by one of the lesser crews. But that made no sense. The Union could wipe them out any time they wanted. Or maybe there had been a break in the truce and this was the start of a war. Whatever the answer, it was not going to be good for the city.

Tony got up from behind his desk, moving his six-foot frame slowly. He scratched the dark skin along his forearm and tightened his ugly tie.

He made his way out of his office into the bullpen to do his morning check. Jim was at the jail questioning Alonzo Fields. Normally, Tony would have sent one of his sergeants but the Fields kid had requested a lawyer. Tony wanted every piece of information out of Fields he could legally get, so he sent Jim.

As Tony entered the bullpen, Brian Lane, a beefy detective, stood up and yelled, "And The Big Nuts Award of the week goes to . . . Inspector Tony Hill!"

The officers burst into applause and whistles.

Tony waved the ovation down. "As you were," he said, trying not to laugh. Tony waded into the officers, slapping fives and pounding fists.

"Lane," Tony said looking at a black officer. "I heard you got that Van Dyke rapist."

"Caught him with his pants down, sir. It's a slam dunk," Lane said.

"Be careful anyway. That don't mean anything these days."

"Heard a big Unionman went down last night," said Steve Patrick, a young black detective.

"Yeah. Floyd Turner aka Big Money Grip."

"Good," said Lisa Meadows, the only woman in the Unit. "One less turd in the sewer."

Tony quickly got oral reports on the assorted killings, drug deals, and other crimes. He just needed to make sure things were stable. Grip's murder smelled like big trouble and if he had to be away for a while, he needed to know things were OK.

Tony was going back to his office when Jim entered. They said hellos then walked in together.

Jim Cole was bright, wickedly handsome, and possessed an ingratiating personality. He was tough, a little hot-tempered, but a fine cop and partner. His only weakness was his genitals. He'd earned the precinct house nickname Stroke because of his sexual escapades.

Once, Jim was having affairs with a young girl and her mother at the same time, and both women knew it. Tony had marveled at the ease with which Jim had handled the situation. The affairs lasted for about half a year and when they ended, mother and daughter were not on speaking terms. Everyone in the Sewer delighted in Jim's exploits.

"Anything on the Fields kid?"

"Nada," Jim said. "But he did lie to us. He was one of The Grip's dealers. Looks like he was trying to rip off his stash. We didn't find any money on the corpse or in his vehicle, but Fields denies taking it. Fields only had a few hundred on him. If he knows anything else, we'll have to find out later. He got a lawyer and wouldn't say much after talking to him."

"But Fields didn't kill Grip, did he?"

"Not probable. The dead guy had been knifed something terrible and our boy Fields didn't have a drop of blood on him."

"Makes sense," Tony said. "I wonder who would be stupid enough to whack a Union roller?"

"I don't know, but whoever did it sure wanted to make an impression."

"I got the most recent info on the Union," said Tony. "It's hard to come by since no one will admit there is a gang. But our drug people managed to dig up a few things. I just have to remember where I put it." He started to rummage through his desk.

"You lost it?" Jim asked.

"No," Tony said a little too harshly. "I misplaced it."

"Take your time, man. Look, I'm sorry about the Belle Isle thing. I had no right to call you out like that," Jim said.

"Forget it," Tony said. "It's your job to watch my ass. Got it!" Tony held a large manila folder. "I'll get one of the guys to summarize this for us."

"Who are you gonna give it to?"

"Martin. He's good at shit work."

"I wouldn't advise that," Jim said. "Martin has been making noise about racism again."

"Really. Well, he can make more noise while he's reading over these reports."

"Tony, you're gonna have to lighten up on him," said Jim.

"Martin is an asshole."

"True, but some of the men are saying that you don't like white cops."

"Who's saying it. The black cops, or the white ones?"

"You know who it is."

"Fuck 'em. This is our department now."

"You're an inspector, Tony. Look man, you know this race shit runs deep. It's the history of Detroit. Black and white been fighting over this city for half a century."

"And we won," Tony said.

"Did we? This city is just as fucked up as it was when the white folks ran it."

"Well, at least we're in control of our own fucking up."

"Tony, you can't just be doggin' white officers," Jim said.

"You trying to say I'm a racist?" Tony said. He laughed a little at the idea.

"All I'm saying is between the brothers you can feel anything you want, but you're in charge here. You have obligations and you can't have an open bias."

"That never stopped them from doing their dirt, did it?"

"Forget it. I should know better than to talk to you about this." Jim paused, then looking directly at Tony said, "You know, I figured out what your problem is."

Tony froze for a second. How could Jim know about The Dream? Hell, *he* didn't fully know why he was having it.

"I don't have a problem," Tony said.

"You know what I'm talking about," said Jim. "You've been off your game for the last few months. I should know, I've been covering for your ass."

"It's just stress," Tony said. "A little time off and I'll get over it."

"No," said Jim. "What you need is to get laid."

"I'll talk to Nikki about it." Tony was relieved. For a second, he thought Jim actually knew.

"You know what I mean," Jim said.

"I'm married—happily."

"All the more reason to get a piece on the side. Man does not live by wife alone."

"Thank you Reverend Jim, but just because you blew your marriage, don't drag me into your shit," Tony said.

"Hey, that woman was bad news. I had to leave her."

"You always do this to me," Tony said. "We start a conversation about work and you turn it into one about women."

"Hey man, life is about women," Jim said.

"Not today. I want a detailed medical report. I called Dr. Roberts and he agreed to see us this morning."

"Can't we just read the damned thing?"

"No. I got a bad feeling about this. When was the last time you saw someone butchered like that?"

"Actually, that was a new one for me."

"Exactly. I don't want this thing blowing up in our faces. So, we'll keep it low key for now."

Tony and Jim walked into the bullpen of the Sewer together. Tony gave brief commands and orders to his people on the way out. He dropped the drug reports on Detective Orris Martin's desk.

They made their way through the gray halls of 1300, saying hello to all the familiar faces.

The building always seemed haunted. The lives of thousands of cops and criminals whispered behind the walls. Tony always felt the constant burden of working in the building. Duty, death, honor, all weighed on his insides. Whenever he was there, he felt heavier, more dense, as if every cell in his body thickened and took on the history of the place.

When Tony was a young man, 1300 was spoken about with fear. There were stories of beatings and the deaths of black prisoners killed by white cops. Those brutal images were particularly relevant to Tony and his family.

David Hill, Tony's older brother was killed by a cop. David was always in trouble. Hard-headed, strong-willed, and careless.

At fourteen, David and a friend got into a fight with an off-duty police officer. The officer shot them both with his service revolver. David had caught one right between the eyes. The other kid wasn't so lucky. He was hit in the heart and lingered in the hospital for a few days before he went.

The cop said they tried to rob him. A switchblade was found at the scene.

At David's funeral, people cried, yelled, collapsed unconscious, and threw fits. Church nurses in fresh white uniforms tended to the fallen with smelling salts and cool towels. When they tried to shut the casket, his mother sprang up, fell on the floor, and had to be taken out on a stretcher. It was the most frightening thing Tony had ever seen.

After David was buried, Tony's mother, Lucy, was never quite the same woman. She seemed always to be a little sad, off-center from normal human contentment. And on the anniversary of David's death, their house turned into a wake. She wore black and would play sad, depressing religious songs. And if the anniversary of either event fell on a Sunday, they spent the entire day at church and by the end of the day, his mother's eyes were raw from crying.

There was an inquiry into David Hill's death, and the police determined that the officer was not at fault. The police committee said that the officer had been threatened with sufficient danger to warrant the use of deadly force.

Tony's father, Taylor Hill, would have none of it. The cop was a white man named Miller, and his father had no love for white people. It was a deep, torrid hate that seemed to run through each moment of his daily life. He just knew that if his son were white, he would still be alive. He would have two children instead of one.

Taylor Hill sued the city and got a generous settlement, but money did nothing to quell his rage. Taylor Hill blamed whites for everything. Layoffs at the plant, Kennedy's assassination and, of course, Dr. King's; inflation, recessions, unemployment, drugs, even bad television was all part of The Great White Man Conspiracy.

Tony's father hounded the cop who killed his son, sending him hate letters with pictures of David and filing complaints. Taylor Hill stayed on Miller's case until the old cop died, five years after shooting David.

When Tony became old enough, his father bombarded him daily with stories of the white man's atrocities. Slavery, rape, castration, lynchings, and beatings, formed Tony's first images of white people in their all-black neighborhood.

Once, his father took him to Hudson's department store downtown to get lunch. A few minutes after they sat down, a white man sat near them. When the waitress came, she went over to the white man first.

His father became enraged. He yelled, cursed, and made a scene, telling the little blond waitress he was there first. When she tried to apologize, he became even madder. "Don't try to patronize me!" he screamed. The waitress began to cry.

Tony was too young to understand his father's rage. It was like a current flowing from him, touching and filling everything that he came into contact with.

"Son, understand that black and white people can't get along with each other because white men refuse to play fair," his father would say. "It's not enough that they've had three hundred years to kill everyone and steal all their money, they have to keep beating us down so that we won't rise up against them. But they can't keep us down. One day, we'll be the ones in the driver's seat and then we'll see how they like it."

Taylor Hill's tough-minded, no-nonsense approach to life and race relations provided Tony with the mettle to overcome the barriers of prejudice. But it also caused Tony to dislike whites. In his mind, it was an eternal battle with definite lines of allegiance. Whites were the enemy. He worked with them and even socialized with them on occasion, but it was never the real Tony Hill they saw. He felt as though they didn't deserve to know that special person. He kept them at a distance, and after a while, he saw them as almost inhuman. They were to be tolerated, but not dealt with as people.

Years after his brother died, Tony joined the police force just as it was becoming more black. He believed that it was his destiny, one which injustice had lead him to.

Tony and Jim reached the lobby of 1300.

"Last chance, buddy," said Jim. "I can hook you up with this fine sister I met last weekend. Legs up to her neck."

"Give it up, man."

Jim shrugged as Tony pushed open the big front doors and walked out into daylight.

4

The Crypt

The morgue was a nondescript building which stood three blocks from 1300. It was an ominous structure made of gray stones. Its front side was windowless, with cracks and chips that made it look like an old tombstone.

Tony and Jim entered. Several sad-looking types sat in the reception area, probably there to identify bodies, Tony thought.

Tony saw Jim tense as they walked in. Jim had an unnatural, almost childlike fear of the place. Tony never understood how a guy who had seen so much death could be afraid of the morgue. Perhaps it was because the death Jim had seen was violent and he was a part of it as an officer. In the morgue, however, you were reduced to spectator status. There was no action, no chance, no roll of the dice. It was death in a vacuum—your death.

They asked the receptionist for the coroner and sat down on the puke brown sofa in the lobby. The young girl fumbled with the phone and its many buttons. She was obviously new on the job.

Tony saw Jim smile. The receptionist was a young, pretty girl. Whenever there was a beautiful woman around, Jim seemed to become a totally different person. His eyes and smile brightened. His hair seemed curlier than normal and his already great body became even greater. The young girl returned Jim's smile and nervously twisted her long, dark hair.

"Nice looking, huh?" Tony asked.

"Real fine," said Jim not taking his eyes from the girl. "You seen her before?"

"No, but I think that's one of the mayor's nieces."

"You shittin' me?"

"Don't think so. There's one way to find out." Tony smiled at the receptionist. "Aren't you Harris Yancy's niece?" he asked.

"Yes, I am," she said brightly.

"Are you working here as a college intern?" Tony asked.

"Yes," she smiled and twisted her hair. "I'll be a sophomore in pre-med at Wayne State in the fall. That's why I'm here. Where else can you watch autopsies at my age?" She let the hair go. "You guys are cops, right?"

"Guilty," Tony said.

"Uncle Harris says you can always tell a cop by his shoes."

She smiled and peeked at their shoes. She was right, Tony thought. All cops wore big, ugly shoes. He laughed.

Jim seemed disappointed. Tony knew that Jim thought of him as a married eunuch, so he loved it when Stroke couldn't get the girl.

"He's ready to see you," the receptionist called.

"What's your name?" Tony asked.

"Wanda," she said.

They got up and walked through a pair of double glass doors. They were going to the cellar of the place they called the Crypt. Jim tightened all over.

"I just did you a favor back there," Tony said.

"Oh, how so?"

"If I hadn't told you that Wanda was Mayor Yancy's niece, you would have had her dress hiked up right now in some storage closet."

"To tell you the truth," Jim said. "I don't think I could get it up in this crypt."

They took the elevator down to the basement. Belly of the beast. How many times had he taken this trip? Tony thought. Too many times these days. He should have an office in the morgue. In the last six years, the murder rate had climbed steadily.

The emergence of crack cocaine had turned the streets into a fast-money shooting gallery in which most of the dead were young black men under twenty-five.

In Detroit, the population was about ninety percent black and many of those lived below the poverty level. To these hopeless underclass, using drugs or selling them was a way to end the days of suffering.

Tony and Jim got out of the elevator and entered the morgue's autopsy room where they found the Chief Medical Examiner, Dr. Vincent Roberts talking with a young Asian assistant over a naked female body on a gurney.

"Your work on this case was substandard, Mr. Kim," Roberts said. Roberts was a plump, bespectacled man of forty-eight with very narrow shoulders. His head seemed too big for his body and looked as if it would fall off at any moment.

"With all due respect, sir, I was very thorough," said the Asian man. "This case was very complicated. Any one of a thousand people could have missed that second wound. It was less than a centimeter wide and—"

"But you did miss it." Roberts lifted the corpse's arm. "And I don't care what other people would have done." Roberts dropped the arm and it made a smacking sound. "You're on late nights under Dr. Neward from now on."

"But when I came here, I requested days so I can finish school," said Kim. "You promised me that—"

"That was before I knew your work was so shoddy," said Roberts. "Take it or leave it, Mr. Kim. Either way, I'm done with you on my watch."

Kim walked out cursing. Tony saw Roberts smile a little.

Tony gave Jim the usual cautionary look as they approached. Roberts was a mayoral flunky and ass-kisser who took himself far too seriously, just like most of the city and county officials. Tony tolerated him, but Jim disliked Roberts almost as much as he did the morgue itself.

"Mornin', Doc," Tony said. Jim mumbled something like a salutation.

"Good morning, gentlemen," Roberts said. He turned, and it seemed that his head was going to detach. "I suppose you have come about our friend Mr. Turner."

"I *suppose* we have," said Jim too quickly.

"Yes," said Tony, cutting the tension a little. "We need the report and any thoughts that you might have on the death."

Roberts rolled his head to the side. "Well, there's not much to tell. He was beaten, and knifed. He died from loss of blood. The weapon was big, probably eight inches or so. I'm told you know that the deceased's hands were removed just above the wrist. We're holding that from the papers. You know how the mayor hates bad press."

Tony knew all too well. It was an election year.

Roberts continued. "The killer used a second instrument to remove the hands, possibly a surgical device. Considering the situation and the lack of light, it was a pretty good job, too."

"And we never found the hands," Tony said absently.

"No," Roberts said. "The wound on the deceased's throat would have killed him eventually, but apparently that wasn't good enough."

"Eventually?" asked Jim.

"Yes. He was alive when the hands were taken, Roberts said. "The throat wound was across the front. The major artery wasn't severed. Painful, but he was definitely still alive. The right hand was taken first. The cut is ragged. There was hanging tissue and jagged bone fragments. The deceased was still struggling, albeit not much. The cut on the left wrist is much cleaner. The subject was probably dead by then. I estimate the time of death to be about eleven-thirty or so."

Tony started to speak but Roberts cut him off.

"And several other things you will be interested in." He paused again, taking his moment. "As I said, the knife was used to inflict the basic wounds, but not to sever the hands. Also, the deceased's left eye was punctured and partially dislodged from the socket with the tip of the knife. There is a cut on the outside of the socket. The eyeball itself was severed. We think the killer pushed the knife into the eye socket."

Roberts smiled a little, taking another moment. Jim shifted on his feet. Tony looked at Jim, making sure he was not about to say something foolish.

"And last but not least," Roberts said, "the killer wounded the deceased in the rectum."

"What?!" Tony said.

"Are you sure?" Jim asked.

Roberts seemed irritated at Jim's remark. "Yes, I am sure. I checked twice. The wound matches the others. The killer jammed the knife into the rectum with great force."

"Was he raped?" asked Tony.

"No. His clothes weren't even removed."

"Then why wound him there?" Tony asked.

"That's one for you guys," said Roberts.

"Any other evidence of sexual violence?" asked Jim.

"None," said Roberts tilting his head again.

"Was he wounded in the rectum before or after the hands were taken?" asked Tony.

"Before, we think. There was lots of blood back there."

Roberts showed them the body. It was a mess—a cold, gray nightmare.

Tony and Jim listened as Roberts went into the more technical aspects of the death. Roberts was an asshole, but he was good. He always gave the cops the story in plain English before he did his civic duty and began to talk like a scientist. Roberts promised a full, written report before he let the technical terms fly. Neither officer was really listening. They both were thinking the same thing.

They had come to investigate a drug hit. Now it seemed they had a psychopath on their hands.

5

Rockin' Eight Mile

Eight Mile separates Detroit from its northern suburbs. It is a huge, multi-lane street with a concrete island running down the middle. To the locals, however, it's more than a street. It's a wall, a barrier, which over the years has come to symbolize the separation of the races.

In a burgundy Cadillac in a parking lot of the Village, a motel just north of Eight Mile, Theodore Bone pushed a shotgun into the rib cage of a blindfolded man. He jabbed the gun into the soft fold just above the hip. The blindfolded man sat on thick plastic that had been draped over the passenger seat of the Cadillac. In the backseat, a tall, handsome man with long dreadlocks held the blindfolded man from behind.

"I don't have a lot of time to waste on your ass," said the man they called T-Bone. He raised the shotgun and placed it under the man's jaw, careful not to raise the blindfold on his face. The man winced as the barrel touched one of several bruises.

In one of the motel's suites, the thick bass of a rap song pumped through the walls. The windows were covered with the shadows of the dancing people inside. Outside the door, three young men stood guard, trying to hide their weapons.

T-Bone had ordered the party because Grip had been killed. The death party was the dealer's equivalent of a wake. Over the years, T-Bone learned that mourning death was for those who were afraid of it. Rollers celebrated death because they cheated it every day.

"I should kill you," said T-Bone to the blindfolded man.

"Just d-don't s-s-shoot *me*," said the man in the backseat. He was Robert Campbell, Big Money Grip's immediate supervisor and one of T-Bone's lieutenants. Campbell stuttered slightly, a problem which contrasted with his handsome face.

"What did it cost to bail his monkey ass out?" T-Bone said.

"F-five thousand after they d-dropped the murder charge on him. The lawyer g-got him out before the c-c-cops knew what was happenin'."

T-Bone had an ordinary face, but it was etched with a hardness of years in the drug trade. When he dressed commonly, most people would think he was a mailman or perhaps a bus driver—a working man. T-Bone glared at the man at the end of the gun's barrel. T-Bone had been told that the blindfolded man was one of Grip's rollers who was there when Grip was killed.

"Where is my money, Mr. Fields?" T-Bone asked the blindfolded man.

Alonzo Fields was silent, still shaking and hurting from a beating Campbell had inflicted on him earlier.

"Speak up, b-bitch!" Campbell slapped the man hard on the side of the head.

"I don't have it," said Alonzo Fields. "The police took everything I had as evidence."

"He t-tried to rob Grip," said Campbell.

"No, he didn't have no money. I was trying to get his rock," Alonzo said. "To sell it and bring the money back to you, but the Hook got me first."

"Who killed Grip?" asked T-Bone.

"I don't know!" Alonzo said.

"Bullshit!" Campbell slapped Alonzo again.

T-Bone moved closer to Alonzo. "Do you know who I am, Mr. Fields?" T-Bone asked.

"Yeah," Alonzo said, his voice falling. "Nobody."

"Correct. I don't exist, just like the Union doesn't exist. So, if you lie to me, I can do whatever I want to you and nobody will care."

T-Bone pulled the gun away, tucking it between his seat and the door. He then reached into the glove box and pulled out a small, cordless drill. T-Bone turned it on. The tiny engine sprang to life with a high-pitched hum. The sharp drill bit spun in a blur.

Alonzo tensed in the passenger seat.

T-Bone looked at the thin drill bit. He stopped the machine, took out the drill bit and put in a larger one.

"Please, I didn't do nothing!" Alonzo said. "OK, OK man, I was gonna take the money, but I didn't kill him."

"Who did?" T-Bone asked.

"I don't know. I swear!" Alonzo cried.

T-Bone shoved the drill into Alonzo's shoulder. Alonzo yelled and kicked and slammed his body against the locked door. Campbell held him from behind. T-Bone kept up the pressure and blood flowed from the wound onto Alonzo's shirt and the plastic.

"Hold his ass!" T-Bone said to Campbell. He kept the drill in Alonzo's arm.

Campbell slipped his arm around Alonzo's neck, holding him in place. "T-tell the man what he w-wants to know," Campbell said.

Alonzo said nothing. He just whimpered like a child. T-Bone gunned the drill's small engine, the bit still embedded in Alonzo's shoulder and Alonzo screamed again as Campbell struggled to hold him.

"All right," said T-Bone. "Now that we understand each other, I'm gonna ask you again. And this time, if I don't like your answer, I'm taking an eye."

T-Bone pulled the drill out of his arm, and poked around Alonzo's eye socket with his finger. Alonzo sobbed, trying to jerk away.

"Who killed my man?" asked T-Bone.

"I swear, I swear on my mama, I don't know!" Alonzo yelled.

"Sorry."

T-Bone turned the drill around and pushed the blunt end into Alonzo's eye. Alonzo screamed. The drill left an imprint on the blindfold, but Alonzo was not hurt. Campbell laughed quietly in the backseat.

"Get him the fuck up out of my ride," T-Bone said.

Campbell dragged Alonzo out of the car and dumped him on the ground. T-Bone wiped the drill clean of prints then gave it to Campbell. Campbell folded the bloody plastic and took it away.

T-Bone caught Campbell's eyes. T-Bone said nothing.

Campbell nodded then dragged Alonzo away.

T-Bone took a deep breath. He disliked dealing with street trash like Alonzo Fields. But Grip's death was important. The sooner he found out who did it, the sooner he could get back to business.

T-Bone controlled the Union, the drug-gang-that-was-not-a-gang. He had helped organize a truce among the rival gangs several years ago, showing the various crews how there was more money in organized dealing. Those who adopted the plan were soon rewarded. Those who did not, disappeared.

After the organization was complete, he naturally assumed the role of leader. But he did not want glory. He wanted cash. So, he set up the Union as a collection of three autonomous crews, each controlled by a strong leader, and then he distanced himself from the illegal activity. T-Bone only met with his most trusted lieutenants, men he called the Big Three. Robert Campbell, who was disposing of Alonzo Fields, was one of them.

T-Bone checked his watch, then pulled out his cellular phone and dialed a number.

"Room thirty-three fourteen," he said.

T-Bone waited, then a familiar voice came on the line.

"Yes." The man's voice was soft and rich with a South American accent.

"It's me."

"I trust you're calling to tell me when I can have my money."

"I'll get you the damn money, but I need more time!" said T-Bone.

"Your time was up three weeks ago, my friend," said the man on the other end.

"I got a problem here. One of my men was iced."

The line was silent a moment, then, "You owe me a great deal of money. That is my only concern."

"I'll get it. I always do, don't I?"

"I need it now. Your government is squeezing my balls."

"I know things are bad. The shortage is fucking with everybody. That's why I need more time."

There was a silence on the line. Only the thin static of the connection could be heard, then, "A week."

"Cool." T-Bone turned off the phone. "Shit," he cursed quietly as he put the phone in the cradle under the armrest.

T-Bone turned his attention back to the shadows on the windows in the suite. The party was really jumpin' but he wouldn't be attending. He never hung out with his street-level people. Hell, most of them didn't even believe he existed anyway.

Grip's death couldn't have come at a worse time. There was a shortage of coke, thanks to the Feds. And for the last year, T-Bone had been hoarding cash to finance an important operation. Now, he had to scramble to get the money for his suppliers without the aid of Big Money Grip, his best roller.

T-Bone had been told that Grip was wasted by some nut, at least that's what someone wanted him to believe. Grip had recently been approached by several other crews about joining up. He had turned them all down. Grip was a loyal man and maybe somebody wasn't happy about it. Fields didn't know anything about Grip's murder and Campbell would find out everything he did know before he got rid of him.

T-Bone turned on the car's ignition and pulled away from the party. He had more important business than Alonzo Fields. He had to find Grip's killer, raise half a million dollars for his restless suppliers, and he needed to continue the next stage of his costly plan to get out of the business.

6

Tony

The Beretta blasted holes in the black target. Tony fired quickly. Years of training had given him a quick finger and soon the clip was empty. He pushed a large black button and brought the target to him. When it got there, he counted the holes. He had scored only one head wound, two in the heart, and the rest on the perimeter. And the worst part was there were only ten holes. Six of the shots had missed completely. That meant six innocent bystanders were gone.

"Damn," he said.

He slammed in another clip angrily and continued. Target practice was Tony's newest line of defense against The Dream. The nightmare was infrequent, but when it did come, it did so with a vengeance. And he could no longer deny what The Dream meant. The past was coming back to haunt him.

A newspaper reporter had started it all three months ago, when she called and asked for an interview. She was doing a story about an old case he was involved in years ago. The woman had been all over him about doing the story. Tony had turned down her every offer.

Tony's career advanced rapidly when he joined the police force. He became a rookie while Detroit's first black mayor, Coleman Young, was in office. The mayor had instituted an affirmative action program that promoted black officers quickly to achieve parity with the whites.

The mayor favored younger black officers, ones who would be loyal to him and still active in the years to come. The quick ascent of the young cops met with animosity from older black and white officers alike.

Tony enrolled in night school soon after his first promotion. He earned a degree in criminal justice. It wasn't long before he had a detective's shield.

Tony took his success with a mixture of elation and misgiving. He often wondered if he would have advanced so quickly if it weren't for the mayor's program. Tony was sure of his talent. He was intelligent, hard-working, and tough. And since he'd taken over the SCU, its capture and conviction rate had almost doubled. He'd even received a plaque from the prosecutor's office. But would his talents have been enough to earn the leadership of a division? Not knowing burned at the very core of his reason. It haunted him like a ghost, mocking his accomplishments with cruel uncertainty. Tony was confident and effective in his leadership, but part of him wondered if he had truly earned anything. Over the years, many questions of his worth came back to this same uncertainty.

Tony reasoned that whites were at fault for this weakness of spirit. If it were not for their racism and oppression, there would be no need for preference programs and the resulting mental wreckage.

Tony ended his shooting practice when he realized that he had run about a hundred and fifty rounds through the Beretta. Sadly, the practice session had not improved anything. If he read the targets correctly, he'd killed forty innocent people in the session.

He left the target range. He had a busy day. The Chief was holding a press conference on crime and Alonzo Fields's attorney had filed a motion to dismiss his case. Tony was scheduled to appear in court at three.

Tony was walking into his office when Detective Meadows approached him.

"Hey, boss." She smiled brightly. She held a newspaper.

"Awful goddamned early to be smiling like that, detective," Tony said.

Meadows just continued to smile as she shoved the newspaper at him. "Happy anniversary," she said and walked away as Tony unfolded the paper. On the front page of the Metro Section, he read the headline:

TEN YEARS AGO TODAY: HERO COP SAVES HOSTAGES

Tony stared at the newspaper in his office. The black-and-white headline seemed twice as big as it really was. Images of the GM incident and The Dream mingled briefly in his mind.

The article told the story of Tony Hill, still a young detective, and how he had saved several hostages from Darryl Simon, a lunatic.

Simon was a brilliant engineer for General Motors who had gone nuts one day and taken hostages on the eighteenth floor of the GM building.

The SWAT team, state troopers, and local police were all in on the show. Tony and his partner, a cop named Sam Kelly, backed up two SWAT guys on the team assigned to take Simon.

Unfortunately for them, Simon was more clever than they knew. He rigged a bomb that blew up a door and killed the SWAT men. Kelly got caught by it too, but was only knocked out.

Tony survived and made his way to the hostage area. He found Simon holding a rifle on a group of hostages, ranting and raving about the end of the world. Simon was a thin, balding white man of about thirty or so.

Tony also noticed several dead hostages piled in a corner. It was later reported that all the dead hostages were black.

When Simon was clear of the living hostages, Tony shot him, wounding Simon in the shoulder. After Tony evacuated the hostages, Simon got to his feet, and attacked Tony. During the fight, Simon jumped out a window to his death rather than be arrested and tried. Soon thereafter Tony became an inspector.

The news article used words like bravery, courage, honor, and hero frequently. Tony's face frowned as he read, his hands gripping the paper tightly.

"What's up, partner?"

Tony was startled for a second. It was Jim. His voice betrayed a mild concern.

"Nothing, I was just reading," Tony said. He put the newspaper down.

"I was just stopping by to say that if you want, I'll go to court with you today, even though Alonzo Fields's scumbag lawyer didn't think I was good enough to subpoena."

"No, I . . . uh, I want you to keep on the Big Money Grip case. The funeral's tomorrow. Could be some action."

Jim took the newspaper. He scanned it, then looked at Tony. "Nice picture."

"Yeah."

"Is this why you look like someone stole your dick?"

"You know I don't—"

"Yeah, I know you don't like to talk about that GM business."

"Then let's drop it," Tony said.

"No, not this time."

"Very funny. OK, I've got some—"

"I want to talk about this," Jim said. "Ever since I've known you, you have refused to discuss the single most important thing that's happened to you as a cop."

"It's none of your business."

"Fuck that. If whatever's wrong with you is connected to GM, I got a right to know about it. Because sooner or later it's gonna cause you to fuck up and I don't want to catch a bullet when you do."

"You thinking of asking for reassignment?"

"I didn't say that."

"You're talking about getting shot because of me. It's the same thing!"

"I just want to help you."

"Then stay the fuck out of it!"

"I can't. Been together too long. Five years in the Sewer. You breathe, I live, you fart, I shit, you fuck up . . . I die. So, tell it, whatever it is, because if you don't, you're only hurting yourself."

Tony walked over to Jim and gently took the paper from him. "OK. You want to know, all right." He pointed to the newspaper. "This is bullshit."

Jim was stunned. "You didn't save those people's lives?"

"No, that part is true. It's the part about how Simon died."

"He jumped out the window, right?"

"Yes, but . . . I let him do it," Tony said. "Simon threw himself against the window three times before he broke it and I just stood there and watched."

Tony walked back to his desk, holding the newspaper.

"And you never told anyone?" Jim asked.

"How could I? Simon was a killer, but he was also a citizen and I let him die. And there were plenty of people who wanted to see him go to trial."

"But he killed those people. Black people. No one would have blamed you."

Tony smiled a little. "I wish it was that simple. The Penal Code says, and I quote, 'Any law enforcement officer or official who either by act or omission allows or causes a person to be killed or die by accident or by said person's own hand shall be guilty of a felony, punishable by no less than five to fifteen years in prison.' "

"I take it you researched this."

"I have a degree in criminal justice, remember?" Tony said. "It's a felony for a cop to let a person kill himself. If I admit I did it, I go to prison and you know the Prosecutor's Office loves to take down cops."

"Yeah, those bastards. Tried to get me once on a shooting."

"And in case you're wondering, partner, now that you know, if you don't turn me in, you're guilty of a felony too."

"Jesus H. Christ," Jim said. "I can see why you're so upset. But look, man, no one knows, so let's just forget about it."

"Easier said than done, partner," Tony said. "I just need some time to sort things out. Time will do it."

"I hear you. I hear you."

There was a knock at the door. Tony said, "It's open," and in walked Orris Martin, Tony's least favorite member of the SCU. Tony and Jim stopped talking, and for a moment, they looked like kids caught in the act.

Martin was about forty. He had sandy brown hair and eyes that were a hard blue. He was a white cop from the old-school days when there were no blacks on the force. Martin had even sued and lost a reverse discrimination case. This fact made Tony dislike him, even though Martin's lack of respect was reason enough.

"Excuse me, but while I was doing my daily shit work, I got a call from that Fields kid's lawyer."

"Right," said Tony ignoring Martin's sarcasm. "I've got that motion to dismiss the hearing this afternoon, thanks."

"You can cancel that," Martin said. "Your witness is gone. Alonzo Fields can't be located." There was a hint of pleasure in his voice.

"What?!" Tony said. "He's in jail."

"Nope. Somebody sprung him. Laid down five big ones."

"Shit," said Jim.

"Dammit. We've got to find him," Tony said.

"Come on, you know he's dead," said Martin.

"We don't know anything," said Jim. "Get a team together," he said to Martin.

Martin left without a word.

"He enjoyed that," said Tony.

"No time to worry about him. We've got to find out what happened to Fields," Jim said.

"I hate to say it, but Martin is probably right."

"Let's not get ahead of ourselves."

Tony dropped the newspaper in the wastebasket, taking a second to look at it as if it would jump back out by itself.

"Jim, I'll understand if you want to reassign yourself because of what I told you."

"I don't know what you're talking about," Jim said.

"Simon. The GM thing."

"I have no knowledge of that, your honor," Jim said.

"Thanks, man," Tony said. "Let's go find our witness."

7

Fuller and Salinsky

Police Chief William Fuller walked the high-wire like a pro. The press was always out for blood and today he was the sacrifice. Mayor Yancy had issued a written report on crime to counter media accusations. Yancy then set up a press conference, lit a fire and put Fuller on the grill. But it was his job. Fuller was the top man in the Detroit Police Department and he answered directly to the mayor.

The room in the Millender Center was filled to capacity. All three local television stations were there as well as both papers and the radio journalists. These were the times when Fuller had to be at his best. He liked the challenge.

Bill Fuller was six foot four and weighed in at two-sixty. He was a big man in every sense of the word. Big body, large booming voice, and a manner that made everything he said a command.

Fuller headed toward the press conference in his dress blues, trailed by his aides, who struggled to keep up with his giant steps. Fuller lead the procession, looking like a military leader.

The Chief's graying hair was barely visible under his cap. That gray was caused in part by pushing sixty and in part by Mayor Yancy.

In this election year, a lawyer named Craig Batchelor was giving Yancy a run for his money. The city's crime problem had gotten worse during the last term. Yancy had even fallen out of favor with some of the unions, and that was bad news in Detroit.

Yancy had only beaten Batchelor by eleven percent the last time and now Batchelor was four years older and ten times wiser. He had young, talented supporters and lots of money. This time, he was for real.

So Fuller had to face the media hounds about the report. It was a shitty document. It contained no hope and even fewer answers for a tired and angry citizenry.

Fuller was briefed by some of the mayor's aides, but he ended the session early. He didn't need those college boys with their trendy-ass ties and red suspenders giving him any lessons in how to be a public figure. Screw the briefing. He worked without a net.

"Chief Fuller! Why was the report issued after unfavorable articles in the media?" asked a television reporter.

"Well, if you guys had given an accurate description of what's happening in this town," said Fuller, "there would be no need for a report. We did it so that the good citizens of Detroit would know the real story."

"Craig Batchelor says the report is an attempt to divert attention from the city's crime problem. Is that true?" asked April Lindsey, a TV reporter.

"I think that statement by Mr. Batchelor was an attempt to divert attention to himself. He's so dull, he needs us to even be noticed."

The gallery laughed loudly.

"Wouldn't you say, Chief Fuller, that the crime problem has gotten worse since the last election?" said a reporter.

"Well, that's one point of view," he said. "As the report states, theft and robberies are up, but murder, rape, and other violent crimes are occurring below last year's totals for this time."

Questions began to come from all directions. Then one voice rose above the others. It was Carol Salinsky from Channel Five. A good reporter, probably too good to be local. Salinsky was tenacious and always seemed to know inside information. She was beautiful, smart, and a consummate professional. Fuller hated her guts.

"But isn't it true that the statistics used don't take into account crimes committed by juveniles, those under the age of majority?" Salinsky asked. "The report deals only with adults. When you add juveniles in, my calculations say the rate of violent crime is up by . . ." she looked at her notes. The gallery was unusually quiet. "Fifteen percent."

Fuller looked uneasy. He stumbled with the answer, and an undercurrent of laughter spread through the gallery. "Your information is obviously not accurate. You are just throwing out numbers."

"That's funny. I was about to suggest that you did the same."

The gallery exploded in laughter. Fuller was upset. He moved on to the next question.

"Chief Fuller," said a radio journalist, "A major street-level drug dealer was just killed. Would you say that it was a hit by a rival gang and if so, does the department expect further violence as a result?"

Fuller's brow furrowed. "I can't comment. We are still investigating the matter."

"Is it true that Floyd Turner, or Big Money Grip as he was called, was mutilated?" asked Salinsky.

Fuller hesitated, then, "I'm not at liberty to discuss any matters pertaining to the condition of the deceased."

Salinsky smelled blood. "Were his hands cut off, Chief?" Salinsky said "Chief" with obvious contempt.

"Look, Salinsky, I said . . ."

"Was he sexually assaulted, Chief?"

"I am not going to answer any of those ridiculous questions!"

The television crews loved it. They got it all on camera. Pictures were flashed, capturing Fuller's frustrated look.

"Well, I guess we know one thing then," Salinsky said. "Whoever killed Big Money Grip was over eighteen, or I guess you wouldn't know anything."

The laughter was deafening. Fuller was going to find Salinsky's contact in the police department if it was the last thing he did. And when he found the leak, he was going to tear that officer a new asshole.

Fuller quickly ended the conference and tried to escape the media, who pursued him into the hallway as he left. He caught a glimpse of Salinsky. She had on a shit-eating grin. Fuller smiled back. The bitch would eat shit one day all right.

Fuller hurried. He would be in the City-County Building in no time thanks to the connecting walk between the buildings. He was supposed to meet the mayor right after the lunchtime press conference to tell him how it went. Yancy was not going to be happy.

8

Yancy and the River

The river was beautiful to Harris Yancy. It was late spring and boaters were happily cruising on the water which rolled and crested as if playing with the wind. The sun added its treasures and the river smiled a wonderful reflection. He loved the river. It was just like him.

He had been mayor of Detroit for two terms. Eight years. It seemed like an eternity. He remembered the city when it was run by whites. Blacks were blocked out of every major avenue of life, openly discriminated against, forced to live in the worst areas of the city, and denied public services. And when Coleman Young, ran that historic campaign, Yancy was right in the thick of it and they had won, beating the whites at their own game.

When Coleman Young retired, Yancy had gotten the call. But it was a struggle to fill his predecessor's shoes. The city was sick and crippled because white people would sooner move their businesses and lives out into a desert before they'd live in a city run by blacks. So Detroit, under black leadership, had not become a promised land for disenfranchised blacks, but a continuation of hardship and poverty.

And so he had taken up the fight with the establishment. He used the old tactics of the Movement to battle the white men who controlled all the money and power. He threw their past atrocities against blacks in their faces. He used race to bait them and beat them down whenever he could.

Some of the younger black leaders questioned this. They said he was only making the problem worse, that it was time to stop making everything an issue of race. But Yancy understood that it was his only tool. Whites had money and power. All his people had was their suffering and the guilt that moved moral men to do the right thing.

Race had given Detroit to blacks and it would be race that brought it back to its former power.

Still, Yancy had thought of retirement. Hell, half his friends told him to think about it. But if he left, who would look out for the people? He provided the means by which jobs were attained, money made, and bills paid. A whole generation of blacks had gone to college thanks to black rule. His machine was a spider's web of familial and personal relationships. It stretched out over two decades of power in the mayor's office.

Yancy regularly discussed leaving office with his wife, Louise. She was a faithful politician's mate, but lately she was yearning to see more of the world. At times, she urged him to think about what he was doing. They were in their sixties. There was wisdom in the idea that they should spend their last years enjoying life, instead of subjecting themselves to pressure.

He could not retire yet. He was needed and that was special. It was like Anthony Quinn said in that movie *Lawrence of Arabia*: "He was a river to his people."

Yancy wanted one more shot at rescuing the city. If he could just get reelected, he could bring the city back and leave the mayor's office with some dignity. If only the people had passed that casino measure. That would have done it. He would have had the money and development he needed. But that damned Batchelor and some ministers had taken to the streets and stopped it.

"Harris, Chief Fuller is here to see you." His secretary, Novelda Reed, cut through his musing.

Yancy reluctantly turned away from the water. This was one of the few moments that he'd had to himself in the last few months.

"Send him in."

Fuller lumbered into the spacious office. Yancy and Fuller had known each other since their service in Korea. They were two of the few blacks who had been inducted into the elite fighting corps of the Green Berets. Yancy and a white soldier named Riggins had carried Fuller for two miles under fire after Fuller was hit in the leg. He still had the limp, a constant reminder of owing his life to Yancy.

Fuller looked upset and Yancy knew at once that his old friend had some trouble at the press conference. Normally, he would have been furious, but the river had mellowed him.

"Problem with the press, Bill?" he asked even before Fuller sat down.

"You heard already?" asked Fuller taking a seat.

"I know you, man."

"Salinsky. That bitch knew about the juvenile deletion in the report."

"I see. And how did she find out?"

"I wish to hell I knew." Fuller turned his hat in his hands. "I'll find out who's tipping her."

"Is that all?" Yancy knew there was more. He could see it.

"No."

"Tell it, man."

"She also knew some sensitive information about the drug dealer who got popped last weekend. She knew about the missing hands and the possibility of sexual abuse." Fuller stared straight at his friend. If there was an explosion coming, it was gonna happen now. Yancy hated leaks.

"Is she certain?" The calmness in Yancy's voice caused Fuller to relax. It was gonna be OK.

"She didn't say she definitely knew, but I know her. She knows. It'll be on the six o'clock news tonight. Hell, if Salinsky knew, Channel Five probably had it on the noon report, thirty minutes before the press conference."

Yancy looked right into Fuller's soul. "Did she know about the samples?"

Fuller hadn't expected that. He had worried that Salinsky knew but didn't think the mayor would be concerned. "I don't think so. She didn't say anything about it and if she knew, she would have to. She's arrogant like that."

"So, no one knows besides you, me, and Roberts?

"That's right."

"Who's on the case again?

"Hill. Tony Hill. A good man. The best."

"Does he know yet?"

"No. He hasn't been told yet."

"Find the goddamned leak, Bill. If this thing gets out, I don't have to tell you what's gonna happen. And tell Roberts that if it gets out, it's his ass."

Yancy let a moment pass for the gravity to sink in. "How about some lunch, Bill?"

"Sure. Opus? Rattlesnake Club?"

"Mario's," Yancy said smiling. It was his favorite place. Best Italian food in the world. Yancy put on his jacket and told Novelda to cancel three afternoon appointments. He was going to take a mini-vacation.

Before he left, he took a last look at his river. He was troubled about Roberts's samples. He had a sense about these things. It idled around the back of his mind, defying his power to ignore it like a sore that wanted to be picked. And not even the river helped.

9

T-Bone

T-Bone gripped her shoulders harder. The girl uttered something hard beneath him then let out a long breath. Her ponytail jostled as T-Bone moved faster behind her. Her hand slipped a bit as she held the edge of the dresser in the dark room.

T-Bone was lost in thought. His frustrations churned in his head as he made love to the girl. Grip was dead, Santana was on his ass about the late money, and his plan to get out of dealing was stalled.

He heard the girl make a pained sound and he slowed his effort and stroked the side of her face. He was not the type to hurt a woman.

He was told the young girl was twenty, but he had the feeling she was younger. In any event, she had cost him a nice piece of money.

T-Bone only had sex with prostitutes. He'd learned that having a regular woman was too much of a hassle. They talked too much, spent too much, and eventually wanted to share your power. Sooner or later you might have to kill her and that would be a whole other set of annoying problems. A call girl was a criminal too, in her own way, and she'd keep her mouth shut. She just wanted the money. It was a perfect relationship.

T-Bone moved the girl over to the sofa where she straddled him. She was full of energy and seemed to be enjoying herself. T-Bone found himself getting into the act, too. He moved her onto her back and slipped between her legs. Soon, he reached a climax.

He rose and planted kisses on her breasts. She breathed hard and made a pleasant little sound. He noticed for the first time that she had a wonderful smell.

T-Bone broke the connection and sat next to her. She stood up. She was beautiful. She was a soft brown with nice full breasts and long legs.

The girl smiled, removed the condom from him, then walked into the bathroom. T-Bone watched her. Jasmine, his supplier of women, had outdone herself this time, he thought. He would have to tell her that this girl was a keeper.

Soon he heard the shower running. He put on his boxers, lit up a joint and stretched out on the bed. He needed to relax. He would figure his way through his current troubles, he told himself. He always did.

T-Bone was from what was considered in his neighborhood a good family. His father was an assembly line foreman and his mother a teacher. He loved his mother dearly, but his relationship with his father had never even approached that emotion.

Theodore Bone Senior was a large, barrel-chested man full of male bravado. He was an auto worker, marine, and football player, he was the Great Father-Provider. And of course his only son had been nothing by comparison. "Little Teddy," they called him. T-Bone hated the name. To his father and his friends he was never quite good enough, never able to match his father's maleness. Big Teddy called his good grades "sissy stuff" and inveighed his lack of athletic ability.

Slowly, his father had turned him away from every normal thought and need he ever had. T-Bone understood that his father didn't really want his son to be like him. Big Teddy cherished his son's failures and wallowed in the knowledge that he would always be the bigger man, the only man in the family.

But that was a long time ago, T-Bone thought. Now his father was old and broken and where an asshole like him deserved to be.

T-Bone credited his father for his turn to crime. Big Teddy had driven him to it as surely as he breathed. T-Bone felt he had to prove he was a man and chose crime because it only accepted real men. Besides, he had reasoned, there were two great truths in the world: only a fool defers gratification, and this country was too racist to ever let any smart black man (who didn't sing, dance, or play with a ball for a living) ever get ahead.

In a different world, he might have been the bright young man on the fast track in a Fortune 500 company. But in this reality, the truth of capitalist America, he was what a smart kid who doesn't escape the ghetto often turned out to be: a drug dealer.

In the old days, the drug business was run by a bunch of old men wearing big, ugly hats and listening to eight-track tapes of Isaac Hayes. It was different now. Most of the really serious dealers were still in their twenties and some of them (though not many) even had style.

T-Bone was in his mid-thirties and still on top in Detroit. If you read the papers or listened to the news, you would think that all dope was being run by a bunch of stupid, random punks who didn't know their asshole from the center of a doughnut. And that's just the way he liked it.

He had worked hard to put together the Union and even harder to put people between him and the law. Most of the street salesmen were juveniles who couldn't be prosecuted as adults and who never saw him in person. If they got busted, they were out in no time.

T-Bone had three main men who distributed the product: David Traylor, Robert Campbell (who was sometimes called Soup), and Steve Mayo. They were tough, loyal, smart and would lay down their lives for him. He had hand-picked and molded them from a young age. You had to get them while they were young, challenge them to overcome their fears, and make them into men.

Each of the Big Three had come from a fatally poor family and had no chance of success in the mainstream. T-Bone had given them the world: confidence, knowledge, money, and women. He was the father they never had. He kept them clean and away from the product long enough for them to respect moderation. He let them get busted and spend time in jail to learn the ropes. They became tough, smart, and faithful to him. Now, they basically did it all, acquisition, distribution, and collection of the cash. He had a bunch of white boys wash the money for him and he was home free. He kept his exposure to a minimum and he only became personally involved when someone was stealing, or in a crisis. Like Grip's death.

T-Bone also had a relationship with the police. There were always cops who took money. People knew, but proving it was another thing. To T-Bone, law and crime were not enemies but brothers. One needed the other to exist. Without crime, there would be no need for police. Without law, crime would be chaos and yield no profit.

He'd entered into a partnership with a cop on the force several years ago. T-Bone paid a weekly amount and his operation was provided a measure of protection. The only problem was, the cops wanted a lot of money and their numbers were small. So, they could only do so much. There were raids, but they tried to tip him off beforehand to keep the damage minimal. T-Bone only talked to the head cop, but had seen him only once. He just paid the money, asked no questions and so far, it was OK.

T-Bone had been hoping that Grip would become his fourth high-level man. It would have been the Big Four, just like the cops called their team of two uniformed officers and two detectives.

T-Bone had risen through the ranks in a now defunct gang called the Black Killers. He'd managed to elude the police and, consequently, had no record. But the cops were not fools. They knew about him, but could never get anything on him. Even the Feds had failed. So far, he had been too smart. And now he was so far removed from the action that they didn't bother him at all.

There was only one group big enough to kill one of his dealers. But the Southend Crew were a bunch of faggots, lightweight punks who were lucky he let them stay around. Their leader, Cut Jefferson, was a man, though. He had taken those sorry-ass punks and made something of them. But he was too smart to fuck with the Union, T-Bone thought.

Maybe it was one of the independents, he thought, or one of the suburban Chaldean Crews. There were only a few of them, but they were crazy enough to try anything. But the Chaldeans were small and mainly distributors. T-Bone made deals with them when he could and kept the peace. Could they be trying to get the two biggest crews to fight, so they could expand after the blood was spilled?

Grip's death was just part of the recent bad news. The Feds had made several major drug busts in Texas, Florida, and California two months ago. The bastards had hauled in enough coke to supply the western world. So T-Bone's suppliers were hurting and growing intolerant of his late payments.

T-Bone desperately wanted out of the business. Not many dealers made it out alive but he was determined to be one of those who did.

About six months ago, he was introduced by phone to a man who called himself the Prince. This man claimed he could revolutionize the drug trade by making a drug like crack that was even cheaper, used less cocaine, and was more potent.

Crack was already cheap to produce. So at first T-Bone was not interested. But then he remembered those who doubted whether crack would catch on. They said crack was too common and would never make money. They were wrong and the revolution caught them with their pants down.

T-Bone had spent considerable time thinking about what this could mean to him. Much of his money went back to his suppliers, and to the cops. So, he was going to meet with the Prince, who was coming into town soon. Nothing big, he just wanted to see who he was dealing with. If the Prince was the real deal, he would find a way to get the money. If not, the Prince might leave town in a box.

The girl came back out of the bathroom dressed in a long, tight dress and high heels. The dress was white with a row of big, black buttons in the front.

T-Bone smiled. Jasmine had remembered all of his preferences. He motioned the girl to come over.

The girl walked slowly over to the bed and spun around, letting him see. The dress hugged her and he could clearly see the outline of her body.

"Nice," he said.

T-Bone removed his boxers and began to unbutton the dress slowly, taking his time.

His beeper went off on the nightstand. He ignored it.

10

Tony, Nikki, and Moe

Tony watched the footage of Grip's funeral with disdain on TV at his home in Detroit's Palmer Woods. A fashionable, upscale neighborhood, former home to Detroit's affluent whites, it was now inhabited by decidedly middle-class blacks. Tony and his wife Nikki together made more than enough to afford their house. Heading the Sewer paid well, one of its few advantages.

Big Money Grip was finally allowed to be buried, thanks in part to Carol Salinsky's ace reporting. The police had to admit that Grip's hands had been cut off and taken. The family had been kept in the dark. They had only been allowed to examine the corpse's tortured face.

Hands. What did that mean? Tony had been thinking about it ever since Roberts's report. Was it just a lunatic's random pattern of violence or was it a clue to his identity?

Carol Salinsky, dressed in a black suit, reported on the funeral. She had a pained, sad look on her face. Tony half believed she gave a damn about Grip's death.

"Here at the Eastside Memorial Baptist Church there is an aura of dread and melancholy," Salinsky said. "Floyd Turner, also known as Big Money Grip, was laid to rest. Family and friends were torn apart by their loss."

There was a shot of Grip's mother, a heavy, light-skinned woman, crying a river on camera for the television stations, and they caught every drop. She was held up by two big men as they left the church.

"Etta Turner refused to comment to this reporter," Salinsky said. "But did say that she's continuing with her lawsuit against the city, for not recovering the missing hands of her son. In case you're curious, the deceased's hands were replaced by the undertaker with hands made from plastic molds."

Salinsky appeared on camera again.

"There is much speculation about the death of the man some say was the biggest street dealer in Detroit. But ironically, the thing some will remember most is the deceased's coffin."

The camera showed a picture of a coffin made to look like a fancy car. It even had hubcaps on it. Tony was disgusted. How could the stations broadcast that garbage into people's homes knowing that kids would see it? This kind of thing glorified drug dealing and the TV bastards didn't care what effect it had on inner-city children.

Tony watched as the pallbearers walked down the church steps with the monstrosity. He could see several of them struggling as they carried it. It must have weighed a ton. Just as he was about to turn off the spectacle, Carol Salinsky's very serious looking face appeared again.

"So, as Floyd Turner is laid to rest, one can only guess how the police will deal with his murder. Some suspect a street war will follow in the aftermath. But more importantly, how many more young black men will be slaughtered by this cunning and vicious killer?"

Tony sighed heavily. She was really laying it on.

Salinsky continued as the cameras went in for a close-up. "And in a fitting end to this day of mourning and fear, the killer of Floyd Turner now has a name."

"What?" Tony said aloud.

"Because of the medical examiner's admission that the killer removed the victim's hands with uncommon skill, a sick joke began circulating within the police department that the murderer is very '*handy* with a knife.' So some are calling Detroit's probable serial killer the Handyman."

"Jesus Christ," Tony said. He switched off the TV. A name after only one victim. Cops had to use sick humor to deal with the job, but journalists didn't have to exploit it.

Carol Salinsky was becoming a big pain in the ass. After her first story exposing the manner in which Grip was killed, Yancy sent Fuller to another press conference where he gave the department's official position on the matter. Fuller told the whole story and released an un-official copy of the autopsy.

The media was having a grand celebration. It was the juiciest story in quite a while and the press sensed what the police already knew. The killing was not over.

Tony was taking the afternoon off in hopes of lowering his tension level. They hadn't found Alonzo Fields yet, and after his revelation to Jim about Darryl Simon, he was feeling more off-center than ever. He leaned back in his old La-Z-Boy recliner and closed his eyes.

Now that the Handyman was an official citizen of Detroit, Tony's life would certainly be getting worse. He had actually thought of tak-ing a vacation until it cooled down, but he knew that was impossible in an election year. The mayor would lean on Fuller, who would lean on him. And besides, he was not going to let someone else catch the killer.

He just wanted to rest now, rest and forget about all of the pol-iticians, criminals, degenerates, and assholes of the world. He slowly lowered into sleep, floating between slumber and wakefulness, the two realities shifted in dominance while he wiggled in the chair trying to find a comfortable position.

When he finally drifted off, The Dream came again and he awoke with a faint cry.

Tony sat there, sweating in his favorite chair in the den, his heart beating like an untamed animal's. He breathed deeply. The events in his life seemed to be under their own power. Killers killed, rollers spread poison, politicians lied to the public, and The Dream tor-mented him without mercy. He straightened his back as his six-year-old son Maurice walked in.

"What's the matter, Daddy?" asked the small boy. He had a round head and big, bright eyes that were a dreamy shade of brown. He was small for his age and had a face that looked as if he would break into a smile at any time.

Tony softened at the sight of him. He could never find words to express his feelings about his son. Moe was the only thing that ever seemed completely right. He was cute, smart, and just bad enough to make a father proud.

"Just had a bad dream, that's all."

"Like the Freddy Krueger?"

"No, not quite. Hey, I thought I told you not to watch that stuff on TV."

"I didn't see it. I heard it, in school."

"Well, don't listen."

"I cover my ears but it keeps getting in," Moe laughed.

Tony fought the smile as long as he could. He embraced his son and fought him playfully from his chair. This was better than therapy. He had never wanted children at first, but when Moe came along, he saw that he had been wrong. This was good, completely good, and there were not many things in life that he could say that about.

Once Moe was born, he realized he had a lifetime of commitment and sacrifice. There were no more spontaneous trips and adventures. Always now, the child came first. But as he gave his life over, he found that his son held magic. He was honest, uncorrupted, and beautiful in his simplicity. Moe brought Tony in touch with great emotion. The miracle of birth and the mystery of life were twins, and while The Great Question was not answered, it was now easier to live with.

But it was also a terrible responsibility. Children were, to some extent, only what you made them. How would he deal with the inevitable questions of race and prejudice that Moe would bring to him? What would he say to his son about the bitter discord in the world?

Nikki Hill entered the den and broke up the wrestling match. Still half-asleep, she hadn't heard her husband's yell. She was thirty-two and very attractive, though she was putting on weight. Her dark brown skin and almond-shaped eyes gave her an exotic, almost Asian look. She pulled her son away from his father, trying not to drop him as he wiggled in her arms.

"What have I told you about beating up your father?" she said.

Moe just pointed at his father making a mean face and said, "Next time, next time," like the professional wrestlers he saw on television.

Tony sometimes felt strange when he saw his wife and son together. It was like he had just awakened from a daydream. He wondered who they were and what relation they had to him. My wife. My son. It did not seem possible sometimes that he had been so lucky.

"Well, Mr. Hill, is this how we rest on our day off?" said Nikki. "You know you need to relax."

Tony knew he was in trouble. Whenever there was a "Mr. Hill" in the house, that meant he was messing up.

"I was just fooling around. Besides, I already slept." He forced a smile.

"I'll get us dinner. You just take it easy," she said then kissed him lightly on the lips and left with Moe in her arms.

Tony sat down in the La-Z-Boy again. He was so lucky to have Nikki, he thought. She was bright and compassionate. She was a manager with Chrysler and made good money. Nikki was a business-woman, a mother, and a wife. She was impressive. Then again, he had always admired her.

They met while he was taking night classes in Criminal Justice at Wayne State. They were both studying in the Law Library Annex, a nice, carpeted area with dull gray cubicles for individual study. Tony had fallen asleep and was snoring loudly. It was finals time and he had worked himself to exhaustion. He was awakened by a beautiful woman, looking down at him over her book.

"You're making a lot of noise," she had said.

Tony sat up and a piece of paper had stuck to the side of his face. He had been drooling and the paper was glued by it. "Oh, God," he said pulling the paper away and wiping himself. He was fatally embar-rassed and he showed it. Nikki covered her mouth, laughing.

"I fall asleep all the time in here, too," she said.

"I bet you don't slobber all over yourself."

Nikki disappeared into her cubicle. Tony had seen her before. She had a lovely face and, quite frankly, the best ass he had ever seen. She always studied alone but was too good-looking not to have a man, so he had never made a move. And now he was introduced to her with spit on his face. Tony Hill: Ladies' Man.

Tony was totally surprised when Nikki returned with a Kleenex. He took it and laughed as he wiped at his face. "Well," he said, "I guess we should make a date to go out."

"Excuse me?"

"I said that . . ."

"Oh, I heard you, I just don't get it. Where did that come from?" She was trying to suppress a smile and he thought it was the most beautiful thing he had ever seen.

"I figure that since you've seen me at my worst, I have nothing to lose. I mean, I can't get any more stupid than that."

"I see your point."

They began to date casually. Although they were strongly attracted, they were wary of each other. They both had battle scars from dating and neither possessed a desire to add more. Nikki was pleasantly surprised at Tony's sensitivity and thoughtfulness. And he was flat-out in love.

After a month of dating, they had gone to a concert and returned to Tony's home early. The soulful, melodic sound of the O'Jays still filled their heads. After a drink, some dull conversation and disguised foreplay, they went to bed. They attacked their endeavor like hungry workers at a long-awaited meal. They surprised even themselves with their intensity and the depth of their own selfish pleasure. They writhed in the covers, minds absorbed with their lust. Only when it was over, did they realize that neither of them had been so involved in a long time.

"So, how long since you did it?" asked Nikki laughing.

"Was it that obvious?" Tony said.

"Eight months," she said. "That's about how long it's been for me."

"Eight months!" Tony said trying to sound surprised. "It hasn't been near that long for me."

"Right. If you had come any harder, the neighbors would've called the cops."

"Do I have to say, I am a cop?"

"Come on, Tony. How long?" She sat up in the bed.

Tony paused, a little embarrassed.

"Four months."

"That's long for a man, right?"

"Yeah, it's like eight months for a woman."

She grabbed him and it started again. The encounter lasted the whole night. They had to make up for lost time. For Tony, Nikki was a godsend. He needed a good woman and he needed sex too. How nice to finally have them in the same package.

"We should do this every night," Tony said. "Screw all that going out crap. Just you, me, and the bed." Tony grabbed her playfully, still in his briefs.

Nikki pulled away gently, looking hurt. It soon turned to a look of mild anger. After an awkward discussion that turned into a bitter argument, she was gone.

They didn't see each other again for a month. They spoke on the phone, but Nikki seemed to want to make him suffer. She gave him just enough hope to call again, but she would not go out with him.

He wanted to write her off, but he could not. Nikki had made him feel whole, given him an essential, primal, part of life that he had needed for so long and he would not be denied her.

Tony became obsessed with her. He sent flowers and cards. He wrote letters and called every day. He tried to convey to her what he was feeling and failed miserably. He tripped and fumbled over every word and statement and he was beside himself with his desire. And then, without reason, she forgave him. She never said why and he was too scared to pursue it. Women. Who knew why they did anything?

Ironically, when they finally saw each other again, they made love. She almost had to force him. He was afraid that it would end badly again, but he was too taken with her and much too weak. They were just as feverish in their love-making the second time. Tony enjoyed it, but could not help feeling that something was wrong. When it was over, he was a mass of confusion—happy, afraid, anxious, and satisfied. Against his better judgment, he spoke.

"I don't understand. I thought that you had a problem with us making love."

"No, it wasn't that."

"Then what?" He was pushing, and was surprised that he had the nerve.

"Well," she said, "it's complicated."

"Try me," Tony said.

"After we made love that first time you said can we do this all the time, like you didn't want me, just sex."

"But I didn't mean it that way."

"I know that now." Nikki smiled.

"I don't know how you get there from an innocent statement."

"I'll tell you a secret," Nikki said. "Life isn't fair to women. We have maybe six or seven years where everyone wants us then it's all downhill. Men mature. Women age. Women get fat. Men get 'that successful look.' Women have children. Men become fathers. Life uses women. It chews up our youth and spits us out into middle age. So we are wary of men—all men. And we are determined not to waste our good years on what we think is worthlessness. So a little thing becomes a big thing, a slip becomes a warning signal. Sure it's paranoid, but it's also safe. No matter how successful or independent we are, we look for some measure of safety from the unfairness of life."

Her voice trailed off. Tony was quiet and he stayed that way. They made love again and not a word was spoken for the rest of the night. Thereafter, they referred to their first fight as Hell Night and it became a continuing reference and measuring device for other incidents in their lives. This or that wasn't as bad as Hell Night, they would often say. After a while, it became a joke and a link to their shared past.

In retrospect, Tony thought that it was Hell Night that truly brought them together. They had probably opened up more about themselves because of it than they would have normally.

Years later, after marriage, he witnessed Nikki's relentless intellect and subtle, manipulative manner, and he wondered whether their Hell Night was planned, contrived by an ingenious mind. When he thought about it, it made sense. She initiated the complaint and framed the issue during the fight. She had let him pursue her, and granted him her favors when it suited her and never told him the reason. And the beginning and end of Hell Night were both sexual encounters, poignant points of reference and subtle statements of trust. Had she played him? There was a pattern: adversity then sex. (Punishment and reward?) He considered the possibility that his wife had constructed an elaborate plan to get him to marry her from the very beginning, and he was exhilarated and upset all at once. Nikki was the kind of woman who could elicit that type of reaction.

"Dinner is ready, honey," Nikki called from the kitchen.

Tony answered and walked toward the bathroom to wash his hands. His mother always made him do that and old habits were hard to break. He was trying to relax, but there was just too much going on inside his mind. He would have to concentrate on just one thing and he knew it had to be his work. It was, next to his family, the most important thing in his life. And Nikki was a true cop's wife. She would understand if he threw himself into this thing. She had been through it before.

Tony entered the half-bath downstairs and ran warm water over his hands. He stared at his tired face in the mirror.

A reflection was a frightening thing, he thought. Just as the mirror doesn't lie, neither can you lie to yourself when you look into it. He saw all of his life's secrets in his eyes behind the glass.

The Dream was a truth that he could see all too well. It was a truth that still haunted him, even after his confession to Jim.

Tony was still concerned about telling Jim the GM story. It wasn't that he worried about being turned in by Jim. Their friendship was too strong. He was concerned that Jim would eventually ask more disturbing questions. Jim was a cop after all, and it was his job to see through a lie.

The familiar frustration boiled inside of Tony. He had saved the lives of many people in the GM building that night, and what was his reward? A nightmare of guilt and fear that was unnerving his very life.

The water was hot and soothing as he lathered his hands. Tony looked at them and thought about the Handyman.

11

The House on Shalon Street

The bright red Jeep sped down Livernois Avenue, jumping up and down as it hit bumps and potholes. Rap music pulsed out of the vehicle's large speakers as it darted in and out of the late-night traffic, changing lanes and passing other cars. It whizzed by the many shops, glowing streetlights, and restaurants as if on a mission.

Inside, Derek Nelson and Jonnel Washington bopped and rapped along to the tune. They were off duty for a while. They had worked all day selling crack and now they were going to take a well-deserved break. It had been a long day and the cops had been out in force. It was like that every election year.

They were both sixteen but hardly ever went to school. There was too much money to be made. They laughed at all those other stupid-asses—studying, joining clubs, and slaving at the local Burger King. They, on the other hand, were getting paid. That's what it was all about.

"Damn, this beat is *phat!*" said Jonnel, rocking to the tune.

"Hell, yeah," said Derek, waving one hand.

They bounced along for half a mile, when Derek leaned over and turned down the music. "So, man, what you think they gonna do 'bout Grip?" he asked.

"They gone find out who did it and fuck his shit up," said Jonnel. "Grip was da man."

"Yeah, he was cool people."

"You know, they gone need somebody to take his place, know what I'm sayin?"

"I heard that," said Derek. "And it's gonna be me."

"You?" laughed Jonnel. "It's gone be *me*. They wouldn't trust the Strip to yo sorry ass. You be in jail so fast, it wouldn't even be funny."

"You gotta be the most jealous muthafucka I know. You know I'm tight with Traylor and it's fuckin' with you," Derek said.

"Right. Only thang tight is yo imagination."

"You know I'm his boy. He gave me a gold watch last week."

"Don't mean shit," Jonnel said.

"All right, man, anything you say. May the best nigga win."

They bumped fists. Jonnel was mad but he didn't want his friend to know it. He wanted Grip's job and he was going to get it, despite Derek's relationship with David Traylor, who was one of the Union's Big Three. Jonnel was determined to do it, even if he had to go through Derek.

Derek made a sharp left turn onto Outer Drive. They were going to his brother's house. He lived just a few blocks from Livernois with his girlfriend, Sharon Borders. Rolan Nelson was a retired roller turned distribution chief. He had hung out with all the big-time guys when he was younger. Rolan would still have been on the street if he hadn't gotten shot and lost his nerve. Now, he was just a storage man, but very well connected.

The house was the main northwest distribution point. The neighborhood was respectable, filled with single-family homes. The lawns were well kept and the street clean. Neighborhood Watch signs hung from telephone poles and trees. Derek and his brother had set up the house with Traylor's help. The Union made distribution runs during the day and took in coke shipments three times a week. For the last year, they had supplied most of the north end of Detroit. That's why Derek knew he had an inside track to Grip's job; things were going well.

Derek turned down Shalon Street and parked in front of his brother's house on the corner.

Jonnel removed a nylon bag from under his seat. It bulged with the currency it held. He took an Uzi pistol out of its hiding place under a panel in the back of the Jeep. The gun was his baby. They were expensive and damned hard to come by. It was totally wrong to carry it in a vehicle, but he couldn't help it. He liked to flash it in front of the young kids and girls. They got a charge out of it. The two young men got out and walked up to the front door. Derek stopped at the door, looking for the right key.

They entered the house. The living room was small and well kept. A long staircase rose from the back, leading upstairs. The dining room was off to the left. It was dark and the light from the upstairs faintly glowed from the top of the stairs.

"Damn, it's dark. Turn the lights on, man," said Jonnel.

"Hey, Rolan!" Derek yelled. "It's us, man." Derek fumbled for the light switch and found it.

The instant the lights came on, both men were blinded for a split second. When their eyes focused, they clearly saw the bodies in the corner. They were naked and twisted as if they had been played with, like dolls. Sharon had a bullet hole in the front of her head. There was a spray of blood on the wall behind her. Rolan's hands were cut off and his throat was a tangle. There was blood everywhere. It looked fresh.

"Sh—, shit! Shit!!" Derek yelled. He began walking toward the corpses.

Jonnel pulled up the Uzi and put the money bag around his shoulder. He pulled Derek back toward the stairway. Jonnel was thinking fast. Derek was out of it and had to be handled. "Call Traylor on his car phone and tell him what happened!" Jonnel said.

There was a phone on a small wooden stand next to a closet at the foot of the stairs. Derek was in a daze. He couldn't take his eyes from his dead brother. "Wake the fuck up, man, and do it!" Jonnel said. "I'm gone check upstairs and then we'll go in the basement to see if any of the coke is missing."

Jonnel turned to go up the stairs when the closet door opened. The creaking of the door was like an eruption. Derek and Jonnel had their backs to the door and Jonnel was thinking in the instant that he should have checked it.

All they saw was the flash of a hand as it went across their faces. Something like sand hit them and their eyes burned like fire. Jonnel dropped the gun, but not before his finger hit the trigger and sent a quick spray of bullets into Derek's side. Derek screamed and fell into the phone table.

Jonnel dropped to the floor. Tears ran from his burning eyes. His mind worked like a whirlwind. He had to find the gun. His vision was blurry and his eyes exploded with pain. He dropped one hand to the floor and felt around. A hard kick slammed into the side of his head. The one to his balls came next. Jonnel could faintly hear Derek crying next to him and screaming his brother's name. Through his burning eyes, Jonnel saw the tall figure cutting his friend's throat. He tried to move away as he heard the gurgle of Derek's life leaving him. He scrambled away, going in the general direction of the door. He didn't make it.

The killer finished off Jonnel then stopped to savor the moment. Rage filled him. More gone. More trophies. He took himself from these pleasant thoughts, knowing he had to leave soon. He'd used a silencer on his gun, but someone had surely heard the other shots and the commotion. He had to move quickly. There was much unfinished business.

He took the money off Jonnel and took Derek's hands, then went upstairs into the master bedroom. There had to be more money somewhere.

In a baby's bed slept a seven-month-old boy named Brian. The killer stared a moment at the infant. He bent over, placing his face close to the child's.

"Detergent?" asked Tony with more than a little surprise. He stared in disbelief at Ralph Neward, the assistant coroner. Neward nodded his head, a blank expression on his face.

The crime scene in the house on Shalon was full of activity. The bodies had been removed and a search of the house had found a mountain of cocaine in the basement. It had probably been cut with something, but it was still worth a lot of money on the street. This house had to be the north end distribution point, Tony thought. The house supplied Detroit's crackhouses with diluted coke. The Narcotics Unit and the feds had been looking for it for about a year. They were in the process of getting a warrant on this and several other houses, but the Handyman had found it first.

This was all he needed in his life, a serial killer. This guy had a thing for drug dealers. Was he a vigilante? A rival pusher? Was he even a *he*? When Tony arrived and saw the missing hands, he knew it was going to be a long summer.

"He threw soap in their eyes?" Tony asked again.

"Yes sir," said Neward. "Just plain laundry soap. At least that's what it seems to be. The soap box is still in the hall closet and there's soap on the floor, in the eyes, and on the bodies of the victims. We think that they were killed at different times. The naked man and woman died at about eleven o'clock. The other two men were killed about an hour later."

"Why the hell would he stick around for an hour?" Tony thought out loud.

"Maybe he knew the other two were coming," said Neward, a little surprised at his own insight.

"Yeah," said Tony. "Yeah, maybe."

"And one of the men," Neward said. "The one named uh . . . Jonnel Washington, and the woman, still have their hands."

"Why didn't he cut them off, too?" Tony said to himself.

"Maybe he didn't have time," said Neward, hoping that Tony would be pleased at the idea. But he just looked through Neward, immersed in thought.

Tony left Neward and went out to the front porch. A crowd of neighbors was standing across the street. Tony remembered when he used to see looks of terror in the eyes of the onlookers. Now, he only saw sadness or anger in their faces. They were getting used to it.

Tony had his own fears about this crime. He lived only several miles from this house and it was probably distributing drugs to all of the crackhouses on the northwest side. But that was the least of his fears. A second killing by the same nut meant that the media would really get in on it. That goddamned Salinsky had slipped by some green rookie and gotten a look into the house. She had already hinted on television that the police were covering up evidence, talking about the people's right to know and all that shit.

And what would the mayor do? The crime rate was a major campaign issue. In a strange way, Tony thought, this killer was doing the city a favor. Taking out the trash, you might say.

Was the killer an Angel or Satan himself? Whatever the answer, Tony understood that his ass would be the first one kicked if the murderer wasn't caught soon.

"Inspector, would you like to question our witness to this terrible crime?" Jim asked. Jim and Tony had both crawled out of bed to come to the call.

Jim had been with a woman, but was in a surprisingly good mood considering the circumstances.

"Yes," Tony said, letting a small grin creep onto his lips. "Bring the culprit here."

Jim and a young female paramedic climbed the stairs together. She was holding a baby in her arms, the child of Rolan Nelson and Sharon Borders.

Tony guessed that the killer wasn't a complete psycho. He hadn't killed the kid. They were all elated to find the child still alive. At a murder scene, any survivor was a blessing.

"You saw it all didn't you?" Tony asked. He smiled at the young boy. "If only you were a little older."

"He wouldn't be here," Jim said. "And you know it."

The paramedic excused herself and took the child away.

"What's the deal on this guy? Is he trying to be a one-man drug enforcement team?" Jim said. "You know how much coke they found downstairs?"

"I know, but again, no money. This must be a rival gang. The Southend Crew has been gaining power lately, according to our sources. Both hits have been on Union people. Their territory is small, they need to expand—"

"Naw," said Jim. "I know you have the same feeling that I have about this. It's too weird. They left the damned cocaine. Besides, gangs shoot, they don't cut throats."

"The girl was shot," Tony said.

"Yes, but the men were not. It's a separate statement, see. It's like—"

"Like shooting was too good for the men."

"Right. And her hands were left on. She was just in the way and unlike the little boy, she could make a positive ID," Jim said.

"But why did he only take the hands off two of the men and not the third?" Tony said.

"Maybe the, excuse the term, Handyman is trying to confuse us, throw us off of something else," Jim said.

"Well, it's working."

Tony looked distant again. This time, there was no evidence of sexual violence. No one had gotten a sharp ride up the ass. Maybe the Handyman was just excited when he did Grip. It looked as though he brought the couple downstairs naked and killed them, probably so he wouldn't have to do it in front of the kid. What a prince. The bastard had taken out three drug dealers without leaving a clue. No prints, nothing.

Jim and Tony were a little surprised when Chief Fuller and Roberts showed up. The throng parted to let them through. Cameras went on, throwing light into their faces. Fuller ignored the questions shot at him. He gave Salinsky a nasty look and got a smile in return.

Tony had seen the Chief come out on a call when it was of the utmost importance. Vincent Roberts, however, *never* came out on night calls. Roberts was the type to be in bed by nine.

As Fuller approached, Tony stood up straighter, like a soldier coming to attention. Fuller was, to Tony, a great cop in the old tradition. Fuller was also, unfortunately, a mayoral appointee and Yancy's official scapegoat. Fuller could be kind of an ass-kisser, but he was still one hell of a guy, ex–Green Beret, president of the National Police Council for three years straight. It was sad to see him on the mayor's string. Tony guessed that Fuller was just too tired to fight anymore. He had the look of a very old man in a younger man's body. A look that came with too much time staring up the city's asshole.

Fuller walked up to Tony and Jim. He looked even worse up close. Fuller was definitely not used to being out of bed at two o'clock in the morning. Before Tony could answer, Roberts brushed by, grabbed Neward and took him away. Neward looked relieved and Roberts began talking to him urgently.

Tony and Jim both turned to watch them. Roberts stared straight into Neward's eyes and barked at him. Tony was moving in their direction when Fuller spoke.

"What we got here, fellas?"

"Well, it's definitely our boy again," said Tony, snapping back to the moment.

"With a few new wrinkles," Jim added.

"Before you start," said Fuller holding up a beefy hand, "I want you to know that this is a top priority for your department. Reassign the other shit. The mayor is deeply concerned. The press will be all over this case and you know how he feels about that. Now, what's the story here?"

Tony and Jim began to give Fuller the story as they knew it. Tony was only half-concerned about communicating the events and his theories of the case to Fuller. Politics was responsible for Fuller's presence. That was totally understandable.

But what the hell was Roberts doing there?

* * *

In the crowd on the other side of the street, a tall, thin black man with reddish hair watched with more than shock or fear in his eyes. He was angry. David Traylor stayed toward the back of the gawkers, making sure that no cops saw him. He was cruising on his regular rounds, checking out the houses and supply points, when he heard the call on his police band radio.

He'd driven to the Shalon house, parking his car on a side street, then called T-Bone on his car phone on the way over. Actually, he'd done what they called shaking the tree. Traylor called an unknown person on a beeper who made another call and so on, finally someone would call T-Bone. It took at least a half hour for T-Bone to call back.

T-Bone had not been happy. He had cursed and yelled and Traylor could hear things being thrown in the background.

Traylor watched as they brought the bodies out of the house. A hush fell over the crowd. He hoped that his boy Derek had taken a piece out of whoever did it. Derek was hard, a real man, he thought.

Traylor felt someone watching him. He looked to his right and saw a young girl, about six, looking at his hand. He instinctively put his hand into his pocket. His right hand was missing the two middle fingers and must have looked frightening to the young girl. He usually cursed anyone who stared, but this was just a child and he didn't want to attract attention.

Traylor moved through the crowd. He heard a television reporter say in her report that two of the bodies had no hands and that the police had found drugs, but no money. He immediately went back to his car and told T-Bone. It was the same guy that took out Grip. T-Bone had exploded with anger again. They had lost four men in less than two weeks and that was unheard of for the Union.

T-Bone thought it was the Southend Crew but he wasn't sure. Traylor knew that it didn't make any difference. Somebody had to pay and he was willing to go along with any plan T-Bone had because he owed the man his life.

Traylor checked his watch. It was after two in the morning. He had to get going. He frowned as he saw the cops carry the cocaine out of the house. How much money had they lost? He walked back toward his car. T-Bone had called an emergency meeting at a motel.

Just like the police, they had work to do.

12

T-Bone Makes a Plan

The Big Three waited. None of them had seen the other two in many months. Union operation dictated that even on the street, they were to maintain their distance. No one spoke as they stood in the dingy motel room in northeast Detroit.

Robert Campbell twisted a long dreadlock, David Traylor twirled his keys on the three fingers of his right hand and Steve Mayo, the last of the Big Three, just sat on the old bed staring at the door.

Mayo was a short, thickly muscled man with a bald head. He wore an earring in each ear. One a gold hoop and the other a diamond stud. Mayo ran the trade out of midtown and the east side. He was the newest of the Big Three.

There was a knock on the door. Campbell walked over to get it, placing one hand on his gun.

T-Bone entered the small room carrying a black leather case and talking on the phone. He put the case on an old desk as he continued his conversation in a low voice.

Walking in behind T-Bone was a boy of about fourteen. The boy was horribly disfigured and looked somewhat like a dog.

The boy's name was K-9 for obvious reasons. He was T-Bone's companion, though no one knew why. Some guessed that he was T-Bone's son, born with birth defects to a drug-addicted mother. Others theorized that T-Bone felt sorry for the kid, that he did indeed have a heart. Whatever the connection, K-9 was a constant fixture in the Union and no one was going to question it.

K-9 walked to a corner where a coat rack stood and leaned against the wall. T-Bone never looked at his lieutenants as he ended the phone conversation.

T-Bone put the phone away and took out the shotgun. He had brought it as a test. He wasn't sure if any of his Big Three were involved in the killings. He wanted to see their reaction to the weapon. If any of them became nervous, he would know something was up. T-Bone watched them as he pulled out the big weapon and began loading it. Traylor and Campbell did nothing. Mayo calmly leaned to one side on the bed, bringing his gun closer to his hand.

T-Bone saw that they were all cool. Mayo, forever the paranoid, made a defensive move as T-Bone had expected.

"We have an enemy," said T-Bone. "It's too much of a fucking coincidence that all the people killed have been Union. My police connections tell me that it's some freak, a psycho. I'm not going for that so fast. I don't know who the fuck is doing this, but I do know that I can't let it ride this time. People on the street are starting to say that we're weak, that we ain't got it no more."

T-Bone walked past Traylor.

T-Bone had found Traylor when the latter was just twelve, living in a run-down, roach-infested house on the east side near Mack and Van Dyke. Traylor's father had left when he was just ten. His mother, who was half-white, drank a lot and kicked his ass when she didn't have any money to buy whiskey. He spent many nights listening to her have sex with her "boyfriends" on the living room couch.

T-Bone changed Traylor's life when he brought him into the Union. T-Bone had taken a special interest in him. He made Traylor read things and taught him about life and the business.

After he'd been with T-Bone for a few months, he came home to find his mother being slapped around by one of her men. Normally, he would have just gone to another room, but after seeing life in T-Bone's world, he had followed the man outside and attacked him. The man pulled a gun and shot Traylor in the hand, blowing off the two middle fingers.

Traylor was taken to the hospital but the fingers were gone forever. A month after he got out of the hospital, Traylor and T-Bone found the man who had shot Traylor and split his head open with a baseball bat.

Traylor worked his way up through the ranks, meeting T-Bone's challenges and overcoming them. He rolled the product and took his lumps from the police. Now, he was one of the Big Three and he was sure that he was T-Bone's favorite.

"... so we have to make sure that our reputation is intact," said T-Bone. "That's gonna take some hard work." T-Bone lifted the gun to his shoulder as he walked past Campbell.

T-Bone had discovered Campbell when he helped to take out a roller named Carlton Williams, whose nickname was Elrock. Campbell was just a kid back then. He was in a small-time gang called the Bad Boys. When the Union started, the Bad Boys, along with various other random street gangs, were absorbed into T-Bone's creation.

But Elrock would not join the Union. He was making too much money. He had several houses and a big crew that he ran, with a number of rollers and his brother, a skinny, dumb-looking kid named Talmadge. Talmadge played tough, but was just a kid hiding behind his big brother. But Elrock was tough. When several rollers defected to join the Union, he killed them himself, strangling the last one with his bare hands.

T-Bone recruited Campbell to join Elrock's gang then turn on him, and that's just what Campbell did.

After setting up and abducting Elrock, T-Bone, Campbell, and the rest of the Bad Boys took the rebel dealer and his brother out to a rural area far north of the city and killed them.

Campbell was afraid at first, but after the others drew blood he became ardent, plunging his knife into Elrock's nonvital areas as T-Bone had instructed. Killing the man wasn't enough for T-Bone. He wanted him to suffer first.

Campbell remembered all the blood on his hands and how black it looked under the moon.

When they finished, T-Bone had another young roller named Butchie shoot Elrock's brother. No loose ends.

T-Bone was different back then. He was brash and more willing to take chances, to be seen with his young lieutenants. Now, they rarely saw him.

T-Bone moved Campbell up after the Union came together. T-Bone always rewarded loyalty. And tonight, T-Bone looked like the T-Bone of old, mean and ready to kill.

"... so I'm demanding more from you now because we need to stop this shit before it gets out of hand."

T-Bone passed by Mayo. He looked Mayo in the eye as he lowered the gun. Mayo returned the gaze and didn't move. T-Bone turned and walked away.

Like the others, Mayo had met T-Bone as a kid. He replaced a roller named DeAndre Dixon in the Big Three after Dixon was shot by his girlfriend at one of the crackhouses. Dixon had given his woman, Sheila, a baby, and after she became fat from the pregnancy, he started dating a young girl named Tina. Sheila was a hard woman and did not take kindly to the affair. She followed DeAndre to the small apartment where Tina lived and while they were making love, she shot them both dead with a .45. She had given them one in the heart and one in the head, just like a pro.

The police and the Union had searched for the woman, but to no avail. The cops wanted to get her to testify and expose the Union and T-Bone's people wanted her dead. But she disappeared along with the baby boy she had by Dixon and soon everyone stopped looking for her.

Mayo was elevated about a year later. Since then, he had seen T-Bone in many moods, but never this angry.

". . . you know that I don't like to ice people over petty shit," T-Bone said. "It's not what people say that bothers me. It's what they do. Pretty soon folks start buying someone else's rock, some muthafuckas decide that they want to break into our network of customers. It starts with a drop and pretty soon it's a storm. So we gotta make sure that none of the other rollers out there are getting any funky ideas and our customers know that we can still kick ass.

"Traylor," T-Bone pointed at him with the gun butt. "I want you to fix that situation on the northwest side. Without Shalon, we gotta hustle. Have you hooked up the camper again?"

Traylor nodded, happy that he wasn't getting blamed.

"Mayo, I want you to pick some people who owe us money out of the houses and enforce the debt. You hear me? Enforce the fuck out of them."

Mayo's expression didn't change. He just nodded.

T-Bone walked over to Campbell, standing in front of him. "I want you to keep a team of rollers on Belle Isle to cover Grip's old job. I don't want any one person to be in that job for a while. And we gonna plan a visit on the Southend Crew. We won't use our people, though. Let's use Frank. He's the man for this type of thing."

Campbell nodded.

T-Bone walked slowly to the door. He looked up at the ceiling for a moment. "This shit is gonna get real nasty. Some of us may not survive. But we all know the deal. This ain't no time for weak shit. If you can't hang, let me know now."

To everyone's surprise, Traylor spoke. "How do we know the Southend is hittin' our people?" He nervously rubbed his three-fingered hand on his leg.

T-Bone was not offended. Traylor was a smart man. No one else would have thought to ask that. T-Bone smiled and eased the tension brought on by the question. "We don't," T-Bone said. "But it don't mean shit. Everybody's already thinking it's them. It's unfortunate for them that they have a big crew."

"But the b-bodies was all f-f-fucked up, hands cut off and s-shit," said Campbell, encouraged by Traylor's statement.

"And I heard that he didn't take no coke from Grip, only his money. That's not like a roller, you know what I'm sayin'?" David Traylor said.

T-Bone looked at Mayo, anticipating a comment, but Mayo said nothing.

T-Bone knew that the Handyman's methods would come up sooner or later. It was not any of their concern how the rollers had died. But he had to calm them, let them know that he had knowledge in all areas.

"Yeah, it's true," he began. "I read the papers. This killer, this Handyman is supposed to be a psycho, crazy. Well, we can be crazy, too. Just 'cause Grip didn't get shot and they left the coke, don't mean that it ain't another crew. Matter of fact, if it was me, that's just how I'd do it, so no one would suspect, you dig? Take the money, leave the coke, cut off hands. It's not a hit. It's a nut, right? Well, what do a nut need with money? The shit ain't fooling me. I been around too long and seen too much to be fooled. We gonna shake things up a little, see what we can see."

The Big Three seemed pleased by the statement. K-9 just shifted in his corner. T-Bone knew he had to hold them together through this. He really had no idea who was killing his people. His connections had given him nothing. But his instinct told him the Handyman was big trouble. But he would find and kill him, whoever he was.

It didn't matter who fucked with the King. The important thing was, everybody should know better.

13

Handyman

The Sewer at 1300 was filled. Tony and Fuller had called a meeting of the officers to give them their assignments on the Handyman. Every day since the Shalon Street deaths, the media had run a story on the killer: MOTOR CITY HANDYMAN BAFFLES POLICE, HANDYMAN: VIGILANTE OR MANIAC? The headlines assaulted the public, causing fear, apprehension—and massive sales.

Fuller sat at the back of the small gathering. He usually addressed the troops himself on big investigations, but this time he wanted no part of it. Fuller looked tired and troubled even though a recent news poll had given Harris Yancy a twenty-five percent lead over his challenger, Craig Batchelor. The mayor was even slated to appear on a radio talk show that night to talk about his lead in the polls. There was joy in Mudville.

"I would like to begin by thanking the Chief," Tony said. "We appreciate you taking the time out of your busy schedule to give us support."

Fuller ignored the compliment. Jim's face soured. Tony knew that look. Jim hated it when he paid homage to the Chief.

"Now for the hard part," Tony continued. "I have assigned teams to various tasks which are designed to find the killer and simultaneously head off a major drug war on the street. Each team will have a platoon of uniforms backing it up. They will be seasoned cops for the most part, use them wisely. You will have as many backup men as you need. We are calling up the reserves to cover the routine work."

"Queen, Bright, and Palmer will be in charge of rousting the Union. We have tips on the location of their crackhouses and members. The regular drug teams in the other precincts will get involved, too. I have been assured by the Prosecutor's Office that the wheels of justice will turn slowly, so as to keep them off the street. Pick them up for whatever you can, and hopefully we can dilute their effectiveness on the street. A drug or weapons charge is great, but we'll take whatever we can get. And let's not have any mistakes. We don't want corpses."

"Hear that, Bright?" said an officer. "You don't get to kill anybody, too bad." The laughter subsided with Tony's stern look.

"May I continue? Thank you," Tony said. "Lane and Meadows will be assigned to check the lesser crews. They will follow the same procedure as the Union contingent. Martin and Patrick will assist Jim and me in running down leads on the Handyman." He paused for effect. "We can't let a war tear through this city. The schools will be letting out soon and the streets will be filled with juveniles with nothing to do but get in the way of a bullet. The mayor and city council will put a curfew in effect and I want it enforced. The ACLU will challenge it, but by the time the lawyers get done yelling at each other, the summer will be over. Let's get tough. We don't need any more weekly body count totals like the newspapers did last summer. That's it. You all have a report on the procedure. We start today."

"Do we have any leads?" asked Patrick. Tony could see that he was a little disappointed at not getting a street assignment.

"Well, no," Tony said. "No real leads. The forensic report is in, but there's nothing in it we can use. Shalon Street gave us nothing new. The killer took hands from some of the victims, so at least he's living up to his name. We do know some things, however. We believe that he is a psychopath so we are checking the department files on known crazies in all the midwestern states and will request a national rundown from the FBI. It's not a pattern we've ever seen before. An expert is doing a psychological profile for us. That's all."

"He stabbed Grip in the ass, so we should be looking for a pervert, right?" asked Orris Martin. The other officers laughed.

"Well, yes and no," Tony said. He tried not to show his irritation at Martin. "Yes, Grip was wounded in the rectum and no, we aren't looking for a sex offender. None of the Shalon Street wounds had any sexual overtones to them. We think that the killer tries to humiliate his victims out of anger, but I'm waiting to see what the profile turns up."

Tony did not like the question and his look must have showed it, because no one had any more. He dismissed the meeting and again thanked Fuller, who hobbled out the door.

"Excuse me, Inspector." said Orris Martin, coming over to Tony. "But I'd like a street assignment on this thing."

"I'm not changing the assignments right now. You'll be rotated in due time." Tony started to walk away.

"I been ridin' the shithouse for over three months now," Martin said, blocking his way.

"Forget it, man," said Steve Patrick, a young black officer and Martin's partner. He tried to pull Martin away.

"Let him go," Tony commanded. Patrick did. "You got a problem, detective?" Tony asked, moving closer to Martin. Tony was much taller than Martin and looked down on him.

"Yeah, I got a fucking problem, *sir*," Martin said, sweeping his hand through his hair. I'm tired of workin' the turd assignments 'round here."

Tony didn't need something like this to bring down the men's morale. Even though he would have liked nothing better than to floor Martin, he decided that it wasn't worth it. He had to end it now.

"The assignments stand, Martin. Now get to it or get transferred."

Martin looked at Tony with contempt then walked away. Tony turned slowly, letting the tension melt away. He motioned for Jim to follow him into his office. Tony closed the door so that no one could hear what he was about to say.

"I would have kicked his ass," said Jim, laughing.

"That's why you're not an inspector," Tony said.

"Ouch!"

"Man, I hate that fucking Martin."

"He's dirty, you know," Jim said matter-of-factly.

"You say that about everyone but me," Tony said.

"That's not true. Fuller. He's as clean as they come. He's a dickhead, but a clean one."

"Lay off the man."

"You really like him, don't you?" asked Jim.

"Yes, I think he's a fine officer and you just said so yourself."

"And Yancy, you like him too?"

"No comment."

"Man, you are quite the politician."

"What are you, a reporter? You always ask me this shit. I'm not political and you know it. I just do my job."

"Bullshit. You may be slick, but you're political. You play the system like a pro," Jim said.

Tony hated it when Jim did this. He thought maybe Jim was a little jealous of him after all. "Hey, Jim," Tony said, sounding a little upset. "Let's use some of this energy to catch our killer, OK?" He paused for a moment. As Jim looked at him, he could almost read his mind. "I want to talk to Roberts again," Tony said.

"I knew it! You saw that shit too! What the fuck was he doing at Shalon Street?" Jim said.

"I don't know, but it's been on my mind since that night. I don't get it. This is important, but Roberts being there don't compute."

"He's gotta be hiding something. And your boy Fuller knows what it is," said Jim.

Tony nodded. He hated to admit it, but it was evident. They each knew Roberts was definitely not the kind to go on midnight calls. Roberts had groomed Neward especially for that purpose. The way he had grabbed Neward and isolated him, it was just too incriminating. Something was up, but what? That was the billion-dollar question.

"It has to be a lead, and it must have some political consequence." Tony's brow furrowed. He was guessing.

"Well," said Jim. "Do we call before we go over to the Crypt, or do we surprise old Boulder Head?"

"Let's not give him the chance to call anyone. We have to be careful here. If Fuller's involved, that means the mayor knows, too. We cannot risk stepping on their feet. Yancy will have Fuller reassign us to West Hell. If the mayor is hiding something, he obviously doesn't want us to know it. Roberts may not spill his guts, but maybe he'll give us a clue."

"Do you wanna be the Good Cop or the Bad Cop?"

"Good cop," Tony said.

Jim stood up and adjusted his gun in the shoulder strap. "I'm gonna enjoy this," he said.

Tony and Jim walked out of the Sewer on the fifth floor and

walked over to the elevator. Jim pushed the down button. The elevator came up slowly, creaking and sounding its age.

"I hate these old-ass elevators," Jim said.

"No need to rush," Tony said. "Roberts ain't going anywhere."

"Yeah, but I really want to get his big-headed ass."

Tony laughed as the elevator came to a stop. The doors opened, revealing a huge black man in a rumpled suit and a black fedora.

Tony and Jim became rigid at the sight of the big man. Jim took his hands from his pockets. Tony stared at the man in the elevator as he entered the car followed by Jim.

The big man was Walter Nicks, leader of Mayor Yancy's team of personal bodyguards. They were nicknamed the SS, because no one knew what they did and they seemed to operate with impunity.

"Well, well," said Nicks. "I thought this car was going down. Guess I was wrong."

The elevator doors closed.

Tony and Nicks had never liked one another. After the GM incident, Tony became a star and had left Nicks in his dust in the department. Nicks was a competitive man, a former football player and army veteran. Nicks never made any secret of the fact that he was jealous of Tony's rapid ascent in the department.

"What brings you down here, Nicks?" asked Tony.

"The normal things," said Nicks. "Hear you boys got a little trouble."

"A little," said Tony.

"Hope I don't have to come in and clean the shit up for you," said Nicks.

"Oh, is that your job for the mayor?" asked Jim. "Cleaning up shit?"

"Only when muthafuckas like you do the shittin'." Nicks took a half step.

"There's no need for any of that," said Tony. "Let's just go on about our business."

Nicks hit the emergency stop button and pulled a .44 magnum from inside his jacket. The elevator car jerked to a halt. It happened too fast for either Tony or Jim to do anything. Jim was caught with his hand halfway to his weapon.

"You crazy ass—" Jim said.

"Be cool, Jim," Tony said. "OK, Nicks. You got something on your mind, say it, otherwise turn the elevator back on and stop wasting my time."

Nicks had the gun out in front of his chest. Tony watched Nicks, looking him in the eyes. Jim kept his eyes on the big gun. Nicks opened the gun, reached in his pocket and brought out three bullets.

"I hate to reload in public, that's all," Nicks said. He put the bullets in, then put the gun back and turned the elevator back on. The car started to descend.

The elevator door opened to the lobby. Nicks adjusted his hat and walked out.

"That bastard is crazy," said Jim.

"No he isn't," said Tony. "He just wants everyone to think he is. He hasn't liked me since I got promoted over him—three times."

"I should have shot his ass."

"He's not worth the trouble," said Tony.

"He carries two of those .44s. I saw the other one when he hit the elevator button."

"It's never good to see Nicks down at 1300, especially when we have a big case. I wonder what he really wants."

Tony and Jim walked out of the building in time to see Nicks pulling away in a black Thunderbird.

14

Roberts on the Hook

Vince Roberts reclined in his soft leather chair. It was imported from London and had been a gift to himself. He liked giving himself gifts. Lord knows that none of his friends or his wife would ever give him such a present. His wife. What a joke.

Paula Roberts, the Eighth Wonder of the World. Her whole life was eating, growing more fat and disgusting, and making his life dogshit. She was every man's nightmare, an obese nag whose idea of sexual gratification was eating a jelly doughnut. She was a cellulite demon, a double-chinned terror from Husband Hell. The very thought of her began to make him ill.

He shifted his mind to his mistress, Barbara—firm, thin, and pretty. She knew how to satisfy a man. So what if it cost him? It was money well spent. He delighted in his memories of their exploits. He kept their meetings secret and that made it all the more exciting. He had a possible rendezvous tonight, and just thinking about it made him quiver.

"Officers Hill and Cole here to see you," said Wanda. Roberts was startled by the intercom buzzer as it went off. He had taken Wanda on for the summer as a favor to the mayor. She was a pest, always asking to observe his work, but she had a great body. If she weren't related to the mayor, he might have given her a try.

Roberts thought for a second about the detectives. What could they possibly want? He had to be careful after the Shalon Street incident. He was always suspicious of cops anyway. His job was sensitive and cops were crude. He didn't like these two at all, especially Jim Cole. He went out of his way to piss him off. Still, it might be official.

"Send them in," he said into the phone's small speaker. He reached into his desk and turned on a small tape recorder that he kept inside. If there was one thing that he learned from being in a political job, it was to always cover your ass.

Tony and Jim entered the office, Tony looking as he always did, serious and tired. Jim, however, looked angry. His eyes were narrowed and he literally swaggered into the room and he never took his gaze off Roberts.

"What can I do for you?" asked Roberts.

"We have some questions for you, Doctor," said Tony. Jim didn't say a word. He sat down hard in one of the chairs across from Roberts's desk and stared at him hatefully.

"Is something the matter?" asked Roberts. He was watching Jim.

"You could say that, Doctor," said Jim, his voice filled with sarcasm. He grabbed a small lead crystal paper weight from Roberts's desk and tossed it in the air.

"Please don't play with that," said Roberts reaching for it. "It's lead crystal and it's expensive." Jim put it down hard on the desk. Roberts winced. "Look, I don't know what this is all about, but there is no reason to come in here and act like this." Roberts sat down. Tony followed.

Jim spat out. "You've got a lot of nerve, after what you did, you—"

Tony raised a hand and Jim sat down. "Let me talk here, Jim." Tony tried to sound like he was angry at his partner. "We just need to know a few things here, Doc. Things about Shalon Street."

"A few things?" said Roberts.

"Yeah," said Jim. "Like what the fuck you were doing there!" He was nearly yelling.

"I thought I told you to let me handle this," Tony said to Jim. They engaged in the very old, very practiced argument. They both watched Roberts out of the corners of their eyes. When Jim asked his question, Roberts had paled and his eyes widened. They took this time to let him stew, maybe try to create a lie that would give them a clue.

Tony finished chewing Jim out and turned again to Roberts.

"Sorry, Doc, but that was our purpose in coming. What were you doing there?" he said.

"My job," he said almost defiantly. "Chief Fuller called me at home and ordered me there."

Jim grunted a short laugh.

"Well, you have to admit that it was strange for you to be there. I can't remember you ever coming out on a night call," said Tony.

"First time for everything," Roberts said. He smiled a little.

"We think there may be something about the killings that you overlooked. Something about Shalon Street and the first death," Tony said calmly.

"That's ridiculous," Roberts said. His eyes darted away from Tony as he spoke. "You have my report. It's all there."

"Fuck the report!" Jim rose and almost jumped at Roberts. "We know you're hiding something!"

Roberts backed up and stood, startled by the explosion.

Tony watched Roberts. The doctor was frightened. He was going for it, then he began to chuckle.

"Nice try, gentlemen," Roberts said. He pulled his chair back. "Nice try. If I were a criminal, I guess this might have worked on me." He adjusted his tie. "Like I told you, I don't know anything and I have nothing to hide. Read my report. It's all in there."

Tony and Jim were silent for a moment.

"I told you this wouldn't work," said Jim, sitting back down.

Tony stood in front of the desk. He looked at Jim and then at Roberts leaning over the desk as he spoke.

"OK, Doc, game's over. I want to know what the fuck you were doing there that night. Why did you grab Neward and take him away?"

"I already told you, officer, the report. Read the report."

"Well maybe Doctor Neward will have a better story to tell," Tony said.

"Doctor Neward is on an extended vacation," said Roberts.

"How very convenient." Tony was right in Roberts's face now. "So he just up and decided to go. Could it be that you'll handle all these murders from now on, so that you can keep your secret safe?"

"I don't know what you're—"

"People are being butchered, goddammit!" Tony yelled. "And you sit here and play fuckin' games with *my* investigation!"

"Come on, Tony, it's not worth it," Jim said on cue.

"I swear, if I find out that you're obstructing justice, you'll be in the county jail before you can say cover-up. You'll be bent over a sink with some bull faggot ten inches up your ass! You hear me, Doc? You hear me?!" Tony was almost on top of the desk. Roberts had slid his chair back again. This time he was scared.

Jim saw his next cue and pulled Tony back. "Come on, let's not waste our time with this loser. We'll go to the Chief, he'll get to the bottom of this shit."

"Fuck!" said Tony, turning to leave. "This ain't over." He pointed at Roberts.

Roberts pulled his chair back. "We can both talk to Fuller!" His voice shook. "We'll see what he has to say about this harassment!"

Tony and Jim stormed out of the office, leaving the door open. Roberts got up and slammed it just as they had hoped he would.

The officers walked quickly to the waiting area just to the left of Roberts's door.

Wanda sat at her desk in the middle of painting her nails. No one else was in the room.

"Bad day with the doctor, huh?" she said.

"Yeah, he doesn't take bad news well," Tony said. "Mind if I borrow your phone?" Tony asked her.

"Oh no, go ahead," she said.

Jim started a conversation with Wanda, distracting her. Tony heard Jim telling her how much older she looked. She giggled.

Tony picked up the desk phone struggling with its short cord. He turned away from Wanda so that she could not see as he covered the transmitter with his hand. He faked dialing and a conversation with his wife consisting of faint "uh-huh's."

Roberts's line lit up, Tony waited a moment, then gently pressed the button.

"Is the Chief in?" Roberts said. He sounded nervous.

"No, he's not," said a woman's voice.

"Well, could you ask him to call Doctor Roberts when he gets in? He has my number."

"Yes. Thank you."

"Bye-bye."

Tony heard the line click. He quickly pressed the button again. He knew that Roberts would not be able to hang up with the additional line on. The line's light went out.

Tony also knew the Chief had a mobile phone. He was sure that Roberts knew it too. He waited for a couple seconds. The line light went on again. He pressed the button again and he prayed that Roberts was finished dialing. He was. A phone rang again. Tony could hear the whine of a car's engine in the background as it was picked up.

"Fuller," said the voice on the other end. Tony smiled.

"It's Roberts, Chief. I have bad news."

"What's the problem?" Fuller sounded concerned.

"I just had a visit from Hill and Cole. They suspect something on the Handyman case. They accused me of hiding evidence."

"What did you tell them?" Fuller asked.

"Nothing, nothing," said Roberts. "They tried to trick me, but they didn't find out anything."

There was a silence on the phone. Wanda laughed loudly, and for a second Tony thought that it was all over. His hand tightened over the transmitter.

"I want you to bring everything to me," Fuller said. Tony sighed softly. "Bring it to me tonight at my house and don't screw it up."

"No problem, no problem," Roberts said.

"Nine o'clock!" said Fuller.

Fuller hung up.

Tony waited for the click then quickly pressed the button and hung up the phone. He was about to put it down, when he saw the line light go on again.

What now, he said to himself. He waited, then listened in.

"Hello," said a female voice.

"Hey, it's me," said Roberts.

"Oh, hi baby," said the woman in a sexy voice. "You're the big winner. We're on for tonight."

"Great!" Roberts sounded almost like a kid. "But I gotta run an errand first. I'll be over around ten or so, OK?"

"OK, but you know how I get when I have to wait." They both laughed at the very private joke.

"See you then."

"Bye."

"Bye-bye, honey."

Tony hung up the phone. He watched the line light for a second. Nothing. "Let's go," he said to Jim.

Wanda looked surprised as Jim broke off the conversation and left hastily.

"What's up?" Jim asked as they walked down the long hallway.

"Everything," said Tony. "Everything."

15

Magilla

Everybody knew it was a crackhouse.

The neighbors knew, the local church and community groups, even the garbage men knew. The traffic in and out was always heavy and shady characters were always around. Occasionally, you could see a transaction on the sidewalk or people lighting up their crack pipes, not able to wait to get home. Yes, everyone knew, but no one did anything. They were all scared.

No one wanted to put their life on the line to close the house. They all had heard stories of people who had squealed to the cops. They had been killed, shot at, or their families terrorized. A man named Walker had called the cops and two weeks after he did, one of his daughters was raped. Nothing was worth that kind of horror and pain. The police had shut it down often, but it just reopened again a few weeks later.

The house was built on Detroit's east side in 1946, after the war. It was a two-story, red brick house with a small, one-car garage in back that was now almost falling apart.

It had first been the home of an Italian immigrant named Angelo Marini. When Marini's fruit stand blossomed into a grocery store, he sold the house to a big, Irish auto worker named Mark Ridley in 1955.

The auto business was good and when Ridley became a foreman, he had the basement finished for entertaining guests. In the sixties, the neighborhood became integrated. Ridley was not crazy about the idea, but he did not move out. He held on to the house until the riots in 1967, when he moved to Southfield and rented the home to a succession of black families. One named Glover stayed there for three years, until the home was broken into for the fifth time in the mid-seventies. Ridley couldn't watch the house effectively from the suburbs. The insurance was outrageous and he couldn't afford to hire a manager. The neighborhood had become so bad that it was difficult to rent. When the property taxes became too much to pay, he let the city take the house. For years, it lay abandoned, boards over the windows and grass rising high to the porch.

When crack hit the city, the home was appropriated by dealers. It was raided several times, until the Union became dominant. After that, the police came around a little less. Now, the house distributed its product freely. The cops still raided now and then but the occupants knew in advance and when the raid hit, the most the cops got was a few rocks and suspects too young to keep in jail.

Magilla West surveyed the basement of the old house with interest. The crack was made and sold upstairs and he had turned the basement into a smoking gallery. The crackheads would come, buy their stuff, and retire to the basement to smoke it. Magilla figured this was a good deal because when they ran out (and they always did), all they had to do was go upstairs to buy more.

Magilla was a huge man who had always been fat. He was light brown in complexion and had terrible acne. His nickname came from elementary school when the "Magilla Gorilla" cartoon was popular.

Magilla was twenty-seven years old and had never finished high school. When he was young, he used and sold dope and tried to chase girls, but because of his weight and appearance he was never very successful. While his friends boasted and told stories of sexual conquests, Magilla lied and masturbated in shame.

It seemed he was always horny and craved sex constantly, but could not find a girl who would submit to him. Only God would curse him with great sexual desire and unattractiveness, he thought.

When he was eighteen, he paid a prostitute for sex and that became his method for relief from the need that plagued him. He soon rationalized that all men paid for sex in some way, so he had no reason to feel ashamed. But he grew to hate women. They were so smug and confident of themselves. They had the one thing that all men needed and they denied it to them unless they got paid for it. Slowly, predictably, he became rough with his women. It was not long before he was requesting kinky sex and paying extra for it.

When he began to run a crackhouse for the Union, he never guessed that it would provide him the means he needed to finally sexually dominate women. Once he got on the job, he found addicted women coming to him and wanting to trade sex for crack. At first he thought it was bad business. The Union didn't like bullshit going on in their houses. But soon, he saw that this exchange was almost a staple of the marketplace. Money and sex were both legal tender in the business.

Now Magilla did it regularly. In fact, he had not paid a prostitute in several years. He had his pick of the neighborhood's young girls and as long as they were not too ugly from drug use, he would have sex with them in exchange for a high. Crack stole a woman's beauty faster than anything in the world and the way he saw it, a man in his position didn't need to deal with scaggy-looking women. He was important now. He was lord of this house and he was entitled to the comforts of a king.

The basement was large and had been bordered with what was at one time expensive wood panelling. It was now a filthy, squalid ghost of itself. The bar had been torn down and old furniture was carelessly scattered around the room. The pipes leaked and the furnace and water heater bellowed their age. There was a bathroom in one corner which still worked and filled the area with the sour smell of urine and feces. It had no door but its users didn't mind. It was not uncommon for conversations to be held while sitting on the throne.

Magilla watched from the stairs. Crack pipes sent fumes into the air. The users smoked and talked furiously; their brains working rapidly from the drug. There were about twenty people in the room and he knew that soon more would come to recreate. Business was good. Not even the Handyman had stopped the crowds from coming in.

"Hey, Magilla, what's the deal on raising the price of the rock?" asked a crackhead named Ron. "Seven dollars for a nickel hit. Man, that's bullshit."

"You heard of inflation, nigga," said Magilla and walked by him.

Everyone was complaining about the new prices, but there was a shortage, and the so-called Handyman wasn't helping things either. People were getting scared to do business.

Magilla couldn't believe that some random nut had killed Grip and busted up the Shalon Street house. Handyman his ass. It had to be some renegade rollers out to break up the Union. He had started keeping his gun under his pillow at night. No one was gonna just waltz in and kill him. He heard a rumor that a war was going to start and he dreaded it. It would mean a drop in business as the heads got cold feet. Even worse, it would mean a drop in his sex life.

In a far corner, a couple were having sex on an old love seat. A dirty sheet had been strung across the front of the area on a wire suspended from the ceiling to shield anyone who wanted to use it. Their grunts and groans were ignored by the others who were busy getting high. Someone was in the bathroom taking a dump and farting like a symphony. In the middle of the room was a drain on the hard tile floor. Directly over it, was a fading, green *R.*

Magilla walked over to the couple on the love seat. As he passed, people looked up. Some in fear, others in a drug-induced carelessness. Magilla waddled his frame over to the copulating pair and hovered above them. The girl's dress was hiked up and the man had pulled his pants down around his ankles. Magilla smiled. The man was a regular, a guy named Phillip who was in his thirties. The girl was new and she couldn't have been more than eighteen.

"Who said you could fuck in my house?" bellowed Magilla, fighting back a smile. He could hear the familiar sound of crackheads laughing in the background.

"What the—" said Phillip looking up and over his shoulder. "Magilla, hey man, cain't you see I'm takin' care of some bidness here?"

The girl looked startled. Magilla could see that she was indeed young and very pretty. Her legs were long and unblemished. He followed them with his eyes as they surrounded the man between them. Her eyes were large, brown, and held the familiar devastation of drug use behind them.

Magilla wanted her. She was young and relatively unused. He needed a new woman. Most of the ones around lately were getting too nasty-looking to have sex with.

"Don't no fuckin' go on here less I say so. You wanna keep doing bizness here, you better shut the fuck up with that shit," Magilla said to Phillip.

Phillip was angry. He knew that Magilla could have any five crackheads beat his ass for one lousy rock. He hated the fat bastard but he didn't want to risk anything.

"Finish up quick," said Magilla as he walked away.

Magilla returned to the room's center and regarded the occupants with hate. They were all fucking assholes. Owned by a little white rock no bigger than a pebble. They would sell their mothers for it, maybe even their souls. He used coke but not that cheap crack. He only snorted real cocaine. But he was not an addict, he told himself. He was only a "recreational user" as he had heard the term used on television. He was certainly not like these fuckheads.

The drug had complete control of them. Sometimes, he had the women perform sex acts for his amusement in private. But never with men, only with other women. He wanted them to debase themselves just for him. After all the abuse that he had suffered at the hands of women, he finally had his revenge. Now he dealt out the abuse and the pain. Time was the great equalizer, he thought. He was happy for the first time in his life.

He heard Phillip reach his climax with the attendant groaning. Magilla shifted his attention to the couple. Phillip rolled off the girl and pulled up his pants. He gave her several rocks of crack. She took it and walked into the bathroom which was now empty. Phillip went with her, pulling at the condom he wore.

Magilla watched the girl pass. She was tall for her age and had a great body. She looked at him as she passed. She knew he wanted her. He winked his eye at her and she smiled. He would enjoy having her. Magilla turned his attention back to the crackheads in the room. Through the haze in their brains, they knew a show was coming.

"Why you wanna do me like that, Magilla?" he heard Phillip's voice behind him. "You know how it is. She's prime stuff, man, I was just—"

"Shut the fuck up," Magilla said. "I could give less than a rat's fat ass about what you think. Now get the fuck out, before I put some of my boys on you."

"Soon as my woman get through in the bathroom," Phillip said, trying to look confident.

The girl had come out of the bathroom and was already lighting up one of the few rocks that she had gotten from Phillip. She had heard the conversation and looked directly at Phillip as she spoke.

"I don't know who you was talkin' 'bout, but I ain't yo woman or nobody's," she said as she lit up.

She smiled at Magilla. She could use him to get all the crack she would ever need and all she had to do was have sex with him.

"Hey, bitch, I was the one who brought you here—"

Magilla backhanded Phillip across the mouth, knocking him backwards onto the floor. Several people laughed as he hit the floor. They were wired out of their minds and anything was funny. Magilla turned and stood over Phillip.

"Don't call *my* woman no bitch, nigga," Magilla smiled at the fallen man. "Now this is the last time I'm gone tell you. Get outta my house!"

"I'll throw his ass out for some rock," said a burly man sitting on a crate and smoking. Magilla ignored the offer and watched Phillip get up and slowly walk to the stairs.

"You know this ain't right," Phillip said holding the side of his face. "You know it ain't." He ascended the stairs slowly disappearing from sight.

The girl walked over to Magilla. She was wearing a tight, black one-piece miniskirt that hugged her body. Magilla almost licked his lips as she approached. Her stomach was flat and her breasts high and firm. Magilla put his arm around her.

"What's your name, baby?"

"Jamilla."

"Come on with me, I got some real shit upstairs."

Jamilla put out her pipe and followed eagerly. She knew what Magilla meant by "real shit." He had some cocaine, probably not even cut, she thought.

As they walked up the stairs, Magilla was bursting inside his pants. He grabbed her ass and she giggled and ran up the stairs. Life was good. He smiled as he thought of all the things that he would do to Jamilla tonight. He heaved as they reached the top of the stairs. Magilla followed the girl through the kitchen where his people continued to make crack using a gas oven and several microwaves. He pointed her to the living room, planning to take her upstairs.

The front of the house was filled with buyers and rollers selling crack to the public over an old dining room table.

Suddenly, Magilla froze in his tracks. Fear seized him and his heart began to race. He saw the smug face of Phillip near the front door, talking to a bald man with a gold hoop earring. The man turned and Magilla stared into the very angry face of his boss, Steven Mayo.

16

Indian Village

Tony and Jim had been waiting for over an hour for Vincent Roberts to come out of the Chief's house. They sat in the unmarked car near the end of Seminole Street in Indian Village, a fashionable neighborhood on a succession of streets named after Indian tribes. Roberts had gone in as scheduled at 9:00. Jim and Tony had just sat and watched since then.

"What's taking him so long?" asked Jim. He and Tony had been watching the Chief's house from an unmarked car parked four houses past Fuller's.

"Maybe they're planning what to do with the evidence they're hiding," said Tony.

"Fuckin' assholes, the both of 'em," said Jim. "Like we ain't got it bad enough trying to do our fuckin' job, we have to fight our own people."

"I'm sure Fuller's got some reason for it," said Tony. "Probably political. To me, it's just something else to get by."

"How the hell can you say that?" said Jim, somewhat angrily. "What he's doing is a crime." Jim was mad.

"I just have faith that he thinks he's doing the right thing."

"Then why are we here? If there's such a God-almighty-fuckin-good-reason, why aren't we both at home giving our women the high hard one?" Jim asked.

"We have to get our information through Roberts. He's the weak link. That woman he talked to today was obviously his mistress. I've seen his wife and believe me, if any man ever needed a mistress, it's Roberts."

"I don't fuckin' believe this. Cops tailing cops. It's like we're those goddamned IAD assholes."

"I don't understand what the problem is," said Tony. "You knew we were coming this afternoon and you agreed. Now all of a sudden, it's all fucked up. You're full of all this law-and-order shit. You know how it is, man. Politics, rule at the top. We just do our job as best we can. What choice do we have? Accuse Fuller? It's our word against his, and he'll deny everything."

They were quiet a moment. Both men felt uneasy about the night's activities.

They watched Fuller's spectacular house with the six-foot wrought iron gate in front. There was a jockey holding a lantern on the front lawn. Its face had been painted white.

"There he is," said Tony, as Roberts walked out of the front door of the house. Fuller appeared in his robe for a second, then he was gone. Roberts walked to his car and got in. He pulled away from the curb and drove to the corner. Tony started the car. "Here we go," he said.

They followed the gray Mercedes 320-E onto Interstate 75. Roberts sped along at eighty as he hurried to his appointment.

"Man's got to have it tonight," laughed Jim.

Tony smiled. The thought of Roberts having a sexual rendezvous was totally comical.

Roberts drove out of Detroit at the Eight Mile border on the freeway. He took the W. P. Reuther Freeway east. Tony was careful not to get too close. It had been a long time since he'd done this.

"Where the hell is he going?" asked Tony, thinking out loud.

Roberts exited and hung a sharp left at a light. He drove for a few blocks, then took a long driveway into an impressive-looking, hilly complex. A huge sign in front proclaimed, "Knollwood—A Condominium Community."

"Hey, I had a woman that lived here once," said Jim.

"You had a woman everywhere," said Tony, keeping up with Roberts. He slowed the police car as Roberts stopped at the guard booth. The guard, a young black man, stuck his head out of the booth's window for a second. The yellow crossing arm lifted and Roberts's car went through.

Tony waited a moment, then pulled up to the guard booth. He saw the guard lean out. He was probably only twenty, Tony thought. His hair was long and curly. It was what the kids called a gheri curl. Chemicals were put into the hair to make it limp and curly. The only problem was that the stuff smelled like battery acid and it was a wet, sticky mess. This guy had a lot of hair and the smell of the curling ingredients was strong.

"Can I help you?" said the guard, smiling.

"Police officers," said Tony showing his badge. "Where did that last car go to?"

The guard suddenly looked frightened. "What's the deal? Is this a bust or something?" His smile faded.

"No," said Tony.

"I dunno. I ain't suppose to give out information on the residents or guests." He looked into the car harder, trying to see Jim on the other side. "He a cop, too?"

"Yeah," said Jim showing his badge.

"Look, man, we ain't here to bust nobody," said Tony. "We just want to know who our boy is going to see, dig? We been after this white boy's ass for a long time. We ain't lookin' to fuck with no brothers. I doubt if there's any out here anyway. We just need a little information, that's all." Tony sounded almost stereotypically ethnic and Jim hid his smile.

"Well," said the guard. "In that case, I guess it's cool. He went into 3117 Terrace Court. He comes here regular."

"You wouldn't happen to know who lives in 3117 Terrace Court, do you?"

"Oh, *hell* yeah!" he laughed. The smell of his hair was overwhelming Tony but he tried to hide it. He heard Jim snicker next to him. "It's a lady named . . . wait a minute," he said as he checked a list. "Barbara Volkarwicz," he said with difficulty, then he laughed again.

"What's so funny about her?" asked Jim from the other side of the car.

"She a prostitute—uh, excuse me, call girl," he said. "Yeah, fine, too. I tried to get some once and she told me it was five hundred. Ain't that a bitch! Two weeks pay for some pussy. Sheed!" He laughed again. "Nothing but Benzes, Beemers, Cadillacs goes in to see her. She high class, man, all the way."

"What kind of car does she drive?" asked Tony.

"Badass convertible Saab, blue one."

The guard gave directions to the Terrace Court unit, then lifted the crossing arm. Tony thanked him and drove along the circular drive. The condos were townhouses. Two-storied, wood-framed units. Each one had a garage and a private yard.

"Boy that gheri curl juice is potent," said Tony.

"I thought you would go blind," laughed Jim.

"They ought to outlaw that shit. I thought it was out of style," Tony said.

"I guess my man there is living in the past," said Jim. He paused a second, then, "You know, I love the way you play that brother shit when you want information from black people."

"What you talking 'bout?"

"We ain't here ta bust no righteous bruh-thahs," Jim mocked him in the stereotypical voice. "We just be needin' some info you dig?"

"All right, all right, so I laid it on a little thick. I got what we needed, didn't I?"

"You sholl did bruh-tha," Jim mocked again.

"Fuck you," Tony laughed as he slowed the car behind Roberts's Mercedes. He noticed a blue Saab convertible two cars away. It had a personalized license plate that read, BADGRL.

"I bet she is, too," said Jim. "Now what, Kemosabe?"

"Well, we can bust in on them. Or we can get the low-down on her from the license plate from the DMV before we move on Roberts."

"You know what I vote for," said Jim.

"Yeah, but let's think," said Tony. "If the Chief is in on this, the mayor knows. If so, then this thing is big, real big. Maybe we should proceed slowly here, feel things out first."

"What? Are you punkin' out on me here? This was your idea you know?" Jim turned to Tony.

"No, I'm not punkin' out," Tony said. "I want to get to the bottom of this just like you, but let's not get ourselves into a lot of trouble in the process."

"I don't understand what all this pussyfootin' is about! Roberts is fucking this bitch, we know about it, so we press his ass until he tells us what we want to know. What else is there?"

"There's diplomacy," Tony said forcefully.

"I don't see anything we need to finesse here," said Jim. "I say we bust his big-headed ass right here, right now."

"You can't let your personal hatred of Roberts guide my investigation." Now he was angry and determined to have it his way.

"*Your* investigation? You pulling rank on me, partner?" Jim asked.

"You know me better than that, man."

"Well, I just want to get the case moving. This clandestine shit is bad enough, but playing politics with Roberts is the ultimate jackoff."

"Look," said Tony putting the car in gear, "I'll compromise. Let's just wait and check this babe out first. If nothing comes of it, then we'll do it your way. OK?"

Jim was still a little angry but he agreed reluctantly. "But remember, if we don't find anything, it's my way," he turned back around in his seat.

They were quiet again as Tony pulled the car out. They were used to having such fights. It made for a good partnership. A difference of opinion provided balance in judgment. They both knew that partnering was a constant exercise of covering the other guy's ass. Tony drove out of the complex, happy that he didn't have to endure the guard's hairdo again.

In 3117 Terrace Court, Dr. Vince Roberts poured two glasses of wine, while a naked Barbara Volkarwicz, on her knees, unzipped his pants and started work on her fifth client that day.

17

Mayo and Magilla

Magilla was frightened of few things, but one of them was Steve Mayo. Mayo was the manager of Magilla's territory and a mean son of a bitch. Magilla remembered about a year ago when Mayo had a fight with his woman and had set her hair on fire, watching her burn. The woman had flung herself on the floor and Mayo had pulled his gun, daring anyone to help her. And now here he was in his house, looking totally pissed.

There was bad blood between the two men and everyone knew it. When Mayo was still just another roller, Magilla had embarrassed him in front of a group of women. Mayo could not read well and he was running down a written list of new houses, when Magilla made fun of his reading. He mimicked his hesitant, clumsy vocalization. The women laughed and Mayo never forgot the incident.

After Mayo became one of the Big Three, he had made Magilla's life hell at every available opportunity. The main reason he didn't get rid of Magilla was that he loved to torment him. That and the fact that Magilla ran the most profitable house they had.

The others in the room sensed the tension. Jamilla, recognizing Mayo, smiled at him, trying to look sexy.

"Hey, what's up?" Magilla said lamely.

"How you gone run a house, when you always in the basement jackin' off?" Mayo answered, going on the offensive.

Magilla was scared and angry at once. He didn't like being humiliated in front of his people but he didn't want to make matters worse by trying to answer the question. He tried an aggressive posture.

"Hey, man, the house is gettin' run just like always," he said.

Mayo looked around in disbelief, as if he were trying to see to whom the remark was directed. He walked closer to Magilla. Several people in the room moved away, jumped, anticipating a fight.

"Who the fuck is you talkin' to like that?! I'll kick yo extra large ass up and down this muthafucka myself!" He was face to face with Magilla. "Answer me, bitch. Who was you talkin' to?"

Magilla trembled with anger and hoped that no one thought it was fear. "Nobody," he said. "Nobody."

"That's what I thought," said Mayo. "Like I was sayin', how you gone run the crib, when you fuckin' off half the time?" Mayo stepped back from Magilla. "Get on yo job and stop fuckin' with this sack-chasin' hoodrat!" Mayo looked at Jamilla. A sack-chaser was a few steps below a whore and a hoodrat was a drug dealer's groupie.

Jamilla stormed out the front door, insulted. Phillip, who was still laughing, followed her. Magilla wanted to stop her, but decided that he would look like a punk if he did. He had to act like it didn't matter. Women were supposed to be worthless to rollers. They were replaceable, things to be used and discarded.

"We gotta talk," said Mayo walking to the front door. Magilla followed like a puppy, not looking at anyone.

Mayo got into his car, a red Alfa Romeo, and Magilla followed. He put in the key and turned on the auxiliary switch. The radio came on. He hit the CD changer and turned down the volume as a rap song blasted out of the speakers.

"I want three muthafuckas that owes us money. I want names and where they hang out," said Mayo.

"Easy," said Magilla. "Just pick three. They all in debt. You know the policy is to keep 'em behind on credit."

"Yeah, well, then gimme three that owe the most."

"What you gone do to 'em?"

"None of yo fat, fuckin' bidness!" Mayo exploded. "Just gimme da names!" Mayo took a pad and pen from his glove box and handed them to Magilla who began to write. A half-smile drifted over his face as he wrote.

"I know what you thinkin', fat boy," said Mayo. "I'll write it, but you won't be able ta read it. Well, don't you worry 'bout it lard ass, just write the shit down."

"How am I supposed to know where somebody hang out? I don't keep up with these heads."

"You ain't shit, you know that? I ask you some simple shit, an' you actin' like I want you to chew off yo fat ass dick." Mayo looked disgusted. "Just gimme the names!"

Magilla continued to write. "Why you always comin' wrong on me?" he asked. "I know we ain't cool an' shit, but you ain't gotta fuck with me every time I see you."

"Yes, I do. 'Cause you fucked wif me."

"Hey, man, that was only one time, all right!" Magilla gestured with one hand.

"One time too many, gorilla."

"It ain't even necessary, you know. That's what I'm sayin'."

"I don't give a fuck! You fucked with me and made an enemy. The worse enemy you could ever make. I may not read good and shit, but I'm still smart. Smart enough to be over yo fat ass, and that's the way it is, life in the big, muthafuckin' city," he poked each syllable out on Magilla's chest. "You fucked up, now live with your shit." He snatched the pad from Magilla.

Magilla glared at Mayo.

"If I was you, I'd get happy quick, bitch," said Mayo. "I don't like yo attitude."

"We'll see 'bout this shit," said Magilla a little too angrily. Mayo grabbed him by the collar and whipped a gun to his nose. Magilla was so startled that his hand automatically reached for the door's handle. Mayo's move was catlike and Magilla had no idea where the gun had come from.

"This ain't school, nigga!" Mayo was leaning toward him. "I guarantee you if you start any shit, I'll finish it quick. We got some muthafucka out there whackin' our people, and you worryin' about what I do to you. You just better smile and say 'yessir' like you always do." He pushed Magilla away. The gun disappeared to its secret place. Mayo looked at the list. Magilla could see he was having trouble reading it.

"Is that it?" asked Magilla, sighing heavily. He'd had enough of Mayo.

"Yeah," said Mayo. "Raise yo' fat ass up outta my ride." Magilla moved quickly to free himself from the car. "And don't tell nobody 'bout the names you gave me. If I find out any of these people knew I was comin', it's yo ass."

Magilla was silent. He stared at Mayo, trying to radiate hate at him. The Alfa Romeo pulled away from the curb and Magilla gave it the finger when it was well out of sight.

"One day, muthafucka," he whispered to himself. "One day."

18

Palmer Park

Amir Hamood pulled his white Mercedes along a side street adja-
cent to Palmer Park, a large public facility on Detroit's fashionable
northwest side. Amir bopped his head to the beat of the music on the
radio. He was a strikingly handsome man whose every mannerism in-
dicated that he had no idea how handsome he was. Disheveled and
tacky, only his extreme good looks saved him from looking like a bum.

Next to him sat Fakir Aranki, his partner and friend. In contrast,
Fakir (who changed his name to Frank because it was more American) was short, average-looking, and immaculately dressed. It was always Frank's dream to wear expensive clothes and drive in the finest
car money could buy. He was not going to waste the fruits of drug
dealing on buying dope like Amir.

There were only a few Chaldean crews in the city. They disre-
garded the territorial domain of the blacks and were generally not
bothered. In the suburbs, however, there were several big-time Chaldean distribution middlemen.

Chaldeans were Iraqis, many of whom were Christian. Next to
their homeland, Detroit had the largest population of them in the
world.

Frank, Amir, and other dealers like them were shunned by their
own community. Drug dealers were just criminals and thugs and were
eschewed by everyone.

But Frank saw dealing as part of the American experience. He had
studied this country in school before his family moved here. America

was founded upon violence and treachery. He had learned that many of the first Americans were not only those looking for religious freedom, but also the scourge and scum of Europe, released from the prisons to the new world. And the country rose to power by murder and ruthlessness, killing the Indians, enslaving blacks, promoting indentured servitude and the oppression of immigrants, imprisoning the Japanese and stealing their money and property for the good of the country. That was how you got ahead here.

Frank was excited by the call from T-Bone. They didn't know the target, but the price was always right with T-Bone. Frank greatly respected T-Bone, whom he considered a true American.

T-Bone had accumulated great wealth and power, even though he was black, in a country that hated him. He was also one of the few blacks they dealt with who respected the Chaldean people.

"Hey, what do you think T-Bone has for us?" asked Amir. His accent was thick.

"It's *what*," said Frank, emphasizing the *t*. Frank tried to suppress his own accent and constantly kept on Amir about his English. Amir's "what" came out "whad" and his "has" came out "hazz." It made him sound like he was fresh off the boat.

"I bet it has something to do with this Handyman," Frank said. His accent was soft. "Word is the Southend is doing this killing. If I know T-Bone, he will want revenge."

"And this is where we come in," smiled Amir.

"*This*, not *dis!*" said Frank, harsher this time. "You have to work harder to stop this immigrant talk. I am getting tired of correcting you."

"So am I," said Amir.

"Why do I try?" said Frank.

Amir turned the Mercedes along the south end of the park. He saw a burgundy Cadillac with blacked-out windows parked by a row of trees. A moment later, Frank's car phone rang.

"Hello," Frank said.

"What's up, man?" T-Bone said.

He sounded funny to Frank, who had only actually seen T-Bone once. T-Bone was a recluse and for him to even be out like this meant trouble.

"I'm OK and you?" Frank asked.

"Cool man, hold on."

A moment later, Frank heard the unmistakable voice of Robert Campbell. Smart, thought Frank. T-Bone let his men do the talking because conspiracy was a felony.

T-Bone's car pulled off and Amir followed in the Mercedes. The cars moved into traffic as they talked.

"I don't have m-much time here," said Campbell. "I need you t-t-to take c-care of something."

"If it's your problem, it's mine, too," said Frank.

"Well, you know that we-we're having a p-problem. It's t-time we let ourselves be heard."

"I see," said Frank. "And who do you want to hear this message?"

"You know."

"They are tough. It will be hard," Frank said.

"Hey, that's why we c-c-came to you." Campbell turned down Seven Mile Road toward Woodward Avenue. "This is special. We'll pay d-d-double."

"More than fair," said Frank rubbing his manicured fingers together. "Do you want the leader as well?"

"No," said Campbell. "N-not him. Say hello to one of his places. And don't take anything, just make 'em hurt. Leave the c-card."

"No problem, my friend."

In T-Bone's Caddy, Campbell clicked off the cellular phone. He turned south on Woodward and cruised along the front of the park.

T-Bone whispered into his portable phone in the backseat. He finished his conversation, ending it with, "Bye, Jasmine."

"Everything cool?" he asked Campbell.

"Cool," said Campbell.

T-Bone rode in the backseat of the Cadillac with K-9 nestled in a corner. "You sure? We can't afford any remote kind of fuck-up with this."

"You know F-Frank, he's smart."

"Yeah, all right."

T-Bone reclined in the soft leather and sighed. He really hated getting this involved in things. But it was necessary. Sometimes, you had to show your face, get things done. It was risky, but necessary. He didn't even trust the Big Three with starting a war.

T-Bone was still working on getting the money together for his suppliers. He had one of his white boys running to dip into his personal accounts to get it. It was costly to move around that much cash, but his hand was forced.

Campbell pulled the Cadillac behind his own car on a side street and got out. T-Bone exited the backseat of the Caddy and climbed into the driver's seat without a word. Campbell got into his car and drove away.

As T-Bone pulled off, K-9 became alert. He shifted into the middle of the long backseat.

"OK, Mr. Nine," said T-Bone. "Repeat back to me, everything Campbell just said on the phone."

K-9 did. Verbatim.

"Cool. Nothing too incriminating in that. It's time to answer some questions for me."

"OK," said K-9 in a soft, almost feminine voice.

"How much money will I lose because of all of this Handyman shit, including what I have to pay Frank and Amir?"

"Gross or net?"

"Net."

K-9 took a second. "Two hundred five thousand, six hundred fifty dollars."

"Damn. And I have to give that fuckin' Santana five big ones. OK, Mr. Nine, the real question. If we can make the new drug at the prices agreed upon with our new friend, the Prince, how long before I will have the money I need to get out."

"A year."

"A year. A long time out here."

K-9 was what was called an idiot savant, like that guy in the movie *Rain Man*. He could do complex math at incredible speed and could remember large volumes of information, but was baffled by the simplest things.

K-9 was another inner-city treasure. T-Bone had stumbled onto the boy after his mother, a prostitute and drug addict, overdosed two years ago. The woman worked for Jasmine, T-Bone's madam. When she discovered what the boy could do, she gave him to T-Bone.

Because of K-9, he never needed to keep records that could be used against him in court. He could eavesdrop on people and never needed anyone to keep track of his money. T-Bone had even used K-9 to catch several rollers stealing from the houses.

Too bad K-9's powers couldn't help him find the Handyman, or pay that blood-sucking Santana. T-Bone had to go the normal route on these problems. A war. It had been a long time since there was a major one in the city.

T-Bone dialed a number on his cellular. He had to let his police connection know that trouble was coming.

19

The Prince

The old, green Chevy Astrovan pulled into the parking lot of the Grand Eight Motel, creaking and chugging as it moved into the parking slot in front of room 11-B. The engine died with some hesitation and three people exited the vehicle. The driver was a tall, bulky white man with a river of lines etched in his face. He clutched a large brown bag.

"Van's on its last legs," he said.

Exiting from the rear was a white woman with a shock of bleached blond hair and a homely and overly made-up face atop a fabulous body. She looked like a store mannequin at Halloween.

"That thing's dangerous. I smell like gas," she said, looking at the van with disdain. She poked out her tongue, tugged at her short skirt, and walked toward the motel room.

Riding shotgun was a short, dark black man. He had a large forehead, a receding hairline, and eyes that looked like cheap plastic. He had arms that seemed shorter than they should have been and teeth dotted with gold.

"Stop complaining," he said to the woman. "Soon, we'll be riding in a limo and drinking champagne." He jumped out of the van full of energy and walked briskly to the room, passing the other two.

The man they called the Prince was excited. His plans had come together ahead of schedule and he was looking forward to cashing out soon. He entered the shabby room and immediately headed for the phone and dialed a number.

The woman, Donna, headed into the bathroom. "I'm sick of this fuckin' dump," she said.

"Nobody asked your ass," said the Prince.

The big white man they called the Professor reached into his bag, opened a bottle of gin and took a drink. "Who you callin'?" he asked.

"My man the dealer, T-Bone. Been readin' about his problem." He laughed a little. "I think he's ready to do business." The line picked up. The Prince gave his number and hung up. "He be callin' back in a little while. Man's got a system."

"I don't know about this shit," said the Professor.

"You don't need to know. I know."

The Prince's real name was D'Terrance Clark, a name he detested because it was his mother's feeble attempt to give her poor son some class. He had always been a slick kid, regularly finding a way out of trouble. He'd talked his way out of a hundred ass-whippings and seemed destined to be a great hustler. He was a natural at the game, a smiling, quick witted one-man show. He'd pulled a thousand scams, from old-fashioned three-card monte to elaborate insurance and social security frauds. And in true hustler tradition, he'd blown each fortune and started all over again. That was the cycle in the game. Hit it, quit it, and get back with it.

What the Prince hadn't bargained for was the savage turn the business took in the '80s. Suddenly, you had to be willing to kill or die just to play the game. It was a setback. At that time, he was not a violent man—talking was his weapon. But eventually, his need to live the adventure in his mind took over and he stepped up to the new order. The Prince found that it wasn't an unpleasant undertaking. Violence was a natural part of the con game. It raised the stakes and increased the risk.

Donna came out of the bathroom. She looked good as she walked by the Professor, who was starting on his second bottle. He never noticed her. Donna pulled out a cigarette, then thought better of it. She was trying to quit. She poked out her tongue, then quickly pulled it back in. She was trying to kick that annoying habit, too. She put the cigarette back and headed for the door.

"Where you think you goin'?" asked the Prince.

"Out," said Donna.

"Naw," said the Prince. "My call's comin' back soon. We might have to get on the road. I need you to be here."

"I hate this fuckin' one-horse, one-dick town. I gotta get into something."

"You be gettin' in a coffin, bitch, if you don't sit yo itchy ass down somewhere."

The Prince smiled and took a step her way. Donna had been with him too long not to know what that smile meant with its insincere corners and dirty flecks of gold. She made a grumbling noise, put her purse down and sat hard on the bed.

The Prince grabbed his crotch, adjusting it, and stepped over to the Professor. "How ya doin', man?" he asked.

"Good. I'm calming down." He took another long swig from the bottle of gin.

"You should be cool on that, man," the Prince said. He pointed to the bottle. "I'm gone need you soon."

"I know, I know," he said and took another drink. "I'm just nervous about all this. I've never—"

"Don't fuck with me!" The Prince snatched the bottle.

"Hey, gimme that, damn!" The Professor stood up. He was much taller than the Prince.

The phone rang. The Prince looked at the white man for a second, then threw him the bottle and went to the phone.

"Hello . . . yes, my brotha," said the Prince. He was animated and seemed to be moving to some music in his head. Donna and the Professor had seen this many times. He was on the make.

It was T-Bone on the phone. "I'm outside. Let's talk. Just you," he said. Then he hung up.

The Prince went to the door. He patted his hair as if he were going on a date. "Don't leave here until I get back," he said. He was looking right into Donna's eyes.

The Prince walked outside and got into the front seat of the Cadillac in the parking lot. He was shocked at the sight of K-9 in the backseat, but recovered quickly, only to be shocked again by the sawed-off pump nestled between T-Bone's legs.

"You ain't expecting trouble, are you?" asked the Prince.

"You ain't gonna give me any, are you?" said T-Bone.

"No, no, not me, my brotha. It ain't my thang. I'm strictly a businessman."

"I know. I had you checked out." T-Bone pulled the car away.

"So, are you ready to deal, my brotha?" asked the Prince with a smile.

"It's gonna take a while. Got a few problems."

"I understand. I read the papers."

"I got business to do first, so you'll have to wait," said T-Bone.

"But my people are restless. We need to move on this thang. We itchin' to make you rich."

"I need all this shit to die down first."

"We can't wait that long. We need to go—"

"I think I'm calling the fuckin' shots here," T-Bone said.

"Yes, yes, my brotha, I didn't mean to suggest otherwise. It's just that we have other people who want to talk to us."

"I'm the only one in this city who can give you what you want. Anybody else is shittin' you."

T-Bone knew he had him. The reason the Prince had picked Detroit was because of its centralized drug trade. No other crew in the city could offer him decent money.

"I mean, we have offers, in other cities," said the Prince.

"Well, I'll see what I can do." T-Bone circled the block and headed in the direction of the motel where the Prince was staying.

"You know, I didn't think I'd get to meet the man himself," said the Prince. "I'm honored."

T-Bone ignored him. He was feeling him out. The Prince seemed like a classic hustler, the kind of guy who was always on the make. T-Bone wanted to know what his angle was. The Prince had told him that he had a chemist who had discovered the new drug. So, the Prince was pimping that man for his knowledge. That made sense. All T-Bone needed was to look him in the eyes and feel what he was dealing with. For now, he was satisfied.

"I want to set up another meeting with all your people," said T-Bone. "At that time, I want to see just how you do what you do. I will need the whole setup and I want in writing how it's done or no deal."

"That's not a problem, my brotha."

"If anything goes wrong, at any time, I'll have to deal with it." T-Bone patted the gun.

"I understand, yes. Everything will be cool."

T-Bone pulled back into the motel lot next to the old Chevy van.

"What do I do now?" asked the Prince.

"Wait, lay low, enjoy our city. I'll get back to you."

"No problem," said the Prince. The Prince got out of the car. He waited outside until T-Bone had pulled away, then he went back into the room.

"Fuck!" he said as he slammed the door. "This muthafucka is pissin' me off! Nigga want me to wait on him. I ain't got time to wait!"

"I say we ditch this place. We're in too deep this time," said the Professor.

"Yeah," said Donna. "This place is wack."

"When did this become a fuckin' democracy?" said the Prince. "Neither one of you muthafuckas can do shit without me, so just shut the fuck up."

The Prince sat down hard in a fading red chair. This was going to be harder than he thought. His mind was working on a thousand different ways to move faster to the next stage of his plan.

20

The Handyman Revealed

Tony entered the Sewer and hustled into Jim's office and found it empty. Jim was probably still out running the check on Roberts's mistress.

Tony sat in Jim's chair and waited. He'd spent the morning running around, fighting thoughts of Darryl Simon and the need to confess to Jim again. Even in the heat of this investigation, he could not shake thoughts of GM and Simon and the people he'd murdered . . . black people . . . Simon's body falling from the building. . . .

"Hey, pardner!" Jim said as he entered.

Tony was startled. "What did you find?" he asked, referring to Barbara Volkarwicz. Tony got up and sat on the desk.

"You gonna love what I got. I ran a check on the plates and the car was registered to her, right? Dead end. Big deal. So, I get her Social Security number and run a make on her through want and warrants and the previous offender files. Nothing. Zip. Zero. Just a few minor hooker busts."

"Yes. And?" Tony adjusted himself on the edge of the desk. He was getting a little upset.

"So, I go to the vice guys and check out their info on call girls. They know her all right, but as far as they know, she's just a hooker. But one of the vice guys tells this story about how he remembers her from a domestic violence case a few years back. Husband tried to choke her when he caught her turning a trick in their bedroom. So I think, Married?"

"Why are you doing this to me, Jim?" Tony asked. "You're as bad as Roberts."

"Well, funny you should mention him, 'cause when I looked up her divorce case, I found out that he's our leak to the media."

"How so?"

"Well, little-miss-blue-Saab's maiden name was Barbara Salinsky."

Tony's mouth hung open. "Well, I'll be damned. I'll just be damned."

Jim smiled. "Yep. Sisters."

Tony's eyes widened. "Salinsky uses her sister to get inside information from her high-class johns. She looks like Joe Ace Reporter in the process. Ain't that a bitch!"

"How can we use this to get what we want, though?" asked Jim.

"Easy enough," said Tony. "We just tell Roberts that we'll give away his secret to the Chief if he doesn't tell us what we want to know. We have to use it on the bastard anyway, to plug the leak."

Jim nodded.

A middle-aged secretary popped her head into the office. "I'm sending a call in here to you, Tony."

"Take a message," said Tony. "We're busy here."

"Well, the woman on the phone has been calling all morning, sir. She says it's life or death."

"It's probably a crank," said Jim. He stepped to his side of the desk and Tony noticed Jim slip a piece of paper under the blotter into his pocket.

Tony thought a second. "OK, Mildred," he said. The secretary disappeared from the doorway.

"Hey, pardner, we gotta get moving, remember? Why are you taking calls from strangers? It's probably some nut who wants to confess to killing Kennedy."

"Well, maybe it's the Handyman," Tony said quietly.

Jim looked at him as if he were stunned at the possibility.

The phone rang a moment after that. Tony reached across the desk to answer it.

"Inspector Hill."

"Hello, Officer Hill," said the female voice on the line.

"Can I help you?"

"No, but I'm here to help you."

Tony recognized the voice but couldn't place it.

"If you don't tell me who you are in two seconds, I'm hanging up."

"I guess I should have called Fuller, he would recognize my voice."

"Salinsky?"

"Bingo! You must be a cop."

Jim came closer when he heard the name. He pointed to the area outside of his door and cupped his hand to his ear, signaling Tony that he was going to listen to the conversation. Tony shook his head.

"What's the scoop?" Tony asked.

"Well, Inspector, I know you guys don't like me 'cause I always know your inside business. But I don't want it said that I have no scruples. See, it takes years of work and savvy to get the connections that I have, and I like to think that I can be called upon to help the cops when they need it."

Tony suppressed his laugh. Salinsky's years of experience were on her sister's back. "Get to the point," he said.

"Well, I have certain information that is vital to your investigation of the Handyman. This is information that you yourself don't have. In return for this information, I want an exclusive if you catch the bastard."

"No deals, Salinsky," Tony stalled. This had to be the same information they were going squeeze out of Roberts.

Jim looked at him with wild eyes. It was driving him crazy not hearing the conversation. It served him right for teasing him like he did, thought Tony.

"Then I can't help you. Bye-bye."

"Wait!" Tony said. "I could get your ass on an obstruction charge you know."

"I know. But by the time the lawyers start to dance, I'll have the information on the air and believe me, you want to hear it first."

"So, no one else knows this information?"

"Well, let's put it this way: people know, but they're sitting on it."

"Why?" asked Tony.

"You'll know when you hear it. That is, *if* you hear it from me."

Tony paused a moment. "If I agree, how do you know I'll keep my word?"

"I don't really," said Salinsky. "But I know your reputation. Your word is worth something and if I get it, I believe that you'll keep it. Besides, if you don't, I just won't bother to call the next time."

Tony smiled to himself. He could see why Fuller hated her. "OK, Salinsky. You have my word."

Jim watched as Tony listened. He had seen Tony in every imaginable state, but had never seen a look like the one that came over his face at this moment. It was like someone had told him that he had two hearts and then pulled open his chest and showed him. Tony said good-bye to Salinsky and hung up.

Jim looked at him nervously. "What? What?" he asked.

"We don't have to squeeze Roberts. I know what he's hiding," Tony said slowly.

Jim waited, holding his breath.

"What Roberts brought the Chief were hair samples taken from the bodies of the Handyman's victims."

"And?" said Jim, about to burst.

"They're blond hairs. Not dyed. Natural, blond hairs."

"What the fu—"

"And Salinsky's gonna tell the world tonight on the news."

"Jesus, do you know what that means in this city?"

Tony was silent. He knew all too well. He glanced at his watch. It was a quarter to seven. Salinsky was saving the scoop for the eleven o'clock report. In four hours, the city would start to heat up.

The gravity of the situation was upon him. In Detroit, where racial polarization was a fact of life and racism itself a political tool, he was facing a serial killer whose targets were young black men. The fact that they were drug dealers would not make any difference. It would be seen as whites killing blacks, the worst kind of murder.

Although violence was a common occurrence to blacks in cities, it offended their deepest and most profound sensibilities when whites killed a black. It invoked thoughts of slavery, lynchings, and other hateful atrocities committed over the years.

It was an intolerable act in a community filled with a history of racial oppression. It was almost inconceivable, and the thing that bothered Tony the most was that he'd never even thought of the possibility. Most murders in the city were committed by blacks against other blacks. It was no surprise. The city was between eighty to ninety percent black. But even with that knowledge, no one would care. Even now that he knew, Tony didn't think it possible.

The Handyman was a white man.

21

Roberts

It was the first time that Jim would enjoy going to the Crypt. He and Tony had decided that the news was too important to waste time on. Tony was going to the Chief and the mayor with the story. Jim was given the wonderful duty of telling Roberts that he was the leak. He was going to enjoy every bit of it, too. Roberts was an asshole and he deserved everything that he was going to give him. He walked faster down Beaubien. He was glad not to be going with Tony. He disliked Yancy more than Fuller, if that was possible. The puppetmaster and his star puppet.

As Jim rounded a corner and walked into the Crypt, he paused a second to rehearse his speech. "Fuck it," he finally said to himself. He was going to wing it. He entered Roberts's reception area and walked past the evening receptionist into Roberts's office.

"Well, you finally fucked up," Jim said, staring Roberts in the eyes.

Roberts was on the phone seated at his desk. He looked startled and quickly ended his phone conversation.

"You had better have a good reason for this intrusion," Roberts said.

"Oh, I do," Jim smiled. "I do. I'm playing a game today, Doctor. It's called 'Guess what I know.' "

"I don't want to play your games, officer. Get out of my office. Some of us have work to do."

Jim closed Roberts's door.

"Look here now," said Roberts standing. "If you intend some sort of violence—"

"What are you gonna do, Doctor, kick my ass?" Jim smiled like the Devil himself.

"If I have to," Roberts said in a weak voice.

Jim roared. "Right!" His eyes narrowed. "You know, Doc, I've never liked you." He moved over to Roberts's desk. The doctor took a half-step back. Roberts was scared and Jim liked it. Jim smiled and sat down across from him. "No, I've never liked you at all."

"Look, Officer Cole, if you don't get out of here right now, I'm going to call—"

"The police. I know. I'll leave, Doctor, if you want me to."

"I definitely want you to go," Roberts said with force.

"Well, OK." Jim stood and looked straight into Roberts's pale blue eyes. "I just came by to tell you that we know you're fuckin' a prostitute named Barbara Volkarwicz, and she's been leaking your pillow talk to the press." Jim grinned in his face. "Still want me to leave?"

Roberts looked back at Jim. Denial and lies passed behind his eyes. Finally, his large head lowered and he sat down hard. He stared into space. He head rolled to one side and dangled at the end of his neck. "I suppose I should have known that she was talking." Roberts looked down at his desk. "Too much was getting out."

"You're fuckin-A right you shoulda known! You idiot! You're stroking this bitch and the department takes the heat because you can't keep your fuckin' mouth shut!"

Then, to Jim's surprise, Roberts reached across the desk and grabbed him at the collar. "You don't have the right to call her a bitch!" Roberts screamed into his face.

Jim pulled free and stepped back, a little startled and angry. "Now you've really fucked up, boy. I've been waiting for this for a long time." Jim moved back to Roberts, fists clenched.

The door to the office opened, and the evening receptionist, a heavy-set woman, opened the door and meekly looked inside. "Doctor, is there a problem?" she said almost apologetically.

"No, Jane," said Roberts. "Excuse our loudness and language. Please, go back to your station."

Jim looked back at the woman, who was giving him a nasty look. He felt ashamed and childish. He didn't really want to fight Roberts. He unclenched his fists, repositioned the chair and sat down. Jane closed the door and left.

Roberts looked sad. He sat down and stared back into space. "My wife," he said in a faint voice. "We aren't—"

"Look man, I—" Jim stumbled.

"No, detective, you came here for revenge, right?" Roberts snapped at Jim. "Well, here it is. Dr. Roberts will tell it all just for you." He looked at him with an intensity Jim didn't think Roberts was capable of. "My wife is a fat, disgusting pig of a woman. She couldn't fuck me even if she wanted to, and if I divorce her, she'll take all the money we've got. Her father is a rich, cheap bastard. He protected her good. So I buy sex from a prostitute 'cause I'm too fucking ugly, dull, and stupid to get it legitimately. Is that what you wanted? A confession? Well, that's it." Roberts's eyes were misty. "I knew she was telling. Hell, I wanted her to. It made me more valuable to her. Sometimes she wouldn't charge me. We'd just do it like we just wanted to be with each other. Can you believe it, officer? She wanted me? Well, it's true. *She wanted me!*" Roberts banged his desk.

"Look, I'm sorry, Doc." Jim almost choked on the words. "I was wrong—"

"Oh no, officer. You wanted this. To humiliate me personally and professionally. You have to listen. It's what you wanted, right?"

Jim tried to get up, but he couldn't. Roberts was right. He had come on a mission, but it had backfired. He owed him an ear.

"I married my wife for the money. I'm a doctor sure, but not a great one. I wanted real money, so I married this plump, rich, spoiled brat. Her family loved it. They thought that they would never get rid of her. Her father put most of the money in a trust that is controlled by the family. She won't get the really big payment until she hits fifty. And we can't touch a dime until then. I thought of knocking her off once. Can you imagine that, detective? Funny thing is, I tried to love her. I figured that this was for life, so I should try." Roberts leaned over the desk. "The sex was terrible from the start," he said. "We never did it until we got married. She was a virgin. Can you believe that? And her folks must have told her to lay off the food until she got married, 'cause after the wedding, she put on weight like nobody's business. She ate everything in sight—"

"Doc, I should go," said Jim getting up. "I have to prepare for—"

"Can't take it, huh?" laughed Roberts. "You come here to screw with me, then you chicken out. You're a coward. Please, sit, Officer Cole," he gestured to the empty chair. "You've earned this."

Jim sat down slowly. He was feeling guilty. He had put his foot in it before, but never had he been in such an awkward situation.

"Before I started with Barbara," continued Roberts, "my wife and I had not had sex for five years. *Five years!* As fat as she was, I still tried to do it with her before then. Then she just stopped one day and that was it. No sex. I held out as long as I could. Cold showers, reading books, television. But you know, nothing can replace sex. Eventually, I rented X-rated movies and masturbated."

Jim groaned.

"Disgusted, detective?" Roberts looked serious. "Well, it gets better. I bought this machine from the back of a porno magazine. It was supposed to simulate oral sex. Damned thing looked like a mouth." Roberts let out a short, dry laugh. "I used the thing right in the house, too. It was more exciting doing it right under her fat-ass nose for some reason. I used it and it was good. Hell, after going without for so long, anything feels good. I did it with that battery-powered mouth as often as I could. One day, she walked right in on me, caught me with my dick in that thing. She just looked at me. There was no shock or shame. She just looked as if to say, You poor stupid bastard. Then she laughed. Can you imagine that? *She* laughed at *me!*"

Roberts looked like he was having a breakdown, Jim realized.

"So, you know what I did?" Roberts continued. "I took my dick out and finished while she watched me. She just grunted and left the room. The big, fat bitch just left without a word. She's not even human anymore, I thought. I felt like I wanted to die, like I was worthless. A man is only half of himself without a woman. You know what I mean? You need a woman to make you whole."

Jim nodded but said nothing.

"I found Barbara soon after." Roberts reclined in his chair and threw up his arms. "Well, you happy? You got me. Dr. Vincent Roberts: Jackass and Pervert."

Jim felt sick. "I'm sorry," he said.

"So am I, officer, so am I," said Roberts quietly. "Well, I guess the press knows about the hair samples then?"

"Yes. We think it's gonna be on the eleven o'clock report." Jim decided that he would not tell Roberts about Barbara Volkarwicz's other name. The information might come in handy. "We'd like it if you wouldn't tell her we know."

Roberts looked amazed. "You mean, you're not going to turn me in to the mayor?"

"Shit no," said Jim. "We respect a man's right to get laid. Just cool out on the information."

"I appreciate this, officer, I really do," Roberts gushed, grabbing Jim's hand and shaking it.

"No problem," said Jim. "No more leaks, Doc."

"Yes, yes, of course," said Roberts. He seemed rejuvenated.

Jim said a half-hearted good-bye and left. He dropped his eyes as he passed Jane. Roberts had been through hell. When Jim thought about five years without sex, he shuddered. No one, not even Roberts, should suffer like that.

Jim walked out of the Crypt into the fresh air thinking that in just three more hours, the city would explode.

22

Yancy on the Hook

Tony and Chief Fuller watched the spectacle with amazement. Harris Yancy's temper was legendary in Detroit political circles—a Mount St. Helens of choler, and it had erupted at Tony's news about Salinsky.

Fuller hung his head when he heard. He apologized to Tony about holding out. It wasn't right, he said, but it was the way life was.

Now the mayor yelled and swore at a television executive on the phone. Yancy paced, gesturing with one hand as if the man were in front of him.

Tony sat and listened, taking in the familiar opulence of the mayor's office. The plush carpet, the rich wood of his large desk, the pictures of rivers that lined the walls. It was glorious.

The show continued. It was typical Yancy, trying to control others instead of dealing with the problem. Yancy still lived partially in the shadow of his predecessor and was frustrated because of it. His rage got in the way of his obvious intelligence, and he could be evil and nasty, even to his best friends. Insiders often whispered that his lack of grace with others would someday be his undoing.

"I don't give a goddamn about your journalistic commitment, Stan. I don't want the shit on the air tonight! Just give us twenty-four hours to prepare a statement and I'll owe you one. Let us get to the people first."

"No can do, Harris," said the distorted voice of Stanley Cramer over the speakerphone. "We've got our interests, too. You tried to hide news and it's our job to expose the whole story."

"*Your job!*" Yancy yelled. "It's not your job to throw the city into a blind panic. You know what's going to happen when it gets out?"

"Well, hell, Harris, it's *going* to get out. *When,* is the question."

"You just don't give a damn do you, Stan?" Yancy said. "You sit out there in Franklin with your butlers and maids and talk about how bad things are in old Detroit."

"Oh, come on, not that old stuff again."

"I know how it is, Stan. You white people think blacks are your entertainment. The violence, death, and drugs, it's all just like a TV show to you. But this time it's different. This affects everyone in the metropolitan area. There will be turmoil in the city, but you just might find people knocking on your door, too." Yancy was breathing hard.

"Are you threatening me, Harris?"

"Take it any way you want."

"I never thought I'd see you sink this low. I'm truly disappointed in you." Cramer's voice was low. "Usually, I just get called a racist honky dog, but never, never have you threatened me. Well, Harris, sadly, it's not going to work. I'm running the story tonight as planned."

"Don't you come to me when the shit gets thick, Stan! I'm serious. You're letting me go this one alone, so I assure you, I'll let your ass fry when the time comes!" Yancy switched off the phone without saying good-bye.

Tony and Fuller were silent. Fuller looked serious. Thus far, the mayor's anger was directed at Cramer but Tony knew the Chief, would have to take part of the blame, too.

"Well, how do you suppose this got out, fellas?" Yancy said. He walked to a wall and pushed a section. His hidden bar appeared. He poured himself a drink and returned to Fuller and Tony.

"We are still looking for the source," Fuller said feebly.

"Source my ass, Bill!" yelled Yancy. Only you, me, and Roberts knew about this. Now, the way I see it, one of us spilled it. Now, I know it wasn't me, so that leaves you and the good doctor. One of you is dirty, and I want to know which one!" Yancy drank a large gulp.

"Excuse me, sir, but there was one other person who knew," said Tony.

"And who is that?" asked Yancy.

"Doctor Neward sir, the assistant coroner," said Tony. "In all honesty, Officer Cole and I were trying to find Neward to ask him some questions about the Shalon Street killings. Neward was there at the house and Roberts grabbed him and took him away. So we figured Neward must know something. Then he disappeared. He may have told someone before he left."

Tony was proud of the story. He had decided to keep his info on Roberts as an ace in the hole. He told Yancy and Fuller about Salinsky's call, but nothing else.

Yancy walked back to his desk and sat.

"Well, wherever he is, he can stay there. Tell the doctor to take care of it, Bill," Yancy said finishing his drink.

Fuller nodded.

Tony stood. "Sir, I didn't say that he did it. I said that he might have. It's a—"

"Sit your ass down!" snapped Yancy. "You don't even begin to have the knowledge to give me advice. Your job does not involve thinking."

Tony sat down slowly. He did not like this mistreatment one bit, but you had to take Yancy's shit. It was the way things were done.

"I'm not saying that he did leak it," Yancy said more calmly. "But someone has to go. I can't let things like this get out without my permission and do nothing. We'll take care of this Neward. He'll get another position, just not in my city."

Tony watched Fuller nod like a robot. It was times like this that he lamented being involved in the politics of his office. It was a sleazy undertaking. The direction of people's lives were changed at the whim of some asshole pushing papers. Say or do the wrong thing and you could wake up in the unemployment line. So he always considered the political consequences of everything he did. Sometimes he wished he could just do his job and forget all the crap, but then, he would be just another swinging dick with a gun and a badge.

Yancy stood up and walked around his large desk. He breathed deeply and faced the large bay windows overlooking the river turning his back on his guests.

"Bill, I want to hurry and feed the story to the other stations," Yancy began. "Let's kill Cramer's scoop. I'm sure he knows that I'm going to do that, so he'll probably try to get it on a special bulletin before eleven, like they did when that nut Simon jumped out of the GM building."

Tony flinched.

Fuller took a pad and pen and began to write.

"When the story hits tonight," Yancy turned around to face them. "I want you to have a statement with our spin on it prepared. I want it to say that we withheld the information for the good of the public and were going to release it in a few days, as soon as we completed our investigation of several suspects. Say that we knew what the impact would be and sought to protect the citizenry. You know all the damn community activist types will be all over us. They live to cash in on shit like this. Then let the public know that a member of the press recklessly broke the story ahead of time. They'll know who it is." He took a deep breath. "And, I want the killings condemned. Let the press have their fun with the racial aspect. Avoid any comment on that directly. Hill, I want you there with him, backing him up. I want it to go to all of the stations, except Cramer's."

"No problem, Harris," said Fuller.

Tony could see that Yancy didn't really mind lying to the public, and he had not expressed any remorse about impeding Tony's investigation. For him, it was now about damage control.

"And get some extra patrols out for the reaction to the news," Yancy continued. "I'm sure that the Brotherhood will demonstrate. I don't want any riots and attacks on white folks because of this."

Fuller nodded again.

Tony sat quietly, like he was in the dunce corner in elementary school. Yancy's comment about Darryl Simon had sent his mind on an uneasy trip. Images of the incident and The Dream filled his thoughts and his head now ached dully.

"All that clear?" Yancy asked.

"Yes, sir," Fuller said.

Tony nodded weakly.

"Officer Hill, could you excuse us for a moment?" Yancy looked at Tony. He was a different man now. The raging madman of a moment ago had been replaced with the kind, concerned father figure.

Tony said "yes" and left. Simon and his creations were running unbridled in his mind.

Tony took a seat in the waiting room among the nervous business types who constantly filled the area.

Tony rubbed his temples. More stress, that was all he needed now. It was times like this that he fantasized about living on a farm somewhere, with puffy white clouds, green meadows, and no assholes. Guys like Yancy made you wonder if it was worth it. If life had any fairness in it at all, he would lose the election and go to purgatory. But if he did, where would that leave Tony Hill? He was tied to him, personality and all. Life was a big, fat, evil bitch sometimes.

Fuller emerged from the mayor's office looking surprisingly relaxed. He pulled Tony away from the constant gallery of onlookers in the waiting room.

"You OK?" Fuller asked.

"Yeah."

"Don't take it personally, you know how he is. I've been taking his shit for years."

"Are you proud of that?"

"Yes. There are hundreds of guys who would kill to be in my position. And if I'm not mistaken, I'm talking to one of them."

"Yeah, but that doesn't make it easier to take."

"You know the game, Tony. Guys like Yancy have made it possible for us to be where we are. We take the good with the bad and all black folk prosper. Better than the old days, right?"

"You know I can't argue with that. It's just that I hate to be treated like shit."

"Life in the big leagues, Tony," Fuller said. He took a few steps away, then stopped. "I really wanted to tell you about the hair, but you know how it is."

Tony nodded. He knew all too well.

"Now come on, we've got a lot of work to do."

23

The Union in the House

Amir checked his gun again. Perfect. He was pumped up and ready. Frank tapped the accelerator of the old Chevy and it responded nicely. Everything was cool. Almost time.

Frank poised the old sedan on the corner of Tireman and Faulkner—Southend territory. He was wearing a running suit and he didn't like it. But he was working and he had to dress accordingly. From their vantage point they could see the traffic going in and out of the fifth house up the street. When a car pulled up, someone would run out of the car, into the house and quickly leave with the purchase. Others just walked in and bought the goods.

"Just like a McDonald's drive through," Frank thought out loud. Amir chuckled.

It was a poor-looking street, peppered with vacant, boarded-up houses. Except for a few homes, the occupied houses on the street were unkempt and depressing. As Frank scanned the area, he laughed. The crackhouse was the best looking one on the block.

If T-Bone himself had not requested the hit, Frank would have left it up to Amir to handle. But any work for T-Bone had to have personal attention. Too important to fuck up. Frank had a reputation, and he couldn't let subordinates ruin it.

"Our men should be coming around any minute now," said Frank. Amir nodded and snorted coke from a small dispenser. "You know I don't like you getting high on a job," Frank said mildly.

Amir was a bum, he thought. He was reckless, used too much

coke, fucked too many women, and talked too much. A dangerous man. But he was a good hitter, as mean and vicious as they came. If their families weren't so close, he would have gotten rid of him long ago. Still, he often thought that the day would come when he would have to kill him. The business was like that and smart men always thought about the future.

"I need some fuel, man," Amir said. "I want to be cookin' when I hit these punks." His accent was thick.

"Right," said Frank sarcastically. "Just be sure that you don't hit our two guys."

"No problem, baby."

The house had two armed guards working near the inside and outside door. If a person they didn't know tried to come in, they would check him out first.

"Here they come," said Frank, pointing to two large men walking up the street, Ty and B-Boy. They were Chaldean and black respectively.

They watched as a lanky roller stopped them on the sidewalk. He was wearing a black raincoat which obviously hid a gun. Frank could tell he was questioning them. They smiled in response and talked with the guard. The guard signaled and another roller who couldn't have been older than twelve came out of the house. The boy-man checked Frank's men for weapons, patting them down right there on the street. He found only the knives that Frank told them to carry. The lanky roller gave them back and continued to talk to the men. When the guard laughed and let them enter, Frank knew they were in.

"Ty and B-Boy are doing good," Amir said, rubbing his gun.

Frank waited. It would be just a few moments before the action started. He breathed deeply. He was not really made for this kind of work. He was a thinker, a planner like T-Bone. He lived for the day when he would not have to do this kind of thing.

"Yes!" said Amir, taking another hit of coke.

"Get ready," said Frank.

The lanky guard in the overcoat ran into the house suddenly and Frank hit the accelerator. Frank stopped the car in front of the crackhouse and he and Amir quickly jumped out and ran inside. Each held an Uzi, ready to fire.

In the house, Ty and B-Boy were on the floor fighting with the knives in a mock struggle. Several people around them watched the fight cheering.

The two guards stood in front of the door. They both enjoyed the fight.

Amir burst through the front door with a yell, knocking over the two guards and spraying them with bullets. His veins pumped adrenaline and cocaine.

Frank followed through the door and turned his gun on the other occupants. Bodies jumped and blood sprayed the walls. One dealer tried to run, but Frank caught him in the back of the head with a burst of fire.

Amir moved into the kitchen, the drug raging inside him. He was electric with energy, his heart pumping like a freight train. He hit the area with gunfire. The three women inside dropped like cut flowers.

He never saw the baby crib nestled in the corner of the room and he hit it before he could stop. He ceased firing. For a moment, he could not believe that he hadn't seen the bed. He was too pumped. His chest heaved with anxiety. Never had he done such a thing. He peered into the bed and turned in disgust. He bent over and tried to stop himself from throwing up, but failed.

"Check the basement!" Frank yelled from the other room.

Amir kicked himself back into action. He stumbled toward the stairs that led to the basement.

Ty and B-Boy grabbed the guns off the dead guards and ran upstairs. Gunfire, yelling, and screams erupted from the second floor.

Two crackheads pushed open the front door and Frank shot them. One was holding a roll of bills, which he tossed into the air when he was hit. The money fell like lumpy confetti.

"Basement . . . clear," Amir said, choking back bile. He ran into the living room, stepping over bodies and breathing heavily.

"Let's do it!" Frank yelled to Ty and B-Boy upstairs. They ran down, streaked with blood and sweating. Amir checked outside. The car was still running in the middle of the street. Amir ran out to it and got into the driver's seat. His hands were sweaty and shaking. He tried to steady them. Ty and B-Boy followed, jumping in the back.

Inside the house, Frank ripped a final salvo of shots into a wall before running out and jumping into the car. Amir hit the gas and they took off.

It wasn't until the police came an hour later that the first neighbor dared come out of his house.

The van roared down the freeway with its human cargo. Steve Mayo sat in the back next to the three bound and gagged prisoners. He had collected his targets, then recruited the necessary help.

Driving the van was a young roller named Larry Drake. He was seventeen and had just dropped out of school. His parents had thrown him out of their house and he was in desperate need of money. He had jumped when Mayo asked him to come on the job. He knew that if he performed well, it might lead to better things.

In the back with Mayo on a makeshift bench were two freelance enforcers named Pit and Nam. Pit was a huge black man with a face marked by terrible scars he had gotten in prison. Nam was a burly, white, self-proclaimed Vietnam vet. Mayo knew that the two men were barely sane, but he respected them. Each had a reputation for ruthlessness, and he could not afford to have any punks with him.

Mayo had thought twice about taking Larry for this exact reason. Drake was new, but he was also smart and eager. This would be a good chance to see if he could stand the heat. If he could take it, then better things were in store for him in the Union. If he punked, this would be his last night on earth.

The three bound captives jumped and jostled on the van's padded floor as it hit bumps. There were two men and one woman. The woman and one of the men cried and begged through their gags. The third captive, who wore a bright yellow shirt, just sat and watched in a drug-induced stupor. Mayo had rounded them all up after he got the information from Magilla.

Larry guided the van on the Lodge Freeway headed downtown. He took the Interstate 94 exit west. He gripped the steering wheel tightly with sweaty hands. He thought he was going to make a drug run with Mayo, but when he saw Pit and Nam, he knew he was in for a much bigger undertaking. He knew them and their reputation. They were hired killers, two of the worst. He knew then that this would be a test for him, to see if he could hang with the big boys. He was scared but determined to make a good showing.

"I say we fuck dis ho," said Pit, indicating the woman. Her eyes widened. A muffled yell came through her gag. Her wide earrings clanked loudly against the van's dirty floor.

"Shut up, bitch!" said Nam pushing her head into the van's wall. "You oughta be glad us soldiers are willing to fuck yo skinny ass. And gimme this piece of shit." He snatched the earring off her pierced ear. She screamed and blood flowed from the wound.

"I want it first," said Pit, holding himself. "She look good to me."

"All right, sergeant," said Nam. "No problem." He threw Pit the earring. He caught it easily. Pit threw the earring back at the woman, hitting her. "Cheap ass, fake gold shit."

"Watch that cursing, sergeant," Nam said and they both laughed.

Mayo was amused. The crazy white boy really thought he was a soldier. In reality, he had never even been in the army. The closest he had probably come was doing drugs with soldiers after they returned home. "Come on, man," said Mayo as he climbed into the driver's cab. "We ain't got no time for that shit."

"Always time for fuckin'," said Pit, unzipping his pants. He went over to the thin woman on the van's floor, stumbling in a crouched walk. He knelt beside her. Her face was streamed with tears and veins stood out in her strained neck. "I ain't gone hurt you, baby," he laughed.

"I don't want this shit!" yelled Mayo.

Pit looked at Mayo with anger, then smiled and backed off, but not before he rammed the woman's head into the van's floor, knocking her unconscious. He and Nam slapped five.

Mayo said nothing. They were going to kill her and the other two, but he had to keep control of the operation. Supervising killers was not an easy job.

Mayo instructed Larry to take an exit and turn north.

"Nervous?" he asked, watching Larry.

"Fuck naw," Larry lied.

"Good. You know the street I want. Just be cool and this shit be over fo you know it."

"What time is it? asked Larry.

"Eight thirty," said Mayo.

Pit and Nam laughed in the back as Larry turned up Holland Street and killed the lights. The seven hundred block of Holland was a short block that looked like a war zone. There were only ten houses on the block and of those, only two were occupied. The streetlights had been shot out and the city had never come to repair them. The darkness and isolation were just what Mayo needed. Larry stopped in the middle of the block, leaving the engine running.

Pit and Nam grabbed the men and took them outside in the darkness. Mayo grabbed a red canister and joined them. Pit unbound their feet and began to beat one of them mercilessly. Nam chose the other man, the yellow-shirted addict. He seemed barely aware of the pummeling. Mayo watched with interest. Larry watched and tried to steady his knees.

"What they gonna do, beat 'em to death?" asked Larry.

"Naw," laughed Mayo. "Just gettin' 'em ready."

Pit and Nam let the men drop onto the ground. Mayo doused the men with gasoline from the canister. They screamed as the liquid hit their eyes and wounds. The muffled cries went unnoticed. Pit and Nam kicked the men and told them to get on their feet. When they wouldn't, Pit and Nam lifted them up. Gasoline dripped on them from their victim's clothes.

"No fun if they don't run," said Pit. He took several steps away from the men so that he would not ignite with them. Nam followed suit. The men moaned and wavered on wobbly legs. Pit and Nam each took a book of matches and struck one. They then lit the entire book, careful not to ignite themselves. Pit and Nam looked at each other and laughed.

"Flame on!" said Nam.

They threw the small torches on the men who lit up the area as they ran, screaming in the night. The yellow-shirted crackhead made a sound that was almost inhuman. The pain awoke him from his high. Even with the gags on, their cries were loud. Larry could smell the burning stink of the cheap nylon scarves that were used to gag them. It was heaven compared to the smell of burning flesh.

"Let's break!" yelled Mayo.

Pit walked backwards slowly to the van. He wanted to see the rest of it. He looked like a disappointed kid.

The van sped off. Larry swallowed hard. He was struggling to hold up.

Nam and Pit slapped five in the back of the van. The woman was still unconscious.

Larry's hands were shaking as he turned onto Van Dyke. "What about da girl?" he asked Mayo.

"She yours," said Mayo.

"All right." Larry's voice almost cracked.

"You didn't just come to drive, did ya?" laughed Nam.

"Sho' he did," said Pit. "He bout ta shit his pants. He ain't never seen no shit like that, have you boy?" Pit said. "Dis is the real shit here. You young boys think you tough. Ha! You been livin' a jackoff! This is pure pussy." He slapped Nam another five. Nam began to make a noise like a chicken.

"Cut the shit!" snapped Mayo.

Larry gripped the wheel harder. He had to show them he was not a pussy, this was his time to shine. If he punked out now, he would never move up. He would be a two-bit roller forever, while he watched others get the big money and the best women. He would show his parents that he was a man and didn't need them. They could keep their cheap-ass house and their Jesus-and-cornbread philosophy. He took a deep breath. He was going to make it on the street and nothing would get in his way. "How do you want me ta do it?" he asked Mayo.

"It's on you," answered Mayo.

Larry pulled the van over. He and Mayo changed places. He gave Mayo instructions. Mayo smiled and drove the van onto the I-94 service drive.

"Go to the overpass," said Larry.

"Awww shit," said Pit and Nam together.

"Boy's a killer!" said Nam.

"Hey, boy," said Pit to Larry. "Why don't you let me snap this bitch's neck an save you some embarrassment?"

"Shut da fuck up!" yelled Mayo. He was seriously thinking of shooting them both.

"Don't worry bout da shit," said Larry. "I'm gone take care of it."

Mayo pulled the van into the middle of the overpass and stopped the van with the engine running. Larry went to the back and pulled the woman to the side door and opened it.

"Wait!" said Mayo as a car went by. "OK, it's clear. Hurry da shit up." Mayo knew what he was going to do. He smiled. The boy had balls after all.

Traffic roared on the freeway below. Larry dragged the woman out to the metal barrier on the bridge. She was dead weight and heavy. The night wind blew around them and it smelled like death itself. He took a deep breath and heaved her up. His whole body trembled with apprehension. He had never been so scared in his life. He debated stopping but he knew that Mayo would probably kill him after going this far.

The woman began to kick. She writhed in his arms, trying to move the gag free from her mouth. Larry almost dropped her. She fell on him. He hit her in the face. She tried to bite him, but the gag was still in place. He grabbed her head and forced it over the railing. He pressed hard and his thumb pushed the back of her other earring into the side of her neck. She groaned in pain.

Larry lifted her back up, and shoved her over the side, into the freeway. He watched in horror as her body hit a car and bounced off onto the concrete with a dull sound. The cars crashing into each other was louder. A large truck caught the limp body in the middle lane and dragged it under the overpass and out of sight leaving a trail of blood. Pit and Nam clapped and whistled their approval. Larry stood on the bridge, terrified, watching the carnage below. He hoped the others couldn't see his knees wobbling.

"Come on, boy," said Nam.

"Let's get the fuck outta here," said Mayo.

Larry was frozen for a moment. He expected to turn around and see the van taking off, leaving him there to take the rap for all of the deaths. But when he did turn around he saw the sick faces of Pit and Nam clapping and smiling. He rushed back into the van, shaking and breathing in short, quick gasps. Mayo burned rubber and they pulled away. Pit and Nam clapped Larry on the back and heaped praises on him.

"Way to go, boy," Pit said.

"Good show, officer."

Mayo said nothing.

Larry fought to keep down the burger and fries he had eaten. He was terrified of what he had done. But he was more concerned with what Mayo was thinking. You had to be tough to be big time in the Union. You had to kill without fear.

Larry eased when he saw Mayo turn to him. He was smiling.

"Good job," Mayo said. "Good job."

24

Story of the Year

Carol Salinsky was a little nervous. She didn't like to be seated when giving the news. She was a street reporter, not a mannequin like the regular anchor crew, and she liked to be loose and spontaneous when she worked. She fidgeted in her chair on the set of Channel Five's Eyewitness News. The lights were hot and it seemed like everyone was about to go crazy. The regular newscasts went smoothly, but whenever there was a special report, these guys completely lost it.

A makeup man fussed over the shine on her nose. A hair stylist made wheezing sounds as she wrestled with her hair. And the director was shouting for her to sit on the edge of her jacket so that her suit would look tapered on camera. She felt like an asshole.

Stanley Cramer paced around behind the camera crew. His fight with Yancy had left him determined to get the story out to the public accurately and before the eleven o'clock report. He knew that Yancy would try to scoop him with a live press conference, so he decided to put Salinsky's story on first. He would interrupt regular programming during the nine o'clock hour, and do a short news segment.

Dane Williams, the station's regular co-anchor, was pissed. She wanted to do the story without Salinsky, but Cramer had insisted that Salinsky be on the air with her.

"All right, people!" yelled the director. "Let's do it in thirty. Dane, you'll introduce Carol."

Williams was getting her makeup checked. She turned to Salinsky. "How does it feel to be in the hot seat?"

"My butt's kinda narrow for it, but I'm sure yours fits," Salinsky said, not looking up from her copy.

"You should feel right at home, Carol. You can move your lips when you read here and it's OK."

The makeup woman fought the smile spreading on her face.

"You know what you can do with that shit—grandma." Salinsky gave her a nasty look.

"OK," the director began. "In five . . . four . . . three . . . two . . . one—"

"This is a special report of Channel Five's Eyewitness News with Dane Williams," said the off-screen announcer.

Williams began, "A shocking revelation has just surfaced in the serial killings committed by the notorious Handyman—"

At the same time, Chief Fuller stepped in front of a row of cameras, but this time Tony was standing next to him. They both looked nervous as the reporters assembled at police headquarters. Fuller patted Tony on the back and smiled at him confidently.

The lobby of 1300 buzzed with chatter. Channel Five's crew was noticeably absent. Chuck Deele, a mayoral assistant, clapped his hands together to get attention. "We are about to start, everyone," he said.

The chatter subsided.

"You all know our two speakers, Chief Fuller and Inspector Tony Hill of the Police Department. Gentlemen—"

Fuller cleared his throat. "We are here to favor the press with information in the Handyman investigation which we feel is vital to the security of the people of this city—"

PART II

SUMMER MADNESS

Chain of Fools

It was hot in the Sewer. The news that the Handyman was white hit the city at the same time an early summer had set in. The humidity typically hovered around ninety percent throughout the summer in Detroit and today, it was also ninety-one degrees.

Tony plucked his shirt from his wet body as he stood at a cubicle in the Sewer, yelling on the phone over the clamor of the office. He was giving new marching orders to the uniform commander on the case. He had given out the wrong assignments, pulled them, then given them out again. It made him embarrassed and angry, but was secondary to keeping a lid on the Handyman fallout.

Jim was out covering the investigation of a Union hit on a crackhouse. They'd hit the Southend Crew, killing several rollers and drug addicts. And they had apparently killed the crackheads just for the hell of it. Clearly, the plan was to reinforce their reputation on the street. A large *U*, the Union's calling card, had been machine-gunned into a wall of the Southend crackhouse.

The war was on.

". . . OK then, I want night teams six and seven to cover the first three sectors and back up my detectives," Tony said. "And I want all arrests processed at local precincts. Don't bring any suspect or witness downtown unless it significantly impacts the case. That's it." He hung up the phone. "Damn," he whispered. He was still upset by having to redeploy the men. Thank God Jim had spotted the mistake in time.

Tony took a moment and sat on the cubicle's desk. The Dream

had come again last night, a maelstrom of guilt. Tony was still slow with decisions as a result and generally screwing up everything he touched. Jim was covering for him like a pro, but it was a big job, and with the added pressure of the Handyman news, people were beginning to notice his blunders.

Tony knew well that one postulate of policework: troubled cops were removed from cases. A cop in trouble, plus policework, equaled disaster. If Tony knew another cop had his own problem, he'd pull his ass off the Handyman case faster than you could blink. But he was in charge and he knew he could handle it.

A small desk fan blew warm air into his face. There were only a few air conditioners in 1300, and the one in Tony's office was shot.

Tony was miserable, as were all the other officers. He picked up the receiver and dialed another number.

"What happened to the A/C units I asked for? We got extra troops on the case, and we're frying," Tony said. "OK . . . ASAP all right?" Tony slammed down the receiver. "Idiots."

The citizenry was going crazy. The city's quiet racial undertow was swirling into a tidal wave. Fights had broken out in several places over a T-shirt being worn by white kids. It read, THE HANDYMAN FIXING THE PROBLEM, and had a picture of a dead black drug dealer at the foot of a white man carrying a large knife. The shirts were banned in schools, but it was a free country. Vendors continued to sell and people continued to buy.

Tony couldn't believe that the killer was becoming some kind of folk hero. It just proved what he always knew in his heart: the races hated each other, and it was a deep, immutable feeling that festered in them all.

Detroit had a long history of using race as a political and financial tool. There were those who would use the Handyman revelation to further the cause of hatred. To these people, the killer was a godsend and would be used to beat white people over the head with their past deeds and extract favors in the process.

Two prominent civil rights groups had already issued press releases saying that the Handyman killings were indicative of today's hatred of blacks. The releases never mentioned, however, that the victims were drug dealers. Both groups had pledged help to the city and requested donations be given to their respective groups to further their cause.

Tony understood that this was how the game was played. Over the years, some blacks had become, in a sense, professional victims. Lacking great financial strength and unable to control their political power, these people resorted to using guilt as a means of effecting change. It was a sorry-ass way to make a needed point. Tony didn't care about the activists' self-serving concern, as long as it didn't impede his investigation.

He reluctantly returned to his office. It seemed that he had put his men into action too late on the Handyman case. And as a result, they had a house full of dead rollers, two people burned to death, and a woman wasted for half a mile on the freeway. And to top it off, the bastards had killed a baby.

Tony looked over the preliminary reports on all of the killings. The Southend crackhouse and the random crackhead killings had occurred within hours of one another. It was obviously a planned effort by the Union.

All this because of the killer, Tony thought. A killer who was as clever as he was deadly. The Handyman's pattern was no longer a pattern at all. He had shot the woman at Shalon Street, but stabbed the men, and only took the hands from two of them. Derek and Rolan Nelson had been separated from their respective appendages but the third man, Jonnel Washington, was spared that treatment.

Tony ran a computer check on the victims, cross-referencing their backgrounds, and ran into a black hole of information. The Handyman's victims had no criminal history in common except membership in the Union. Everyone speculated that the Handyman just didn't have enough time to take the hands off Jonnel Washington and the timing of the deaths suggested that this theory was the best possibility.

In public, Tony supported the city's position on the killer, that the Handyman was just another criminal, and would be apprehended in the normal course. Privately, however, he was angry. It was his job to bring in black criminals. That's what they had fought for in Detroit, the right to self-government and policing and freedom from the old days when black men were victims of white men's justice.

The Handyman case stirred feelings of contempt in Tony, and his attempts to rationalize it failed because his feelings ran too deep. All he saw was whites slaughtering black men again. How many had to die before somebody did something?

Like what you did to Simon?

As quickly as the thought vaulted into his head, Tony tried to push it aside. *The case*, he thought. He had to focus on the case.

Tony checked his watch. It was almost nine a.m. He had a meeting with the Chief at the mayor's office. Yancy had been everywhere recently, playing down the significance of a white serial killer in a black city.

Tony was sure the meeting would mean more bad news and he wasn't looking forward to it. But at least the mayor's office would be cool.

The lobby of the mayor's office was flooded with reporters, politicians, and several community action groups. There was so much chatter that it was difficult to hear. Tony stood by a group of businessmen waiting for Fuller. It was cool in the waiting area, but the large number of people seemed to suck up the cold air, making it warmer than he would have liked.

Since the Handyman was revealed, everyone with a political agenda had descended on the seat of power. There was a rumor that Yancy was doubling his security and sending his wife on a quick vacation.

Tony knew for sure that Yancy was calling in favors all over town to get positive spins wherever possible. Misinformation was spread about, and Yancy's people even greased a few palms at the TV stations to get advance copy of news reports. Fall was around the corner, and the mayor's race would soon be in full swing.

Chief Fuller walked into the lobby waving at friends and waving off reporters. "Hot as hell out there," Fuller said.

"Early summer. The worst. We're baking in the office," Tony said. "So, I can guess what the mayor wants this time."

"I already had *that* meeting with him. This is my meeting. I've got some bad news to deliver."

"What is it?"

"The less you know, the better. I just need you here because you're running the hands-on part of the investigation. Besides, the mayor doesn't like it when other people know things he doesn't," Fuller said.

"I hear the FBI might be brought in," Tony said.

"Not true. This is not their turf. Their office put out that story to let us know that if we can't control this situation, they will make up a reason to come into the case."

"Probably civil rights violations."

"That would be my guess," said Fuller.

A pretty woman of about forty came over and smiled at Fuller. "He's ready for you," she said.

"OK," said Fuller. "All right, Tony. Hold on."

Fuller and Tony entered the office. It was cool, almost chilly inside. He felt a slight breeze from the central air and caught a floral scent now and then. Tony let the cold air wash over him.

Yancy was there with several of his aides. The aides looked like a law firm in their five-hundred-dollar suits and crisp white shirts. Their faces were fearful and nervous, like spectators at an execution.

Tony fixed his eyes on Yancy, who was moving wildly, frantically, like a child who has to use the bathroom.

"I don't care if the subpoena came from God himself," Yancy said. "I want don't want people rummaging through city papers! They can't be in my business at a time like this. They're just fishing for dirt."

"But sir, they are entitled to access by several federal laws," said a young aide named Dillard.

"Fuck the law! I don't care how you do it. I just want them away from the files until this thing blows over. Is that so goddamned hard to do?!"

"But sir," said Dillard, "We've exhausted all of our administrative remedies and—"

"You're fired," said Yancy.

"But sir, I—"

"Get out. I don't need my own people putting limits on me."

"Well, maybe there are some things we can do to—"

"Get the fuck out!!" Yancy walked from behind his desk and pushed Dillard out the door. The room was quiet as he walked back to his desk.

"Sir," said Henry Underland, a longtime mayoral assistant, "I'll take care of the document access problem."

"I want it done now," said Yancy.

"Whatever it takes, sir," said Henry. He got up and hurried out of the room.

Fuller caught Yancy's eye. Tony watched as Fuller gently nodded his head. Yancy returned the gesture.

"Take ten, fellas," Yancy said. The aides almost trampled each other heading for the door. Tony could see their expressions turn to relief as they passed by. He also felt their stress pass into him.

"Whatcha got, Bill?" Yancy asked.

"Harris, we have another problem. I—"

"Spit the shit out, man. I already got problems, in case you haven't noticed."

"The hair samples," Fuller said. "They were being tested at T-Labs. They have a contract with the city."

"Yeah. They find something? What?" Yancy looked excited.

"No, sir. They apparently lost the samples and the test results."

Yancy sat down slowly. "Jesus fucking H. Christ."

"Actually, sir, the samples are still there, but the labels were screwed up by someone, mixed up with forensic samples in several criminal investigations. The prosecutor is pissin' mad."

Yancy buried his face in his hands. He took a deep breath. "OK, here's what we do. Fire the lab, have the city lawyers sue the company and everyone connected. Stop payment on all monies going to them. Then hire another company and get their president to make a press statement. We'll start a rumor that we obtained some leads off the samples before the screwup, then go to the media—today. I'll have my aides tie up any other loose ends."

"Got it," said Fuller.

"Who knows about this?" asked Yancy.

"So far, the head of the lab, the prosecutor, and us. Inspector Hill here is just finding out."

"OK. This one's on your head, Bill."

Tony was about to say something but thought better of it.

"Yes, sir," Fuller nodded to Tony and they walked out as the nervous aides rushed back in.

"Holy shit," Tony said.

"I said it was bad."

"This will demoralize the men. I'll have to do some damage control of my own.

"Got anything we can be happy about?"

"No. We're still investigating the hit that was made on that crackhouse on the southwest side and the other murders."

"This is gonna be tough on all of us. The state troopers will help out, but for the most part, it's our show." Fuller took a few steps. "I thought the loss of those hair samples would kill him. He's probably gulping down pills like nobody's business."

"Pills?" Tony asked.

"The mayor has a mild heart condition. Listen, don't repeat that. He's concerned about his image."

"No problem."

"I know we have some big hurdles, but the harder you work, the sooner we get this fuckin' guy and be done with it."

"Yes, sir."

They shook hands and parted company. Tony walked past the gallery in the waiting area feeling like every eye was on him. It was a rotten break, Tony thought. An unbroken chain of evidence was paramount to a criminal investigation. You could not convict without relevant, admissible, untainted evidence.

The evidentiary chain had been broken by a chain of fools. Now, even if they had a suspect, they could not match his hair to that of the samples. Hair had been found only on the first victim, Floyd Turner, so there were no more samples to be had.

Tony left the mayor's office and went back to 1300. He entered the Sewer and was hit by a wave of heat. All the windows were open but it was still hot. Jim had not returned yet but had called in. He would not be happy when he heard about the blunder at T-Labs.

Tony took a moment and delivered the bad news to the men. They groaned and cursed their frustration. Tony assured them that this was a minor setback and returned to his office, still angry.

There, the day's mail overflowed in his in-box. One letter had been placed in his chair. The assistants always put what looked to be personal mail aside. The letter had no return address and was addressed only to "Officer Hill—Detroit Police." Tony looked at the postmark. The letter had been written over six months ago.

"What the—"

He opened it. It was several pages long and written in a scrawl that was barely decipherable. He went to the last page to see who wrote it.

Tony stopped breathing for a moment as he read the name Irene Simon, Darryl Simon's sister.

2

Set Up

T-Bone loved the heat. He was wearing nothing but a pair of shorts as a warm breeze caught him on the outdoor deck. A light sweat glistened on his arms and legs.

T-Bone studied the notes he had made on the Prince's plan to make the new drug. It was a great idea, but it would be costly and dangerous. Many people might die and fortunes would change forever.

The house in Southfield was one of T-Bone's many unofficial residences. He liked to come here when it was warm. The small house had a large yard and caught the morning sun. K-9 nestled quietly under a tree in the large backyard, looking at the sky.

He hadn't slept well since the child was killed in the crackhouse hit. He was a great many things, but not a baby-killer. He had chewed out Frank, all the while knowing that Frank's whacked-out partner had done it.

The pressure from the cops was unbelievable. You would think that someone assassinated the President. His rollers were picked up all over town and he couldn't call in his police connections to help. That was the rule with the cops. Cooperate for the money, but extreme situations didn't count.

He hated being powerless this way. So many of his people were in prison that sales were going down and the suburbanites were getting afraid to come into the city, and that was much of his market.

The killings did, however, have a good side. People were more afraid of the Union now than ever before.

More troubling to him was the fact that the Handyman had been identified as a white man. How could that be? In a city like Detroit, any white man would stand out. This troubled T-Bone. Now he began to think that the person behind the killings was no mere rival.

T-Bone suspected Santana at first. Even though he had scraped together the money to pay him, Santana was an evil bastard who carried grudges, sometimes to fatal extremes. But Santana assured him that he was not behind it, and had confidence in T-Bone despite their recent problems. But T-Bone understood that the South Americans were liars by trade and sometimes sent warnings of just this type.

Recent events had left T-Bone feeling like a loser, just like his father had always called him. Big Teddy always said the word like it was an undeniable truth. And whenever things went bad, T-Bone heard that voice mocking him, tearing away at his heart. He supposed that he still had something to prove to his father.

He laughed at the thought. Big Teddy was a mindless old wreck in an old folks home, eating oatmeal and vanilla wafers for lunch. And yet, his father was often on his mind, taunting and laughing at him each time he failed. This time, however, T-Bone was gonna get the last laugh, on Big Teddy and everyone else in Detroit.

T-Bone had contacted the Prince again and set up a meeting for next week, more eager than ever to begin his ascent out of the business. T-Bone understood that meeting with the Prince was dangerous, but these were dangerous times. If the plan worked, he would move into production of the new crack, avoid the cocaine shortage, and have plenty of money to pay that bastard Santana.

T-Bone was by no means a poor man, but he wanted much more than others were willing to settle for. Even a successful dealer didn't make the kind of money he needed. He pictured himself as a multimillionaire, owning shopping malls and Lear jets, a world traveller.

Several years back, T-Bone had visited a legendary dealer who everyone called Captain Jack. Captain Jack had been in the military when he started his drug business. He'd gone on to make a vast fortune, which he invested in legitimate businesses.

When Captain Jack retired, he threw a party. T-Bone was lucky enough to be invited by a silly cokehead named Jimmy, who was from a rich family.

Captain Jack lived in a spectacular house in Florida, overlooking the ocean. Guests arrived in limos and flew in on helicopters. Unbelievably beautiful women dripped with gold, diamonds, and sex. The party was a picture of contrasts: congressmen mingled with killers and movie stars with thugs. T-Bone was struck by the sight and he suddenly saw what it was really all about. If you had enough money, legitimacy could be bought.

Captain Jack had talked with him that night and given him the dealer's philosophy, always careful not to make any definitive statements. He said that dealers operate in a different economy. An underground economy that fuels the legitimate one. He said that all business is corrupt. The only difference between a dealer and a CEO is a dealer fucks better women.

But T-Bone didn't have Captain Jack's kind of money, at least not yet. But when he did, he would leave behind second-rate cities like Detroit and inject himself into the big time. The world would be his playground.

Many great fortunes could be traced back to crime, he thought, and in his case, it would be no different.

He finished reading the notes on his plan, then he struck a match and set it on fire. The flame consumed the paper quickly, turning it into dark ashes.

3

Lunch with Lincoln

"I've always wanted to know, Tony. Why do you hate white people?"

Tony was caught off guard by the question. He adjusted his chair. The Traffic Jam restaurant was noted for its fine hamburgers and ambience, but the chairs were very uncomfortable.

Tony sat across from Dr. Louis Abraham Lincoln, an old instructor of his from the night school at Wayne State University. They had struck up a friendship while Tony was taking Lincoln's class on criminal psychological behavior.

Tony had almost forgotten about his monthly lunch with Professor Lincoln until he saw it on his calendar, but he was pleased to see him. He didn't get to visit with Lincoln as often as he'd have liked and he needed this break from the investigation.

What Tony loved about his meetings with Lincoln were their conversations. Even when they disagreed (which was often) they enjoyed discussing and debating the issues of the day. It was a guilty pleasure, because no one seemed interested in actually sharing ideas anymore. People these days got their wisdom from TV or pie charts in *USA Today*. The lost art of conversation lived at their meetings, even if only for an hour at a time.

Lincoln was a long, gangly man with a scruffy beard and an ever-present pipe. He looked younger than his sixty years and his face had an inquisitive look, one that made you feel he was always suspicious of something. And he was constantly moving, long smooth motions that suggested a gracefulness in spite of his size.

Lincoln asked the question about white people casually and out of the blue, his face never rising from his Caesar salad.

"I never said I hated them," Tony said.

"I've known you for years, Tony. You never have anything good to say about white people and today you seem unusually hateful."

"People get on my nerves," Tony took another bite of his burger. "You know how it is."

"Yes, I do. So, how do you feel about the Handyman being a white person?"

"It makes my investigation that much harder."

"No, no. I mean, how do you feel personally. What was your first thought when you heard the news?"

Tony paused a moment, then, "I thought: again."

"Whites killing blacks again."

"Right. Seems like it never ends, you know."

"Blacks kill their fair share of whites," Lincoln said.

"It's not the same. I mean, that's a natural function of being oppressed." Tony gestured with the burger as if it were part of his logic.

"Come now, Tony, you're evading. Every black murderer is not oppressed. Let's forget black political correctness." Lincoln's voice was playful, even though the words were not. "Is it really worse for a white man to kill a black one?"

"It is if you're black," Tony said.

"Did you know that thousands of years ago, black men controlled the world?"

"Yes, I did. We were the cradle of civilization."

"But did you know that during that time, black men, the leaders of the known world, had oppressed people of all colors, held them as slaves, raped their women, killed them for pleasure, and threatened to wipe out their races?"

"But that was ancient times, not like now. We're civilized," Tony said.

"Those ancestors were not animals. They knew exactly what they were doing. And since then, thousands of other people have been massacred over the years. Why is it then, that *American* slavery is this eternal sore spot with us?"

"You should know the answer to that. You're black, too."

"In fact, I do know the answer," Lincoln said. "It's because we have not accepted that our pain is a ripple in the ocean of humanity. Racism is not about race, it's about humanity."

"That doesn't make it easier to take," Tony said.

"You should know. You hate white people."

"OK, I admit there's no love lost for them with me, but it's only because of all the things they've done to us."

"And you think your hate is justified?"

Tony paused. "Yes. But hate is wrong."

"Even if justified?" Lincoln asked.

"Sure." Tony was beginning to feel uncomfortable. Lincoln always did that to him sooner or later.

"I have another question for you, then." Lincoln regarded his pipe. "Have you considered why they hate us?"

"That's a good question," Tony said. "To tell you the truth, I've never thought about it before. I guess it's because they can't make us do what they want anymore, use us for their own benefit and treat us any way they want."

"You think white people want us to be slaves again?"

"No, at least not like it used to be. I think that they want to keep us beneath them, powerless and poor. And we won't stay. We demand equality and that pisses them off."

"But that does not justify hate, does it? I mean, it's not logical to hate because you can't subjugate a person."

"I know, it doesn't make sense, but that's how they are, how we are, human beings that is. We sort of enjoy hurting each other."

"Is that it, you think? Or is it something deeper?" Lincoln looked angrily at his salad as if it had offended him. "I've been teaching a course on racism in the jury system, and it occurred to me that people grow up with a basic morality in them. Even when exercising racist beliefs on black defendants, many white jurors think they're doing the right thing."

"That don't make a difference to all those brothers in the joint." Tony smiled a little.

"The important thing is, whites think of themselves as moral people. The results of my test made me think deeply about race relations. Have you seen *Gone With the Wind*?

"Yes, many times," Tony said. He couldn't wait to hear what that question would lead to. "Why?"

"Well, in the movie, you remember, Scarlett O'Hara's father tells her to protect Tara because land is the only thing that lasts. The earth is the one thing that defies the passing of time. I suggest to you that there is another: history. It binds one generation to the next. It is the fabric of human existence, the soul of our self-realization. The greatest sin of slavery was the robbery of our history. A person with no history is lost within himself, left to the feeble, thin perceptions of the individual."

"History then is the *land* of a culture," Tony interrupted.

"Exactly, exactly." Lincoln reached for his pipe, but changed his mind. "You see, more than money is inherited with each generation. History also passes. Morality, conscience, self-knowledge go along also—and so does the legacy of slavery, its evil, shame, and guilt."

"I have experienced that guilt," Tony said. "But it seems to get thinner each generation."

"Perhaps, but because we think of ourselves as moral, whites have had to justify their own morality to themselves. Though they may not have perpetrated slavery or discrimination, they undeniably have its benefits, and they have the burden as well. It tears at the fabric of their morality and self-esteem. So blacks, especially males, become the repository of white self-loathing. We are suddenly the cause of all societal ills: crime, drugs, fear, death. Thereby, in their minds, we *deserve* to be hated."

"Because they want to feel good about themselves?" Tony asked.

"Yes, yes. We as humans must be good, so blacks must be hated to purge the sin of immorality. Fascinating, eh?" Lincoln reclined in his chair.

"It's very hard for me to think of prejudiced white people as good," Tony said.

"Try thinking of them as human first."

"So, I should accept the Handyman's race as an inevitable event. I shouldn't be pissed off by it?" Tony asked.

"No. You just shouldn't be pissed because he's white." Lincoln looked at his watch. "Time's up." he said. He always said that at the end of their meetings as if it were a class. "I have an afternoon lecture."

Tony picked up the tab and they said their good-byes on the sun-washed sidewalk of Second Avenue. The air was thick with the clinging humidity of the early summer.

Lincoln started away, then approached Tony, standing close to him and looking him straight in the eyes.

"I know you're troubled, Tony," said Lincoln. "You have the same look you used to get when you ran out of money in school and you thought your whole life would crumble. Or that time after the GM incident when the reporters were camping outside of your house."

Tony was silent. He thought of lying, but decided against it. It was hard to lie to Lincoln. "Yes, I am troubled. That is . . . it's the case and . . . other things."

"Then I'm worried. Because I've seen you upset before, but never have I seen you despair. As a friend and a doctor I suggest you get to the bottom of whatever it is. Share it with your wife, or a colleague. That will help."

Tony was pleased that his friend cared enough to push the subject. "I will," he said. "I will."

Tony walked to his car. He got in and pulled out the letter from Irene Simon and read it again.

4

The Brotherhood

The crowd wanted blood.

Outside Detroit's City-County Building, a thousand people massed together, stopping traffic on Woodward and Larned, which bounded the corner of the building. The throng swelled at the steps of the building's entrance. Uniformed cops patrolled the area, mingling inside the crowd; mounted police kept to the rear and the perimeter.

It was a lawful gathering, but the cops had not expected so many people. The group varied in age and background. Doctors, professors, and children mingled with the unemployed and homeless. Expensive Italian suits stood next to common garb which stood next to African dashikis. It was a diverse crowd, but everyone had two things in common: they were all angry, and they were all black.

Tony and Jim stood in the back of the crowd. Tony had a good view of things and could clearly see the speaker, Daishaya Mbutu, the leader of the Brotherhood, a local militant group.

Tony and Jim had run into a dead end on the Union hit and the other murders. They were clean, professional, and quick. And as usual, no one saw anything.

Tony's department had been tipped that Mbutu was going to disclose vital information on the Handyman case in his speech. Jim felt that it was a publicity stunt by the Brotherhood, but after talking it over with Fuller, Tony had decided to come to the rally. They had very few leads on the case and at this point he would take anything he could get.

Tony's head was throbbing. He must have read the letter from Irene Simon twenty times since receiving it. The letter was a waking nightmare, every bit as deadly as The Dream. It was occupying a vast region of his mind, as it conjured up demons and deeds of the past. Now, he was afraid to sleep, fearful of what his conscience might release.

"I feel like an asshole being here," Jim said. "This guy isn't going to say anything."

"We'll see," Tony said.

"I hate this damned Muboto."

"It's Mbutu," Tony said. "He commands a lot of respect in the neighborhoods, so he could know something."

Tony watched as Daishaya Mbutu spat venom. He stood out clearly against the Brotherhood backdrop, a large picture of two black fists, breaking the shackles on their wrists on a field of red and green.

Mbutu was well over six feet tall and commanded attention. His skin shined in its darkness as he spoke. His long dreadlocks draped the shoulders of his African shirt and his eyes were a deep brown, fired by the emotion behind them.

". . . and Mayor Yancy," Mbutu said. "Our leader. He tells us to just be cool about the white Handyman. 'Be cool,' he says. 'We got it under control. The police is gonna take care of everythang,'" he mocked. "Be cool, while white men kill black brothers like animals. Be cool while black babies are shot in drug wars. Be cool while your houses fall down and the garbage piles up in the alley. Be cool while we stick it to you right, up, your, ass!"

The crowd erupted in laughter and applause.

The sound of the crowd was a muted roar to Tony. He was looking into the distance and saw himself running into the GM building. . . .

The crowd cheered again. A group of men jostled each other and for a moment it looked like a fight would start.

"Tony!" Jim said.

Tony watched as some of the uniforms went to the disturbance area. The men stopped whatever they were doing. The uniformed commander looked at Tony. The fight might be enough to disperse the meeting. But Tony knew that would only make matters worse. Tony returned the commander's gaze and shook his head.

"He still hasn't said anything," said Jim. "Let's get out of here."

"Not yet," said Tony. "Let's hear the man out."

". . . and you know the Jews are in this with Yancy," said Mbutu. "Hell, the Jews are in everything that harms black people!" There was more applause. Mbutu had his own brand of anti-Semitism, which he always called his "aggressive truth." In his mind, Jews were the cause of many of the ills of black folk and he took every chance to bash them for it.

"Listen to the mayor," Mbutu said. "Laughing at you. Sittin' in the white-owned Renaissance Center, in a white-owned restaurant, with a white waitress, drinkin' a White Russian and laughing at the stupid-ass, dumb-ass, black-ass people of Detroit!"

The crowd exploded with its approval. The officers looked for signs of trouble.

Mbutu quieted the crowd. "You all know my philosophy. Only a few black people benefited from the civil rights movement. And these house niggers promote themselves and subjugate the weak. The result is poor blacks now have to fight a black and white oppressor and claim freedom from everyone who would take it away."

Tony drifted again. He was closing in on Simon . . . he saw his victims, all black, piled in a corner. . . .

"The Handyman is a blessing," Mbutu said. "He's cast a light on the continuous ineptitude of our leaders. The enemy is black, he is white, he is whatever he has to be to keep you down! Now, I know that some of you are thinking, Mr. Mbutu, the murderer just killed some lousy dope dealers. But this is deeper than dope! A man's worth to the world is not defined by his occupation, and nothing becomes legal until white men find a way to keep all the money to themselves. The value of life is limitless, and the value of *black life* is unimaginable! *Every black person is precious!*" The crowd erupted again.

"We are going into the fourth century of racism in this country," Mbutu continued. "Four hundred bloody, desolate years, and still white men are killing black men at will. The only difference now is that there are other black men helping them to do it!"

The crowd was eerily silent. The air was electric with emotion and tension. Tony marveled at the spell Mbutu cast. He was good, Tony thought, and dangerous.

"The Brotherhood will not tolerate this senseless slaughter of black men," Mbutu said. "We will fight the white oppressor and his black lieutenants. We will patrol the streets, help the helpless, and turn this killer back across Eight Mile where he came from!"

"I'll be damned," said Jim. "This fucker's gonna start his own police force. Hey, man—" Jim looked at Tony who was lost in thought. "Tony—"

"Wha— yes."

"You OK?"

"Yeah, yeah."

"This asshole is going to start a vigilante force."

"Like hell he is," Tony said. "We'll just have to have a talk with him before he does."

"Now you talkin'."

Tony was concerned that Mbutu's actions could find many of his vigilantes in the path of a bullet. More importantly, if Mbutu's people managed to catch the Handyman, it would be embarrassing for the department and the mayor. That was not going to happen.

"My people will pass out fliers to any men who want to join our cause to catch this killer," Mbutu said.

Several men went into the crowd and began to pass out fliers. There were some takers but not many.

"Let us end by reciting our oath," Mbutu said. He started and many in the crowd joined in.

> I am the justice of my people.
> God help me in my quest for freedom,
> And God help those who oppose me.

Mbutu descended the podium to wild applause as his followers took down the Brotherhood banner. The shackled black hands wavered and folded as the banner fell.

Mbutu entered the crowd which parted like the waters of the Red Sea and closed around him like a lover's embrace. He shook hands and gave various handshakes to people.

The officers eased a little. The event was going to be over soon.

Tony watched the crowd before him fade into images of the dark GM building . . . he was running up to Simon . . . taking his gun away . . . struggling with him . . . Simon's bloody face, falling out the window into a dark abyss . . . Irene Simon's letter rose from the blackness. . . .

"This is for the people!" yelled a small black man as he lunged at Mbutu.

The man pulled a gun and Mbutu's two big bodyguards moved into action.

Tony came back from his thoughts. Jim's call to him echoed faintly in his head. Tony looked up to see every other officer on their way to the disturbance.

"Damn!" he cursed then followed.

A shot went off.

People scattered and now Tony could clearly see the shooter being held by one of Mbutu's bodyguards and the other holding the gun up high over the shooter's head. The gun had discharged into the air and no one was hit.

Mbutu was whisked away in a car. The bodyguards were beating the man as the police came and pulled them away.

Tony ran into the middle of the commotion, his Beretta drawn. "Everyone back away!" he yelled.

Jim was already there, separating the shooter and Mbutu's guards.

Two uniforms cuffed the would-be assassin and pushed Mbutu's bodyguards away. One of the officers took the gun away from the bodyguards.

"Take them all in," Jim said. "All of them."

The officers complied. Mbutu's bodyguards went peacefully.

"I'll get Mbutu in," Jim said to Tony. "We'll need him as a witness."

Tony was silent. He was thinking that if the others hadn't responded so quickly, Mbutu or others might be dead.

"Tony, you all right, man?" Jim asked.

"Yeah. Yeah, I'm OK."

Tony walked away. He put his gun away and heard the rustle of Irene Simon's letter in his jacket pocket.

5

Prince's Court

T-Bone waited in the dimly lit room with K-9, Steve Mayo, and a big, muscular roller named Chick. Chick was a little light in the brain but physically imposing, and T-Bone liked to bring a big, mean-looking son of a bitch to meetings to intimidate the other side.

T-Bone picked Mayo to spearhead production and distribution of the new drug. He was the least bright of the Big Three, but he was the most ruthless, and T-Bone would need his strength to start in the new business. He could supply the brains himself.

They waited for the Prince in a burned-out building on Grand River Avenue that had once been a department store.

T-Bone stood on a mannequin platform, tapping his foot. He didn't like to be kept waiting by anyone.

Mayo had brought two large flashlights which illuminated the room. K-9 stood in the shadows, looking off into the darkness.

They heard voices echo off the burned walls and feet crunching debris. Chick and Mayo pulled out their guns. K-9 cowered in a corner behind the gunmen. T-Bone moved neatly into the shadows.

"OK, my brothas," the Prince said. "We are here."

Donna and the Professor followed the Prince, who stepped lively and smiled as he entered. The Professor pulled a large trunk on wheels.

"You late, muthafucka," said Mayo, putting his gun back. Chick kept his gun out, on T-Bone's signal.

"I don't like to wait," said T-Bone.

The Prince and his people strained to get a look at him.

"I am sorry," said the Prince. He walked over and offered his hand. Chick blocked his way.

"We ain't here to talk," said T-Bone. "Let's get this shit on quick."

The Prince grinned, showing his gold teeth. "I like that. I like that. Straight to bizness. OK, my brotha, let's do it."

The Prince turned to the Professor and Donna. "This is Ron. We call him the Professor 'cause he smart, you dig? And this is Donna."

Mayo's face brightened as he looked at Donna. Her face wasn't much, but she had on a tight, black dress that showed her true talents. Her chest was large and stood straight up. Her hips were narrow and even in the darkness, you could see that her legs were near perfect. She returned his look and he would have sworn that she poked her tongue through her lips slightly.

The Professor sat the trunk on its side and opened it. T-Bone instructed Mayo to check it out. The white man was big, but looked like a user to T-Bone. The Professor had a familiar devastation behind his eyes. Even in the dark he could spot an addict. And T-Bone didn't trust anyone who let drugs get control of them.

The inside of the trunk was a small lab. Chemicals and containers sat inside, tied down by ropes. A small battery was also inside. The Professor took out a small zipper lock plastic bag and held it up. It contained about forty crystals, which glimmered dully in the light.

"This is the shit, my brotha," said the Prince.

"Don't look like much," said T-Bone.

"Looks are deceiving," said the Professor.

"Oh, you talk?" smiled T-Bone.

"Man can do it all." The Prince laughed.

"I'll take it from here," said the Professor.

T-Bone was beginning to see the game. The Prince got the connections with blacks in the cities and the white guy played dumb until the time was right. Always, the white man was in control of drugs. Always.

"Our product is a crystalline cocaine," began the Professor. "It uses only one-tenth the cocaine used to make crack."

"How?" T-Bone asked.

"It's simple. Our chemicals attach to the cocaine molecules, in effect creating a new substance."

"So, why do you need the coke then?" asked T-Bone. "Can't you make this shit from whatever you got in there?"

"We tried that," said the Professor. "The result was something that was nasty and gave the user a headache. But when cocaine reacts with it, the result gives the user an intense, short high. The user's head gets lighter and he feels more uninhibited, but he gets less coke and when it's over, he wants it again, right away."

"And the money rolls in, my brotha," said the Prince.

Mayo watched Donna. She took a deep breath and her chest strained the dress. She looked good, he thought, real good.

"What is the shit made of?" asked T-Bone, keeping himself in the shadows.

"Various chemicals," said the Professor. "I was fired from the Ladley Research Corporation several years ago. I was working with a team to invent a new, cheap pain reliever. We failed. What we came up with got you high and didn't last nearly as long as needed. We tried to modify it, but it still wasn't right. The company scrapped the project. I was fired later, but I took the formula with me."

T-Bone didn't have to guess why the guy was fired. He was a drug addict and probably got caught taking his work home with him.

"After that," the Professor continued, "I tried to find a use for it. One day I just decided to see what the chemical would do to cocaine. I mixed it with some raw coke, cooked it, and gave some to a friend. He told me a week later that he had been high for four straight days and needed some more, the high was better than coke and he needed it badly. Then I knew I was on to something."

"So, you cut down on the amount of coke," T-Bone said.

"Right," said the Professor. "I found that you needed very little cocaine to produce the desired effect."

"Which is to get plenty fucked up," the Prince laughed again.

T-Bone looked coldly at the Prince. He was too goddamned happy for a drug dealer. T-Bone just wanted him to be quiet and let the white man talk.

"We called the chemical Syndoxyl," said the Professor. "It was never approved by the FDA, but Ladley tested it and it was safe." The Professor held up a quart jar with a bluish liquid in it.

"And when you mix it with coke," said the Prince, "it'll fire you up, like funky cold medina."

"I'm not sure about chemicals," said T-Bone. "Who knows what this shit is."

"No," said the Professor. "This is just a booster, a glorified cutting substance."

"Like baking soda with an attitude," said the Prince.

"Medina," said T-Bone softly. "Just like that rap song. I like the name. It'll play good on the street."

"If it didn't need cocaine to work, it wouldn't even be illegal under current FDA rules," said the Professor. "We are offering you our formula. We can make several bottles of it to get you started. I will also train one of your men to make it on your own. It's really very simple. I'd like to show you briefly how easily we make it." The Professor pulled out a small bag of cocaine.

T-Bone went cold, as if he only just realized that a crime was taking place. He never liked to be near drugs if at all possible.

Mayo knew what he had to do. "I'll go watch out for the cops," he said.

"Cool," said T-Bone. He relaxed a little.

Mayo moved away from the gathering and took out his gun.

The Professor looked at the Prince who looked at Donna. "I'll go, too," she said flatly.

The Professor began to talk about the ingredients while Mayo and Donna went off together.

Mayo couldn't take his eyes off her. Her face was plain-looking. Her skin was poor, features dull and common. Her hair was cropped short and dyed a sad blond. Her green eyes had red around them which suggested she wore colored contacts. But her body. It was as if an artist had drawn her.

The dress tantalizingly suggested her nudity underneath and when she moved, the fabric was pushed and pulled tighter hugging her and showing even more. She walked ahead of Mayo and he enjoyed every moment of it.

"You really look good in that dress, baby," he said finally.

"I know," she said.

"Oh, I dig. You know you got it, right?"

"I know you want it, that's for sure."

"You got that right." Mayo almost stumbled in the dark.

"Well, you can't have everything."

"So, you his woman?"

"Who? The Prince?"

"Yeah."

"I guess."

"You ain't for sure though, huh?"

"No, I'm sure."

"So, why was you lickin' yo tongue at me?"

"Oh, I always do that. It don't mean nothing."

"Yeah, well maybe—"

"Hold it," Donna said, stopping. "I came here to do some business with my man. I'm lookin' out for the cops with you 'cause we don't trust nobody. That's all. None of this is yours." She passed her hand over her body. "So just cool yo shit out before I cool it out for you." She pointed her finger in his face.

"OK, baby, OK," said Mayo a little embarrassed.

Donna walked ahead and up a flight of stairs.

Mayo watched her legs flex as she climbed the stairs. Too bad, he thought. Too bad.

They stopped in a large room at the front of the building. They could see the street from their position but it was probably difficult for anyone outside to see in. Old counters and displays surrounded them. Mannequin limbs littered the floor, spotted with burned patches that looked like sick, unattended wounds.

Mayo put his gun back into his waistband and watched the street. Donna looked at the street too, unaware of his presence.

He tried to keep his eyes away from Donna but it was hard. There was something about her face on that fabulous body that made him crazy. She was like that statue of the lady with no arms. He'd seen it on TV once. It was a beautiful statue but it was flawed.

Donna walked slowly past Mayo reaching for something in her purse. She moved across the room, her black pumps making crunching noises. She stopped at a scorched counter and leaned back against it, facing Mayo.

He tried not to watch, but it was useless. The woman commanded attention.

Donna parted her legs, stretching the short dress between them. The dress rose to the top of her thighs and created hills and valleys in the shape of a triangle. She ran her hand over her middle, down the front of her dress to the hem. She looked at Mayo and grinned, poking out her tongue. Then she pulled the dress up and over the back of her head. She was, as Mayo had suspected, completely naked underneath.

Her body was exquisite. Her legs were long and trim, moving smoothly into the slight flare of her hips. She had a flat, muscular stomach, and her breasts were high and firm, each nipple coarse from her excitement. She braced one hand along the edge of the counter. In the other, she held a condom.

"Come get it," she said.

The Professor took the tray out of the battery-operated oven. The smoking contents formed a dry, hard plane with crevices in it. He sat it on the top of the trunk to cool.

"Looks almost like crack, but it's blue," said T-Bone.

"But you use less coke," said the Professor.

"A lot less, my brotha," said the Prince.

"If you give a little away at first," said the Professor, "The people will get hooked and eat the stuff up." He reached into the trunk again and pulled out a bottle of gin and took a long swig. His hand shook slightly as he did and he never bothered to offer anyone else a drink.

He was indeed an addict, T-Bone thought, an alcoholic.

"We chose you to try out our product on a big scale," said the Prince. "We done it in some small towns, but this is the first big one." He laughed nervously. He had told the Professor not to drink until after the sale was made.

"Looks like your man here is nervous," said T-Bone.

"That's enough, man," said the Prince. "We got bizness."

"No problem." The Professor wiped his mouth.

"I'll give you twenty-five on faith and the rest when the product starts working on the street," said T-Bone. "If it don't, you won't get shit and I'll be looking for you, understand?"

"We dig, my brotha."

"When it works," said the Professor, "then we get the rest of the money right? Three hundred thousand."

"Yeah," said T-Bone looking at the tray. "But it'll take time. That kind of cash is not just lying around. I've got a lot of people to pay. Is it ready now?"

"Yes, just about," said the Professor who took the tray and covered it with a lid. "You should break it before it cools completely. That way, you don't get a lot of small crystals. There will be some tiny ones, however, but they can be sold and smoked, too." The Professor took the covered tray and slammed it into the top of the trunk's lid twice. When he opened it up, there were a hundred or so crystals about the size of a dime.

"We made this for less than a tenth of what it costs to make this much crack," said the Prince. "You could sell a nickel bag for fifty cents."

T-Bone had already done the math earlier with K-9. A nickel was a five dollar bag of crack. With Medina, he could sell a half-dollar's worth for that much. Hell, with the shortage, he could get seven dollars.

"What does the stuff cost to make?" T-Bone asked.

"Each batch makes about a hundred crystals. For each, you need a few dollars worth of the chemicals. It's made from things that can be obtained easily."

"By five finger discount if necessary," said the Prince. "This is the real shit, my brotha, all the way."

"I'll try it if you want me to, Bone," said Chick.

"No," said T-Bone. "I don't want my folks fuckin' with this shit until it's tested out."

T-Bone was excited. Crack had innovated the drug trade as the poor man's cocaine. He would do it again with Medina.

When crack came on the scene, many got rich and many died in its wake. Ideally, he would like to wait until this Handyman business was settled, but he couldn't afford to let someone else get the jump on this.

The drug game was risky, and at some point you couldn't know everything. You had to rely on instinct. He was rolling the dice again—and he felt lucky.

6

The Crew Strikes Back

The black Chevy Grand National rolled down Cullen Street, the driver careful not to follow the camper ahead too closely. It was the fastest production car made in the U.S. They needed speed. They had been following the dirty white man for several hours. He was the Union's new delivery man. This was not his lucky day.

John Jefferson sat in the passenger seat of the car. He wore a Tiger baseball cap and cradled a small machine gun in his arms. He was silent, keeping his eyes on the small camper.

"Turn down the music, Doc," said Jefferson.

Doc, a heavy-set man with round glasses and tiny dreadlocks turned down the pulsating rap tune in the CD player.

John "Cut" Jefferson was the leader of the Southend Crew. He was about twenty-six, thin, and very dark. He was called Cut because he had a reputation for being a expert at diluting or cutting drugs.

Cut isolated his own territory and started small. Soon, most of the users in the city and near suburbs on the southwest side bought exclusively from him. The town belonged to the Union, but he made the Southend Crew a force to deal with.

Until lately. The Union hit was on his best house. And they were sloppy. They killed a baby, and not even a drug dealer was that fuckin' evil. He would show them how it was done.

The camper stopped at a corner and picked up a roller who looked about eighteen or so. The driver was a white man about forty.

They were going to make deliveries, at least they thought they were, Cut said to himself.

"Hey, Cut, what about the other guy?" asked Doc.

"Fuck him. He busted, too. You think I give a shit 'bout some nappy-headed roller?" Cut's southern accent was whisper thin under his anger.

"All right," said Doc. "No prisoners."

The camper stopped at a house. Cut kept his distance, but watched carefully. The white man pulled up and blew the horn a short blast. A young girl ran out of the house and took a grocery bag from the young roller. Quickly, she was back in the house.

"Smooth," said Doc. "Groceries. I can dig it. People might think it's one of the churches with that free food for the shut-ins shit."

"Ain't that a bitch," said Cut. He pulled up the machine gun.

"This is the move, Cut," said Doc. "The Union ain't the only ones who can make a hit."

"Shut the fuck up and drive the car. Get ready to pull in front of his ass."

They waited until the camper was away from the house. Cut understood that the Union had rollers with guns on this block. If you fucked up, a shot might catch you from any window.

The camper left the block and entered the next. Cut had Doc speed up. The black Chevy swerved around the camper and stopped suddenly.

The scruffy-looking white man inside hit the brakes and the old camper screeched to a stop. Cut jumped out of the car and quickly sprayed bullets into the windshield, shattering it. He saw a red spray lift into the compartment. The white man's body jumped as each shot slammed into him. The young black roller's bright blue shirt became purple as the blood spread. Cut yelled as he walked toward the camper, still shooting.

After the clip was spent, Cut stopped shooting and ran to the camper. He had to get the cocaine and leave before someone saw him. This was still Union territory. He opened the door and the roller fell out onto the pavement. He saw the white man, his head tilted into the window as if were looking for someone. He wore a bloodied shirt that read, SHIT HAPPENS.

7

The Rookies

Tony pumped harder. It had been a while and he was out of shape. Sweat rolled from his body as he changed positions on the Universal machine at the gym. He needed to blow off some steam and decided to do it at the officers gym.

The investigation was moving slowly and the cops were busting heads all over town but getting nowhere. Putting the rollers in jail was of no use. Most were too young to be kept in prison and were released and back to work selling poison within hours.

"Gotta keep your mind on the weights, buddy," said Jim, wiping sweat from his face. He had come to work out with Tony to help ease the tension.

"Don't you know it's dangerous to talk to a man while he's lifting?" Tony kept working.

"Sorry." Jim sat down.

Tony finished and sat on the machine's orange seat, breathing heavily.

Tony was ready to start another circuit when he saw two young men, one black, one white, coming their way. The black man was tall, good-looking, and muscular. The white guy was pale with short blond hair and light blue eyes. They were both dressed in crisp uniform blues and carried new department gym bags.

"Hello, Inspector Hill, sir," said the tall black man.

"Do I know you?" Tony asked.

"We're rookies," said the tall black man. "I'm Fred Hampton. This is my partner, Pete Carter." He pointed to the white guy.

"Good," Tony said. "This is my partner—"

"Oh, we know who he is," said Hampton, smiling. "James Cole, cited for bravery five times, wounded in the line of duty twice, three times officer of the year."

"OK," said Jim. "Now tell me what my blood type is."

The young officers laughed again. Jim did too, but seemed uneasy that they knew so much about his record.

"You have to excuse him," said Carter. "He has a good memory and he likes to show off."

"I know you guys," said Tony. "You guys graduated at the top of the last academy class, right?"

"Yes, sir," said Hampton. "I was fourth, Pete here was number two."

Tony nodded. He'd seen these law-and-order cadet types before. A few years on the streets would kill that shit, he thought.

"Yeah, but Fred was the top marksman in our class," said Carter.

"We're first-team uniform backup on the Handyman case," said Hampton.

"I know. I requested you," said Tony.

"We were just on our way back to duty, but I thought we'd come by and say hello and thanks for requesting us," said Hampton.

"No problem," said Tony. "I need all the help I can get catching the Handyman"

"Well, we really don't want to catch him," said Carter. "He's doing a fine job." The rookies laughed.

"You're kidding, right?" Jim asked.

"Oh, no," said Carter. "The guy is cleaning up the streets for us." He high-fived Hampton, who echoed his opinion.

"So, you guys think it's OK for a man to just kill someone 'cause he's a criminal?" Tony asked.

"No," said Hampton. "But if he's a vigilante, maybe he's trying to bypass our slow and fallible legal system by dishing out a measure of justice."

"What if a cop is in the way the next time he kills?" Tony stood up. "Is it OK to kill him, too?"

"Of course not," said Carter. "But no one cares about these dealers, they're—"

"I don't believe I'm hearin' this," said Jim. "A dealer is a citizen, too."

"Calm down, Jim," Tony said. "I think they're right."

"What?" said Jim.

The rookies seemed surprised, too.

"Well, we see it differently, but I agree that the Handyman has done some good. He's got the dealers scared, but he's also causing the death of innocent people. And I know," Tony cut Carter off, "that if a few innocent lives are lost in the process of getting rid of drugs, it's a good trade-off. And haven't we all dreamed of just popping a dealer? But tell me fellas, where does it end? We get rid of the drug dealers by just killing them, then what? Shoot drunk drivers? Income tax cheats? Cut off the hands of shoplifters?"

"With all due respect, you're way out there, sir," said Hampton.

"I know, it's extreme," said Tony. "But the reason we have laws is to put limits on ourselves. Sometimes, when you point your gun at somebody, you feel like God—you have the power of life and death."

Tony smiled a little. He knew that the rookies all recognized the first line of the old Police Academy poem.

"Since you guys studied at the academy, I'm sure that you know that the first police were soldiers," Tony said.

The rookies nodded in unison. It was eerie to see, Tony thought.

"They fought wars as well as policing the cities," Tony said. "Today, we're still soldiers, only it's an urban war. You never know if the car you stop has a joyrider in it or a killer with a gun between his legs. Wars are fought for honor. Without honor there is no good or bad, just death. So, we have to be part of the system, because to not be would be disaster."

"OK, sir," said Carter. "Since we are talking theory here, I say honor won't solve the drug problem. The system is just a training ground for criminals and drastic measures are needed. Look what the Chinese accomplished—"

"The goddamned Chinese killed drug pushers *and* users by the thousands!" said Jim. "What the hell good will it do to waste a bunch of sorry crackheads?"

"Cut out the demand," said Hampton flatly.

"That's it. I'm outta here," said Jim. "You *rookies*," he said the word with contempt, "have a lot to learn." Jim walked away.

"Excuse my partner," said Tony. "He has this crazy belief that innocent people shouldn't be killed."

"And you?" asked Hampton. "What do you believe, sir?"

Tony stood again. "I believe every rookie thinks he can change the world. I did and I still became part of the system that I condemned. You see, experience is the big dick around here. You get screwed to the ways of the world and you change or you get rejected. That's the way it works. Trust me, 'cause if you ever fuck up, I'll be one of the guys that puts your ass back into civilian clothes."

Tony's beeper went off. He checked it. It was a call from 1300. He mumbled a curse. "Gotta go fellas. But remember what I said."

Tony walked away, looking for Jim. The young officers said half-hearted good-byes.

Tony found Jim and told him they had a call. They quickly went to the locker room and grabbed a shower.

Tony turned on the hot water. The heat felt good as the water ran over his tired body.

The rookies bothered Tony. He hoped the academy was not turning out a lot more like them. A cop should never admire a killer.

When Tony was rookie he was arrogant, but not like these guys. His arrogance was born from a belief that he could play by the rules and just do a better job than the next guy. These guys were obviously out to change the rules altogether. Their success at the academy made them believe they knew better than street-seasoned old warriors like him.

The rookies were idealists and most cops were cynics. An idealist with a license to kill scared Tony.

Tony and Jim got themselves together and went to the call—a murder on the northwest side that could possibly be related to the Handyman.

8

Body Bags

Tony and Jim pushed through the crowd on Cullen Street. They walked toward the camper with a sense of dread. They were informed on the way that this was not a Handyman death, but looked to be an escalation of drug dealer animosity, a not-so-subtle euphemism for a war.

The dead bodies were where the killer had left them. The young black roller was on the street face down and the white man was in the camper, sitting in the driver's seat.

Tony struggled to remain focused. He promised himself that he would follow Lincoln's advice and tell someone about his troubles with Darryl Simon. But he didn't know where to begin.

Pete Carter and Fred Hampton approached Tony as he walked to the crime scene. Tony remembered that they said they were going straight back to duty after their workout. They both looked serious, but their eyes betrayed excitement.

"Sir. No one saw anything, although one witness says he thought he saw a black car drive away," said Hampton.

"Good. Where is he?" Tony asked. He tried not to stare at Carter's blond hair.

"Well, sir," said Carter. "He's over there." Carter pointed to their police cruiser. In the backseat was a shabby-looking man of about forty. He was slumped against the window.

"We want to talk to him," said Jim. "Wake him up."

"Sir, he's not asleep," said Hampton. "He passed out. Drunk."

"Great," said Tony. "Take him to dry out and if he remembers anything, take a statement."

"Yes, sir," the two rookies said, almost in unison.

"What else?" asked Jim. He was not happy to see the rookies again.

"The camper has what appears to be a drug residue, but no drugs were found," said Hampton.

"It looks like a theft and a hit," said Carter.

"No shit," said Jim.

"We wanted to talk to the forensic guys if it's OK with you, sir," said Carter. "We can give you a report."

"Sure," said Tony. "Go see what he—"

"Partner," said Jim. "We have that order from City Hall we need to take care of. Maybe these uniforms should take care of it."

Tony looked at Jim and for a second he was confused. He was not aware of any City Hall mandate. But the look in Jim's eyes was one he had seen a lot of lately. It said, "I'm covering your ass."

Tony realized he had no business letting a rookie be first on his forensic evidence in the middle of a big investigation. Especially after the T-Lab fiasco. Another fuck-up, Tony thought.

"Yeah," Tony said. "City Hall wants constant news containment. Make sure the cameras don't get turned on. We'll get back with you later."

Carter and Hampton walked away. Carter took off his hat and quickly swept his hand through his hair. Hampton cast Jim an evil look.

"I'd like to punch one of those bastards," Jim said.

Tony was silent as they walked over to the forensics team. The leader told them to wait and he would have a preliminary report in a few minutes.

Tony scanned the crowd. The faces all looked angry, as if he had let them all down somehow. He turned away and looked at Jim, who was trying not to make eye contact.

"I want you to know that I'm gonna get it together," said Tony. "It's just this case, it's a bitch."

They stood silent a moment. "We gotta get something going or we'll be yanked from this," said Jim.

"I don't think that will happen," said Tony. "Fuller is behind us."

Tony noticed a man waving in the crowd. The cops pushed him

back, but the man stepped forward again and waved, yelling something.

Tony moved toward the man and recognized his face. He signaled to the cops to let the man through. They did and the small man walked toward Tony and Jim.

"Is that Blue?" Jim asked.

"Yes," Tony said. "The dead kid must be one of his."

Sullivan "Blue" Jones was an ex-con and one of Tony's former street informants. He was also a good friend. Blue ran a neighborhood youth center on the west side.

Blue was dark-skinned and about fifty. His most striking features were his bald head and blue eyes. Tony had seen blacks with blue eyes before, but never one with skin so dark.

Blue walked up and shook hands with Tony and Jim.

"This boy, Melvin, was one of my kids," said Blue. He had a soft Jamaican accent.

"We thought as much," said Tony.

"I'm sorry, man," said Jim.

"It's OK. I wasn't doin' so well with him," said Blue. "He liked the money and the girls too much."

"You want to ID the body for us?" asked Tony.

"Sure. His mother will have a heart attack if she has to do it. I'll tell her myself."

"How are the people at the center taking all this?" Tony asked.

"Terrible, terrible," said Blue. "At the neighborhood meetings, the people are angry. Angry at white people, the black people who run the city, the drug dealers. Everyone. And those who didn't already own a gun, are buying one."

"Man oh man," Jim said.

"Will you come and speak to them again, Tony?" Blue asked. "They always respond well to you."

"Blue, I don't have the time right now, but I'll come back as soon as I can."

"I'll hold you to your word."

"Come on, Blue, I'll take you to the officers," said Jim.

"Good," said Blue. "Don't be a stranger, Tony."

"I'll try not to."

Tony watched Jim lead Blue away. Tony had great affection for the man. He was a success story, a hard-ass street dealer who went to jail and came out a better man, dedicated to helping the community he'd hurt. They should have Blue's picture on the front page, instead of Handyman headlines.

A forensic cop walked up to Tony, looking dead-faced. His hollow heels sounded like horse hooves on the dry pavement. "Sir, it looks like we got nothing. It was a clean kill."

"Go over it again before we take the vehicle in," said Tony.

"But sir, we—"

"Just do it, OK?" Tony said.

The forensic guy clumped off. Tony exhaled heavily as two coroner's assistants brought the young boy's body past him. It was covered by a stark white cloth dotted with blood.

Tony stopped them.

"Why is that sheet on him," Tony asked. "Why isn't he—"

"An administrative screwup somewhere, sir," said one of the assistants. "Apparently, there are no more body bags."

9

Campbell's Secret

Rosedale Park is located on the far northwest side of Detroit. It is an integrated, upscale enclave of huge houses, winding streets, and lush, tall trees. Many of the city's yuppie employees live there as well as many of Detroit's high-ranking policemen and firemen.

On Edinborough Street, in a large two-story house at the end of the block, Robert Campbell made love to the married woman who lived there.

The bed in the master bedroom made soft, easy sounds as the dark couple thrived in their occupation. Campbell had been seeing her for over a year and he enjoyed these little visits in the afternoon. Doing it to someone else's woman in their own bed gave him a charge that was as good as the sex itself.

Campbell worked on Lisa Martin with slow, steady rhythms and she clung to him with her usual hunger. Sweat glistened on his chest and sides. She pushed back into him, whispering something he couldn't hear. He slipped his hand around her thigh, then under her, teasing for a moment, and she responded loudly. Campbell smiled and continued, pleased with himself.

They had met at a supermarket in Southfield. She commanded attention in her tight skirt, high heels, and wedding ring. Campbell knew that whenever a married woman wore that kind of stuff, she was looking for some kind of action. He followed her.

She walked down the aisle, taking items and walking smoothly in the too-short skirt. He actually got an erection when she bent over to check a cereal box.

Campbell struck up a conversation and eventually walked her to her car. She told him she was married. He said that it didn't mean anything 'cause he wanted her and that was just something to get around.

Lisa had not even flinched when she heard his stutter. He liked that. Almost everyone he met showed some sign of shame or surprise at it. But she didn't. She just smiled at him, flirting with her eyes.

Campbell gave her his phone number. She took it, still pretending not to be interested.

Campbell was good-looking and knew it. His classic features were covered with smooth dark skin and he had a rock hard body. And he could tell Lisa Martin was instantly attracted to him. Most women were.

After a few days, she called him and it wasn't long before they met in a hotel and made love.

Campbell knew women. Lisa had money and a pretty good life, but she wanted back those days when everybody wanted her, those days when her sex was power and she had men waiting on their toes to be chosen by her. He had given it all back to her.

Campbell tightened his grip on the woman's waist and quickened his strokes as he reached his orgasm. He took a deep breath and blew it out slowly, then kissed her moist back.

Lisa rose up from all fours and threw her head back. Her long dark hair hit him in the face. It smelled good. She pushed her body against his and he hugged her from behind.

Campbell kissed her cheek, then broke the connection and lay next to her, breathing in slow deep breaths.

"Good job, sir," Lisa said. "Good job."

"I'll s-s-send you a bill," he said.

"Ha, you should be paying me for this good stuff you're getting."

"I ain't g-got that kinda money," he smiled and kissed her.

"Good lie."

Campbell got up and went into the bathroom. She whistled at his ass and he did a dance for her. He was happy. And not many things made him happy these days.

Campbell had started to tell her many times how he made his living, but he didn't want to scare her. She was too respectable. He told her that he ran a store with his brother and that's why he always had cash on him and carried a gun. She probably didn't believe it, but it was good enough for now.

Campbell sat on the toilet in the neat little bathroom. The drug war was on and the cops were all over them in the streets. The jails and Juvenile Hall were filled to the rafters with their people.

Campbell felt strangely sad in the nice, family house. He never had a place like this as a kid. He wondered if his life had been different, would he still have been in the Union. There were rollers from nice families, so it didn't really matter that you had a father with a good job. If you wanted quick money, you sold drugs. And once you made that choice, there was no going back. It was a one-way ride.

Campbell accepted the fact that he would die in the business. But like all dealers, he had a plan to get out. He had been saving his money and had an open airline ticket. At any moment, he could be on a plane and out of Detroit. But the business was seductive. In a way, it was fun. You had power. The kind of power and wealth you could never get in society. No one could touch you.

But still, if he'd had a choice, he might have lived differently. He could have gone to college, gotten a degree of some kind, and then a good job. A respectable life. He could even have been like Lisa's husband. He laughed out loud. No, he could never be like that, a limp-dicked office boy.

He didn't feel any guilt taking another man's wife. It was a sin, but that whole marriage thing was bullshit. He could never promise to only have sex with just one woman. It was a lie he couldn't even bear to think about. He didn't know why women believed it.

Campbell flushed the toilet and looked at his handsome face in the mirror. Lisa had reminder notes posted on it: "Get Chuck's suits," "Pick up carpet cleaner." Campbell laughed. She had forgotten one: "Have sex with my man."

Campbell walked back into the bedroom thinking that he had time for one more round with Lisa before he had to get back to the street. School would be out soon and business usually picked up then.

As he entered the bedroom, Campbell saw the man holding Lisa. She was on her knees, tears streaming down her face onto her naked body, wet and shiny.

Campbell's mind clicked in rapid succession. Life, death, and fear sped through his brain. The imposing figure stood over the helpless woman and Campbell's gun in his gloved hand pointed at Lisa's head. The Handyman cocked the hammer.

Campbell stood there naked, looking at Death, then yelled a battle cry and lunged at the Handyman. The killer sidestepped, and Campbell was tripped, falling hard on his face.

Campbell heard a shot and a body hit the wall. He got up and lunged again, not wanting to see where Lisa had landed, but the Handyman hit him in the face, sending his body flying onto the bed.

The killer fell upon his mark like an animal. Campbell struggled as the attacker cut into him. He screamed, stuttering an endless word. He fought, but the killer was too strong. And his last living sight, was the Handyman's face, descending toward his own.

10

Lafayette Coney Island

Tony and Jim watched as the forensics lab techs went over every article in Lisa Martin's bedroom.

Charles Martin had come home late to quite a surprise: his naked wife shot dead with a murdered man who was obviously her lover.

Charles Martin cried like a baby as an officer tried to interview him and no one could tell which had been wounded most, his heart or his pride.

Tony examined the spray of blood, bone, and tissue on the wall with cool detachment. He'd seen worse, but when they put Lisa Martin's body into a thick, plastic bag, he suddenly felt sick. The dead woman was about Nikki's age and the thought that the Handyman might kill his Nikki snaked through him, leaving him cold. The dead man was typical of a Handyman killing. No hands and his throat slashed. Tony would bet his life that no blond hairs would be found on these bodies either. The Handyman was too smart to make that mistake again.

The psychological report said the Handyman was a maniac, a killer who fed on power and domination, and that his obsession with hands was a sign of his need to control.

But the killings were too clean, too planned to be done by a psycho. Tony didn't care what the damned shrinks said.

The pressure from the murder spree was rising to an intolerable level. The phone lines at 1300 had to be rerouted because of the calls pouring in, and the press was floating a rumor that Chief Fuller would be replaced.

"What's up, partner? You with me?" Jim asked.

"What? Oh, yeah," Tony said. He realized that he was standing in the middle of the crime scene, daydreaming. Tony moved aside as the lab techs worked around him.

"Do you know who this guy is—uh, was?" asked Jim. "Robert G. Campbell."

Tony's eyes widened. "Shit," he said. He knew the name. Campbell was one of the biggest dealers in Detroit. The city had about five or so top dealers who supplied it, three of whom, it was believed, composed the loosely formed gang known as the Union.

"This is it, my man," Jim said. "This city's going to break wide open and I don't think we can stop it. We can't find Mbutu since that guy tried to whack him, but the Brotherhood's passing out vigilante fliers, saying 'protect yourselves from the black *and* white killers.'"

"And there have been over thirty violent incidents between blacks and whites in the last week," Tony said. "I need some air."

Tony walked out of the room and then out of the house and Jim followed.

The air outside was soothing to Tony. It was evening and the heat was tapering off. The summer days were hot and sticky, but the nights were pleasant.

"I figured it out, you know," said Jim, putting his hand on Tony's shoulder. His voice was low.

"What?"

"Your story. Simon. You letting him jump. It's a lie."

Tony stood silent and looked his partner in the eye. Tony thought about Dr. Lincoln. He had to tell somebody and Jim was the best friend he had on earth, next to his wife.

"OK," Tony said. "But let's get the hell out of here. There's nothing to do until the reports come in."

Detroit's Lafayette Coney Island is famous for two things: great chili dogs and all the cops who eat there.

Jim and Tony sat down in a corner booth. The place was rather empty, only a couple of teens, their girls, and the assorted bums having coffee. Jim ordered four coneys with onions, two Cokes, and told the waiter to get the two homeless men at the counter two bowls of chili.

"So," said Tony. "How did you know?"

"I didn't," said Jim. "I was guessing. You partners with a guy for a few years and you just know. Besides, I waited to see if you would get back on your game after you told me, and you didn't."

The waiter brought the food. They ate in silence for a while, then, "I murdered Darryl Simon," Tony said. "I threw him out the window."

Jim stopped chewing. He looked at Tony as if he were seeing him for the first time. "But how? There were cameras and SWAT guys all over the place."

"Simon had all the shades pulled and lights dimmed so our snipers couldn't get a shot at him, and the SWAT guys were blown away by Simon's little booby trap, remember?"

"Right, he was some kind of engineering genius."

"Electrical engineer. Anyway, they were killed and my partner was knocked unconscious. It was just me and him."

"And you just threw him out?"

"No, I apprehended him first. When he put the gun down, I pinned him, got the hostages out." Tony was perspiring a little. He wiped it away. "I was going to take him in, then I saw the black hostages. He had only killed the black ones! He smiled at me. 'End of the line for niggers,' he said." Tony shook again as he said the line from The Dream.

"I hit him, he punched me back," Tony said. "The next thing I knew, he was sailing out the window."

"Man," Jim leaned back. "I don't really know what to say. We all have things we wish we could take back."

"I don't want to take it back."

"Well, I would have done the same thing. Fuck him. He didn't deserve to live."

"That case put me where I am today, Jim. I murdered my way to the top, partner."

"Don't do this to yourself. You can't bring him back. If this is all that's bothering you, screw it, man. Simon was a low-life. Some lawyers would have gotten him off on a psycho anyway. It's better this way."

"That's not all," Tony said.

He removed the letter from his pocket. He had taken to carrying it around with him. He didn't want anyone to find out about it and no matter where he put it, the letter didn't seem safe.

"A few days ago, I got this in the mail. It's a letter from Simon's sister." He held it out.

"So what?"

"She knew."

"How could she—" Jim took the letter and read.

Dear Mr. Nigger Hero,

It took me a while to find you but I did it. I paid good money, too. I know you killed my brother. Darryl was afraid of heights and he would never have jumped out that window. I tried to tell that to the other nigger cops but they wouldn't listen to a dumb piece of trash like me.

I know you wanted Darryl to die for killing those niggers. Well they deserved to die for making my brother go crazy. You people get everything in the world you want and nobody cares if regular people get it up the ass as long as the damned niggers are happy!

Well, Mr. Hero, you killed more than my brother. After he died we had nothing no more. Darryl was all we had in our family. We didn't get no insurance 'cause he killed himself. Just a little money from his job. My mamma and me we had to sell our house and move downriver. We ended up in a run-down housing project. We got on the welfare for a while but after Mamma got sick, I had to get a job to get money for her. But my job at the restaurant just wasn't enough for us to live, so I had to get dates with men to make it up. That's right, I whored myself. I sucked off men to keep my mamma alive while she was sick, I took it up my ass and learned to like it. I even dated some women. I did it 'cause Darryl was gone and I never been smart or nothing. And all the time I thought about you. Every time some greasy, fat trucker climbed on me, I thought about you. Every time some young kid came in my face I saw your face. It was always you. You were doing it to me, every time.

I was doing it with a mechanic one time and he tried to take the money back. He pulled a knife on me. But I always kept a little gun in my purse. I shot him dead. He had about five hundred bucks on him, so I took it. And listen to this, Mr. Nigger: Darryl talked to me. He came into my brain and helped me kill that piece of shit.

After that, we killed some more just for the money. Me and Darryl. After a while, we did it just for the hell of it. I forget how many, but it was you we thought about. It was you we was killing.

"Damn," Jim said looking shocked. "The boys downriver never did catch that killer, did they? What was that?"

"About a year and a half ago," said Tony. "Four men dead in all."

A woman had gone on a killing spree in the suburbs downriver a year ago, shooting men in the head and in the groin each time. The police suspected she was a prostitute, but could not get an ID on her. The Detroit Police, Wayne County Sheriff, and the state boys had put together a combined task force, but had come up with nothing.

"Jesus, why didn't you—" Jim stopped and kept reading.

Mamma died a little bit ago and I tried to kill myself. I cut my wrists in the bathtub. Would have gone too, but my best friend Cheryl Ann saved me. My wrists hurt 'cause I just got out of the hospital a few days ago. I got stitches and they look like Franken-stein shit. That's funny, huh?

I see now about life. I see what it really is. I guess 'cause I almost died, I know more than other folks do. Life ain't no good without love. All my love is gone and I'm already dead. I can't love nobody 'cause I gave it all up when Darryl and Mamma died.

I know you did it. I know you killed him. God knows it, too, and he ain't gonna let you get away. He'll take all your love like you took mine and then you'll be dead, too.

When you get this letter, I'll be gone. I'm gonna make sure this time. I got a whole bottle of Jack Black to get my nerve and there's a train that runs regular, close to my house. I'm gonna drink that Jack Black and let that train take me back to my family. I'll be back with them soon in heaven and that makes me happy, but I feel sorry for you. You have to go through what I did.

I hope nobody stops you when you want to die.

                                                    Irene Simon

Jim put the letter down. "Did she do it?"

"No," Tony said. "I made some calls. But she disappeared. Clean, just gone."

Tony was a tough cop but his morality had him by the balls. He felt like he was drowning and no one could save him.

"Remember the poem all the cadets learned at the academy?" Jim said. "The one you started when you were talking to those asshole rookies at the gym? 'We with the power of life and death—' " Jim trailed off. He could see in Tony's eyes that he was going back to those days.

"We with the power of life and death," Tony recited:

> Cannot be weak, must not regret.
> Be strong in the mission wherein we delve.
> And kill for others, and not ourselves.

"Damned right," said Jim leaning in to Tony. "I know it's a silly cadet's poem, banned by the instructors and all that shit, but every cop still knows it. *We have the power, Tony.*"

"But I didn't kill for the public. I did it for me, Jim. *For me!* And that's not what the poem says, is it?"

"No, Tony. That's not right. You don't understand what the poem really means. You did it for those brothers Simon wasted and the others that he might have."

"And look what happened. You know me, Jim. I threw the entire white race out that window with Darryl Simon. For all the shit they've done to me and our people over the years. I'm no better than the assholes fighting each other over the Handyman being white. Irene Simon murdered innocent men. Their blood is on my hands, too. All of them."

"I know it's bad," said Jim touching Tony's hand. "But we got a new guy out there killing brothers. The public needs us and you ain't got time to live in the past."

"I know, don't you think I know that?! Every day I wake up knowing that the Handyman is out there, that he's got some sort of plan, and all I can do is wait for him to make a mistake. In the meantime, the bodies pile up."

"Back on the horse, Tony."

"It's not that easy, Jim. I killed a man."

"So what? He wasn't the first or the last."

"But this was different. He was helpless. I murdered him, Jim, there's no other word for it."

"That's bullshit and you know it."

"Look, I've been able to live with it so far, but my conscience has been beating me. I've had the same nightmare at least ten times since that news story came up. This Handyman thing has really fucked me up 'cause it's all about race, too. I feel like I'm back at the GM building but this time, it's me going through the damn window."

Jim got a match from the waiter and burned Irene Simon's letter in an ashtray. "That's what I think about that bitch and her brother," he said.

"No matter what we think of ourselves, we are not gods, Jim," Tony said. "I'm just a man, accountable to the law for his actions like every other man."

"What are you going to do? Go to prison? You'll last three seconds before some con puts a sharpened spoon in your heart."

"I don't know what I'm going to do, but I've got to do something."

"Promise me you won't do anything before you talk to me."

"Why?"

"Because I'm your partner, goddammit. I shouldn't even have to ask."

"All right, but don't act like I'm unstable. I just need to take it easy."

"I can help. I'll take on more responsibility if you want."

"You're already doing enough. Just keep watching my back."

"Always, man. Always."

11

Dead Presidents

T-Bone wrapped another rubber band around the bills and stacked them. He was hustling to get the Prince's money together. The cash came directly from the dealers, so it was all in small bills. Washington, Lincoln, and other dead presidents lay on the table.

T-Bone counted the money in a small flat on the east side, another of his many living places. K-9 sat quietly to the side, watching.

T-Bone was dreaming of his life after drug dealing. After Medina had made him wealthy, he might come back to Detroit, buy a politician, and run the city. That would be the ultimate revenge. His father, Big Teddy, had always dreamed of becoming a city power broker. T-Bone would do it, then rub it in his sorry-ass face.

T-Bone's beeper went off. He checked the number, then called Traylor.

"Yeah," T-Bone said.

There was a moment's hesitation, then, "Campbell's dead."

T-Bone dropped the money. Bills fell to the floor. He instinctively searched for his shotgun.

"What? How did it happen?"

"He was fucking some married bitch and he got caught by the Handyman."

T-Bone couldn't speak for a second. He was thinking what this meant to his plan.

"OK, OK," said T-Bone. "Get with Mayo and cover Campbell's territory. I'll call you later."

T-Bone switched off the phone, then threw it into a wall, smashing it. K-9 jumped and moved away. T-Bone fumed and walked over to the table of money and turned it over.

"Fuck!"

T-Bone pumped a shell into the chamber, put his finger to the trigger and looked around, breathing heavily.

He took a second.

Then another.

He lowered the weapon and sat on the chair by the overturned table and scattered money. He put the gun on the floor. He could not afford to lose it now. He was too close to freedom.

T-Bone set the table back up. He had to keep his plan moving. The first order of business would be to get Medina on the street and take over the city. His prices would fall and by the time the Prince and his people could convert the other major cities, he would be on a sandy beach somewhere with a ton of money and the finest woman alive.

T-Bone was sure it was an external force at work on the Union and he had to find it. He was going to have to help the police catch the killer. Then again, he'd had a system of communication and payoffs in place for a long time now. He paid them monthly, giving money to rookie bagmen who spread it around like Christmas bonuses. He would have to let them know what he was about to do.

T-Bone began counting the money again. With Campbell gone, money would get tighter and he still had to pay the Prince, keep Santana and the South-of-the-Border boys happy, and fund the Medina project.

Of course, it would be easier to just have the Prince and his people eliminated, he thought, but that might not be good business. You should never kill a man who's doing business straight up unless he crosses you. And he didn't know who else the Prince might be connected to—maybe someone who might not take kindly to his death.

"Damn," he said again. The Handyman was ruining his life, he thought. White people were a pain in the ass.

12

Mayo and Donna

Steve Mayo had set up the Medina production as well as any Harvard MBA. He had his people working all through the last week, careful not to let any of the grunts steal a sample.

His orders were to send the new drug out in the suburbs to the wiggers, and to start pumping it into the city. They were raising the price about twenty percent over the old stuff. With the shortage, there would be a run on the new drug.

The summer had come early and that meant plenty of recreation, fun, and getting high. Mayo hated the hot, muggy Detroit summers but they were always good for business.

Mayo supervised the production in an abandoned warehouse on the upper east side. They had turned out a carload of the stuff. Mayo made sure that the production was swift and clean. Medina seemed even easier to make than crack.

The mixture was the hard part. The Professor had whipped up several large bottles of the stuff. But they would need more. They trained a young kid named Dennis, who was a college dropout and claimed to be a former chemistry major. Whatever he was, he was smart, and the Professor had been impressed with how quickly he learned the process.

They set up a team of rollers to buy or steal all of the ingredients the Professor had told them they would need. The Union could now create the drug.

Mayo would kill the Prince and end the relationship right where it was if he were in charge. But T-Bone had not given the order, so the deal would probably stand.

Mayo swore that he had gotten high from the fumes once while it was cooking. He made everyone wear the little cloth masks at the Professor's insistence, but when he took it off briefly, he got a contact. He took a few deep breaths and put the mask back on. The rush was swift and wonderful. It faded inside of a minute.

The Prince and the Professor were there. Donna walked around, intentionally ignoring him. She wore a pair of jeans that looked painted on, and she corralled her breasts in a tight, leather top. He didn't understand the woman. After making love in the burned-out building, he thought she would be friendlier. But who knew women?

Mayo began to give the rollers their assignments. There were about thirty of them in all.

Campbell's death had shaken Mayo and that was no small feat. Campbell was a pretty boy, but he was smart. He was a pro and the last person Mayo expected would get taken out.

But Mayo knew that the woman was a factor, too. Women had been the end of many a good man. He couldn't count the rollers who got iced fucking with a bitch. He thought about Donna and what they had done. He knew it was wrong. One roller never screwed another's woman, but he couldn't help himself. She was sexy and provocative, and the danger she brought only made the sex better.

Mayo dispatched the rollers with the Medina. In a week or so, he thought, they would know whether the stuff was real or not.

"When can we expect the rest of our money, my brotha?" asked the Prince. He jingled his keys in his hand nervously.

"When the shit hits with the people. I told you already," said Mayo, trying not to look at Donna, who was bending over.

"I know that, but who decides when it hits, as you say?"

"T-Bone." Mayo looked at the noisy keys in his hand and then gave the Prince a nasty look.

"I do know, it's just that we have many other places to go with our wares." The Prince smiled and placed his keys on a crate, noticing Mayo's annoyed look.

"Fuck it, go on and go. We be here when you get back." Mayo smiled.

"Oh, no, my brotha. That's not acceptable. We must have the money in order to travel."

"Well, I'm sorry 'bout that, but I ain't the man." Mayo walked away and instructed the remaining rollers where to take the formula.

Mayo disliked the Prince. He was overly friendly and phony, a sneaky little bastard. And he was dangerous. Mayo had been around enough killers to recognize that the Prince would cut your throat and order dinner while you bled. Mayo had met his kind before and it was never good.

As the Prince and the Professor left, Donna said something to the Prince and they allowed her to stay behind. She strolled by Mayo, poked out her tongue at him and walked behind a stack of large crates.

Faintly, Mayo heard a zipper being undone. He quickly sent the last rollers away and went to her.

Behind the crates, he found Donna topless and smiling. She wiggled out of her tight jeans and leaned over a crate.

Mayo almost fell in his run over to her. He cupped his hands over her breasts and licked her hard back. She pulled his hands away.

"Hurry up," she said not looking at him.

Mayo fumbled with his pants and was soon inside her. He made love to her, his pants around his ankles. He was loud in his passion and she smiled, happy with her control over him.

They never saw the Prince watching them. He had come back for his keys.

13

Courting Medina

Magilla squinted as he looked at the dull crystals that had been dropped off at the house. They were hard to see in the dimness of his basement. This was the new thing everyone was buzzing about. Magilla had only heard rumors of the Union's leader and had never met him. But whoever he was, he was a genius if the shit was half what they said it was.

He was glad that Mayo had not brought the new drug called Medina. He was not in the mood for his abuse and he was feeling scared after Campbell's death. Whoever the Handyman was, he had no fear of dealers and that was enough to keep anybody up nights. Magilla had taken on even more bodyguards at the house. But he trusted no one and he slept with a loaded gun in his room.

Magilla's first order was to give some of the new product to the biggest crackheads. He told them to rave about it as instructed. They had not even asked what it was. They would smoke anything.

Magilla watched as a head named Quinten popped a rock of Medina into a pipe and lit it up. He took a long puff and closed his eyes. A contented smile spread over his face and he took another long puff. He then smoked furiously until it was gone. He immediately put another rock in the pipe.

"Man, this is the shit!" Quinten exclaimed loudly as he began to smoke again. "Cold Medina!"

Magilla smiled and watched. The other crackheads all talked with

Quinten and took hits on the pipe. Magilla couldn't tell if the stuff was good or if it was just good acting on Quinten's part.

There was only one way to find out. Magilla borrowed a pipe and after wiping it, lit up a rock of the Medina and took a long drag.

Magilla's head went light and a rush of sensation hit him. His fingers and toes tingled and he felt the unmistakable sensation of an erection coming. His body was hit by a host of commands as the drug sped through his cerebrum. He felt stronger than he had ever been. He could do anything. He was attractive and virile. Suddenly, the world was a place that he was in total control of. *He* was The Man and no one else. He possessed power and no one could deny it. He smoked the first rock and lit another right away. He ran his hand across his chest. He was horny. He looked at the women in the basement. They were ugly and skinny but he wanted them anyway. And he could have them if he wanted 'cause he was in control.

As Magilla smoked rock after rock, he thought of things that he had always wanted to do. He dreamed of screwing Ms. Phillips, a woman who lived next door to him when he was a kid. Hers had been the first breasts that he had seen as a young man. He thought of making two men freak off with each other and watching. He wasn't a fag or anything, but he always wanted to see that.

And he thought of Steven Mayo. The things he could do to him. He thought of tying him down and beating the shit out of him and pissing in his face. Or making him watch as he screwed his woman—or his mother. Yes, that was better. The day would come he thought when he would have him right where he wanted him.

Magilla walked around the basement of the old Ridley house and stood over the large *R* in the center of the floor. He took a long puff and threw his arms into the air.

"This is my muthafuckin' house!" he yelled.

The crackheads looked at him through glazed eyes. One young crackhead sitting on an old sofa snorted a quick laugh. Magilla puffed the pipe as he stepped toward him. Magilla smiled, took another puff and kicked him in the face. The man reeled back. His head hit the muddy brown wall and made a dull sound. His eyes rolled up into his head and he slumped into the sofa.

"I said, this is *my muthafuckin' house*! Don't nobody fuck wif me in here."

Magilla walked around smoking another rock, smiling. This stuff

was good, too good for fuckin' crackheads, he thought. His house was
set to get the stuff used to make it. He couldn't wait. He prided himself on not being a crackhead, but this stuff might change his mind.
He could feel the high slipping already, like water running out of a
container. The stuff was good. The high was strong, unusual, and it
didn't last long.

Magilla instructed his people to distribute more of the Medina to
the users, but he made sure that he had a good amount for himself
and there was plenty upstairs to sell. He smiled and lit up again.

The users smoked up the Medina as quickly as it was given out
and raved about its powers. There was only one thing a crackhead
liked more than drugs, and that was free drugs. When it was all gone,
the basement was buzzing with requests for more.

Magilla ignored them. He was busy smoking.

"You can buy the shit upstairs," was all he would say.

After it was apparent that no one was getting any more free, they
opted to purchase the product. There was almost a stampede up the
stairs.

Magilla laughed at the silly-ass addicts as they stepped over each
other to get high again. A crackhead didn't realize that he spent most
of his time smoking dope. If he wasn't smoking, he was stealing to get
money to get high, or fucking somebody for it.

Quinten lumbered by Magilla holding his head. "Thanks for the
shit, man. It was good at first, but it gave me a headache."

"You want some more?" asked Magilla.

"Oh, hell, yeah!" said Quinten and pulled out his pipe.

"Get the fuck outta my face," said Magilla and laughed in his
face.

Quinten took the advice and left the house quickly. Outside, the
hot summer air hit him.

"Hotter than a muthafucka out here," he said.

Quinten rubbed his temples. His head did hurt after smoking the
Medina. In fact, it began throbbing as the humidity choked him.

"Damn," he whispered. "I need some damn aspirin or something."

He stumbled on an uneven patch of concrete and steadied himself
next to a telephone pole, then staggered on. The pain grew worse as
his high slipped away. It was like a tiny cannon being discharged inside his head. There was a moment of terrible pain followed by a

short moment of relief. The anticipation of the next assault only made the waiting worse.

Quinten grabbed his head and fought tears as he sat down on a bus stop bench at Chene Street. The bus would be here soon and then he could go home and get some aspirin. In his pain, he thought that if he got high again, it would go away.

"Shit fucked me up," he said to himself as the bus approached. He reached to get the fare from his pockets and was hit by a wave of convulsions. He shook and twitched, moving uncontrollably. His head thundered with pain and a tiny drop of blood welled in the corner of his eye. He stumbled in front of the bus before it could stop. The impact lifted him right out of his shoes.

The shocked bus driver cursed as she watched the man's body fly into the air. Quinten landed with a thud. His head hit the pavement first. The rest of him flopped down afterwards with a wet thud.

The bus's brakes locked the wheels and the huge vehicle skidded on the pavement. The passengers were thrown forward like rag dolls, screaming and clutching at the support bars. The driver ran out to the injured man after calling for an ambulance on the radio. She stood over Quinten's body with a large first-aid kit. Quinten still shook violently and blood poured from his head and face. The driver had never seen so much blood. She knelt next to him and told him to be calm.

She removed a blanket and covered him with it. She was crying but didn't seem to notice. Quinten gurgled something, then stopped moving. The passengers crowded around the body. The driver turned to them, sobbing.

"He just fell in front of me," the driver said.

"Sho did, I saw it," said a man.

"I got to get to work," said a woman.

"Damn, lady, have some sympathy," said another passenger.

"I can't pay my rent with sympathy. Can't nobody help him," she said pointing. "Look at him, he as dead as you can get. He ain't even breathing." She stormed off to hail a cab, cursing on the way.

Thirty minutes later, a police car rounded the corner, lights flashing. The crowd instinctively stepped away from the scene. In the distance, an ambulance wailed.

14

Tony and Mbutu

"**W**hat is this shit, candy?" asked the crackhead. He took the bluish rocks into his hands.

"It's base, fool," said the young dealer. "They call it Medina, like funky cold medina. You remember that song?"

The head examined the Medina on the steps of an old abandoned church. The sun was hiding behind some clouds, but the humidity was still high.

"Yeah, heard about it. Is it as bad as they say?" asked the head.

"Best you ever had, now come on. It's too damn hot to be jacking off with you out here. You want the shit or not?"

"OK," the crackhead took the rocks and slipped the dealer a bill. "Peace," he said and left.

The dealer pocketed the money and walked down the steps. The new drug was moving like nothing he had ever seen. Once someone got a hit, he was hooked for life.

The young dealer headed toward a group of kids playing on a nearby playground. The sun came back and the street heated up again.

"That ain't the way, young brother."

The young dealer turned to face Mbutu and two of his men. They wore African garb.

"Look, man," said the young dealer, "I don't wanna hear none of your save-the-race shit today. Just let me do my thang."

"That can be dangerous these days," said Mbutu. "Some white man is killing people in your line of work."

"I can take care of myself. So fuck off."

"OK, we will. Just give us all the drugs you're carrying. As long as this white killer is out here, we can't let him kill any more black men."

"Kiss my ass," said the young dealer and started away.

One of Mbutu's men pulled out a gun.

The young dealer stopped. "OK, here, take the shit," he said. "But you know what it means."

The dealer gave Mbutu a small plastic bag containing some regular crack.

"Where's the new drug, the Medina? We know you got some," said Mbutu.

"Don't know what you talkin' 'bout," said the dealer.

"Give it to me or my fellas will take it."

"Man, if I give it to you, they be comin' after my ass to kill me tonight!" said the dealer.

"Give it up—now." said Mbutu.

The man with the gun took a step toward the dealer.

The young dealer was about to pull out the Medina, when a police cruiser pulled up. A short blast of a siren sounded.

"Stop where you are!" said a voice over the car's speaker.

All four men took off running.

The police cruiser's doors flew open and the officers inside gave chase.

The young dealer ran, tossing his drugs along the way. He was soon overtaken by an officer and stopped, throwing up his arms.

"OK, OK," the young dealer said. "Don't shoot, man!"

The officer ran by him and tackled Mbutu. They struggled a moment, then the other officer came and soon they had him handcuffed.

"Hey, what is this—" said Mbutu.

"You know what it is," said an officer.

The dealer watched in amazement as they took Mbutu back to the cruiser and pulled away.

He watched the police car disappear, then began looking for his Medina.

"This is bullshit!" said Mbutu. "I want to see my attorney."

"Fuck an attorney," said Jim. "You're not under arrest. We just want you for questioning."

"Y'all ain't shit, you know that," said Mbutu. "You look like brothers but you just puppets for the white man. He's got his hand right up your ass."

"Save the speeches," said Tony. "We need to talk with you for a while, that's all."

The interrogation room in 1300 was warm and quiet. The mugginess of the summer seeped in through an open window. Jim and Tony sat across an old table from Mbutu.

Mbutu settled a little. He rubbed his wrists where the handcuffs were, pushed back his dreadlocks and let out a small chuckle. "Black cops. Savior of the people."

"The man who tried to shoot you is in custody. Why haven't you been here to press charges?" Tony asked.

"Because someone is always trying to get at me," said Mbutu. "Comes with the job of speaking out for my people."

"Let's talk about your people," said Jim. "We want them to back off the vigilante stuff. It's causing a problem."

"I don't see how."

"Your people are making citizen's arrests on dealers and chasing down men they think are the killer," said Tony. "It's only a matter of time before one of them catches a bullet."

"They're in the struggle," said Mbutu. "They die, they do it for the cause."

"Who are *you* to send someone off to their death?" Jim asked, pounding the table.

"I am a black man, a real one, not a house nigger like you!"

Jim stood up and threw his chair aside. Tony grabbed him and whispered something in his ear. Jim turned and left the room, giving Mbutu a cold look.

Tony sat back down in front of Mbutu.

"That good cop/bad cop shit is played out, my brother," said Mbutu.

"We're not playing. He was going to kick your ass."

"My lawyers would love that."

"Let's talk, me and you. Forget all the political stuff, let's get to the one thing we have in common," said Tony.

"And what would that be, officer? The liberation of our people?"

"We both want the Handyman."

"I want him dead," said Mbutu. "You want to use him to cover yourself in glory."

"Makes no difference. Call your people off and let us do our job."

"I have to look after the people of this city. You so-called leaders are just promulgating the white man's power."

"Get off your fuckin' soapbox," said Tony. "I'm black too."

"But some of us are blacker than others."

"You people make me sick. It's easy to sit on the sidelines and criticize, race bait, and complain about everything that happens. You don't produce anything, all you do is piss and moan and pretend to be in charge of something. You're no better than those so-called community activists looking to line their pockets over this thing."

"Now who's on the soapbox? Look, I was brought here to make a statement. Let me make it and I'll be on my way."

"I can get you on obstruction of justice, interference with a peace officer, not to mention possession of an illegal substance."

"I took that crack off a dealer and your men know it," said Mbutu.

"Don't fuck with me. I'll grind your sorry ass up and put it in jail as sure as I'm standin' here."

"We all gotta do what we gotta do."

Tony got up and opened the door. "Take his ass away."

Two uniforms came in and took Mbutu to the door.

"What do we do with him, sir?" asked a uniform.

Tony looked Mbutu in the eyes. The man was obviously on the other side of the whole issue of race. Mbutu had graduated from hating white people, to hating black people, to hating all people. He would go to jail before he would abandon his cause.

"Let him make his statement," Tony said. "Then let him go."

The uniform pushed Mbutu toward the door. Mbutu stopped them.

"You know what your problem is, officer?" Mbutu said to Tony. "You love white people too much."

The uniforms took him away.

Tony cursed under his breath and walked back toward his office. He was startled as Jim and several detectives rounded a corner in a run.

"We got something," said Jim.

"What?" asked Tony.

"One of the Union killings. The murderer of that woman who was tossed off the bridge."

"Where is he?" asked Tony.

"He's holed up in a house on the west side," said Jim.

"What's the situation?" Tony was getting his jacket.

"He's got a gun and apparently there's a woman and a kid inside with him," said Jim.

To one of the detectives, Tony said, "Tell them I don't want anybody to do anything until we get there."

Tony and Jim ran out of the building, passing Mbutu, who was being taken to make his statement.

Tony and Jim sped along in their cruiser headed for Six Mile and Greenfield on the west side of town. Tanya Hale, the woman who was thrown from the overpass, had put up enough of a fight to get her killer to touch the back of her earring and leave a fingerprint. A big, fat, beautiful thumbprint.

The felony files had turned up nothing, but, thank God, Jim had remembered to check the old juvenile files, too. And when they did, Larry Drake's rap sheet came out.

They had forgotten about Mbutu and his street police; they finally had a break.

"This fucker could give us what we need to crack this thing," said Jim, gunning the car faster. "If he's in the gang, maybe he can tell us what the Union knows about the Handyman."

Tony didn't respond. He was deep in thought. Mbutu's barb and his confession had only added to the recurring sense of depression he felt. The Dream was now gone, but it was replaced by random thoughts of his guilt and Irene Simon's victims.

Jim stopped the car on a street on the near northwest side. The street was illuminated by the cherry lights of three marked police cruisers and an ambulance. There was also an unmarked detective's cruiser.

Six uniformed officers were outside the house. The cars were in the traditional barricade line. Tony had been informed that there were three cars with six uniforms backing up the rear. A small crowd was being dispersed by an officer. Tony got out of his car, kicking himself into high gear.

"Shit," said Jim, as they approached.

"What?" Tony asked.

"The gang's all here."

Tony looked at the line of cars, and sure enough, there was Orris Martin holding a bullhorn with his partner, young Steve Patrick, next to him. Tony had rotated them to Handyman street duty.

Fred Hampton and Pete Carter held guns over the hood of another car.

Also in the crowd, Tony saw several of Mbutu's men. The black fists against a sea of red on their shirts.

"Great," said Tony.

They walked over to Martin and Patrick. Patrick seemed happy to be rotated to the street. Martin was dour as usual.

"He's inside," said Martin. "And he's armed. There's at least one other person inside, a woman we think. We don't know if she's armed or a hostage."

"Contact?" asked Tony.

"None," Martin said. "I'm gonna ask him to give up." He tilted the bullhorn.

"I'll take over from here," said Tony, grabbing at the bullhorn.

"OK, already." Martin pushed it at him.

"What's your fuckin' problem?" Tony asked.

"Somebody needs to take over this investigation," Martin said. "Everyone knows you're screwin' it up."

Tony felt someone grab at his arm. He turned to see Jim holding the fist he was planning to hit Martin with.

"Martin, get your ass back there and do crowd control," Jim said.

Martin walked away mumbling. Patrick followed him. Three other squad cars pulled up and more cops got out with guns drawn.

Tony turned to the other men. "I'm gonna talk to him. No shooting unless he starts, and in that case, you only fire on my signal." Tony lifted the bullhorn. "Larry Drake, I'm Inspector Hill. There's no way out of this. Come out now and I promise you that you'll be treated fairly."

Silence.

Someone walked by a window in the house.

"We're willing to stay here all night if necessary," Tony said. "There's nothing you can—"

A shot hit the side of a cruiser. Tony and Jim drew their weapons, then Tony gave the signal and a barrage of police fire slammed into the small house, shattering windows and splintering the flimsy door.

"Hold!" Tony yelled out, holding up a fist. The shooting stopped.

There was a scream from the house. "No! No!" yelled the voice of a woman. The front door flung open and out came a young girl of about twenty holding a small girl by the hand.

"Don't shoot, please!" She yelled with tears streaming down her face. "We ain't with him!"

Fred Hampton ran from behind a car toward them.

"What the fuck—?!" yelled Jim.

"Get away!" Tony yelled through the bullhorn.

Hampton rushed the woman and young girl to safety. They were put into a patrol car. Tony was on his way to tear Hampton a new asshole when Drake spoke.

"All right, all right!" Drake yelled. "Fuck this, I'm coming out."

"Throw out the weapon first," said Tony on the bullhorn.

Drake threw out a handgun, then walked out of the house with his hands up high. He looked at the angry faces of the police on the street.

The officers rushed out and grabbed Drake. Carter got to him first.

Tony and Jim went over and pulled the officers off him and instructed several officers to go into the house to secure it. The officers complied and Larry Drake watched closely as the cops poured into the home. Only Tony, Jim, and three uniforms remained with Drake.

Jim put away his gun. "Man, for a minute there I thought we were gonna have a stand off," he said.

Carter read Drake his rights while he cuffed Drake's hands behind his back. Carter was rough and punched him in the side. Drake uttered a groan.

"That's enough," said Tony. "Go inside with the others. This man is ours."

Carter was finishing the cuffing of the struggling man when Tony walked up next to Drake. Tony's gun hung lazily in his hand.

Drake jerked his right hand free of the cuff, which was only half on, and grabbed at Tony's gun.

Tony tried to pull his gun back, but Drake had it. Tony grabbed the gun and got a grip on it. They struggled, doing a weird dance on the yellowing lawn.

Carter yelled something. Drake lifted the gun up with Tony's hand still on it, and sent off a shot that whizzed past Jim's face. Jim fell to the ground.

Tony's hand slipped and Drake pulled the weapon away. Drake jerked his body away from Tony and stumbled back, the gun wavering in his hand. Drake fumbled with the weapon raising it at Tony's chest. He pulled the trigger.

For a second, Tony thought it was all over. He saw Pete Carter step in front of him. The bullet caught Carter in the chest and sent him crashing into Tony. They both fell to the ground.

Drake was moving away when his chest exploded in a burst of red. Tony looked up to find Fred Hampton in the shooting stance, his gun barrel still smoking.

"He's down!" yelled Hampton.

"Dammit!" yelled Jim. He raced to check Tony. "You OK, man?"

"Yeah, but the rookie got hit. Get an ambulance."

"They're already here, partner," said Jim.

Tony moved Carter over. He was unconscious. The paramedics descended on him. "You'll have to move away, sir," said a woman.

Tony rolled to his feet, dazed.

Jim went over to check Drake. "Shit, shit, shit!" he cursed. "He's dying!"

"Are you all right, sir?" Hampton asked Tony.

Tony didn't answer. The gravity of what had just happened slammed into him. The flashing police lights bombarded his eyes in succession. He was frozen as he watched Jim desperately try to save Drake.

Tony's gun lay mockingly next to Drake's hand. The other officers rushed out of the house, weapons drawn. Tony watched, unable to move as Jim screamed for help and their only lead in the case bled to death on the lawn, surrounded by police.

15

End of the Line

Tony sat across from Chief Fuller in Fuller's office. It was cool inside, a perk of being in charge.

Since he blew the collar on Larry Drake yesterday, nothing was the same. Hampton was cleared for the shoot—justified homicide—and Carter was in stable condition in the hospital. The bullet had broken three of Carter's ribs under his flak jacket, but no penetration. Lucky bastard.

After the medics pronounced Drake dead, Tony had the horrible realization that Drake had almost killed Jim and would have gotten him if Hampton hadn't shot first.

"Tough break yesterday, Tony." Fuller had a big cigar in his hand. It was not lit.

"Yes, sir," said Tony. "I take full responsibility."

"The mayor was not pleased, but since we killed the bastard it looks good for us, like we took out one of the bad guys."

"Sir, I . . . I haven't been performing lately."

"Don't worry about it. We're all feeling the—"

"I'm resigning from the force, sir."

Fuller put the big cigar down. "Why in God's name—"

"I don't have it anymore, sir."

"I know you don't mean it, Tony," Fuller said. "It's just the pressure, that's all."

"No, I think I do mean it, sir."

"Tony, I need you on this investigation. The mayor will—" Fuller thought better of whatever he was about to say. "OK, take a little vacation, but promise me you'll come back."

"I can't do that. I've decided to leave all this to men better suited for it."

"OK, Tony, so you fucked up on that Drake kid. Everybody fucks up, man."

"I got a cop shot and my partner was almost killed. An inch more and we'd be at Jim's wake right now. And if it wasn't for the Carter kid, you'd be at mine. Not even the greenest rookie would have left his weapon so close to a suspect, even if he was being cuffed," Tony said.

"OK, I'll put you on a desk," Fuller said. "You can supervise the investigation. I can fix this. Just give me a chance."

"I'm afraid the problem is where only I can fix it, Chief, but thanks anyway."

Fuller stood up and Tony was reminded of how big he was. He limped from behind his big desk and faced Tony.

"Don't give up, Tony. We can work this thing out."

"I'm sorry, Chief, I have to do this. I appreciate everything you've done for me. I owe you and I can never repay." Tony took off his shield and put it on Fuller's desk.

They shook hands. Fuller pulled Tony to his massive chest and bear-hugged him.

"I'm considering this a paid leave, Tony," said Fuller. "I know you'll be back."

Tony was silent. He just turned and walked out of the Chief's office. He went to Jim's office and waited.

A half hour later, Jim walked into his office to find Tony sitting at his desk.

"Hey, man," Jim said.

"Hey."

"I, uh, got the info on that new drug. It's spreading fast. It's like crack, but it's selling for more on the street. The state troopers are analyzing some of it, our people are too, and . . . are you OK?"

"I'm quitting the force."

"Jesus." Jim sat down.

"I know what you're gonna say. I've been through it all with Fuller. I need to—"

"Come on, Tony, don't do this to me. Don't let the bastard beat you! You can't give in now. It's just a matter of time before we break this case."

"The bastard" Jim referred to was the street. The street was like a person, the toughest son of a bitch and the most beautiful woman you ever met. It was seductive and brutal at the same time. It offered pleasure, but at a very high price.

Tony knew, however, that the street had not beaten him. He'd beaten himself. He murdered a man and he had to pay for it. But how? He guessed that answer would come from God.

"You can beat this," Jim had said. "I know it. I know you fucked up with Drake, but—"

"I almost got you killed."

"It's as much my fault as it was yours. I knew you weren't a hundred percent. I should have been looking out for you."

Tony loved Jim more then than he ever had. It was almost a believable lie.

"I never told you this, but—" Jim looked away for a moment. "I admire you. I know I seem like I don't give a shit about anything but my job and my dick, but I . . . I really need our friendship. It's important to me. You know how this job is. I need my other half."

Tony stood and shook Jim's hand. Jim's grip was weak. And he couldn't bear to look at Tony as he walked away.

"Call me any time you wanna talk. I'll be here."

"I know that," Tony said. "You know, if Carter hadn't jumped in front of me, I'd be dead."

"I know. He's OK after all, I guess."

"Yeah." Tony laughed a little. "After all I've been through, a white man saves my life."

Tony left, walking through the corridors of 1300 for the last time. He was flipping the script, as the kids said these days. Soon, he would see what the next chapter of his life held.

As he neared the end of the hall, Walter Nicks came out of an office, putting his fedora on his large head. He seemed startled at the sight of Tony. Tony didn't stop. Nicks was about to say something, but Tony passed by him without a word.

Tony got on an elevator and was soon at the front door in the lobby. He waited a moment, then pushed open the big door.

He stepped outside and the humidity wrapped itself around him. The weight of the world was gone, lifted away like a cover from a sleeping man.

16

Tumult

Medina took the city. T-Bone and his minions pumped it into every neighborhood, every school, every place of business they could. It flowed out of the city and into every walk of life. It was embraced from the nearest neighborhood to the outer reaches of the metropolitan area and the money rolled back in.

Medina became the drug of choice and the people couldn't get enough. But with the high-volume usage, there were odd occurrences. For every twenty who used it, one would have a violent reaction.

Some would have seizures and die instantly, while others would break down mentally and hurt themselves or others. No one noticed at first, because strangeness was within the nature of drug use, but slowly, steadily, the new drug began to leave its mark.

In the suburbs of Birmingham, a young art student killed herself by drinking a can of paint.

In the downriver suburbs, a man who thought he had superpowers lost a race with a train and was cut in two on the tracks.

In Detroit, a young man drowned, after having a seizure while trying to swim across the river to Canada.

On the east side, a mother sold her eight-year-old daughter to a man for a hit of Medina, then killed the man when he tried to molest the young girl.

The hospitals were filling up with cases of people sick, unconscious, and just plain crazy from contact with the drug.

Medina was selling fast, but the users were dying off or going crazy just as quickly. It was an inner-city nightmare, a high-tech plague, out of control.

The police force had been focusing on the Handyman but now they had an even bigger worry—the new drug was causing acts of random violence. Manpower was diverted from catching the Handyman, who could now operate in the center of the chaos.

Carol Salinsky stood across the street from the police scene. A young girl had been taken to the hospital, her dress soaked with blood. Police questioned three teenagers while photographers took pictures. A crazed student had ambushed her and several others with a lead pipe after school let out. No one knew the reason for the attack.

Her unit director prompted her, "OK, Carol, we're live in three, two, one."

"The summer came early in the city. The heat driving everyone into shorts and T-shirts. But summer won't be coming for young Shauna Williams. She was killed by a lead pipe–wielding assailant only moments after Taft Middle School let out for summer recess. A massive manhunt is under way for the killer."

Salinsky walked over to a school crossing sign covered with graffiti.

"I have learned that this is another drug-related slaying," Salinsky said. "Several rocks of the new street drug called Medina, or cold Medina, were found at the scene of the crime. The city, county, and state police have verified that this new drug is cocaine-based and creates a strong, hallucinogenic effect."

Salinsky walked over to a crowd of kids.

"Street sources tell me that Medina drives some users insane," said Salinsky. "The drug picks its victims at random and the streets are filling with danger. Police warn that Medina is ten times as addictive as crack and dangerous. And with the Handyman still at large, the summer looks like a vast graveyard, waiting to be filled—"

17

The Prince Breaks Wide

The Prince was quiet as the bright new van rolled down Interstate 94 toward Chicago. The Professor drove, happily sipping beer from a long, swirling plastic straw that led to a bottle on the floor.

Donna and the Prince sat in the rear of the van, counting part of the large bundle of cash that T-Bone had paid them. Small bills. Drug dealers always gave you small bills.

The Prince was glad to be leaving Detroit. It had been a fruitful enterprise, but if they had stayed a week longer, they would all be dead. They had left a time bomb ticking in the drug-using populace.

"How long before the shit goes off?" the Prince asked the Professor.

"Probably a few weeks before people catch on."

"Then all hell breaks loose," said the Prince, laughing.

"We were lucky to get out. I read the papers every day looking for signs," the Professor said. He took a big sip of his drink.

"Yeah, like that bitch who drunk that paint," said the Prince. "She was so fucked up on that shit, she probably thought it was a milkshake."

"That's actually very likely," said the Professor. "The drug would produce a hallucination like that."

"I'm just glad to get away from those damned drug pushers. Those boys are some mean-ass muthafuckas," said the Prince.

"I kinda like them," said Donna, as she placed the money in neat stacks. "They grow on you."

"You fuckin' bitch!" said the Prince, knocking some bills from her hand onto the floor. "You gone just sit up here and say that shit right in my face." His eyes narrowed to evil slits.

"Yeah, so what?"

"I was gone wait until we got to Chicago to call yo ass out, but since you wanna dis me, I'll do it right here."

"What? I don't even know what you talkin' 'bout!"

"I can't believe you gone sit there and lie right up in my face."

"I ain't lying. I ain't gotta lie to you."

The Professor withdrew his attention from them. They always fought like this, swearing and sometimes even coming to blows. The strangest thing was they were married and had been for about five years. Married drug pushers, fighting like the goddamned Honeymooners. It was funny, yet there was also a sickness about it.

"I don't know what you talkin' 'bout," said Donna.

"Bitch, don't try to play me, I saw you."

"Saw me what?" Donna said, smiling.

"I saw you fuckin' that dog-assed drug pusher in the warehouse."

"I'm sorry, baby." Donna began to take her top off.

"Bullshit!" yelled the Prince. He was shaking with lust and rage. "Was that the only time you fucked him? And don't lie to me. I know you."

"Yes."

"Lying fuckin' bitch!"

Donna closed the partition separating the driver's cab from the van's rear.

The Prince tore at his clothes and forced Donna on the carpet. Stacks of bills fell on them. He faked hitting her, slapping his hands together. She yelled and smiled under him.

Donna grabbed her husband and forced his head into her bosom. He loved it when she lied and teased him. The only thing he liked more was watching her have sex with other men.

Donna smiled as the Prince kissed her hard stomach. He would not ever want anyone to know his secret. It was contrary to everything that he represented. He was a badass, a pusher, dangerous. He had to keep up his image at all times. What would people think if they knew he was impotent?

Poor bastard, thought Donna. Liked to watch his wife get screwed by other men, then go down on her while she told him about it.

It was an ideal marriage. Most normal married couples spent their whole lives lying to each other and playing games. The men acted out the loving husband role while fucking every waitress and secretary they could find. Wives spent years getting half-assed sex and fighting their desires for satisfaction. But not Donna Ann Mayfield. Hers was a marriage based on personal honesty and selflessness.

The Prince's affliction was a tragedy, but they made the most of it. She began to whisper to him about Steven Mayo as he raged between her legs.

The van roared down the freeway into Jackson, Michigan. Detroit was a memory as they departed, leaving their troubles behind them.

PART III

COLD MEDINA

The Other Side

Tony sat on a bench in Palmer Park and watched parents and their children on an old playground. It wasn't yet midday but it was already starting to heat up. The heatwave was still on, and soon it would be too hot and muggy to be outside.

Tony thought about his son Moe and how happy the boy was to see more of his father since Tony had left the force.

Nikki was understanding about his decision and very happy. She could see that he was better for the decision.

Maybe he had made the right choice after all, he thought. He was sure Orris Martin and idiots like him thought so. The official word was that Tony had taken an authorized paid leave. There were stories in the newspapers about his departure. He refused to read them.

Tony's existence on the other side of the badge was only two weeks old, but seemed longer. Without the hustle of police work, the days dragged. He was painfully aware of the passage of time. The part of him that missed the job nagged him daily.

And the job missed him. The city was on fire with a new drug called Medina. Violent crimes were up, the police were scrambling to handle the increase. New rookies were turned out of the academy early to help. Reserves were called in. And all the while, the Handyman was still at large.

Tony tried to forget these things and enjoy his day. It was no longer his official concern. He just wanted to rest and savor civilianhood. But soon, other, more terrible thoughts came into his mind. He saw Irene Simon's haggard, tortured face, her tired body, having sex with men and then murdering them in cold blood.

I hope nobody stops you when you want to die.

Leaving the force did not stop these demons. Part of him felt that by quitting he was trying to cheat the debt he owed society for the death of Darryl Simon. Tony had snuffed out one of God's creations and that action had resulted in even more death. He was accountable for the lives of Darryl Simon and his sister's victims.

Murder was against everything that he believed in, everything he stood for. Tony had dedicated his life to stopping people who did such things, and now he was one of them.

I hope nobody stops you. . . .

He had seen death and killed in the line of duty, but it had always been justified. But not with Simon.

His father's rage dwelled within him for many years and it finally poured out upon Darryl Simon with fatal consequences. People go through life knowing very little of what they are truly capable of, Tony thought. Under the proper circumstances, anyone could do what he did.

. . . when you want to die.

Tony walked back toward his car. The temperature had already gone up several degrees in the last few minutes. Others sensed the change too and started to leave.

Tony spotted a woman playing with her daughter, tossing a colored ball back and forth. A few feet away, a man smoking a cigarette by a dumpster watched the lady and her child.

Tony pegged the man as a drug addict. He was thin, nervous, and moved sluggishly. One of his hands was shoved inside the pocket of his dirty jacket.

The addict watched the woman and her daughter and moved a few steps closer, stopping by a tree.

Tony changed direction and circled around behind the addict.

The addict moved in closer to his prey. There was something different about this guy, Tony thought. Most crackheads were scared. They had to push themselves to action. Drugs stole their confidence, making them apprehensive about their chances of success. But not this guy. He seemed sure of himself as he did his slow drug-addict walk toward the woman. Tony moved closer to him, careful not to make any noise.

Tony realized then that he'd left his gun in his car. No matter, he thought. He was not going to let this guy attack an innocent woman and baby. He would stop him, somehow.

The addict was about ten feet from the woman and her daughter now. Then he suddenly burst into a run toward them. The woman looked up and saw the addict coming. She pulled the little girl to her chest, stood and backed off, but by then, the addict was upon her.

"All right, bitch—"

The addict was yanked away from the frightened woman and fell backwards on his ass.

The addict looked up to see Tony's angry face, framed by the midday sun.

"You and me, asshole," Tony said.

The addict looked at Tony, and for a moment it seemed as if he would take him up on the offer. Instead, he scrambled away.

Tony watched the addict leave, making sure he would not return. Then he turned to the woman, but she was gone. She had run away during the altercation. Smart woman, Tony thought.

Tony went to his car. He'd never seen an addict so bold and certain of himself. Then he remembered the new drug. Medina. He'd read that one of the effects was bolstered confidence. Jesus, he thought. The only thing worse than a crackhead was a brave one.

Tony got into his car and drove away from the park. He wanted to get into the neighborhoods. That always made him feel better. He was in his cruising car, an old Ford that looked like a piece of shit, but had a good engine and air conditioning. Tony used it to drive the inner-city neighborhoods. He couldn't afford to take the good car where he was going. Many of the more clever rollers also used such old cars. They called them hoopties. The rollers drove the hooptie when making drug deliveries because if they were caught by the police, their cars were often confiscated and sold in forfeiture.

Tony drove to the east side, turned onto a residential street, and cruised. He checked his Beretta under the armrest.

He drove slowly. He suspected criminal activity all around him. Many houses were gutted, burned-out, or abandoned. Waist-high weeds and garbage were common. No wonder the young boys chose drugs, he thought. This would drive anyone to desperation.

Tony drove for about an hour before he found himself on Anglin

Street. He parked across the street from his old childhood house, settling in behind a car with three flat tires.

Tony looked at the burned-out shell that had once been his home. The grass was three feet high, the windows boarded up, and he could smell the stench of rotting garbage.

He closed his eyes and imagined the street as he had known it as a child: bright with color and loud with activity. It seemed his old street had always been filled with kids playing, laughing, and getting dirtier by the minute. The sky was blue and clouds passed in wonderful shapes. The wind whipped leisurely, bringing the smells of trees and cooking food. Easy life then, play was work and the day seemed endless, filled with fun, adventure, and friends. What awful fate could have ended all this . . .

A shot rang out. Tony focused in the direction of the explosion. It came from an inhabited house about three doors away from his old house. Tony remembered that a family named Reed had lived there. He removed his Beretta.

Probably a crackhouse, he thought. But there was not the great activity that you usually saw in a dope house. It could be a supply station or a money drop-off point, he reasoned.

Tony watched the front of the house. The door was flung open and two men wrestled outside. One of the men was young, eighteen or so. The other was older, about forty. They fought as the older man tried to take a gun from the young man's hand. About six other people, all black, followed them as they fell off the porch and onto the ground.

The men writhed in the dirt as a startled woman screamed in horror. The young one pushed off his older attacker and stood in front of him with the gun.

Tony watched and fought the urge to identify himself. He was not technically an officer anymore. Before he could make up his mind, the young man fired a shot into his would-be assailant, wounding him in the leg. The woman fainted and another man carried her back into the house.

Tony watched several young boys drag the wounded man back into the house as two other men laughed and slapped each other five.

Tony froze in the car. His eyes widened and focused on one of the men. It was difficult in the clothes he wore, but Tony was sure of the face. It was Fred Hampton, the hotshot rookie. The other man, a black man, Tony did not know, but Tony would bet that he was a cop, too. Hampton's regular partner, Pete Carter, was still on sick leave from taking the bullet that was meant for Tony.

The cops had to be dirty, he thought. They had just witnessed a shooting in what was probably a dope house and had done nothing. Hampton and the man went back inside.

Tony waited. He was angry and curious. Dirty cops were a plague on the force. And even though Tony knew they existed, he just had to know what this was all about. Deep down, he admitted that he was just trying to be a cop again. But he had every right to be a concerned citizen, he reasoned.

A half hour later, Hampton walked out of the house with his companion, laughing and carrying a small satchel.

Hampton and the other man got into a car and drove away. After they reached the corner, Tony followed them, careful not to look at the drug house as he passed.

Tony had forgotten about the shooting he'd witnessed. He was after much bigger prey now. The rookies were assholes, but he never expected one to be on the take. There had to be money in the satchel. He would follow them and see where that package went.

Tony thought about his first days as a new officer. Soon after you started, the dirty cops would approach you to see if you wanted to join up with them. Once you were in, that was it. There was no turning back.

As long as there had been cops, some took money from the bad guys. Everyone knew about it, but no one did anything. Cops were loyal to each other, even if one cop was dirty. Most played it straight, even though the pay was shitty.

It used to be that the cops would only take from gamblers, the numbers men, and the pimps. Those were "good" crimes, easy vices that left no guilt behind. Now, they took money from these vile drug pushers, many of whom were like the Devil himself.

Tony spent the rest of the morning tailing Hampton, despite the fact that he had mixed feelings about trying to bust a man who had helped save his life. Hampton had hit Larry Drake off-balance and under pressure. Dropped him with one shot.

Then it occurred to Tony that Hampton did not have to shoot Drake. Drake was falling, trying to hold that heavy gun. Hampton dropped him before anyone else could even draw a weapon. There was no warning, Hampton had just shot. Maybe Drake was shot because Hampton was afraid of what he might say if interrogated.

Tony followed Hampton and his friend like a pro, hanging back in traffic, spinning off on side streets, and taking the chance to pick them up again on main thoroughfares.

Tony grew angrier as he saw them stop and dispense the money among the police force. It was like watching the rollers sell their wares. Slick handshakes while passing a wad of cash, smooth exchanges in cruisers.

It had to be a regular payoff run, and since this was Union territory, it was not a mystery who supplied the cash. What bothered him most was that it was almost impossible for rookies to put this kind of thing together by themselves. There had to be officers in it somewhere.

Tony followed the discouraging trail to the west side of town. The other man was indeed a cop. He seemed to know all the officers they paid off. The pair turned south onto Dexter Avenue. Tony caught a red light. But their car went only halfway up the block and stopped. Hampton and the other cop got out of the car and walked into a building.

Tony didn't have to keep following them. Once he saw the familiar red, black, and green sign and the huge hands breaking the shackles on their wrists, he knew. It was the Brotherhood's Mother Chapter.

2

Mexican Village

Detroit's Mexican Village is located on the city's southwest side. It is a small district, created by the city's small Latino population. Restaurants line the streets, boasting colorful designs and beckoning diners to come in and spend their hard-earned cash.

John "Cut" Jefferson walked out of the El Grande Restaurant filled with spicy food and beer. He had not been in public since he made the hit on the Union van. He was no fool. Even with the Medina surge, T-Bone would be looking for him.

Medina. He was sick of hearing the name. The Union was running the whole damned city with that shit. The popularity of the drug had surpassed crack in its intensity. He couldn't even begin to get his hands on whatever they used to make it. He thought about having it analyzed by a scientist or something but he didn't even know where to begin.

Cut had gotten a few rocks of the new drug and tried it. The shit was bad. The high was intense, unusual, and very short. It took a great effort of will to keep himself from smoking any more. But he was strong. He'd resisted drugs for years.

Cut became obsessed with learning Medina's secrets. After his experiment, he banned its use in his crew and started asking about the drug on the street. So far, he'd learned nothing.

Cut had closed one drug house and more would probably follow. He was becoming poorer by the minute. His profits were down and he was losing customers and rollers to the Union. After years of successful drug dealing, he was becoming just another punk with a high in his pocket for sale.

Cut had even thought about joining the Union, becoming one of the supervisors, but that was not an attractive proposition. He was used to being a king, and once you had a taste of that, nothing else would do. Besides, he reasoned, he had killed two of their people. He couldn't just walk up and ask for a job. He would be dead before the words got out of his mouth. No, he would ride out this feud and work harder to get into the Medina game. Sooner or later, he would find an opening. He just hoped that there was something left for him to be in control of when it was over.

Cut walked to the parking lot with his bodyguards on either side and stood a safe distance away as one of them started his car. He waited a moment while it ran to make sure that it wasn't wired with a bomb or some shit. Although a car bomb was not the usual style of drug dealers, he wasn't taking any chances. After several minutes, he got in and relaxed in the plush backseat, closing his eyes.

"Back to the crib," he said lazily. "And don't be speedin'. I don't need no shit from the cops." He closed his eyes, took a deep breath, and listened to the car's engine hum.

It was good to be out in the world, Cut thought. He was not the type who could stay isolated for long. Maybe he would take a little cruise around the neighborhood before he went back to his home. He had been staying at six different places since the hit on the Union. It would be nice to get back to a stable place of residence.

Cut heard a butane lighter ignite in the front seat, followed by the stinging aroma of Medina.

"Hey, I know I don't smell that—" Cut opened his eyes.

Laughter came from the front seat.

"What the fuck is so funny?" asked Cut.

"You, you dead-ass muthafucka," laughed one of his bodyguards.

Cut saw a smoking pipe of Medina in one of the bodyguard's hands, and in the other he held a gun, pointed at Cut's face.

3

Termination

"I mean it!" T-Bone yelled into the phone. "I don't care what the fuck they say. Pull the shit, all of it! Kill them if you have to, but just do it!"

He slammed down the phone and threw a chair against a wall. He kicked another chair and cursed when he hurt his foot.

K-9 walked out of the room in the Southfield house as quietly as he could.

Things were falling apart. Medina had proven to be just what he first expected—a great product, profitable, and popular. But in the several weeks since introducing it, the bodies were piling up. People were dying or slowly going crazy and there was no profit in corpses. Even worse, his workers started to use it and became addicted. And now, they were deserting him, going crazy from the drug.

The Big Three, no Big Two he remembered, were still loyal, but their people were killing each other, robbing houses, stealing money, doing anything to get their hands on Medina.

T-Bone ordered a stoppage in production, but the way it was set up, the dealers were able to keep making it. He had Mayo take Dennis, their makeshift chemist, off the production line, but not before Dennis had made several large batches of the chemical and sent them out. So T-Bone was scrambling to stop the hysteria that was out there and restore order.

He realized he was close to losing everything. He thought about his father and the man's lifelong belief that his son was destined to be a screwup. T-Bone's hatred burned as he threw more furniture.

The drug was out of control and the money had stopped coming in. Santana and his men were paid up, but they would want more soon. He was going to try to save his business but had to face the fact that he might fail.

T-Bone had several emergency plans for situations like this. They were each different in concept, but all involved one common step.

He got up and went to find K-9.

He had to keep the boy close until he knew for certain that he had to close down his business. In that event, K-9 would have to disappear. K-9 was a wonder, but possessed too much dangerous knowledge. T-Bone would have to make sure the boy did not leave his sight.

T-Bone walked into the small back room where K-9 lived. It was like a child's room, messy and colorful. There were two televisions and comic books littered the floor. But the boy was nowhere to be found.

T-Bone panicked for a second, then calmed himself. K-9 often hid himself in closets and other darkened areas when he was afraid and lately, T-Bone had been yelling and screaming like a madman about everything.

T-Bone looked in the room's closet. Nothing. T-Bone's heart began to race. He knew that K-9 was not stupid, indeed he was a genius of sorts. Maybe he had figured if T-Bone's business was crumbling, that his life wasn't worth anything.

That was silly, T-Bone told himself. K-9 was not dumb, but he was not smart enough to come to that conclusion.

T-Bone searched the house, going from room to room, calling the boy. Still no sign of him.

T-Bone grabbed a gun and searched the outside of the house, then got into his car and cruised the area. But the boy had vanished.

T-Bone went to a pay phone and dialed a number.

"Hey, it's me . . . yeah I'm on a pay phone. Look, my little friend is missing . . . no, I don't want him back. I want his ass eliminated. Put the word out, a hundred thousand for his little fucked-up ass . . . I want him gone!"

T-Bone hung up, then drove back home. He hit the dash of the Cadillac angrily. Everything was going wrong.

He picked up his car phone and dialed. He had another job to attend to. It was time to get in touch with the police.

4

One in a Million

The girl danced seductively in front of Magilla. Her long braids, dirty and frayed at the ends, covered her drug-ridden face. She stumbled as she did her drugged-out striptease for him.

The girl was down to her last stitch of clothing, a pair of silk panties. She wriggled out of the underwear and fell on her side. She laughed a little then got up, standing naked before him.

Magilla sat on the end of the bed, unaroused by the dance.

He looked different these days. His face had deep lines etched in it, his cheeks were hollow, his skin ashen. He was thinner by some thirty pounds and actually looked better for it.

Jamilla came to him. She had left her sometime boyfriend, Phillip, and taken up permanent residence with Magilla.

She tried to walk seductively, but still looked high. She got to Magilla and knelt between his legs.

He took a rock of Medina and lit it up for her. She smoked it quickly.

Magilla put her on the bed and put his hands to her throat. She didn't resist. He often liked kinky stuff.

"Come on," she whispered as Magilla squeezed harder, but soon she couldn't breathe and she fought him, slamming her fists into his face and body.

Magilla shifted his weight on her and tightened his grip. He could almost hear her heart racing inside her, struggling to work against the lack of precious oxygen. Soon her pounding fists were harmless love taps on his sides.

Magilla stood over her body for a few minutes, running his hand over the corpse, his eyes closed.

He let the power of the dead girl fill him. Soon he was exhausted and lay down next to her, contented.

A few days ago, after smoking a huge quantity of Medina, Magilla had solved the riddle of existence.

Life was not a sun-soaked happy existence, filled with family, friends, cookouts, and shit. That was a dream. Real life was a painful, intense, and mostly unhappy existence, a shadow zone of despair, doubt, and hopelessness.

He began to see the profundity in life's simple things. The beauty of an open wound, the art of a knife edge, the depth of blood. Yes, his eyes had opened in ways that he'd never dreamed possible. Regular people could not see it, but he had sight beyond normal comprehension—he could see into the human soul.

Magilla had figured out how to drain the life out of a person and make their life force his own. For a while, he thought that he was becoming a crackhead, that his newfound knowledge was drug-induced. He used Medina almost nonstop each day and he even occasionally had blackouts, blank periods when he couldn't remember what he had done. He figured that it was just lack of sleep. He stayed up for three days straight last week, thinking and planning how he would use his new powers.

But he wasn't an addict like those dog-assed crackheads who frequented the house. His use of the drug helped to fuel his already formidable intellect. He had taken to reading the dictionary every day and using new words that he found. He began reading the newspaper and even watched public television to expand his mind.

Medina was getting scarce due to its popularity, but he had hoarded a great deal of it to keep the house going and was still making it every day with that chemical stuff. He still had a lot of it left in his bedroom for his own personal use.

The phone rang. Magilla picked it up and heard the voice of Steven Mayo.

"I hear you still selling the shit, gorilla," Mayo said. "I told you to stop it."

"And I told you. I don't take orders from you. I answer to a higher power—me."

"You dead, muthafucka."

Magilla laughed.

"I'm not playing, fat-ass bitch!" Mayo yelled.

"I know," Magilla said.

"You fucked up on that shit right now, ain'tcha?"

"If you mean Medina, yes I use it, but not like you think."

"Stop selling it. That shit is killing niggas left and right!" Mayo said.

"That's not my problem."

"Oh, yes it is, lardass."

"I have a question for you," Magilla said.

"What?"

"You think you could read better if you got Hooked On Phonics?"

"Fuck you! OK, dead muthafucka. This was your last chance. Now, I'm coming to get you myself."

"I'm counting on it," Magilla said.

Mayo hung up.

Magilla laughed and looked for another hit of Medina. This was Mayo's third call today. He was on a mission to stop Magilla from producing Medina and to destroy the chemical used to make it.

Magilla had seen some people flip out after using it, but they were just weak. It took a real man to use like he did. Mayo was just trying to keep him down. He could say anything he wanted about Medina, but the people wanted it and he needed it. So fuck Mayo. Medina was a mere high in the hands of weak, foolish crackheads, but Magilla knew its deeper powers.

He found a stash of the drug in a sock under his bed. The pale blue crystals clinked together as he lifted it.

Magilla had assembled his own team of bodyguards, paid with Medina or money, to protect him from the Union. He laughed again. Soon, there would be no Union. Because of Medina, everyone was going their own way, making their own deals, and Mayo and his flunkies were scrambling to keep up, trying to keep what they called order. They would see that Medina was greater than anything they had ever known.

Magilla looked at the girl's corpse. Her power was so sweet when it rushed into him. He alone knew the secret of life's power and how to absorb it. It was like drinking water for him. He had not shared the information with anyone. They wouldn't understand. Only he had the power to make it work. He simply opened his mind and let Jamilla's life force course through his body. She was as sweet in death as she had been in life. Now he had all of her, forever.

Magilla had no idea why he was not affected by the drug like some of the others. He figured he was just special. And he was right. If he had gone to a doctor, he would have learned that he was an extremely rare individual, possessed of a metabolism that could handle the drug in large quantities. One in a million.

Magilla lit the rock of Medina, took a long drag, and thought about seeing Steven Mayo.

"Come and get me," he said.

The Conversation Piece

Tony walked up to the apartment of the rookie Fred Hampton. Hampton lived in a nice complex on the west side, near Wyoming Street.

Since he'd seen Hampton doling out the payoff money, Tony was undecided about what he would do. He thought of going to Jim or the Chief, but he had to make sure first. Besides, he reasoned, it didn't make a whole lot of sense.

But then it had come to him, like the name retrieved from the tip of your tongue. The money. That was the only thing about the Handyman crimes that didn't make sense.

He had asked himself, Why did the killer take money from drug dealers, but not their drugs? Where did the rookies get the money for payoffs? Why would the rookies be working with the Brotherhood to pay off cops? And how could a white killer walk unnoticed in Detroit's ultra-black community?

The answer he got made sense. The killer could be a cop. And not just one.

It was a long shot, but it made sense to Tony. The cops killed the drug dealers, stole the money, and made the murders look like a psycho committed them. The blond hair sounded like a Mbutu idea. He had a PhD in racial politics.

So Tony decided to talk to Hampton and make sure there was a connection. If there was, then he would bust Hampton and go to the department. If not, well, he didn't care about a bunch of dirty cops.

Tony rang the doorbell. The door was opened by a surprised Fred Hampton.

"Come on in, sir," said Hampton.

Hampton looked shocked, but then again he should have been. Tony had no reason to be there.

"You'll have to excuse the place. I'm a bachelor, you know."

"Thanks," said Tony. He swept past Hampton and surveyed the room with phony interest. Tony had his interrogation attitude on, and he was trying to infuse his every movement with it.

"Can I offer you something to drink?"

"No," he said in a hard voice, then, "Thanks," as an afterthought. Tony sat down in a chair and stared at Hampton.

Hampton sat down on the sofa opposite him. He looked uncomfortable.

"Well sir, what brings—"

Tony removed his gun.

Hampton's eyes showed fear. Tony's eyes were filled with great energy.

Hampton looked at Tony as though the latter had gone crazy. Now Tony knew he had the man's full attention.

Hampton breathed a little easier when Tony put the gun on the coffee table and sat back. Tony stared at Hampton, then at the gun, then back at Hampton.

Realization showed on Hampton's face. Putting the gun on the table meant it was a Conversation Piece, an archaic police tradition that started in the fifties when there was a big corruption investigation in which over forty cops were indicted.

During the interrogations, the investigator would slam his piece on the table in front of the suspected cop and begin to question him.

It was an act of disrespect and aggression. The meaning was, if the suspect was guilty of betraying the police code of honor, he should just kill himself and get it over with.

Tony was certain Hampton knew what the Conversation Piece meant. It was information every rookie was told in the academy.

"What's going on, sir?" Hampton asked.

Silence. Tony stared him down.

"I don't get it, sir, what do you want?"

Another look, even colder.

"Well, if you don't want to talk, I'll—"

"You know," Tony said.

"Look, sir, this is my day off and I want to try to enjoy what's left of it, so—"

"Taking some time to spend your payoff money?"

Hampton was shocked but did a good job covering it. After all, he was a pro. He knew that whenever he was threatened, aggression was necessary.

"I think you'd better get the fuck out of my house before I kick your ass out—sir." Hampton stood, clinching his fists.

"I don't think so," said Tony. He reached into his jacket again and Hampton looked at the gun and was about to lunge for it, when Tony dropped a videotape on the table.

"I don't feel like playing with you," Tony said. "I saw you on the payoff run and I videotaped it. This tape is the story of a cop who distributes drug payoffs to other cops. Are you getting the picture?"

Hampton sat down and stared at the tape and the gun. He had a look that said his young life was over.

"I know a great deal about what you do, and what I don't know, you're getting ready to tell me or this tape will find its way to Internal Affairs."

Hampton grabbed the gun and pointed it at Tony. He looked at Tony and froze, his fingers trembling on the weapon.

Hampton looked at Tony fiercely, but the stare wavered and he began to shake even more.

Tony smiled a little. Hampton was obviously guilty. And Tony was an expert on guilt lately. He placed his hand on Hampton's trembling one, removing the gun.

Then he fired point blank in Hampton's face.

Hampton jumped as the hammer struck. The impotent clicking of the weapon was like someone jabbing a needle into his skin.

"I guess no one ever told you about a Conversation Piece. It's never loaded."

Tony put a clip into the gun, cocked it, and rested it on his lap.

"Now that we understand each other, let's talk."

"You working for IAD?" asked Hampton. He was still shaken.

"Don't insult me, Hampton. I'm a cop."

"Then what do you want?"

"I want to know if cops committed the Handyman murders for the money."

"Wha—what?! No."

"No?"

"What I said. No. We ain't killing nobody."

"Bullshit!" yelled Tony. "The killer slips in and out of black neighborhoods and he's white with blond hair?"

"We ain't—"

"Did you know that we were getting a search warrant for the Shalon Street dope house right before the Handyman knocked it off?"

"So what?"

"So, rookie, only a cop could know these things, do these things in Detroit and never be suspected."

"I'm telling you man, we ain't killing nobody for the money."

"But it is drug money?"

"How do I know you won't tell on me anyway?"

"You don't, but you do know I will give the tape to IAD if you don't talk."

Hampton waited a moment, then, "This ain't got nothing to do with the Handyman."

"Is it drug money?"

"Yeah."

"Where from?"

"I don't know. We just pick it up, different places."

Tony knew he was probably telling the truth. The rookies never knew anything, in fact, there were probably very few cops who had an abundance of information. It kept any one person from giving it all away. But somewhere, there was a person who had all the answers.

"If you don't know where the money comes from, how do you know it's not the Handyman money?"

"I don't. Like I said, we just pick it up."

Tony put his gun away. If Hampton tried anything, he could still get a shot off. He poised for the big question. Hampton was holding back and he was going to see how much.

"Why did you go into the Brotherhood's headquarters on your last run?"

Hampton looked away from Tony for a moment, thinking. "I need a drink." He started to get up.

"No drink, Hampton, answer the question."

"I'm a member."

"No, I checked that out," Tony lied. "Now that you've used up your one lie, tell me the truth. How is Mbutu in on all this?"

Hampton looked as if someone had told him that his whole family had been murdered.

"There are a couple of cops who are members. And don't ask me who. You want to turn me in, fine, but I'm not giving up any names. Look man, this thing's been going on long before I was even a cop. I don't know anything but where to take the money."

He was telling the truth, unfortunately, thought Tony. These dirty cops were just like the goddamned criminals. They were smart. They kept the bagmen out of the loop.

"OK, let's say I believe you for now," Tony said. "Now I want to know if you had to shoot Larry Drake or did you want to shut him up?"

"He was trying to get off a shot at you!" said Hampton. "I had to get him. For Christ's sake, I saved your life!"

"Maybe," said Tony refusing to show any compassion.

"Why are you doing this? You're not a cop anymore. Everyone's saying that you went nuts on the job. Is that why you're doing this?" asked Hampton.

The question made Tony angry. He was doing it because he still *needed* to be a cop, despite his fall from grace. But that was none of Hampton's business.

"It's none of your concern why," said Tony. "I just want to know one more thing."

"What?"

"It's been my experience that cops on the take hang out with drug dealers, so they know a lot of shit they can never tell. Who's making this new drug?"

"The Union. It's a real gang, you know," said Hampton.

"But why are they poisoning their customers?"

"I don't think they knew what they were getting into. Anyway, their whole operation is falling apart. They even got a special contract out on some guy."

"Special, what's special about it?" Tony asked.

"It's for a hundred grand."

"A lot of money for some lowlife. Who is he and why do they want him killed?"

"I don't know," said Hampton. "I just heard the rumor. It could be anything—money, drugs, a woman. They're all over each other."

"If you do find out, I want you to contact me."

"What am I now, an informant?"

"In a word, yes."

"Fuck that."

"Have it your way, but if I find out you've been holding out on me, I go right to IAD. I'll be leaving now. You've been a gracious host."

"So, that's it?" asked Hampton.

"Yeah, I guess."

"What about the rest of it? You're not going to say anything?"

"No."

"I don't believe that. I want some kind of . . . assurance."

"You're not in a position to demand anything. You're a dirty cop. You've given up all of those rights."

"I should've let that Drake kid shoot your ass."

Tony grabbed Hampton, but Hampton managed to shake free and take a step back.

"It's not too late for you to be a cop again," Tony said. "I'm sure it's not easy to get out, but if you don't, you'll be looking over your shoulder for the rest of your career."

"I can take care of myself."

"Really? Well, my experience has been that this kind of thing catches up to you one way or another, sooner or later. You've got to get out before that happens and just hope for the best."

"So, you're not going to tell," said Hampton. "You're going to be generous to us all, huh?"

"I made my choice about taking money a long time ago."

"What about the tape?"

"Keep it. I don't need it anymore," Tony said.

"Is this the only copy?" Hampton grabbed the tape.

Tony just laughed, then left.

Tony left the apartment and quickly got into his car. Hampton seemed to be just another stupid rookie in over his head. Hampton's interrogation hurt his theory that cops were committing the Handyman murders. But just because Hampton didn't know who was doing the killing, didn't mean some other cops weren't behind it all.

Tony drove away, his mind still working on his damaged theory.

Inside, Hampton put the tape in his VCR, fumbling with shaky hands. He wondered what exactly Tony had filmed. He held his breath when the picture came on screen. He looked at it and began to fast forward. He didn't believe his eyes. He went through the entire tape, determined to see everything that was on it. Once he reached the end, he stopped, turned off the television, and threw the remote against the wall.

The entire tape was old episodes of *The Cosby Show.*

6

Boston-Edison

The Handyman watched the red door with intensity. The houses in the historical Boston-Edison district were huge and ornate, dating back to a time when the city's elite lived there.

The killer stood behind a row of trees at a house next to the big colonial house with the red door on Boston Street. Soon, his next target would come through that door. This one would be more difficult than the others, but he understood that the remaining targets would be the hardest to get. But he was confident. After all, he was the Handyman. He was no murderer as the newspapers said. He was an avenger, but they were too stupid to see the difference. Still, he liked the name. It was amusing.

The killer had followed this particular one off and on for several days, watching his moves and routines. The target was careful, but he would be killed, just like the others.

His victims were evil men, he thought. They sold poison, killed innocents, and hurt women and children. They should welcome him and the death he brought. Their sin was a hundred times worse. They had created him.

The killer tensed as his target, a fat man in a white shirt, exited the house along with his bodyguards. One guard was huge, the other was a thin man. Their weapons bulged under their coats. They looked around, then flanked the man in the white shirt and walked down the long walkway to the Lexus at the curb.

The Handyman flipped the knife, catching the blade in his gloved hand. He could use his gun and maybe hit one of the guards, but it would alert the other two and then he might lose his prey. He didn't care about the guards, but the white-shirted man could not be shot.

He was about twenty-five feet away from the men. He moved closer to the three men, careful not to make any noise.

The three men moved closer to the Lexus. The killer readied himself, waiting for an opening.

The small guard checked out the inside of the car while the big guard scanned the area.

The killer was closer now, about fifteen feet away.

"It's OK," the small guard said, then headed for the driver's door.

The big bodyguard opened the door for the white-shirted man.

The Handyman threw the knife at the big guard's head. It struck the big bodyguard in the side of the neck as the car's engine started.

The killer raced toward the man in the white shirt, who jumped headfirst into the car, but didn't quite make it. His lower half dangled out the door, his expensive shoes hitting the curb.

The bodyguard pulled the knife from his neck. Blood ran from the wound. He staggered in shock, but managed to reach for his gun.

But the killer was upon him. He placed his gun in the big guard's face and pulled the trigger.

The man in the white shirt pulled himself further into the car yelling, "Drive, goddammit!"

The car took off, knocking the Handyman to the ground. He dropped his gun. The killer scrambled to his feet, grabbed his gun from the ground, but the car was gone.

The killer was angry. Then he noticed lights being turned on in the darkened houses nearby.

He ran.

The killer moved through backyards, jumping fences and avoiding dogs, until he came to Woodward Avenue. He pulled his hood tighter in the light, making sure no one could see his face. His gloved hands were shoved in his pockets.

He walked for a block. Pain from an old wound in his shoulder flared up. He cursed himself for failing to get his man. Now the man in the white shirt would be even more careful.

The killer darted into an alley where his car was parked. He headed toward it, then saw a man trying to force the door. The killer gripped the gun that was still in his jacket and pointed it toward the man.

The car thief saw the killer and walked toward him, holding a crowbar.

"This your car, ain't it? Gimme the keys," said the man. The thief had a haggard, angry look.

The killer pulled the trigger inside his pocket and his jacket exploded. The man took the slug in the chest and fell backwards, hitting the car.

The killer got into the car and pulled off over the man's body. He backed up over the corpse again, before driving into the night.

7

The Prince in Chi-Town

"**Y**es. No problem my brotha," said the Prince with a smile into the telephone. "We will be there tomorrow at six a.m. sharp with the product." He hung up and turned to Donna and the Professor. "We are in. They are eager to meet with us and do business."

He was making a deal to distribute Medina with the local Chicago gangs, and these guys made the Detroit dealers look like schoolboys. Chicago's black gangs had a long history, stretching back before the Movement to the days of Capone.

Recently, one of the gangs had a split in its ranks after its leader went to prison on a rape charge. Women would get you every time, thought the Prince. Now the rival gangs were trying to put each other out of business. The Prince smiled as he thought of making deals with both of them. By the time he got to Atlanta, he would be set for life.

Donna was dressed in a hotel robe, watching television. She was thinking about the bellboy she'd screwed in the hotel's service elevator last night. "That's good, baby," she said offhandedly to the Prince.

The Professor was halfway through a bottle of gin and it was only eight a.m. "I still think we are too close to Detroit," he slurred a little. "The drug should be in full swing by now and they will have caught on."

"You worry too much," said the Prince. "They don't know shit. Besides, they won't care what happens to a bunch of crackheads. When the ones they have now die off, some more will come to take their place."

"You got that right," said Donna.

"Besides, they have their hands full trying to find out who's killing their people," said the Prince. "The Handyman."

"We were lucky they didn't think we were behind all that," said the Professor. "We were a new face in the game."

"Hey, I'm a bizness man," said the Prince. "I only kill somebody when it's profitable."

"Look, all I'm saying is this is the first time we've done this to this magnitude and dealt with these kind of people," said the Professor.

"Fuck 'em," said the Prince.

"I did," said Donna, laughing.

The Prince gave her a look and she stopped.

"These Chicago gangs are dangerous," said the Professor, taking another drink. "I've heard that they torture their enemies before they kill them."

"Well, we'll just give them Donna if it comes to that."

"I'm serious here," said the Professor. "I think we should one, get further away from Detroit now and two, lay low for a while until this thing blows over." He took another drink.

"Fuck that," said the Prince. "I got a plan and I'm stickin' to it."

"I don't want to die," said the Professor.

"Hey, this shit is starting to scare me," said Donna. "Maybe he's right. Maybe we should just keep moving."

"What the fuck is this, a mutiny? I'll decide if and when we move on," said the Prince.

"That's bullshit, baby. If I think I'm in trouble, I'm outta here," Donna said.

"You're out when I say you are, bitch!" The Prince stepped closer to her, clenching his fists.

Donna knew he was for real. He'd been full of himself since scoring in Detroit and he was capable of anything. She kept a razor in her purse, but had left it in the bathroom. She backed away from the Prince.

"Let's not fight among ourselves," said the Professor, catching the Prince's arm. "We're on the same team here. I was just trying to talk about alternatives."

"Yeah," said the Prince. He turned, but gave Donna a nasty look before he did. "This is what we'll do. I'll meet with their leaders alone first and if I think anything is not right, we split. Agreed?"

"Agreed," said the Professor.

Donna grunted something and went into the bathroom, where she placed the razor into her robe pocket, returned, and continued to watch television. If the Prince came at her again like that, he would be putting his face back together.

They all jumped at the knock at the hotel room door. A moment passed as they each looked at the door, dread snaking its way among them.

"See who it is," the Prince said to the Professor, who was in midswig. The Professor got up and slowly walked over to the door.

The Professor looked out the peephole and saw the face of a shabby-looking white man. His face was obscured by the glass in the peephole. It bent his visage into that of a ghoul. It reminded him of one particularly bad, three-day binge in Kalamazoo.

"Yes, can I help you?" The Professor asked through the door.

"Y'all with the con-vention?" asked the man in a Southern drawl.

"No. I'm sorry," said the Professor.

"Who is it?" asked the Prince.

"Some guy, asking about a convention."

The Prince remembered vaguely that there was a convention in the city. Farm equipment salesmen or some shit like that.

"Is he black or white?" asked Donna.

"Hey, I'll ask the questions around here, OK? You shut up and close that robe. Your titties are hanging all over the place."

Donna's response was to open the robe and flash him.

"Is he black or white?" asked the Prince.

"White. Talks like he's from the South."

"Get rid of his ass. We got things to do." The Prince walked over to the small refrigerator and grabbed a soda.

The Professor turned to the peephole again. "Look, I'm sorry—"

He fell silent a moment, then applied a shaky hand to the doorknob, slowly opening the door.

The Prince had the word "wait" on his lips when the door was kicked in with such force that the Professor fell on his ass by the bed next to Donna.

The shabby-looking white man removed his gun from near the peephole where he had threatened to shoot the Professor's eye out and entered. He was followed by a huge black man, wielding a gun. The big black man almost licked his lips at the sight of Donna in her robe. It had opened again, and one of her breasts hung lazily. The third man through the door was Mayo, followed by T-Bone himself, who motioned Pit and Nam to lower their weapons.

"Game's over, *my brotha*," he said.

8

Child of Chaos

Tony kissed his son good night and dimmed the light. Moe hated to go to bed, and Tony had to read him three stories before he fell asleep.

Tony quietly got up and left the sleeping child. He had been unable to reach Jim to tell him about the Hampton incident. Jim was practically living at 1300 now and was a tough man to find. Really, he didn't know what he would tell him. Hampton's information seemed meaningless, but another cop might see something that he'd missed. Ultimately, he felt that it could wait.

Tony walked down the stairs into the den, where Nikki was watching television. She was in a long gown, feeding her face with microwave popcorn.

Tony sat beside her and she leaned back into him. He felt good. Family was what life was really about and now that he was back to his family full-time, he wondered if he could ever return to the force. He stroked Nikki's hair, then kissed her. She pulled him on top of her and pulled at his clothes.

The phone rang.

"Touch that phone and I'll choke you," Nikki said opening her gown.

"Yes, ma'am."

Tony kissed her and began disrobing.

The answering machine picked up on the fourth ring.

"Tony, it's Blue, man . . . I know you there. I heard you quit . . .

Tony I need your help. I found a kid and he's . . . well, you gotta come and see him—now. He's got a contract out on him—"

Tony rose up, but Nikki pulled him back down.

This must be the kid that Hampton had mentioned, Tony thought. He was involved in the Medina trade somehow.

Tony rose up again. "Nikki honey, I gotta talk to him. Just for a second."

Nikki reached into his half-opened pants, took out his penis and began to rub it on her breasts.

"Maybe tomorrow," he said.

Tony pulled the rest of her clothes off then got naked himself. He made love to his wife on the sofa then took her to bed and did the same.

After she was asleep, he got up, put on his clothes and walked to the door.

"Be careful," Nikki said from the bed.

"I will."

Tony drove his old Ford, his hooptie, further into the west side. He noticed that the car was pulling to one side a little. He gripped the wheel tighter and drove on.

Tony stopped in front of the Jones Youth Center. The building was nestled between an old abandoned building and a small supermarket.

Tony was let inside by Blue. He looked tired. His eyes were bloodshot.

"What the hell happened to you, Tony?"

"I got caught up. So, where is he?"

"In the back. He's a mess."

Blue took Tony to a small back room. It was dark and smelled of whiskey.

Tony scanned the area and saw K-9 in a corner. The boy stood when he saw Tony, then he lost his footing and stumbled against a wall.

"It's OK, Earl," Blue said. "This is the friend I told you about." To Tony, Blue whispered, "He found the liquor bottle in my desk. He's drunk."

"What's wrong with him?" Tony asked.

"He's deformed, dummy. Probably a crack baby. And he's got a price on his head. Union boys have been trying to kill him. It's all over the street. He was in an alley, eating trash when some of my people found him."

"I heard about the contract on him. He's connected to the new drug, Medina."

"Tony, he's more than that. This boy is amazing. He can do math like a computer. And his memory! He can tell you what he had for breakfast three years ago today. And, he might know who your killer is."

"The Handyman?"

"Yes, but he's afraid of cops. He says they kill people for money. So, I called you. You're not technically a cop anymore, right?"

"No, I'm not." Tony almost didn't want to say it.

"OK, then. His name is Earl, but they call him K-9."

Tony could see where the boy got the nickname. His deformity made him look like a puppy.

Blue pulled the boy from the corner. K-9 resisted.

"Tell him what you told me, boy," Blue's Jamaican accent was thicker in his excitement.

K-9 was silent.

"Tell me or out you go. I mean it."

K-9 looked at Tony. Tony fought the urge to look away.

"Tryin' to kill me, gotta . . . run," said K-9. His voice was high-pitched, almost like a girl's.

"I know. I'm here to help you," said Tony.

"I know everything, that's why they . . . wanna kill me. It's all messed up now . . . can't control it."

"What's messed up?" Tony asked.

"Medina."

"I see, I see. Who's in charge of making the drug?"

Silence.

"Who?"

K-9 tried to run. He fell again, but Tony caught him. He sat the boy down in a chair next to a table. He knelt in front of him.

"OK. Forget that for now," said Tony. "Who is the killer, the Handyman?"

"I don't know."

Tony looked at Blue. "Blue, this is not—"

"Tell him the story, Earl. Tell him what you told me."

K-9 shifted in the chair. For a second, Tony thought that he would fall again.

"The dead ones . . . were all in a gang a long time ago. Big Money . . . Campbell and another guy . . . but he died a long time ago."

"What's the name of the gang?"

"I don't know . . . no one ever said it, or I would remember."

"OK, then. The dead guy, what's his name?"

"They called him Baby Knife . . . 'cause he carried a little one."

"What about the others? The ones killed at Shalon Street. Were they in this gang too?"

"No . . . not them."

K-9 turned away from him. Tony put his hands on the boy's shoulders and made him face forward.

"Listen carefully," Tony said. "Is the Handyman killing off this gang?"

"Yes, but they don't know it yet."

"Are there any more of the gang left?"

"Butchie and another one . . . the big dealer."

"What's Butchie's real name?"

"I don't know."

"OK. I can check that. What's the other one's name, the big dealer?"

"He'll kill me."

"Look, I'll protect you. I swear. I'll take you to the station house and—"

"No!"

K-9 stood up again and tried to run. Tony grabbed at him, but he slipped away. K-9 fell and hit his head on the side of a table. He was out. Blood leaked from the wound. Blue ran over to him.

"Damn," said Tony.

"Shit, Tony," said Blue. "Why'd you have to spook him. I told you he's afraid of the cops."

"Sorry, I was just trying to get to the bottom of it all."

"Shit. It's bleeding pretty bad. I'll have to call an ambulance. He needs a doctor," said Blue.

Blue ran off and returned, carrying a towel and a first aid kit.

"Hold this over the wound," Blue said, giving Tony the towel.

Tony pressed hard against the boy's head. Blue grabbed a phone and dialed, leaving the room.

Tony stared at the boy's deformed face. What in God's name was he doing with drug dealers?

Blue returned ten minutes later with a male and female paramedic.

"We'll take over here," said the young woman.

Tony got up and let her tend to the boy. He and Blue moved away.

"They got here fast," Tony said.

"I got connections," said Blue. "The ambulance company's owner had a son on crack. I helped his son beat the addiction."

"Nice to know someone still gives a damn," said Tony.

"Well, what you gonna do about what he said?" asked Blue.

"I'll pass it along to—"

"No, Tony. I told you what he said. You can't trust the police. They kill for money."

Tony felt he was right. After witnessing the payoffs, he could honestly say that some of his fellow officers could no longer be trusted.

"OK, I'll look into it myself, but if I find anything, I turn it over."

"Fair enough," said Blue. "Look, I'm going to the hospital with him."

"Call me if he says anything and don't tell anyone who he is."

Blue left with the boy. Tony went behind them outside. He stood by his car and watched the ambulance drive off. Then he got into his car and wrote down all that K-9 had told him.

Tony headed for home. The first thing he planned to do when he got there was phone Jim and tell him this story.

If what the boy said was true, then perhaps the Handyman was eliminating drug dealers with a common link. He would need the department's computer to be sure. Tony remembered that when he checked the computer before, there was no common link between the Handyman's victims, except that they were all in the Union. If he could identify the next victim, maybe he could catch the Handyman in the act.

Tony looked at the notes he'd taken. He had scribbled Butchie . . . a dead man called Baby Knife . . . a gang with no name and big dealer.

The first three might be easy to find, but he had no clue to the man called the big dealer.

There were many drug dealers in Detroit. The Union was really a collection of drug crews. If the boy's big dealer was some kind of

leader, maybe he meant Theodore Bone, the man who was often re-
puted to have founded the Union.

Even though Tony had to turn over this information to the department, he was excited. He felt like a cop again.

Tony noticed the hooptie was pulling to one side even more. He
needed to put some air in the tire. He might not make it all the way
home if he didn't.

"Great," he said to himself.

He stopped at the first gas station he saw. As he pulled in, he no-
ticed a skinny man on a pay phone. Probably a drug deal, he thought.
No one used pay phones on the street unless they were up to no good.
Tony pulled around the back to the air hose.

The back of the gas station was dark. There was a house next to
it and the window facing that gas station had thick, black iron bars on
it.

Tony got out of the car fishing for a quarter to turn on the air
machine. His left front tire was low. Suddenly, the skinny man walked
up behind him.

"Don't move, muthafucka," he said.

Tony stopped. His back was to the man. Tony put his hands up
and measured the distance to his gun. A second or two and he could
have it out, but it might be too late.

"OK, bitch!" said the skinny man. "Wallet, watch, and keys."

"OK," said Tony. "I'm putting my hands down." He lowered
them.

"Hell no! Turn your ass around, slow," the man said.

Tony turned, knowing that after he saw the man's face, the robber
would shoot him after he had his valuables. Tony turned. He didn't
recognize the man's face, but he was obviously high, probably on that
new drug.

"OK," Tony said then began to take off his watch.

The robber reached for the watch and Tony grabbed his hand,
jerking him forward. The robber was off-balance and stumbled. In
that moment, Tony kicked forward, catching the man in the stomach.

The robber grunted then started to bring the gun toward Tony,
but Tony caught his wrist and they struggled. Tony lifted a knee into
the robber's groin and he doubled over. He slammed his forearm into
the side of the man's face and sent the robber stumbling backwards.
Unfortunately, the robber still had the gun.

Tony pulled his weapon out quickly and pointed it at his attacker. To Tony's surprise, the skinny man rose in the air, lifted by a big shadowy figure. The big shadow grabbed the robber's head and twisted his body. A dull snap of the skinny man's neck followed. The big shadow dropped the limp body to the ground.

"I'm a cop. Don't move!" Tony yelled at the big shadow.

The man just stood for a moment and Tony knew he was contemplating his next move.

"So am I," said the man, moving into the light.

It was Walter Nicks. Tony tensed. He was more shocked to see him than the robber.

"What are you doing, following me?" said Tony. He kept the gun up.

"I just happen to be out tonight."

"I think you've confused me with someone who doesn't know you."

Nicks laughed. "OK, I'm tailing you, but it's lucky for you I am. That jacker would have burned you for sure."

"I had it under control."

"Yeah, you kicked his ass a little, but he would have got off a shot. So, why did you go to see Blue Jones?"

"He's a friend."

"Who was the ambulance for."

"That's it. I don't owe you any answers."

"Really? You're a civilian and carrying a concealed weapon is a felony." Nicks stood with his hands at his side.

"Fuck that. I have a gun on a man who could be a robber, so you had better talk. Why are you following me?"

Tony was worried. Nicks and his men could do anything in Detroit. Nicks could shoot him dead and no one would ask any questions.

"I'm on my own Handyman investigation, per the mayor's orders. This is an election year and white vigilante killers don't exactly make people want to vote for him. So, I'm checking out anything unusual."

"What the hell does that have to do with me?"

"When the inspector on the case resigns, I call that pretty fucking unusual."

"Well, I'm not involved," said Tony. He let the gun drop to his side.

"Why did you resign?"

"None of your goddamned business."

"Everything in this city is my business. You been in the life a long time, Inspector. Too long to quit, unless you were up to no good."

Tony laughed. "You wouldn't know good if it walked up and yanked your dick."

"You don't wanna fuck with me, Hill. You know who I am."

"I don't give a wet shit. You'd better leave now."

"Not until I get some answers."

"No, I think you're leaving or I'll have to do a lot of explaining to the cops tonight." Tony raised the gun again. Tony knew it was a risk, but intimidation was all men like Nicks understood.

"You fucking assholes think you got it made don't you?" Nicks said. "Well, I earned my position. I ain't no affirmative action baby like you. You just another candy-ass pretending to be a warrior. I'm for real. I've killed enough people to fill Tiger Stadium. I eat real men for breakfast and shit out muthafuckas like you."

"Then if I shoot your ass, it won't even hurt, right?"

"You ain't got the nuts."

Tony fixed his eyes on Nicks and he couldn't waver. The slightest break and the big man might try him.

Nicks backed up.

"Next time, I'll let the jacker kill your sorry ass." He walked to his car and pulled away.

Tony looked at the body of the would-be carjacker on the ground. He knew that reporting it would lead to all kinds of entanglements and he didn't need any of that right now.

Tony rolled the body into the dark with his feet. He filled the leaky tire and drove away. He took a long out-of-the-way path back home and checked his rearview mirror all the way.

Tony got home and immediately phoned Jim, but his answering machine picked up. Tony started to leave a message but thought better of it. Walter Nicks and the mayor had been known to tap phones and bug offices. Tony hung up without leaving a message. He tried several more times but kept getting the machine. He would have to see Jim first thing in the morning.

Tony slipped into bed with Nikki but could not sleep. Images of Walter Nicks coming through his window kept surfacing in his mind. And when he finally dozed off, his Beretta was on the nightstand.

9

Cleaning House

T-Bone sat in the shadows of the old vacant building in Detroit as the two killers worked on the Prince. He would be dead soon and then he would question the Professor. He needed fear on his side in order to get the answers he wanted. Once the Professor told him what he needed to know, he would kill him, too.

Nam stood by as Pit beat the Prince. Mayo and Traylor watched from across the room. They stood by Donna and the Professor who were bound and watched on their knees.

T-Bone had reluctantly shut down production of Medina and all hell had broken loose. Some of the houses had refused to return the product and continued to sell it. Chaos. Rebellion in his houses! It didn't seem possible. And K-9 was gone and no one knew where he was.

The Prince was a useless mouthpiece so he would die first. Then he'd ask the white man if he could make Medina without the side effects. T-Bone didn't care about the girl. Pit and Nam had tried to rape her during the return ride. Mayo had threatened to kill them if they had.

They had retrieved the money, but he didn't care about it. It was chump change compared to what he had lost. These assholes might have cost him everything.

Pit slammed his fist into the Prince's side and felt another rib crack. He was wearing gloves with brass knuckles on them. Blood flowed over the gloves. Tiny pieces of flesh stuck to them. Pit hit another solid blow to the chest and the Prince's body began to jerk spasmodically, then it stopped. It wouldn't be long now.

The Prince's face was a tangle of blood and pulpy flesh. Both eyes were closed and all of his front teeth were gone. When he breathed, he made a wheezing noise through his broken nose and the air made bubbles in the blood which ran from it.

The Professor and Donna watched in horror as Pit attacked his victim. Donna had been relieved of her razor and allowed to put clothes on. Neither of them struggled. Even if they could get free, they would be killed before they took three steps.

Donna's eyes were red with tears, but not for the Prince. He was her husband but she did not love him. She had known that sooner or later he would get his. All drug dealers did. But she never expected to go down with him. She had always been smart enough to stay out of harm's way. She could usually smell trouble and made herself scarce at those times.

Once in Tennessee, some dealers had shot at the Prince in their cheap motel room, but she had been out shopping. In New York, they had tried to knife him, but she was at a hotel with a man she had met the night before.

She'd had a bad feeling about Detroit, but had not expected them to come so quickly. It was her fault. She had gotten too far into the sex with Mayo and told him they might go to Chicago. Now she feared what they were going to do to her. She kept looking at Steven Mayo, but he would not return her gaze. It was obvious that her fate was in the hands of the leader. She thought to herself that she should have had sex with T-Bone instead.

Pit struck a blow to the Prince's sternum that made a dull, cracking noise. Nam dropped the Prince and his body fell to the floor, uninhabited.

Nam quickly bent down to check his pulse. He raised his head and smiled broadly. "That's all, folks."

Pit immediately looked at Donna. He pointed a bloody finger at her and walked toward her.

"That's enough," said T-Bone to Pit.

"I want her, man," said Pit. "Just let me—"

"I said no, dammit!" T-Bone yelled. Mayo and Traylor put their hands to their weapons but did not raise them.

Pit's anger grew. Why were they protecting this *bitch*?!

"Cool, cool," he lied. He went over to Nam and slapped him five with his bloody hand.

T-Bone walked to the Professor whose face was filled with terror. He had not had a drink for hours, and he was literally shaking.

"I blame all this on your boy," said T-Bone calmly. "I know you two were just following orders. So, I'm only going to ask you once. How do we take the side effects out of the Medina?"

"There's got to be a way," the Professor said. "Let me work on it! I'll do it! I swear!"

T-Bone signaled Traylor who brought him the blue steel sawed-off pump shotgun. He pointed it at the Professor's head.

"Don't lie to me. *Is there a way?!*" T-Bone placed the shotgun under the Professor's nose. "Lie to me and I'll blow your fucking face off, one ugly piece at a time." He looked the Professor straight in the eyes. He would know if he was lying.

"Yes, I can do it!" the Professor almost yelled.

"How?"

"I'll break it down . . . to its base elements and . . . eliminate the hallucinogenic effect."

"How?"

"By . . . uh, I'll have to do tests first. I need a drink. I can't think—"

T-Bone pushed the gun hard into the Professor's nose. Blood flowed out of a nostril. T-Bone pulled the gun back then knelt down next to the Professor, who was sobbing like a child.

T-Bone moved his face close to the crying man and whispered. "I'm not an unreasonable man. The Prince hustled me. Goes with the territory. But you, I need you. We need to take some time out and find the answer to the drug's problem. Then everything will be cool."

T-Bone pulled out a pint of gin. The Professor's eyes brightened. He reached for it, but T-Bone pulled it back.

"I'm a businessman," T-Bone said. "I need Medina to work. You help me and I'll let you live. But don't lie to me. It's insulting. Now, is there a way to fix the drug?"

"No, but we can find a new drug. I just need some time to work on it."

"Cool," T-Bone said.

T-Bone gave the Professor the bottle then stood up. This drunk couldn't help him. He probably never even worked on the formula at all. But it was too late to change any of that. If there was one thing that he had learned in the business, it was when to cut his losses.

T-Bone shot the Professor dead. The blast shattered the bottle on the Professor's lips and tore his head apart.

Donna shrieked until T-Bone pointed the weapon at her and pumped it, discarding the spent shell and loading a new one.

"Hey now, Bone, don't waste her until we can get some," pleaded Pit. "She too fine to just kill."

"Yeah," added Nam. "Let the troops have some R & R." Pit and Nam smiled at each other and high-fived, rubbing themselves.

T-Bone turned the gun on them both. He shot Pit in the chest. He fell backwards, a look of surprise on his face. T-Bone quickly pumped another shell and shot Nam. The blast caught him in the leg. Nam fell to the floor. T-Bone pumped the gun again and moved over Nam, put the gun in his face and fired.

"Shut up!" T-Bone said. He turned back to Donna, who was crying with her bound-up hands over her face. T-Bone pumped the gun again. Donna jumped but did not lower her hands. T-Bone waited a moment, then handed the shotgun to Mayo.

"She's yours," he said and walked away.

Mayo tightened. He hoped that T-Bone would allow Pit and Nam to take care of the woman. He was prepared for that. He also knew that Pit and Nam would have to be disposed of. They had seen T-Bone commit murder and neither of them was reliable. But he certainly had not expected T-Bone to waste them now.

T-Bone had his back to Mayo, but Mayo knew he was waiting to see what he would do. Even at a time like this, T-Bone tested your loyalty. The woman was harmless, but she had stolen from them.

Traylor took a step toward the woman. He saw Mayo's hesitancy at his opportunity to show what he was made of. He pulled out his gun.

"I'll take care of her—"

T-Bone stopped Traylor, putting his hand on his chest.

"Man's gotta make up his mind," T-Bone said. "Who's it gonna be, Mayo, the bitch or your crew?"

Mayo pulled his gun and went over to Donna, handing the shotgun to Traylor.

Even half-crazy and covered with blood she looked good. She wept like a child in front of him. He couldn't deny his feeling for her. But women were never allowed to come between men and their business.

He pointed his gun at the space between her eyes. He didn't want her to suffer. He pulled back the trigger and saw her jump at the loud click.

"Gotta be this way," he whispered.

His shot was point-blank.

10

Turnaround

At seven a.m., Tony surfaced into downtown from the Lodge Free-way. He was headed to 1300 in his old Ford. The all-news radio station predicted no end to the current heatwave.

Tony thought that last night would never end. He'd been restless, waiting for the morning to come.

Maybe Nicks was telling the truth. Maybe he was just making sure Tony was clean for the mayor. Well, whatever he was doing, Tony thought, it would not stop him from getting to Jim and giving him the information he'd obtained last night. With all that had happened lately, only Jim could be trusted.

Tony parked on the street and walked up to 1300. He quickly went inside.

In the lobby, he was hit by a wave of feelings. The look, the feel, even the smell of the place made him sad. Officers moved about on their daily business. He stood in the middle of the floor for a moment, looking like a man who had lost his way.

"Sir?"

Tony turned to see Detective Meadows, his only female officer in the Sewer.

"Meadows. How are you?"

"Fine, sir. What brings you here? Are you coming back to us I hope? Place isn't the same without you."

"I, uh, just need to see Jim."

"I'm sure he's not in yet," she said. "But you can come up if you want. Everyone would love to—"

"No, no. I don't think that would be . . . I'll just wait for him down here."

"OK, sir," Meadows started to walk away. "By the way, I'm sorry about your friend."

"What friend?"

"That guy who runs the youth center, used to be one of your street people, the guy with the blue eyes."

Tony grabbed Meadows. "Blue? What happened to him?"

"He was killed last night. They killed some kid he was with, too."

"Oh, Jesus, no—"

"They were shot right in the damn hospital and—"

"Who . . . did we catch who did it?"

"I was gonna say some of the staff said they saw a strange black man running down the stairs, but no one could give a good description. The perp must have used some sort of silencer, because no one heard anything."

. . . he's afraid of cops, he says they kill people for money . . .

Tony pulled away from Meadows. He looked around the big lobby. Suddenly, this place he'd known for so long felt like a prison. The faces seemed foreign, threatening.

He moved quickly to the front door, only to see Walter Nicks getting out of his car with two other men. Nicks started up the steps, adjusting the big gun under his jacket.

Tony backed up.

"Sir," said Meadows. "Are you OK? Can I—"

Tony turned quickly, walked by Meadows and out the side entrance.

Tony got into this car and drove away. He went up Jefferson to the near east side and pulled into the parking lot of a Big Boy restaurant. He went inside and called Nikki at work.

"Hello, it's me . . . yes I'm fine. Look, I want you to do me a favor. Get Moe out of school and go to your mother's house, right now."

"Tony, what's wrong?"

"I can't talk right now, just do it."

"But what about my job? I've got meetings," Nikki said.

"Tell them you're sick."

"But mama lives fifty miles away in—"

"I know. Just do it—now!" Tony said.

"Tony, what's wrong? Are you in trouble?"

"I'll explain later. And don't go back home. Go straight to your mother's and call home and leave a message when you get there, but don't say where you are."

"You're scaring me," Nikki said.

"I'll explain later, OK?"

There was silence on the phone. Tony knew his wife. Nikki was thinking that if she didn't go, she could be here for him. She could hide Moe with a friend, then help. Tony didn't feel like having to talk her out of that.

"All right," Nikki said. "But call me at mama's."

"OK. As soon as I can."

"Please be careful. I love you."

"Me, too."

Tony hung up and raced back to his car. He headed away from 1300. He was going to take the next step alone. And now, he trusted no one.

Jim let his mind wander while his new partner went into the third boring story of the day. It was early and he needed rest. They were coming back from another drug-related death. Two rollers had killed each other over a considerable quantity of Medina. It was hard to get these days and worth its weight in gold—or blood.

Since Tony was unofficially retired, Jim had been forced to partner with Jerry Burns, a fat, thirty-five-year veteran who was full of stories of the old days. Burns had been activated from desk duty, due to shortages.

". . . so one time, me and Kelly collar this spic who thinks he's a badass. So we put the damn beaner in a cell with a big colored . . . uh, bla . . . uh, African American guy named Rondell Jackson, a big, six-seven, two-fifty, jailhouse faggot. Well, after ten minutes, old Jackson's ridin' this wannabe badass spic like a goddamned racehorse! I ain't never laughed so hard in all my life!"

Burns paused and Jim knew it was coming.

" 'Course we did that back in the old days," Burns said. "Now, you could never get away with it. Goddamned Jewish lawyers would sue you for every penny you got before the dick went in."

"Would you stop the racist names please?" Jim said.

"What? You ain't no Hebe are ya?"

"Just cut the shit out, OK?"

"Jeesh, no need to bust my chops. I was just making conversation."

"Fuck the old days, all right?" said Jim. "Let's just stick to what we have to do and keep the racial remarks to a minimum. No, change that. Keep them to yourself."

"All right, partner. No problemo." Burns was angry but said nothing more. Burns turned the car down Grandriver. They stopped at a light and Jim saw an old car pass by slowly. He might not have noticed the car's driver if he had not been with Burns and looking for anything to take his attention away from him.

"Hey—" Jim said wrenching his neck to get a better look. He stamped his feet to the floor as if hitting an imaginary brake.

The old car moved past and Jim desperately tried to get a look. He wanted to turn around and make certain of what he had seen, but they were on a call.

He turned himself back around and stared out the windshield. He was certain that he had the right face. It was haggard, but it was the right face. The only question was, what the hell was Tony doing in this neighborhood, cruising in that ragged car?

11

Divorce

T-Bone drove his Cadillac along, looking for the place he had to be. Since his return from Chicago, the Union had practically dissolved. The streets were dangerous, chaotic, and he hadn't slept in the same place for the last week.

The only bright spot was that K-9 was out of the way. Someone had spotted the boy in the hospital and waxed him. Took out some other guy with him, too. The news said it was one of those neighborhood do-gooders.

Several people had claimed the reward for killing K-9, but T-Bone wasn't paying anyone. The work was done and he had bigger things to attend to.

He spotted the party store on Eight Mile and pulled into the parking lot. A black Michigan Bell pay phone stood in the back near a dumpster. T-Bone pulled the Caddy over to it, got out, and waited.

The phone rang and T-Bone recognized the voice instantly. T-Bone assumed the cop was on a pay phone, too.

It had taken a long time just to arrange this. The cop had refused to meet in person. That kind of thing was no longer a possibility, he was told. T-Bone's old cop friend was now at the head of the payoff chain and he was smart to keep his distance. It was crunch time and he would need help if he was going to get through this mess.

"What do you want?" asked the cop.

"You know what's been happening," said T-Bone.

"No, I don't know."

"My people are getting knocked off left and right, that's what! I pay you all that money and what do I get for it?"

Silence for a moment, then, "I think you have the deal wrong, my friend. I never agreed to protect you. I agreed to set you up to take over a business and that's what I did. If your people are getting hit, that's your problem. Just keep the money coming and you'll have no problem with me."

"I don't . . . You ain't gonna help me?"

"And what do you want me to do? The police are trying to catch him. It's just one man after all. Your other problems were your own fault. *You* brought that poison into the streets. *You* tried to make more money by selling that crap. *You* started the war with the other dealers. *You did it!* So don't try to bring me into your shit-pool. You made it, you swim in it." More silence, then, "By the way, we never asked for a bigger cut of your larger profits either."

"If I go out of business, your money gets cut off. Ever think about that?" T-Bone said.

"Someone will take your place."

"I see, you gonna kill me if I don't pay you?"

"Your words, not mine."

"It's all the same, no matter who says it."

"I don't have time to play this game with you. What do you want? My time is important."

"You know what the fuck I want. I want this killer, whoever he is, off my back and I want you to help me get the city back together."

"What am I, your mother? You want me to wipe your snotty-ass nose and put you back on your feet? Well, like I said, that ain't my job."

"Look, you've got a lot to lose here, too. I make lots of money for you."

"I know. You're late with your current payment."

"Well, you may not believe this, but I've had a few problems, OK?!"

"Don't yell at me. Don't you ever fucking yell at me!"

"You'd better do something or it's all over."

"You don't get it, do you? A lot of people rely on our arrangement."

"Yeah, I know. You all living large off me."

"No it's more than that. We feed and clothe our families, pay bills, send our kids to college. In case you didn't know, what we are doing is illegal and we all have a lot to lose. We walk the line every fucking day, just like you. So we can't allow you to get out of control."

"Me? The whole damn city is out of control. Pick up a newspaper."

"I don't know what you thought you were getting into, but this ain't like selling shoes. You don't just say I'm gonna do this and to hell with everybody else. You ain't got that kind of juice, my man."

"What I got is a problem!" T-Bone yelled. "Some maniac is killing my people. I want to know what you know."

"We don't know anything."

"Look, I got a little behind with the South American guys. I think it may be them."

"I haven't heard anything to verify that. And if it was them, they would have killed you first and you know it."

"If this guy is a psycho, he may be after me, too."

"That's not my problem either."

T-Bone pulled the receiver away for a moment and looked at it as if he'd never seen one.

No other dealer had brought down the kind of money he had. The cops were just as ruthless as the drug men, and in some ways even more so. He had always known that sooner or later he would get into deep shit. All the great dealers did, but he had hoped to have reached his goal of being filthy rich long before then. It was time to reevaluate his position.

"Have it your way," said T-Bone calmly. "But remember, I came to you first."

"Keep the money coming. Don't make things worse for yourself."

"Fuck you." T-Bone hung up.

He quickly picked up the phone and made another call. After all his time in the business, it was time to disappear.

12

Abduction

David Traylor sat at the table in his apartment, packaging bags of crack. He refused to sell Medina. These days, it was more trouble than it was worth.

Traylor had been trying, without success, to contact T-Bone for several days. Word on the street was T-Bone was gone for good.

The Union was officially dead and there was chaos. Rollers fought each other, and the crackheads were after anyone who might have money or Medina. The same guy who bought drugs from you might come back an hour later and try to slit your throat.

The house chiefs had hired their own bodyguards and their own rollers. They were all basically independents now. Traylor had his own crew, a few loyal followers who were still doing business for him, but he was back where he started. He had to put together the stuff himself. He was surprised how you never forgot.

Traylor finished the last bag, then got up and found his keys. He removed a .45 automatic from his refrigerator. He couldn't remember the name of the movie where he had gotten the idea from. He stuck it in his waistband.

Traylor walked to the front door and was about to open it when the door was kicked in. He saw the unmistakable blue uniforms of Detroit's Finest. He reached for his gun, but he was too late. Something covered his vision in a flash of white, and he slipped into unconsciousness.

* * *

Traylor came to and found himself blindfolded and sitting on a hard, cluttered floor. He could smell stale beer, urine, garbage, and burned wood. He could have been anywhere. He was not bound, but he could sense others about him, so he did not try to take off the blindfold. He waited for his captors to make their move. He knew if they wanted him dead, he would be by now.

"Take it off," said a voice.

A moment later, the blindfold lifted. He saw that he was in a large, dark room. A flashlight sat on a crate, but it did not give off sufficient light to see everything. Two uniformed officers, one white, the other black, stood before him. Their faces were shadowy under their hats and their badges shone dully. Their name tags had been removed.

Behind the uniforms, stood another man. Traylor could not tell if he was black or not. But he was definitely not wearing a uniform. Traylor put his hands up in the air. The uniforms laughed.

"Are you surrendering?" said the plainclothes man. It was his voice that had ordered the blindfold removed.

"I'm just tryin' to cooperate, officers," Traylor said.

All the abductors laughed this time.

"Good," said the plainclothes cop. "That's very good. We will get along fine as long as you keep that attitude. Put your hands down."

Traylor lowered his hands. He shifted his weight on the floor.

"I'm only going to say this once, so listen carefully. I am—was T-Bone's police connection. Or more correctly, he was *my* street connection. We had a deal, as I am sure he's told you. That was another of his problems, a big-ass mouth."

The uniforms laughed, but stopped abruptly when the plainclothes officer looked in their direction.

"T-Bone will be dead in about a week or so," the man continued. "You see, he reneged on our deal. He put that poison in the streets and stole money from me and his suppliers. I was patient with him, but his friends from South America were not so nice. When T-Bone screwed them, they sent the Devil here to teach him a lesson. I'm sure you've heard of him. He's called the Handyman."

Traylor stiffened. Now, it all made sense. It was no secret that T-Bone wanted to retire. He skimmed money and when he was found out, a killer was dispatched. But why didn't they just kill T-Bone? Why cut up people?

"So, you have nothing to fear from the killer," the plainclothes man said. "We have to get the street back and reestablish our deal. I have picked you to take over. What do you think?"

"Beats the fuck out of dying," Traylor said before he thought about it. He eased a little as they all laughed again.

Traylor understood that with the police on his side, he could take the city back and bring back the Union. He also knew that if he said no, he would never leave the filthy building alive.

"You will have a week to get rid of any competition you might have," said the plainclothes man. "I only deal with one man, understand?"

"Yes. Can I go now?" Traylor asked.

"Sure," the plainclothes man said. "The officers will take you anywhere you want."

Traylor was escorted out by the uniforms. Traylor went outside and got into a police cruiser. It was the first time he had used one as a taxi.

The cruiser pulled away. Traylor looked through the back window and saw the plainclothes man come out. He was still just a shadow in the night.

"Hey," said one of the uniforms.

Traylor turned to see the cop in the passenger's seat holding a silvery .45 in his face.

"What's up with this?" Traylor asked. "I thought we had a deal."

"This is your gun," said the cop in the passenger's seat.

Traylor took the weapon and despite himself he laughed.

He'd been in cars with police before, but this was the first time he could remember enjoying it.

The cruiser rolled down the street. Traylor never saw the other police car pull up to the building with two more uniformed cops and a blindfolded Steve Mayo in the backseat.

13

The Snitch

Tony hated computers. Even though he knew one day you wouldn't be able to take a dump without one, he fought their necessity in his life. He wished that he had taken time to learn more about them as he struggled with the machine.

All the cops called the Information Access Unit main computer the Snitch because it gave the story on every criminal who had ever been arrested in the city. He was happy that no one had canceled his clearance to use the thing.

The boy K-9 had been very helpful. There were more potential Handyman victims out there. Tony had four leads, but only three of them could be traced: Butchie, Baby Knife, and the gang that all the Handyman victims belonged to. The big dealer would remain a mystery for now.

The leads sounded good, but what made no sense was the men at Shalon Street. They were the missing link. Rolan Nelson and his brother Derek were slaughtered in typical Handyman fashion, but Jonnel Washington was simply shot. But according to K-9, the Nelson brothers were not in the gang.

Tony asked the computer to give him the files on the Nelson brothers. He had seen this information before, but had obviously missed something. Tony typed in the request. He asked the computer to retrieve any known drug or criminal gang member among all the Handyman victims. The computer screen went blank, then:

ERROR. DATA LOST.

"What?"
Tony accessed the files on all known felons, then typed:

RETRIEVE: ALIAS: BABY KNIFE

He hit enter and watched the screen go blank. It would hopefully give him any felon with that alias. After a moment, the screen went blank and spat out a message.

ERROR. DATA LOST.

"Shit!" he said.
Tony settled, then typed:

RETRIEVE: ALIAS: BUTCHIE

The computer screen read:

ERROR. DATA LOST.

Tony hit the computer a solid blow.
"Why you in here, cussin' out my baby?" asked Rosalie Young, an IAU computer technician.
"This is impossible, Rosie," said Tony. "I got the command right, but this thing's telling me there's no information. There's gotta be."
Rosalie looked at the screen. "Maybe not. We lost a lot of information recently on a computer glitch. But this system's got an automatic back up. Saves any information that's erased intentionally or by accident."
"The information that was lost, was it an accident?"
"Oh, it must have been an accident. The system keeps track of requests to erase data."
"When did it happen, before or after the Handyman investigation started?"
"After. Anyway, we got most of it back, but we must have missed whatever it is you're trying to find. Let me try." She sat down next to Tony and began to type rapidly.

"Tony, I'm not gonna ask why you looking up names of the Handyman victims. I won't even ask why you in here when you supposed to be on leave."

"That's why I love you, Rosalie."

"Hopefully, it's not gone. The system will only keep erased info in memory backup for about a month, then it gets discarded."

"Ask it to pull up all known gangs in common to the victims."

Tony looked at the screen. It read:

ALLEGED GANG CALLED "THE UNION."

He already knew that. He was looking for a different, possibly older gang, but apparently the cops had never catalogued it.

Tony had Rosalie look up information on Theodore Bone. Bone had no known address and an almost nonexistent record. He had some juvenile offenses, but several plans to prosecute him as an adult had ended in nothing. He was clean.

"Rosalie, ask it for an alias called Baby Knife."

Rosalie complied, then:

ALIAS ID: "BABY KNIFE"—THELLIS, RANDALL MARK.

"Yes!" Tony shouted. "OK, Rosalie pull up his rap sheet."

Rosalie did and the computer spat out felony after felony that started in 1980 for Thellis, ending in his death at the hands of a cop named Hansed. Nothing else in the file was of significance.

"Rosalie, ask it for the alias Butchie."

Rosalie typed and the screen listed thirty-three names.

"A popular alias," said Rosalie.

"Damn," said Tony. "Print that list of names for me. I guess I'll have to find this guy the old fashioned way."

"Does this help you?" asked Rosalie.

"Yes, but by the time I track this guy down, he might be in a body bag. Can I get a printout of the Thellis file too?"

"Sure. You want all of it?"

"What do you mean all of it? Didn't I just see it all?" Tony asked.

"No, there's a criminal file and a file for all personal information."

"Let me take a look at Thellis's personal info."

Rosalie pulled up the personal file on Randall Thellis alias Baby

Knife. The file listed his mother's address on Orleans Street. Marabell Thellis was his only relative.

"Well, well," said Tony. "His mother is only fifty-two. She might still be alive."

"I can skip trace that address if you want," said Rosalie. "I'm sure she's moved in all these years."

"Please," said Tony.

Rosalie went to a phone and dialed. She read the address and they waited.

"OK," Rosalie said into the phone. "Thanks, Denise. Well, Tony, your witness now lives on Dequindre."

"Thanks, Rosalie. I owe you."

"They all do."

Tony took the address and left the data center, stopping only to call Nikki at her mother's in Ypsilanti. His family was safe.

Tony stepped outside into the heat of midday, hoping that Thellis's mother had not moved away in the last ten years. He could no longer deny what he was doing. He was conducting a murder investigation, even though he was no longer a cop. This was a dangerous undertaking, as Walter Nicks had shown him last night.

Tony pulled away from the building and circled the corner and waited, making sure he was not followed.

14

Disappearing Act

The only thing that scared T-Bone more than being killed was being poor, and he'd lost a fortune. His people could no longer be trusted. Rollers were skimming and dealing on the side and most houses were not sending in any money at all. It was now officially chaos in the street, every man for himself. Even Traylor and Mayo could no longer be trusted. He wanted to bring the Prince back to life and kill him again.

T-Bone walked around the motel room, thinking of how many things he had to do. He was taking quite a chance being so close to Detroit. The small motel in Redford was only minutes from the city. The cops were looking for him for sure, but he didn't plan to be around for long. He'd been living out of his car and motels for the last week.

T-Bone had hoped to exit the business gracefully, but now he had no time for grace. The police would send a hitter to get him or bribe one of his own to do the deed. He wasn't about to wait around for that.

T-Bone had spent the past few years routing cash out of Detroit to the west coast. He sent it in boxes by a private shipper to storage houses in California. He had saved a couple of million. That would last him for a while.

He was waiting for his banker to get the rest of his money, then he could leave. The white boys were taking a big cut for laundering the money, but he didn't have time to argue. Before anyone knew anything, he would be in LA soaking up the sun, breathing smog, and planning his next move.

Fuck Detroit, he thought. He was tired of it anyway.

The Handyman watched T-Bone get into the old car. He had to keep track of T-Bone for a while, then he would take him. He would not kill this one right away. T-Bone was special and he would die spectacularly.

But first he had to get Butchie. He'd been close at Butchie's home in Boston-Edison, but his damned bodyguards had gotten in the way. He slammed his fist hard into his dashboard. He'd failed with Butchie. He hated failure. There was no room for mistakes. He had to be perfect from now on. Failure was for lesser human beings. He was special, and he could not afford any more slipups. He'd come too far.

T-Bone was supposed to be the last to die, after Butchie, but he might have to take T-Bone now and kill him later.

His plan had been helped by the drug called Medina. T-Bone's gang of poison-pushers had only poisoned themselves with it. The resulting chaos destroyed all allegiances and forced T-Bone out into the open. And now that he'd found him, he would not let him get away. He'd follow him until Butchie could be obtained. Then he'd rip him from the face of the earth.

The Handyman thought about how he would kill T-Bone. No quick death for him. It would be slow, painful, beautiful.

He watched as T-Bone drove away. He waited, then followed. Contempt filled his heart as he trailed the drug dealer at a safe distance.

He had the dirtiest hands of them all.

15

Traylor Makes His Move

David Traylor outlined how the Union was to take back the city. Ten of the Union's top rollers filled the small dining room of a former crackhouse on the west side. Several pizzas were on the table, their scents filling the room.

After his abduction by the cops, Traylor had moved fast to assemble a team of dealers. Mayo had to be dealt with, but Traylor had people out looking for him.

Traylor's new team was young, ambitious, and ready to rebuild the Union's dominance. They knew that Medina would not last forever. Sooner or later it would run out and crack would again be the drug of first choice. And when that day came, they would find themselves on top of the whole city.

"First, we get our best houses back in business," Traylor began. "Then we get rid of the muthafuckas causing us trouble by being in business for themselves. We give 'em the chance to get back with us, and if they don't, we pop 'em just like the others."

"What about T-Bone?" asked a roller named Norman. He was one of Traylor's new, hand-picked lieutenants.

"He's out of business. It's time for a new day in Detroit. I got a deal with the cops to protect us," Traylor said. "That's right, I got the cops with me!" He checked the eyes of the audience. Having the police on your side was essential to running the street. "In a year, we'll be pulling down big money and won't nobody be able to do shit about it."

Steven Mayo was going to be a big, nasty problem. Mayo had his own crew running. And Traylor realized that he had to get rid of Mayo or face a rival gang. Mayo was not a genius, but he knew the business and would make a formidable enemy.

"Why you?" asked Norman.

Traylor wasn't angered by the question. He had told him to ask it. He knew that it would be on everyone's mind. So he brought it out on his terms. He learned his lessons from T-Bone well.

"Because I got the money, the product, and the police. Can't be done without that combination." Traylor feigned anger. "Anybody else got it, I be happy to step aside, follow you." The room's silence told Traylor he was in.

"What about this Handyman?" asked Norman, again on cue.

"The Handyman was T-Bone's shit all the time," Traylor said and the faces of the rollers showed shock and disbelief.

"Yeah, that's right. T-Bone was fuckin' up so bad, that the boys from South America sent a professional hitman to ice our people to teach him a lesson. He kept it from us, but now that he's gone, I know the truth."

The real truth was that Traylor didn't believe what the cops had told him, but it served his purposes here. He half expected T-Bone to return any minute. To that end, he'd sent several rollers looking for signs of his former boss. They were to kill T-Bone on sight.

Traylor vowed that he would not make the same mistakes as his predecessor. He would not be greedy, poisoning the masses for his own gain like T-Bone did. And he was going to get out of the business alive.

The meeting was adjourned and the rollers broke into conversations about killing renegade rollers and the Detroit Pistons chances for another basketball championship. Traylor prompted the rollers to leave while he and Norman made preliminary plans to raid Magilla's drug houses.

After the plan was set, Traylor got into his car with Norman at his side. Traylor could only afford one bodyguard and Norman was strapped with a nine millimeter.

Traylor was grabbing for his gun when Steve Mayo appeared in the driver's window, holding a gun in each hand, pumping shots into the car.

16

Mother's Grief

Tony's ass stuck to the thick plastic covering on the flowered sofa in the living room.

Marabell Thellis was a thin woman who looked like every substitute teacher he ever had in school, and she had a tendency to ramble on about nothing.

Marabell took her religion seriously. The living room, crammed with symbols, crucifixes, Bibles, nativity scenes, and velvet paintings of Jesus, crowded Tony as he sat on the sticky couch.

". . . you see, that's God's plan. He's testing us right now, but he's coming soon. Are you saved yet, officer?"

"Yes, ma'am. I hate to cut you off, but I need to ask you some questions. I'm investigating the Handyman killings."

"Oh Lord."

"Your son, Randall, is connected somehow."

"I'm not surprised. He was filth, just like his brothers. Not surprised that they were killed, too."

"Randall had brothers?" Tony set his cup down. "Ma'am can you tell me their names?"

"Rolan and Derek."

"Nelson?" Tony asked.

"Yes, how did you know? They had different fathers than Randall. I don't like to talk about that."

"Holy shi—" Tony caught himself. Derek and Rolan Nelson were killed instead of their brother, Randall Thellis, who was already dead.

"I'm sorry, ma'am."

"No bother. They was filth, all of them." Marabell took a gulp of coffee. "I wouldn't even let them in my house. Both of 'em left me you know. Nate Thellis, then Robert Nelson. I was married to Nate. Robert I sinned with. This is my punishment. All my sons dead. Well, hopefully they're in a better place, though I doubt it."

"Help me, Ms. Thellis. I need to know if your son Randy was in a gang a long time ago."

"The Devil seems to be everywhere these days," she said. "I hear people testify in church about what their kids are doing and I die a little. You know, there was a time when I would have pulled out my heart for my children, you know, like Jesus did for his disciples, but I had to let Satan take them."

For a moment she was silent. Tony could see that she had suppressed a great deal of pain related to her sons and husbands. He had seen the look before. There was nothing more heartbreaking than the loss in a mother's face. Her eyes misted and she removed her glasses.

"Ma'am please concentrate. Was there a gang?"

"Yeah. There was always a gang. Randall's was called the Bad Boys."

"Please tell me, do you see all the Bad Boys on this list?" Tony held out the list of all the Handyman's victims.

"There's one missing," Marabell said.

"Just one? Are you sure it's not two?"

"No, just one."

"Who is he?" Tony asked.

"He's still here in Detroit, the snake. The moment I saw him again, I knew. Calls himself a preacher. Got a so-called church over on Eight Mile next to a Burger King! Right where a church like that belongs."

Marabell got a tissue and wiped her eyes. "Leon Palmer," she said. "Everybody called him Butchie. But he changed his name to Reverend Joe B. Henderson when he came back."

"I know this was hard for you." Tony took her hand. "But I promise that whoever killed Derek and Rolan in that house will pay for it somehow."

"What do you mean by somehow?"

"Well, he might go to jail or, I might have to kill him if the situation calls for it."

Marabell put her glasses back on and straightened her back. She sniffed, fixing her hair and composing herself.

"If it's God's will," she said, looking Tony straight in the eyes, "blast his butt good!"

17

God's Magnificent House
of Miracles

The church is an integral part of society in the black community in Detroit. It is not only a religious institution, but a powerful political force. Despite the growth of black business and academia, ministers are still the undeniable leaders of the race.

God's Magnificent House of Miracles was a small church on Eight Mile Road. Small by Detroit standards. In comparison to some of the money-rich churches, its congregation was tiny.

Tony went through the heavy, gold-colored doors. The service room was ornate. It was dressed with hand-carved wood, thick carpet woven with religious symbols, and stained glass that glowed in vivid color. Behind the pulpit was a stained-glass Jesus, whose face had been tinted black.

The Reverend Joe B. Henderson preached for the Thursday night service. Henderson was a large man with a full head of thick hair and a jowly face. He preached in the unmistakable cadence of the Southern Baptist preacher: lumbering, sonorous digressions easing into singing elevations of voice.

There were only about fifty people in the church, but it seemed like three times that number. The congregation yelled, answered the reverend where appropriate, and clapped for the better parts. The church organist kept time with riffs between pauses. Deacons with large, golden donation plates worked the crowd.

Being in the church made Tony feel good. The church reminded him of better times. He absorbed the familiar electric atmosphere and said a silent prayer for himself.

". . . and where is God?" Henderson said. "If he exists, then why don't he just wave his hand and make everything all right? We know, the Devil is here."

"Watch out, now!" yelled a woman in the front row.

"His work is everywhere, kids killin' each other, sellin' dope, havin' babies all over the place. But where—is God?"

Henderson stepped back from the podium microphone, wiping his face. The organist hit a riff.

"He's here, right here in this church—in your heart! If you let him in," Henderson said. "Let him in, and the world can go to hell, and you'll live forever!"

The congregation erupted, the organist played, and the deacons passed the plates.

Pretty good for a former drug dealer, Tony thought. As the choir came on, Henderson left the stage. Tony worked his way to the front of the church only to be intercepted by a very large deacon. He told the man he was a cop. The deacon asked for ID. Tony was prepared for that. He'd brought along an old detective's shield. He flashed it to the deacon. Tony was then escorted to a waiting area by the minister's office. Tony waited as the big deacon talked to Henderson.

Joe Henderson's office had a large mahogany desk in the center. Exotic plants adorned the corners and abstract paintings covered the walls. The only religious item in the room was a large gold Bible on a wooden stand.

"Come in, officer," said Henderson. "Have a seat."

Tony sat down in a very expensive leather side chair.

"Nice place. Can we talk alone?" Tony looked at the big deacon.

"You can go, Oliver." Henderson smiled at Tony. His hands were covered with gold rings sprinkled with diamonds.

Oliver left and Tony's face took on a serious look.

"How can I help you, officer?" Henderson said. "Is one of my parishioners or their son in trouble?"

"No, Butchie, you are."

Henderson was caught off-guard and showed visible shock at the mention of his old moniker. He adjusted himself in the large black chair and tried to look unaffected by the name.

"You may as well get to the point, officer," Henderson said. "That part of my life is dead."

"Funny you should talk about death, 'cause that's why I'm here."

"Officer, I made my peace with God and now I do His work. If I can help you, I will, but you don't have to beat me with what I was. I know, and I live with it every day."

Tony was almost affected by the speech. He was raised in the black church and looked upon it with reverence and great respect. He believed that a man could be redeemed, that God could forgive any sin no matter how terrible, if the man was truly repentant. And wasn't that what he was seeking to do? Wasn't he trying to absolve his own sin by doing a good deed? Yes, he answered himself, but all the more reason to be even harder on Henderson.

Henderson was a reverend, but he was still a pro, Tony thought. His manner and his clever, sympathetic counterstrike at the mention of his secret identity gave him away.

Henderson was just plying his trade in a different arena, that's all. Instead of selling drugs, Henderson was now selling faith.

"My name is Inspector Hill. Have you been reading the papers lately, Butchie?"

"That is no longer my name. I am a man of faith now."

Tony leaned in toward him as if he were going to strike him, and Henderson instinctively recoiled.

"A lot of your old buddies are dead, killed by a psychopath. Only I don't think he's so crazy. I think he's got a plan. See, all the men he's killed so far have two things in common."

Tony looked deep into Henderson's eyes, ready to read the reaction. "A gang called the Union—and you. So, I'm wondering, Reverend, why you aren't dead, too?"

Henderson started to breathe heavier and a thin layer of sweat emerged on his brow. He reached into his desk and Tony's hand jerked toward his gun.

Tony settled down as Henderson pulled out a bottle of whiskey.

"I can see I'm gonna need one," he said. "Care to join me?"

18

The Big One

Steven Mayo drove down the street, houses passing by in a blur. He was still pumped up from finishing off Traylor. It had been easier to kill Traylor than he thought. He was now the ruler of the street, just like the cops had told him after they kidnapped him.

After the cops let him go, Mayo tracked Traylor down, then followed him.

He did not believe the cop when he said T-Bone would be dead soon. After all, T-Bone was the smartest man Mayo had ever known. If anyone knew how to survive, T-Bone did. Still, the cop had seemed so sure.

The cop who had done the talking wore no uniform, probably a detective. He tried to convince Mayo that T-Bone had brought the whole Handyman thing down on himself by breaking promises to his suppliers, who retaliated. Mayo thought it was bullshit, but he wasn't about to say it to three armed men.

So he had been handed the whole city on a silver platter. And after Medina faded away, he would own Detroit.

If T-Bone was gone, good, he thought. But if he came back, Mayo knew he'd have to kill his former boss.

Mayo would not miss Medina. No one was making it and only the truly foolish even wanted it. It was death. Dennis, the would-be chemist, was the only one who knew the formula. Mayo had taken him off production, then instructed some of his men to make sure Dennis never made the chemical again.

Now all he had left was Magilla. He had to take the house back and kill that fat bastard. The house was their most profitable, and he didn't want Magilla to grow into a rival. Magilla also had a large quantity of Medina. That alone was reason enough to take him out. It would not be easy, though. Mayo hated to admit it, but Magilla was smart and he had an army of rollers working for him.

Mayo turned his car onto the freeway. He vowed long ago not to make the same mistakes as the others. The fact that he was still alive proved that he was smarter than the rest.

It had been the Big Three and now it was just him, the Big One, and he was not going to die.

19

Transformation

Tony watched Henderson go from a confident man to a shaking, scared wreck. Just the mention of the dead men had released ghosts that haunted him.

"I do read the papers, officer," said Henderson. "And I did notice that my former friends have been taken away by some kind of avenging angel."

"So, do you want to go to a police station, or can we talk here?" asked Tony.

"No," said Henderson. "That won't be necessary. The men who were killed were all drug dealers with me a long time ago. They were just kids when I knew them."

The Reverend took another drink and Tony noticed his clean, neatly manicured fingers. He realized then that Henderson was immaculate. His suit was expensive looking, his hair was so groomed that it almost looked fake.

The office was clean, too. No, spotless would be a better word. If nothing else, the Reverend was tidy.

"So, how'd you get out?" asked Tony. "Usually your kind leave the business in a box."

"God saved me. I went to federal prison for trying to rob a bank in Minneapolis. I was lucky enough to get transferred to minimum security. It was like summer camp with armed counselors. There, I found the Lord. After I was paroled, I came back home."

That explained why he was so neat. Many ex-cons come out of

prison obsessed with cleanliness. It's a result of the discipline of incarceration. And cons also feel dirty from having been in prison, so they need to keep their world clean.

"And why did you do that? Wasn't it dangerous?" Tony asked.

"There were only a few people left who knew me," Henderson said. "Most of my friends were either dead, in prison, or deeply involved in selling dope. I knew I'd never see them traveling in normal circles."

"But you changed your name, so you suspected trouble, right?"

"Yes, I wanted to start over. I took the name of the prison pastor who made me his apprentice in Minnesota. See, God don't give you reasons for why he does things and if you're smart, you don't ask questions, you just do as He commands." Henderson rubbed a spot from his desk.

"I still don't see why you'd come back here unless you had some sort of agenda."

"I was a sinner, officer. As evil as they came; I sold and used drugs, I used young women and I hurt people. I had to go into the eye of the storm, prove my worth to God and myself. I came back home because there's no better place to battle the Devil than where you first met him. And no one better than me to know what evil people have in their hearts. When they listen to me preach, they know I'm telling them the real deal. They know it's sincere 'cause I've lived it."

Henderson paused and finished his drink, looking at the empty glass. "I will tell you what I know, officer, but if you think I will testify against any drug dealers, you're mistaken. They'd kill me and I will not let the Devil win that way."

"I'm not interested in you, Reverend, unless you're the Handyman, or you helped whoever is," Tony said.

"Fair enough, officer. When I was a drug dealer, the city was an open market. There were gangs, but they were small. It was fun. We had money, women, everything. But then the Union came. Everyone was forced to join. If you didn't, you just disappeared. Our little gang, the Bad Boys, was nothing, so we joined right up, no problem. But there was this guy, a dealer named Elrock. He refused to join, so he was killed. Elrock's real name was Carlton Williams.

"He was tied to a tree and cut to pieces, like an animal. I remember when they cut Elrock open. Sometimes, I still see his insides spill-

ing out. We were all there, me, Randy Thellis, Floyd Turner, and
Campbell. Turner and Campbell were just kids, babies, at that time."

Henderson poured another drink, gulped some of it and steadied
his hands on the desk.

"Elrock's brother had been brought along, too. He was just this
skinny, dumb-looking kid. Well, he got loose and ran, and that's when
it happened. He told me to go and kill him."

"Who gave the order to kill Elrock and his brother?"

Henderson hesitated. "Theodore Bone. We called him T-Bone."

Now all the pieces fit in Tony's mind. He was killing all the Bad
Boys one by one. T-Bone, the future leader of the Union was there,
so he was going to be killed, too.

"I won't testify against T-Bone. I'll deny it all if you take me in.
I have a wife and kids now."

"Your new wife doesn't know about your past life, does she?" Tony
asked already knowing the answer to the question.

"No, officer, and she never will." He wiped the desk again.

"OK," Tony said. "Then just tell me the rest."

"T-Bone gave me a gun," Henderson continued. "He had to make
me do something so that I would not squeal to the cops. I was a
chicken, a mascot really. I liked the action and the women, but I
wasn't no killer. I wanted to run—they would have killed me before
I got ten steps. So I took the damned gun and went after the boy."

Henderson stopped and took out a handkerchief. He wiped his
face, which was now covered in perspiration. He was no longer Reverend Joe B. Henderson, he was Butchie Palmer, hanging with the
wrong crowd and in over his head.

"Elrock's brother was tall. He ran fast, but he'd been beaten, so
it didn't take me long to catch up to him. I pointed the gun and
squeezed off a shot. He fell but he was still alive. I had hit him in the
shoulder. I was going to shoot him in the head, but I couldn't bring
myself to do it. So, I shot again into the ground and grabbed the
wounded part of his shoulder at the same time. He screamed loudly.
I shot again for good measure. When I came back to the others, no
one questioned that I'd killed him. I left him there in the woods and
I didn't know if he would live or not. All I knew was that I didn't kill
him."

Henderson wiped away more sweat. "But this year, when the others started dying, I knew. The brother is not dead."

"A boy killing drug dealers?" Tony said.

"He's not a boy anymore, not after all these years," Henderson said.

"And the brother, what was his name?" Tony asked.

"Talmadge. Talmadge Williams."

"They were black, these brothers, Talmadge and this Elrock, who were killed?"

"Yes."

"Then why is the Handyman blond?"

"I . . . I don't know. I'm not a police officer, but you can buy hair if you wanted to plant it, couldn't you?"

"You seem to know an awful lot, Reverend," Tony said.

"You don't think I did it, do you?"

"Maybe you did kill that Talmadge Williams and now you're trying to right what you did in those woods. You kill somebody, Rev, and the act festers in your heart and mind. It will destroy you if you don't get it first, and you will do anything to be yourself again, to be human again."

Tony knew what he was talking about. He killed Darryl Simon and it wrecked his life.

"No," said Henderson. "I'm a sinner, not a killer. I was wrong, but I would not compound my sin in order to rid myself of it. There's only one way to cleanse the heart, through the Lord Jesus Christ."

"OK, Rev," Tony said. "Your story makes sense to me. But I think you should come to the police station with me and tell them your story. You're not safe."

"I know. He's already tried to get me."

"How? When?"

"He tried to kill me outside of my house on Boston a few days ago. He killed one of my deacons. A good man. I told the police that it was an attempted robbery."

"Rev, you should go into protective custody."

"I can't leave. I have too many obligations. God will protect me, and my wife can't know about any of this."

"I think she might get suspicious at your funeral."

"You find Talmadge Williams and I won't have to die."

"Back again, huh?" said Rosalie Young.

"Yes," said Tony. "I need the Snitch to get more information." He didn't feel the need to tell her that he was still on the Handyman.

"You look like shit, Inspector."

"I feel like it, too," said Tony. "Rosalie, I'm gonna need your—"

"I know. Let's do it."

The Snitch showed that Carlton Williams had a long and impressive arrest record. He'd been routinely picked up on numerous felony offenses, but the computer showed no convictions.

"Couldn't keep this one in jail, could we?" said Rosalie.

"No. And it doesn't make sense. Look at this—drugs, assault, criminal sexual conduct, even a simple weapons charge didn't stick."

"Looks like he had a friend."

"Or a lot of them," Tony said. He was thinking about Hampton and the payoff run. "Look up Talmadge Williams."

Rosalie did, but as Tony had suspected, Talmadge Williams had no record at all.

Carlton Williams's personal file showed a mother, Roberta Williams, who had a few minor drug convictions. Tony took down her last known address.

"I'll trace a current address for her," Rosalie said. She picked up a phone.

Talmadge Williams had only been a kid around the time Butchie Palmer claimed Carlton Williams was killed. So by now, he'd be a man. The computer showed no death record for him.

"Sorry, Tony," Rosalie said. "This address on Hempstead is the last one we got for Roberta Williams."

"Thanks, Rosalie."

Tony printed out all the information and left. He got into his car and found the address for Roberta Williams on Hempstead Street. That would be his next stop.

20

Saying Goodbye

T-Bone spooned another mouthful of applesauce. It was very dangerous to be here like this, but he had to take the risk. He was vulnerable in the big dining area at the Concord Retirement Home on Detroit's far north side. His father, Big Teddy, ate sloppily and smiled like a baby as T-Bone fed him.

T-Bone could not help but smile every time he saw him here like this. Big Teddy, the big stupid invalid. The same Big Teddy who had hounded him about being a man, who had tried everything in his power to convince T-Bone that he was lacking.

When T-Bone became the neighborhood drug pusher, it drove his mother to an early grave. He and his father had both done it, really, T-Bone thought. His mother had not been able to control either of them, so she checked out.

After her death, Big Teddy indulged himself with liquor and women (the same women he had been seeing while his mother was alive). He tortured himself with his guilt, and soon Big Teddy was a wreck, a poor and helpless drunk consumed by grief and sin.

T-Bone had relished the chance to come back into his father's life and save him, as if preserving Big Teddy would sustain his victory over him. His father was now an invalid, a semi-mindless child, wrecked by alcoholism and incapable of connecting with anyone. He was safe in a retirement home, where T-Bone could treat himself to the sight of the Great Theodore Bone Senior, fallen and helpless, whenever he wanted.

T-Bone fed another spoonful of applesauce into the happy child-face of the old man. His father's eyes were wet. He seemed to be sad, but he could only grin stupidly to the world.

Big Teddy was still in there somewhere, T-Bone thought. Beyond the sickness and disease, he was in there, mocking him and hoping for his son's failure. But his father would not have the last laugh. T-Bone was running away, but at least he had a life to run to.

"I beat you," he whispered to his father, just as he did every time he came to see him.

"I know you're in there," T-Bone said. "I beat you. Life beat you. I win."

T-Bone kept his voice low. He burned with his failure and looked with hatred at the sick, helpless man before him.

"And when I leave you here and stop paying your rent, I'd hate to be where they're gonna put you. They'll turn you out into the street, a homeless bum, where you'll freeze to death if you're not eaten for dinner by the other bums first."

His father laughed, a grunt really, but it thundered into T-Bone's head. He grabbed the old man by the collar of the cheap robe he wore.

"Don't you laugh at me! Don't you fucking laugh at me!"

Several orderlies ran to pull T-Bone away from the old man, but T-Bone pulled a handgun. The orderlies fell to the floor. Someone screamed. T-Bone looked around and knew he had made a mistake. The hospital people would call the police and then they would know that he was still in Detroit.

T-Bone looked at his father, who had fallen to the floor. T-Bone trained the gun on him. His hand trembled, then he put the gun away and ran.

T-Bone went into the underground parking lot. He stopped to catch his breath in the dim light of the structure. It was cold and a draft snaked at his ankles. He walked to his car.

A car raced toward him. It had backed out of a space across from where he had parked. T-Bone tried to jump out of its path, but it hit him, lifting him off his feet and sending him across the lot. T-Bone hit the concrete with a thud. He tried to get up, but he was disoriented and his legs felt like they weighed a ton.

"Dammit, dammit," T-Bone cried, reaching for his gun, which was gone. It was a police hitman, he thought. Once again, his father had managed to screw up his life, only this time, Big Teddy would cause him to die.

T-Bone heard footsteps and soon sensed a presence standing behind him. He waited for a gun to be thrust against his head and the sound of an explosion, fading into nothingness, but it did not happen. Instead, he was lifted to his feet, where he saw the grown-up face of a man, a face that once belonged to Talmadge Williams. Who should have died in the woods long ago.

"Oh, God—"

The Handyman held T-Bone's gun, which had dislodged when he was hit by the car. The killer hit T-Bone in the face with the weapon, taking his victim into a cave of darkness.

21

Finished Business

Magilla watched Steve Mayo divide the last of the drugs and dispatch the fresh-faced kids to sell it. Magilla's eyes were red with ruptured blood vessels from Medina use. He wanted to take a hit now, but he only had a little left. No one could make Medina anymore, so he had to make it last.

Magilla's clothes hung from his frame. He always wanted to be thinner, but could never muster the willpower to stay on a diet. Now, he could not remember the last time he had eaten. It did not matter really, because he was evolving, becoming a new and more powerful form of human being.

Magilla was motionless, his breathing was in slow, measured rhythm as he watched Mayo through a crack in one of the boarded-up windows.

It had been difficult to find Mayo with all of the chaos in the street. Everyone was hiding out, waiting for the craziness to be over. It had cost Magilla some of his precious Medina to get the necessary information, but it was worth it.

Medina's latest miracle for Magilla was his new invincibility. He'd acquired the power to withstand great violence and heal himself instantly. He'd been thinking that Mayo might try to kill him, but now he had no worries. Nothing could hurt him now.

Just last week, Magilla had stepped in front of a car to test his new abilities. He was hit, but had gotten up unharmed. Several people in the crowd gasped in amazement. He ran away quickly before someone tried to hold him for the police, the news people or worse, doctors. He would not share his new powers, at least not until he used them to kill Mayo.

At first, Magilla thought the test with the car was a dream, because right after it was over, he found himself at home in bed. But he had been blacking out a lot lately (a minor side effect from his new powers). He had probably had a spell right after he got home.

He would kill Mayo with his bare hands and absorb all of his life energy. He'd known all along that Mayo's life force was special. Mayo was evil, powerful, and when Magilla had Mayo's power inside of him, there would be nothing that he couldn't do.

After the young kid left with his drugs, Magilla walked up to the door and went inside.

Mayo was sitting on an old lumpy sofa. When he saw Magilla, he stood and pulled a small .22 automatic from his waistband. His face showed his shock.

"Glad I didn't have to come lookin' for you, gorilla," Mayo said. "You cost me a lot of money and I want it back, all of it."

Magilla smiled lazily, pointing at the gun. "That ain't gone help you now, muthafucka." Magilla walked toward Mayo. "I got you now."

Mayo fired two shots into Magilla's chest. Magilla stopped as if waiting. He placed his hand on his chest and fell to one knee. He coughed loudly, then fell on his back.

Mayo's heart beat wildly. Why had this fool just come in and let himself get shot?

"Must be crazy on that shit," Mayo said out loud.

Mayo wiped the gun clean of fingerprints and threw it into a corner. Then he gathered the drugs and got ready to leave. He didn't have the time or the desire to get rid of Magilla's body. He quickly moved to the door, thinking that he'd have to find a new location soon.

Something scrambled behind him—movement, like a weight shifting.

"What the—"

Mayo turned and saw the drug-ravaged face of Magilla. Two bloodless holes were on the front of his large shirt.

Mayo dropped some of his cargo in shock and stared, transfixed by the dead man. Then his eyes went to his gun in the corner, a million miles away.

Magilla smiled, his teeth red with blood.

"Now, it's my turn," he said.

Tony approached the old abandoned house on Hempstead. It was nearly dark outside. He rolled his Ford up the street, dodging the big potholes.

The block looked like it had been hit by a bomb. Only a few houses looked habitable.

Tony stopped his car a few houses away from the Williams house. He got out and crossed the street to survey the situation.

The Williams house was a wreck. The aluminum siding was buckled and rusted on its steel screws. The chimney had collapsed, there was a big hole in the roof and the lawn was waist high in weeds. He walked to the porch of another house that looked to be uninhabited and waited for signs of life in the Williams place.

Few questions about the case remained for Tony. The Handyman had spared the women and Jonnel Washington's hands at Shalon Street because they were not in the group of men who had killed his brother, Carlton Williams. The Nelson brothers were killed because they were related to Randy Thellis. The Handyman could not kill Thellis because he was already dead.

But Tony could not figure out why the killer collected the hands of his victims. Perhaps the Handyman felt as though he punished them beyond death by taking them. The blond hair had to be planted to throw everyone off track. The computer had confirmed that Carlton Williams was black, so his brother was, too.

And the money. Well, everybody needs money, even a killer.

After about twenty minutes, Tony decided to go inside. He crossed the street and went around the back of the house through the thick weeds.

When he got to the back of the one-story house, Tony saw a door. Every other opening was boarded up and yet this one was still functional.

Tony pulled his Beretta and walked carefully to the door. He did not want to kick it in because if there was no one inside, he would be leaving a clue of his visit. He tried the doorknob and the cheap door opened without even a creak. He entered, walking in a shooting crouch, his gun in front of him.

The stench was incredible. It was as if every toilet in the neigh-

borhood had backed up and flowed into the house. Tony squinted in
the darkness of the room. The boards on the windows cut off the
light, and very little came in from the fading sunset outside. He held
the gun in a shooting crouch for a moment, looking for a shift in
shadow, the sound of movement.

When his eyes adjusted to the light, he saw that the back door
had opened into a kitchen that was foul and dirty.

And definitely inhabited.

Talmadge Williams gripped the steering wheel so tightly he felt he
would crush it. Blood and adrenaline raced through him, making him
a little dizzy.

He slowed the car down. He could not afford to be stopped by the
police. They might find the man in the trunk.

He'd screwed up on Butchie, but he was going back for him tomorrow. He would have to keep T-Bone alive until Butchie could be
obtained and killed. He could kill T-Bone now, but that would ruin
everything. They had to die in order—first the flunkies, then the
leader. That's how he'd seen it in his mind so many times.

The dealers had killed his brother, Carlton. He was made to watch
Carlton die and, after it was done, the dealers had shot him and left
him to die. But he did not die.

He managed to get to the highway that night and passed out. He
was picked up by a man driving a semi.

Two days later, he awoke in a county hospital bed with tubes flowing out of his body.

The nurses kept asking him his name, but he would not answer.
When the police came to question him about the gunshot, he had
pretended to be unconscious.

Talmadge had escaped from the hospital three days later, still in
pain. He stole an orderly uniform, begged for money on the street,
and caught a bus home.

When he got home, he found his mother unconscious from drinking. He didn't know what to do, so he called his mother's boyfriend,
a man who came around every once in a while.

When he found the killers, Talmadge wanted to kill them, but he
couldn't. He was just a skinny kid back then. So, he waited. Patience,
that was his greatest asset. He planned his revenge. He trained at a
special place and grew bigger, stronger, and smarter.

When his mother discovered that Carlton was dead, she cried for hours, then got drunk. The next day, she ran a warm bath, got in, and cut her wrists. She left a letter which said Carlton's death was her fault.

Talmadge was grief-stricken. The drug dealers had taken everything from him. And that's when he began to dream. He saw the deaths of the killers each time he closed his eyes. He became obsessed with them and carefully and meticulously planned their deaths.

Talmadge trained, grew stronger, and dreamed of finding and killing the drug dealers. He lost sight of everything else in life. He lived only for the day when they were all dead. And soon, Big Money Grip lay on the ground at Belle Isle, cut to pieces.

And each time he killed, he took their hands as a reminder of his brother's death. Each night he dreamed of how Carlton was killed. He saw his brother tied to a tree, his body being ripped to pieces, the dealers' murderous faces and their hands—covered with thick lines of blood.

Mayo tried not to look at the gun in the corner. The weapon was closer to Magilla. Mayo kept his eyes on Magilla, trying not to attract attention to the weapon.

Magilla took a step toward Mayo, then jerked suddenly to his right and picked up the gun from the floor. Mayo turned and ran toward the back door.

Mayo was hit by a bullet. It entered his left shoulder. He fell and landed on his face and heard himself grunt loudly.

"Now—" said Magilla standing over him. "You will die, just for me."

Magilla put the gun to the back of Mayo's head.

Mayo's shoulder ached as Magilla turned him over on his back and sat on him. Magilla pinned his arms down. Magilla's crotch was right in front of his face and it didn't smell good.

Magilla was thinner, but still a heavy man. He stuck the gun under Mayo's nose and laughed.

Mayo stared at the barrel of the gun. He started to yell to Magilla to shoot and get it over with, but he would not give the bastard the satisfaction. He was not going out like a punk. The pain in his shoulder flared up and he felt tears welling in his eyes.

Magilla breathed heavily as he shifted his weight and pulled the gun back. He then removed the clip and placed it in his pocket. Magilla then dropped the gun beside his victim and began to choke him.

Mayo gagged as the fingers closed on his throat. It was a tight grip, but not the crushing one that he had expected. He was weak, thought Mayo, weak 'cause he was hit twice. Mayo struggled beneath the larger man, trying to free his good arm.

"Yes, yes," Magilla whispered, as if he felt pleasure.

Mayo moved his mouth to Magilla's hand and bit into it as hard as he could.

Magilla screamed and gripped harder momentarily. Mayo sank his teeth in deeper and felt a section of the hand separate. Blood spilled over the corners of his mouth and down his neck.

Magilla wailed again and yanked his hands from Mayo's neck, leaving part of one in Mayo's mouth. Magilla rocked to the side and Mayo used all of the force he had to dislodge him from his chest. Magilla toppled from him, landing on his side, screaming.

Mayo spat out the meat in his mouth and faintly heard it hit the floor. He stood and forced air into his lungs. He retrieved the gun and turned to see Magilla lunging at him.

Mayo raised the gun with his good arm. He pointed it at Magilla's face and pulled the trigger. The gun's last bullet, still loaded in the chamber, fired and blew a hole in Magilla's forehead. The bullet tore through Magilla's ravaged brain and lodged here.

The big man landed on Mayo and they both fell to the floor. The gun flew out of Mayo's hand. Magilla lay on top of Mayo, gurgling incoherently. Mayo pushed the dead man from him and scrambled away.

Mayo got to his feet. A rush of pain and dizziness almost sent him to one knee. Mayo collected himself and stood, pushing his hand into his shoulder to stop the blood.

He fished the clip from Magilla's pocket and put it back in the gun. Good thing Magilla didn't know anything about guns except how to pull the trigger. An automatic loads a bullet in the chamber after each shot.

Mayo fired two more shots into Magilla's head. Then he tore off part of Magilla's bloody shirt and wrapped it around his shoulder.

He saw that beneath his shirt, Magilla wore two heavy, quilted vests. Mayo recognized the name "Mt. Carmel Hospital" printed in bright red. Those were x-ray vests, Mayo thought. He'd had to wear one after getting shot once. He laughed a little. Magilla thought the vests would protect him.

Mayo headed toward the back door. He was wet with blood and stank of sweat. He was going to try to drive, but he was not looking forward to it.

A police siren cut through the silence with a short blast.

"This is the police," said a female voice. "Throw out your weapon and come out with your hands on your head."

"Shit!" Mayo said.

Usually when people called the police, the cops came late. And with all the disorder in the streets these days, they picked now to be on time.

Tony was careful not to touch anything in the room. He could see roaches scurrying over the surfaces and walls.

The house was crudely constructed. The back door opened into the kitchen which opened into a dining room which opened into a living room. The two bedrooms were off the dining and living rooms.

Tony entered the dining room. It was empty, except for several pieces of old furniture and garbage.

The living room was right next to the dining room, separated by a large archway. It contained only an old sofa and chair. Tony could see partially into the kitchen from the living room.

Tony checked the one-story house's two bedrooms and found the master bedroom surprisingly neat with an old mattress and covers on it. The other bedroom was empty.

Tony was about to go in the basement, but he found the stairway leading to it completely gone. The house was secure. He hoped.

Tony went back into the dirty kitchen. The room was dark, save for a little light coming through the boarded-up back door. He hit a light switch and to his surprise, the light came on, dimly illuminating the room.

He opened the refrigerator and checked the contents. It was filled with junk food. In the back of the freezer, Tony saw a large, plastic container covered with tin foil.

He held it up to the light, careful to hold only the edges but couldn't see anything. He understood that anything he found would not be admissible in court, but he was beyond that now.

Tony set his Beretta down on the kitchen table and opened the container. Inside, neatly sealed in plastic bags, were the missing hands of the dead men.

He opened the container to make sure of what he saw. The hands were grayish with blood caked at the ends. His stomach churned.

Tony was placing the tin foil back on the container, when the back door opened and the faint sound of it was like an explosion. Tony turned and saw the silhouette of a big man holding up another man.

Tony managed to grab his gun from the table, but the big man was moving toward him and shoved the man he held at Tony. The weight knocked Tony down. Tony's gun fired, and he felt the hot streak of a bullet enter and leave his side. Tony dropped the Beretta.

Tony was propelled backward, through the doorway that separated the kitchen and the dining room. He landed in the latter.

Tony pushed at the body on top of him and saw a man's bruised face. Thick adhesive tape covered T-Bone's mouth and his eyes were wide with fear.

T-Bone screamed, stretching the tape across his mouth. Tony pushed him up, using him as a shield, waiting for bullets to fly.

Blood spilled from Tony's wound and down his leg. T-Bone's hands were tied behind him and he desperately tried to hit Tony, realizing what he meant to do. T-Bone kicked, but Tony held him tight, knowing that shots would be fired at them.

Tony heard steps approaching. He felt the weight of the body being pulled up and off him.

Tony looked up and faintly saw the face of his attacker. This had to be him, Tony thought, Talmadge Williams, the Handyman.

The killer aimed a gun at Tony's head.

And T-Bone ran for the door.

The killer turned and grabbed T-Bone, shaking him and yelling. "Nooo!" The killer's voice was raspy, hard.

Tony reached up and grabbed for the killer's gun hand. He missed and fell to the floor.

T-Bone raised his knee into Talmadge's groin and the killer yelled in pain. T-Bone broke free and took several galloping strides around the killer and out of the dining room into the kitchen.

The killer followed T-Bone into the kitchen. He grabbed the drug dealer and punched him hard in the side. T-Bone groaned pitifully and fell against the refrigerator.

The killer prepared to strike him again, but T-Bone managed to evade the blow and kicked the killer in the leg. The Handyman fell to one knee. T-Bone kicked again this time catching him in the side of the head. The killer raised the .38 and fired into T-Bone's chest twice. T-Bone hit the floor hard and lay still.

"Sh . . . No!" The killer said in shock. He stood and ran into the dining room where Tony was frantically trying to find his lost weapon.

"You ruined everything!" the killer yelled. "All my planning, my *patience* . . . ruined!"

The killer raised his gun, then stopped and put the weapon into his waistband and took a large knife out of his jacket.

"You'll take his place now. You have to. I have to finish the plan." He stepped toward Tony who was pushing himself backwards on the floor.

Tony could see him now. He was big and muscular. Not the skinny kid he'd heard about. He probably had a handsome face, but it was contorted from his rage. A shadow fell across it, masking his eyes in blackness.

"That's enough," said a voice from behind the Handyman.

The killer halted in his tracks.

Tony pushed himself backwards, away from the killer. He was gripped with shock at the sound of the voice he heard. He was so stunned that for a moment, he forgot the pain in his wounded side. Behind the killer, he saw a man's silhouette and heard the voice of his partner, Jim Cole.

Mayo sat down on the old sofa. The cops called to him from outside, but he said nothing.

If he surrendered, he thought, they charge him with murder and possession with intent to sell drugs. With his record, he'd be lucky to get a hundred years.

Prison. So many times he had nightmares about it. Nasty food, hard work, no women, and muscle-bound faggots around every corner. He knew a guy once, a tough mean bastard, who had gone to Jackson prison and came out three years later a flaming gay. They turned his ass out good.

Mayo heard the cops at the front door. He just sat there, holding the gun.

"Last chance. Come out!" said a woman's voice from the other side.

Mayo said nothing.

The policewoman kicked in the door and stood in a shooting crouch in the doorway.

"Stand up, put the gun down, and place your hands over your head!" she said.

Mayo stood, holding the gun at his side.

"It's me, Johnson," said a cop from the room behind Mayo.

"I got him!" yelled the woman cop.

Mayo heard the cop behind him move away, out of the line of fire.

"Put the fuckin' gun down or I'll blow your head off!!" the woman yelled.

Mayo looked at her, smiling. She meant it. Her gun was locked out in front of her. Her eyes had fire behind them.

At least he would go out like a man, Mayo thought.

Mayo jerked the gun up, and the woman officer fired, the bullet hit Mayo in the chest. The second shot caught him in the head. He dropped to the floor.

And landed right next to Magilla.

"Move away from him," said Jim.

The killer was motionless.

"Put your hands where I can see them and back away from the officer—*now!*"

Tony was holding his breath and didn't notice that blood trickled through the hand on his side. He knew Jim would shoot in another three seconds if the killer didn't drop his weapon.

Talmadge Williams dropped the big knife and reached for his gun in a shockingly swift move.

"Gun!!" yelled Tony.

The killer turned away from Tony, and Jim shot, hitting him in the side of the head. The killer fell, falling a few feet from Tony, and his gun discharged into the floor.

Jim rose from his shooting crouch and advanced into the dining room. Tony scrambled over to the Handyman's body and quickly grabbed the gun next to his hand.

Jim knelt down and checked the killer. He was gone. The shot was right on the money.

"You OK?" asked Jim. "Is the house secure? Are there any more of 'em?"

"You just shot the Handyman," Tony heaved a little, adjusting himself on the floor.

"What?" Jim asked.

"That's him right there. How did you find me?"

"I saw you driving around in an old car. I was curious, so I got the license and followed you. When you went into IAU, it wasn't hard to figure out you were on to something. I laid back until I—"

Tony groaned and held his side tighter. Jim saw that he was bleeding.

"Stay put," Jim said. "I'll get you an ambulance. You can fill me in later."

"No, don't leave me in here," Tony said. "Get me out."

"All right."

Jim stooped and helped Tony to his feet. Tony stood but got dizzy and fell against a wall.

"Maybe I should stay behind," Tony said. "But hurry."

"OK, partner. Hold on." Jim set Tony on the floor, then walked out of the dining room into the kitchen.

A shadow entered the back doorway in the kitchen. Jim pulled his gun, but was shot before he could get it out.

Jim was pushed backwards through the doorway between the kitchen and dining room. He fell back into the dining room, landing on his back.

"What the fu—"

Tony stood and hobbled out of the dining room into the living room. Another shot sounded and the light exploded.

"Police officer!" Tony yelled, pushing himself behind an old sofa. "Whoever you are, you just shot a cop you son of a bitch!"

"It's OK, Tony. I didn't know."

Tony nearly dropped the gun. It was the voice of Chief Fuller.

22

Domino

"**W**hat's up, Orr?" asked a passing uniformed cop.

Orris Martin reclined in his chair. Things were chaotic, but soon order would be restored. These damned black drug dealers were so hard-headed. Seemed like every five years or so he had to have one killed. It wasn't bad enough that he had to work for Tony Hill, the black Golden Boy, but he had to deal with punks in the street, too. They were all a pain in the ass.

"My dick, same as always," Martin laughed.

"Hey, what's the deal on all the brass circulating around here?" asked the uniform.

"Don't know, maybe they're comparing their dick sizes."

"Should be a short contest, huh?"

Martin laughed at the joke and the uniform walked away, pleased with himself.

Martin didn't know which of the drug dealers would kill the other and it didn't really matter, he thought, as long as there was only one to deal with. He couldn't stretch things to cover two gangs.

This was by far the worst time for him since he became the organizer for the payoffs. He remembered how bitter he was when he lost the lawsuit for reverse discrimination against the force. He had been passed up for promotion by black officers after twelve years. He was not the greatest cop, but he had at least been around long enough to know what he was doing.

The new black mayor was promoting green, young black cops and putting them in charge of white cops who had more experience. The black cops were trained by the white ones 'cause they didn't know anything.

After Martin lost the lawsuit, he was exiled into a Back-to-the-Streets Program the mayor dreamed up. He was forced to wear a uniform again, the ultimate humiliation.

He hated the department and so he got in with the cops he knew were taking money. If the system was gonna screw him, then screw the system, he thought.

After a few years, he became the point man and negotiated the deal with that asshole T-Bone, who had seemed like a smart boy. But he was like all the rest of them, stupid and unable to see past his dick and his bankroll.

"Hey Orr, Deputy Dawg wants to see you," said another detective.

Martin got up. Good old Deputy Chief Noble. Another black, do-nothing Yancy bureaucrat. What could he possibly want?

Martin walked to the Deputy Chief's office and found it filled with Federal Marshals and several large men in suits who had to be FBI and IAD.

In a chair, he saw his partner, Steve Patrick, in handcuffs.

Martin didn't make a sound. He knew what was up. Someone had broken the chain. There were many cops between him and the street rookies, but it was the domino theory. One cop breaks, spills his guts and so on up the chain of command. He might not ever know who'd turned on him.

"Orris James Martin," said one of the suits. "You're under arrest for violation of the RICO Act."

As they read Martin his rights, an officer took Martin's gun and cuffed him. They would walk him and his partner in disgrace through the halls of 1300 to the lockup.

But before they did, Deputy Chief Noble took out his own service revolver, removed the bullets, and slammed it down hard on the desk.

23

The Battle of Saints

"**C**hief?"

"Yeah," Fuller said. "You can come out. I didn't know you were cops until I heard your voice. God, I'm sorry." Fuller was out of breath.

"What are you doing here?!" asked Tony, raising the gun. "If you didn't mean to shoot, what the fuck are you doing here?! *How could you know to be here?!*"

Tony refused to be taken in by anything at this point. Jim had followed him here, sure. But Fuller, too? Not a chance. Fuller was too good a cop to have fired without knowing who was in the room. Fuller never identified himself as a cop, he just fired. Yes, it made sense that Fuller was dirty. But how? That was the question.

"I'm still a cop, Tony. I followed the same leads you did. That's how I got here."

"Bullshit! Let me see your weapon on the floor and we'll talk!" Tony said.

If Fuller was willing to expose himself, then he had no intention of letting Tony get out alive. No one would believe Fuller mistakenly killed a cop on an investigation which the Chief knew nothing about.

"Hey, what is this?" said Fuller from the kitchen. "You don't think I—"

"Let me see your gun on the floor or you'll have to kill me!" Tony screamed. "Or I'll kill you."

Tony looked at the front door. It was boarded and nailed shut. No chance of getting out that way, he thought.

Tony saw Fuller swing himself into the doorway between the kitchen and dining room and fire. One of the bullets hit the sofa, but Tony wasn't hit. The other went into the living room wall.

Tony fired a quick shot but missed. The recoil jerked the gun from his hand.

"Shit," he whispered.

The gun had fallen only a few inches away. Tony leaned over and picked it up and pain shot into his side. He was getting light-headed. God help me, he thought. The goddamned Chief of Police—his friend, his mentor was going to kill him. Two cops shooting it out, a battle of saints.

Tony hoped someone had heard the shots, then he remembered the vacant house next to the one he was in. It was not likely, he reasoned.

"Talmadge Williams is dead," Tony called, then he moved to the other side of the sofa. "He shot T-Bone and he tried to kill me, but he caught a bullet in the process."

Then he heard something that he did not expect. He heard Fuller crying. He listened to make sure he was right. The Chief was sobbing like a child.

"There's no way out, Tony," Fuller said, still crying. "This is my battleground. My life has meant nothing. After all these years, this is what I have. Service, honor, it's all bullshit."

"Let me help you, Chief," Tony said. "Whatever it is, I'll help you through it."

"Too late, Tony. I'm too old. Too old and too tired for help. Every man's got secrets. Mine are gonna die here in this house. The only hope I had, I destroyed a long time ago, and tonight you killed my last son!"

Fuller fired a shot that missed. Tony was about to shoot when Fuller moved out of the doorway.

Tony was shocked again. Fuller was Roberta Williams's lover and the father of Carlton and Talmadge Williams. He'd plotted with the Handyman to avenge Carlton's death.

Fuller stepped into the doorway again and fired another shot into the living room. He emptied the shells from his gun, sliding his big body along the wall, backing way from the open doorway to reload.

"Wall," Tony said to himself, hearing the faint sound of Fuller's large frame moving against it and the spent shells hitting the floor.

Tony looked at the killer's gun. It was a .38. Powerful enough, he hoped.

Tony opened the gun cylinder and saw that there were only two shots left.

Tony stood up with all his energy and shot through the wall just left of the doorway, where he thought Fuller's body was. The bullets struck, throwing pieces of plaster and wood into the air. Dust rose into a cloud that swirled in the dim dining room.

Tony heard a loud grunt and then a heavy thud. Slowly, he stumbled into the kitchen, keeping the gun out in front of him. He had no bullets left, but Fuller didn't know that.

He stepped over the corpses of T-Bone and Talmadge Williams and found Fuller was down. His head had been hit and was bleeding over the dirty floor.

Tony kicked the gun away from the Chief's corpse. He went to Jim and checked him. His partner's abdomen was wet with blood, but Jim was breathing. He tried to lift him but did not have the strength.

Tony stumbled out the back door, then into the front yard and headed for Jim's cruiser down the street. The night air was soothing, and for a moment it invigorated him.

Then he started to shake. Tony steadied himself against a ratty fence and it passed. He reached Jim's cruiser and got in.

Tony sat in the police car and held the transmitter to his face. He fumbled for the switch. The control panel faded in and out. He felt the vibrations of words in his throat.

Darkness fell upon him, and he could not remember if he had called for help or not.

24

Dead Alive

Tony's eyes opened to a brilliant white light and he knew in an instant he was dead. Everyone knew about the swirling white light at the end of the Tunnel of Eternity. But as his eyes focused, he saw that the light was made by large fluorescent lamps over his hospital bed. He coughed and felt wires and tubes striking his arm.

"Tony!" he heard Nikki's voice say. A second later, he saw her beautiful tear-stained face appear over his, smothering him with kisses.

"I'm OK," he managed to say. His throat was dry and his head pounded like a drum. He sat up and made himself into a liar as pain shot through his side.

"Take it easy," said a small nurse. "No quick movements for a while."

Tony eased up and hugged Nikki. He was glad to be alive and still with her. She cried and he tried to comfort her as the pain crept back.

"Is Jim OK?" Tony asked.

"Mr. Cole is down the hall and doing a lot better than you," said the little nurse as she untangled Tony's IV.

"You've been unconscious for a day. Take it easy. The doctor will want to see you." The nurse left.

Tony smiled and Nikki hugged him tightly. He looked over her shoulder and noticed for the first time that there were other people in his room.

Near the door, he saw three huge men standing watch. His mind raced as recognition hit him.

Tony clutched Nikki protectively as Walter Nicks stepped forward.

25

Questions to the Grave

Tony and Jim ate the hospital food and it tasted good. They sat in a hospital lounge and talked with Deputy Chief Vernon Noble. Tony and Jim had been in the hospital for three days and were feeling better. Tony even managed to talk with Carol Salinsky, who demanded the exclusive he had promised. Tony assured her she would get it as soon as he was released.

Nikki's anguish had been about more than his injuries. After the police arrived at the Williams house, Tony and Jim had been placed under arrest. No one knew what had transpired except that the mayor's longtime friend and chief of police had been killed. So Yancy put his guard dogs on Tony.

When Jim came to the next day, he cleared it all up, or at least as much of it as he knew. Jim never saw Fuller shoot him. When Tony filled in the rest, the SS men disappeared.

Nikki was relieved and went home only after Tony forced her to.

Yancy never called or came to the hospital. He was too busy trying to keep his reelection campaign going.

"I'm sorry, guys," said Deputy Chief Noble. "I had to put the guards here. Mayor's orders. With Orris Martin, the police corruption thing, and this, he just wasn't taking any chances."

"I understand," Tony said between bites. "Martin had a lot of officers on his payroll. Martin and his partner were my men. Poor Steve Patrick. He was a good kid."

"Screw him," said Jim. "He was a dirty cop. We don't need any of 'em."

"Anyway," said Noble. "I'm glad you understand."

"You ought to do your homework before you go jumping to conclusions," Jim snapped. "We were almost killed and we get treated like criminals."

"How were we to know?" asked Noble, wringing his hands.

"Tell us what you got, Chief," Tony said with a little discomfort. Noble was appointed acting chief of police. Calling him by the title reminded Tony of Fuller.

"The Union is all but dead. They had some kind of internal war and killed each other off."

Tony and Jim applauded.

"Fuller was the father of both boys. He had birth certificates for Carlton and Talmadge Williams in his house," Noble said. "And hold on to your nuts. The Handyman was in the police academy."

"Jesus," said Tony.

"He was there through basic but quit right after," said Noble.

"Makes sense," said Jim. "Fuller sent him there to get stronger, learn the game."

"Or maybe to straighten him out," said Tony. "After his first son died, maybe Fuller tried to do right by the last one."

"What I can't figure," said Noble, "is why Fuller didn't just have a couple of bad-ass cops blast the guys who killed his son."

"I think I can answer that," said Tony. "Fuller said his life meant nothing, that he'd destroyed his hope a long time ago. Fuller had failed as a father. I think Talmadge wanted to kill the dealers himself, and Fuller was so racked up with guilt over the lives he'd helped destroy, that he kinda went crazy too."

Tony and Jim exchanged a look. Tony was speaking from experience.

"Well, he didn't go too crazy. That blond hair stunt was ingenious," said Noble.

"Yeah, he was a regular Einstein," Jim said angrily. "Fat bastard shot me."

Tony laughed but the pain made him stop.

"Did Fuller engineer the loss of the hair samples, too?" asked Tony.

"Maybe," said Noble. "Or it might have just been a screwup."

"Well, I hope he's lucky in hell," said Jim. "You hear that, you prick!" Jim shouted at the floor. "Damn, I hurt."

"We couldn't find anything leading to the body of Carlton Williams or why the victims' hands were cut off," Noble said. "Those secrets were buried with Fuller. You can read my report if you want."

"No thanks," said Tony. "The next thing I read will be a plane ticket to Jamaica."

"I heard that." Jim and Tony slapped five.

"Tell me," Tony said. "Did you ever find out who killed Blue Jones and the boy?"

"No, but we figured it was because the boy had a price on his head, like you told us," said Noble. "The boy came through the emergency room, and at that time, it was probably filled with drug addicts because of the Medina thing. I'm sorry."

"Don't worry, Tony," said Jim. "We'll find whoever did it."

"Well, have fun, relax, and get well," Noble said and walked to the door. He turned and came back. "I forgot." He looked at Tony. "Fuller had this on him when he died. I believe it's yours."

Noble reached into a pocket and brought out Tony's gold police shield.

"But why was he—"

"Don't know," said Noble. "I guess he was waiting for you to come back to the department. Anyway, here you go."

Tony took the shield, feeling like he was lifting it from the grave.

"If you want to come back, Inspector, the Detroit Police Force would be proud to have you." Noble left the room.

A moment passed as Tony stared at the badge.

"Did I say thank you for saving my life?" Jim asked.

"Only about a hundred times," Tony said. "The way I see it, we're even. I don't think the Handyman was about to sing to me when you showed up."

"Yeah, I guess we both done good." Jim took a step and groaned. "I'm much too old for this shit. Hey, let's go flirt with the nurses."

Tony kept looking at the badge, turning it in his hands.

"I can hear all the stuff you're thinking," said Jim. "So, what are you gonna do with that thing, partner?" Jim pointed to Tony's gold shield.

"The only thing I can."

26

Higher Ground

*D*ecember.
        Deputy Chief of Police Tony Hill relaxed as the frozen Detroit River came into view. Large chunks of ice floated downstream, swirling in the river's current.

He was having lunch with Dr. Lincoln at the Summit, a trendy restaurant at the top of the Renaissance Center's Hilton Hotel. The food was good, the prices steep, and the whole place rotated, one half-turn, then back.

Tony was outfitted in his dress uniform. The uniform was deep blue, filled with medals and gold braid. He liked wearing dress blues. It made him feel official.

"So, Tony," said Lincoln. "Are you ready for your big debut today?"

"I guess," said Tony. "I've been avoiding a press conference since I got this lousy job."

"I read about that. Six months and no one has been able to get to you. Except that TV woman, what's her name?"

"Salinsky. I owed her."

"Right. But even she said she felt cheated, that your story was nothing more than was released by the department," Lincoln said.

"I just want to forget about all this."

"Come on, you're famous. People like to touch heroism."

"The press just wants to bring the whole Handyman and Medina business up again, sell a few more papers. We're trying to get it behind us. The killer is dead and the drug has faded away, thank God."

"You're very cynical. I guess public life doesn't agree with you," Lincoln said.

"I deserve to be Deputy Chief, but part of it was just another trick by the mayor to help him get reelected. It worked, too. Three terms. Yancy's almost like a king now."

"But the office seems to suit you. You look pretty good to me."

A waiter came by and Lincoln waved off any more coffee.

"I'm glad to be off the street," Tony said. "This gig is a million miles away from the Sewer. Jim's having a time getting his unit back together after the corruption probe."

"I read about that. I looked for your name."

"You thought I was dirty?"

"No, it's just human nature. I had to make sure you weren't in trouble."

"I helped break the corruption, actually," said Tony. "I prompted a rookie named Fred Hampton to turn state's evidence."

"So, what don't you like about your new job?"

"It's OK I guess. I just wish I didn't have to deal with so many idiots every day. Manpower reports, crime stats, requisitions, joint operations, state, federal, county. I almost want to go out and run down a drug dealer just for the fun of it."

"OK then, I'll change the subject. How was Jamaica?"

"Great. My son had a blast. He'd never seen an ocean before."

"And Nikki?"

"Well, we spent a lot of time off of our feet," Tony said. He smiled and took a drink of water.

"And do you still hate white people?"

Tony choked on the water a little. "Where did that come from?"

"You told me that a white cop took a bullet that was meant for you. I'm curious how that's affected you," Lincoln said.

Tony took a moment. He'd spoken with Pete Carter, but all he did was thank him. It was respectful and pleasant, but nothing more.

"No, I don't think so," Tony said. "I mean, this whole Handyman mess was irrational. People were at each other's throats, and for what? A strand of hair. We should have been ashamed of ourselves. It was totally ridiculous."

"As ridiculous as hating because of color?"

"Yes. You know, when I hired my staff, I made sure that there were some of them on it."

"Them?"

"Yes, them. White people."

"It's difficult to change behavior, Tony," Lincoln said. "Real change comes from within, where only you know it exists."

Tony signaled the waiter for the check. Lincoln reached for his wallet. Tony stopped him.

"No more taking turns, Doc. I have an expense account now."

Tony gave the waiter a credit card and turned back to Lincoln.

"The answer to your unasked question, Doctor, is, yes, I'm really changing," Tony said. "I have to. Chief Fuller failed his sons. My son is the most important thing in the world to me and I want my legacy to him to be love, knowledge, and humanity. I've lived the consequences of a legacy of hate. It's not good."

"Good, good," Lincoln said. "Well, time's up."

Tony and Lincoln left the Summit just as the restaurant was turning to a view of uptown.

They parted in the lobby of the Hilton and Tony started the long trek to the City-County Building and the press conference he dreaded.

Tony went into the shining expanse of the Renaissance Center, headed for Tower 200 which was linked by an enclosed bridge to the Millender Center, which was in turn linked to the City-County Building.

After the Handyman case was closed, the seasons had changed quickly. Fall had passed in a flurry and now it was winter, with a new year around the bend.

Tony had not started an investigation into the Brotherhood. Hampton had taken money there, but his story had checked out. Two of the officers on the payoff run were also members there. They were indicted along with Orris Martin, Steve Patrick, and fifteen others. Mbutu denounced the arrest of his members as racist.

Hampton was given probation and had probably left the state. Poor guy would never be a cop again. Peter Carter was clean. Tony was glad about that.

Tony had been tempted to confess to Darryl Simon's murder while still in the hospital. But when he thought about Nikki and Moe, he abandoned the notion. Nothing would ever bring Darryl Simon back or the men Irene Simon had killed. Jim was right. He would let the dead stay dead—all of them.

Tony moved into the long bridge that separated the Renaissance and Robert Millender Centers. The bridge's heating system had failed and it was cold inside. People rushed to get to the next building. He picked up the pace.

Tony entered the Millender Center. The bustle of the lunchtime crowd was ebbing. Black businessmen hurried. Beautiful women walked along in groups, talking and laughing.

He smiled a little. He loved his city. He loved it even though it was a place as much affected by the actions of his own people as it was by anyone else's racism. He loved it because it was the only place that could ever be home to him. He saw in the city his own humanity and evolution.

The city's latest paroxysm had taken many lives, a good friend, and perhaps a bit of his soul. But he was tied to Detroit, and he lived as the city itself did, despite internal wreckage.

Tony walked into the long hallway to the City-County Building. A young officer saluted as he walked by.

A young black woman rushed up to him from the other end of the hallway.

"They're ready for you, sir," she said. "We're holding the press conference in the lobby."

"OK, Stephanie. What do I need to know?"

"Nothing you don't already know. You have your speech memorized, I hope. Just remember to mention the mayor, the governor, and thank the President for passing the Crime Bill."

"Got it. So, does the press look hostile?"

"Well, sir I—"

"Forget it. Let's just get this thing over with."

They walked to the lobby. Every news crew was there, even CNN. Tony stopped and collected himself.

He walked to the podium and the crowd broke into a thunderous round of applause. TV camera lights and flashbulbs exploded in an electric brilliance.

Tony smiled, surprised and embarrassed by the adulation. He motioned the crowd to stop, but they cheered even louder. Curious passersby stopped and watched, joining the crowd.

Finally, Tony gave up, and let them continue the ovation.